back up and give you room to get out the front door. But if you come one step closer, I'll shoot you dead on the spot. I mean it, Ricky. And if you ever show up here again, I'll shoot you on sight, understand?"

Ricky trembled. Sam couldn't tell if it was from fear or anger. "Yeah, I understand," he said, his voice shaking. "I'm leaving, Sam, but this ain't the end of this. Just don't get jumpy. Point that thing somewhere else, will ya?"

Sam shook her head. "Not on your life, Ricky. Not on your life."

"About thirty-grand," he lied.

She paused and thought for a moment. Then with steel in her voice she said, "That's enough for you to get a fresh start. I'm sorry, Ricky, I can't help you. If you were dead broke, I'd give you enough to get out of town, but that's all. If you leave right now, you'll have nearly a three day start. I suggest you leave tonight. You could be all the way across the country by Monday, or even be in Mexico or Canada.

"I have to ask you to leave--now! I'll pray for you. But I intend to try to forget that you and I were ever husband and wife. I told you before that I never wanted to see you again and I meant it. If you ever try to see me again, I'll take legal action against you."
Ricky was stunned—stunned and angry. "You'd do that to me?" he asked.

"You've done this to yourself. In fact, I tried my best to keep you from it. I paid you a lot of money on the condition that you never contact me again. You've broken that agreement. I want you to leave my house—right now!"

Ricky abruptly stood, sending his chair careening across the floor. Sam flinched back. "Who the hell do you think you are, Sam? You think you can just throw me out, and I'll go away? That's not how it works, lady. You owe me." He took a threatening step forward.

Sam backed up three steps, reached into the hoodie pocket, and pulled out the pistol. She pointed it straight at Ricky's chest. He recoiled, raised his hands protectively and backed away saying "Holy shit, Sam. You going to shoot me?"

"If I have to. I have a restraining order against you, remember? Cass knows you're here."

As frightened as he was, Ricky was still defiant. "That restraining order isn't worth shit here in West Virginia, and you know it."

"But it would be *prima facie* evidence in my favor if I shoot you inside my house. And you're perilously close to that. I'm going to

ALL THE

PRETTY
DRESSES

STEVEN J. CLARK

Published by New Horizons Press/Publishers, LLC

REVIEWS

WHAT *READERS* SAY:

Gayla E: "WHAT THE HELL? Your book should be at the top of the New York Times Best Seller's list. I read a lot and this is the best by far...I LOVED IT!!!!"

Laci W: "It holds you right to the end and won't let go. I enjoyed every minute of it."

Shar H: "It's got everything; mystery, suspense, romance, and terror. I couldn't put it down. Clark owes me more than one night's sleep."

Lynne H: "Anyone who wants a thriller that makes them sit on the edge of their seat and wonder what is next, will find this book a *must read*. I was unable to put it down and consequently lost some sleep wanting to find out just who the 'Freak' was going to be. Clark is a wonderful writer and I will be at the top of the list to see what he has in store for us next."

Lauri C: "Great book. It grabbed me at the beginning and wouldn't let go. I was particularly taken by the twist in chapter 66 when I thought the danger was nearly over and suddenly a whole new layer is introduced. A couple of the chapters are a bit long but are broken up nicely so they don't read so long. Characters are easy to identify with, particularly if one is a divorced woman trying to make it in a male dominated world. This is a very good book."

WHAT OTHER *AUTHORS* SAY:

Jim Collins, Author of *Gallagher*

"I loved this right from the start. Yours is an excellent story, told clearly and concisely with no wasted wordage, and your grammar, punctuation and use of language are spot on. This is Jack Reacher without the excessive overuse of plot-slowing descriptions. I liked your main character straight off and your uncluttered picture that you painted of her and her abilities...The pace of your story is perfect...I think that this is a really well-written and readable tale..."

REVIEWS (CONTINUED)

Dawn Carter, author of *Heart of Vengeance*

"This is well written…I love a murder mystery and you succeeded in keeping my attention. I am bookmarking this. Kudos."

Jack Hudson, author of *Warm-up Kills*

"All The Pretty Dresses is an exceptionally well-written thriller that keeps the reader on the edge of his seat and unsure of exactly who the serial killer is until near the end. Action scenes are exciting and well written. The author proves that off-color language is unnecessary to create tension and realism. High stars."

Erin Davis author of *A Lethal Choice* and *A Driven Vengeance*

"Right away I found the character of Cass Rosier very interesting and very much like detective Kate Beckett on TV's "Castle." I see a lot of the same determination to be taken seriously as women in a more dominantly male field.…I think the twist on having the husband cheat on Cass with another man as opposed to just another bleach-blonde, big-boobed bimbo is definitely interesting and fresh. Nice job. I love the relationship Cass has with her daughter.…Ok, just finished chapter 13 and found myself moving from a relaxed, seated back position to full straight up and only a few inches from my computer screen…hoping the girl could finally make an escape from the killer. When it mentioned that she was looking for her car and only saw his pickup truck, but she had left the keys inside, I found myself saying out loud—"Rookie mistake, girly." Then as she was running away and heard the truck start up, my heart started to beat faster, then I actually yelled out, "Oh you're kidding me"…BEAUTIFUL JOB WRITING THAT SCENE…Steve, my friend, you definitely have a gift!"

Joanne Kendrick, author of *Chance Inheritance*

"…Your writing is succinct and engaging, giving the perfect tone for the story. The characters are well written and believable. Dialogue flows well and is natural.…I would expect this to do very well across multiple genres.

DEDICATION

This book is dedicated to my wonderful wife, Lauri R. Clark, who came to know what it means to be an author's widow during the writing of this book. Thank you for your patience, support and belief in me.

SPECIAL THANKS

I wish to extend special thanks to those who had a hand in enabling me to bring Pretty Dresses to publication. My wonderful and supportive beta-readers, Shar Hess, Laci Warby, Gayla Eakins, and Lynne Harris, I love you all. Thank you Kathleen Lyon, Shirley Bahlman and Bob Bahlman and Sue Player for your editing expertise. You've all taught me so much. Thanks to my dear friends, Terry and Suzie Eustice and Kathy and Dennis Phipps. Your early belief in me as a writer helped propel me forward to this day.

NOTICE

All The Pretty Dresses is a work of fiction. Any resemblance of the characters or events portrayed herein to any actual person, living or dead, or to any actual firm or event is strictly coincidental.

Chapter 1

Only eight ten in the morning, and Cass had already ruined someone's day. The someone was Robbie Hess, owner of the pizza parlor in Mt. Zion, a small town on the southwest shore of Summersville Lake. The business was being sued by a customer who claimed to have broken a tooth on one of his pizzas. *God, I hate serving summonses,* she thought.

Making things worse was the fact that even with an extra mug of morning coffee, she still wasn't fully awake. She'd been up half the night with the love of her life—her irrepressible, red-headed, precocious daughter, Katy, whose excitement over her seventh birthday party in just two days kept her awake until after eleven.

Then there was Katy's cold. Nothing serious, sniffles and a mild fever, but after the little girl finally drifted off to sleep, Cass was up every couple of hours to check on her fever and make sure she was breathing ok.

This morning Katy had protested in her sleepy little voice, "Mommy, I don't want to go to Grandma's. I want to stay here with you."

"I want that too, KK, but Mommy has to go to work."

"But we have to get ready for the party."

"We'll have time for that, sweetheart. The party isn't until tomorrow. We'll start working on it tonight as soon as I get off work, okay?"

Fortified by her second mug, Cass bundled Katy up and delivered her to Mom's house for the day. Thank God for Mom and Dad. Otherwise she would be delivering her precious Katy to some anonymous day care. *Damn, being a single mom is hard.*

With her thoughts more on Katy than her job, after serving Robby his summons Cass forgot to turn her shoulder radio back up. As she stepped into her patrol car she caught the tail end of a radio call; something or other going on at the lake.

Summersville Lake was the largest body of water in West Virginia, and attracted visitors from all around the state. If Cass responded to the call, it might get her out of summons duty for a while. She keyed her radio mic and said, "Dispatch, unit 10. Could you repeat that last call?"

"10-4, unit 10. We have a 911 request for response to Camp Fork Beach. Something about …"

A loud burst of static drowned out the rest of the dispatcher's response. Someone else on the network had keyed their mic, interrupting the call. When the static cleared Cass, heard, "Unit 1, Unit 10." Sheriff Clint Long wanted to talk to her directly.

"Unit 10," she replied.

"Standby, Unit 10. I'm going 10-21 for you."

In a matter of seconds, Cass's cell phone rang. "It's me," she answered with her standard non-identifying greeting, just in case it wasn't the sheriff.

"Sorry for blowing you off the air," Sheriff Long apologized. "I didn't want dispatch blaring that call all over the county just yet. What's your 10-20?"

"I'm in Mt. Zion serving that pizza lawsuit summons."

"We got a 911 call a few minutes ago. A woman said there's a dead body down at Butt Beach. I'm over in Craigsville, so it'll take me a half-hour to get there. You better go up and see what's going on. Maybe this is the chance we've been looking for to take advantage of that Police Science degree of yours."

"I'm on my way," Cass said as she reached down and switched on the light bar on top of her car. "Sure will beat the hell out of serving summonses. I'll keep you posted."

*

Dust billowed behind her as she drove as fast as she dared down the bumpy dirt road toward the northwest shore of Summersville Lake. The official name of her destination was Camp Fork Beach, known to locals as Butt Beach. It was a remote, secluded stretch of sand where Camp Fork Creek emptied into the lake at the far north end. The more uninhibited naturist souls of the area used the place as a hideaway where they could sunbathe in the buff.

Most of the time deputies treated the practice with a wink and a nod, much to the sunbathers' relief. Social nudity was a recreational activity frowned upon by many in the prudish, predominantly Born-Again Christian County.

There was no easy way to get to Butt Beach. Camp Fork Road would have been shorter but it was a four-wheel drive roller-coaster ride that ended on a ridge a half-mile short of the beach. County Road 9/5 off of County Road 23 was a longer, rutted, twisty dirt road, but at least it could be negotiated by car.

Cass was the first officer on the scene. Vehicles of various descriptions were scattered about the field that comprised the beach's unofficial parking lot. Awaiting her was a fortyish, slightly overweight, big-busted woman with coarse, straw-colored hair nearly to her waist. She was dressed in a thin, vaguely see-through linen wrap and no underwear. She practically ran to the police car as Cass pulled up, her unconstrained bosoms swinging freely with every step.

"Thank goodness you're here," the woman said breathlessly as Cass exited the car. Then she pulled up short as she realized she was looking at a woman rather than a *real* deputy. "Why'd they send you?" she blurted.

"Because I'm the biggest bad ass on the force," Cass replied testily. "My dispatcher said you found a dead body. Where is it?"

"Down here." The woman pointed toward a path leading down the creek and into the woods.

Tall stands of oak, ash, pine and sycamores canopied the trail which was bounded by impenetrable tangles of brambles and vines. As the woman led the way to the lake, with mountain ridges all around them, Cass worried about getting a radio signal out of the area. She depressed the 'talk' key on her shoulder mic and said, "Unit 10 is 10-23 at the end of County Road 9/5. Give me a signal check, over."

"Your signal is 5 by 5, Unit 10." the dispatcher replied.

Good. Communications would not be a problem. "Dispatch, I'm proceeding on foot to Camp Fork Beach. Can you give me a 10-77 on the arrival time of back-up units, over?"

"Approximately seven to ten minutes, Unit 10. Unit 3's still four miles out and Unit 6 is right behind him. Unit 1 is on his way as well."

"Copy that," she replied.

Cass emerged from the forest onto the sandy beach. The shoreline was still a hundred yards distant. The hippie-looking woman nodded toward a large, round, flat rock near the water's edge. "She's right over there. Looks like Sleeping Beauty, but she's as dead as a doornail."

A crowd of a dozen or so gathered around the rock. Not all had bothered to don clothing. *Pretty brassy*, she thought. *I hope nobody's messed with the body.*

As Cass approached, everyone began talking at once. She raised her hand and said, "Please, I can only hear one person at a time. This is now a possible crime scene. Please stand exactly where you are and do not disturb anything. I need to look at the victim. Anybody know her?" Her inquiry was met by silence.

The body lying on the rock was a lovely young woman who looked to be in her mid-twenties. She was dressed in a beautiful, full-length, chiffon lace over a rich scarlet-colored satin evening gown that daringly revealed the woman's considerable décolletage. It was a dress one would expect to see at a prom or the opera, not adorning a dead body on a flat rock in the middle of a nude beach.

She had long, blonde hair and a delicate, beautiful face. Her makeup and manicured fingernails were exquisitely done. A distinctive, inch-wide scarlet and black lace ribbon festooned with embroidered white daisies and fastened with a pretty pearl pin was around her neck.

She was laid out in a classic death pose—her hands placed one atop the other below her breasts. One hand held a small bouquet of what appeared to be real daisies accented with a sprig of baby's-breath.

The woman looked as if she'd simply climbed up onto the rock and gone to sleep. Only the pallor of her impossibly pale skin gave any hint that something was amiss. When the gentle morning breeze blew a wisp of hair across the woman's face, Cass instinctively wanted to brush it back to stop the tickle.

Cass had to get up on the rock for a better look. She donned a pair of latex gloves, scrambled up on the rock and placed two fingers against the girl's neck to see if there was a pulse. The instant she touched the woman's skin, she knew there would be none. The body was cold: far too cold for any life to be left in her.

There was no blood, no visible bruises, nothing to indicate to Cass how she had died. The body was fresh enough that the tell-tale signs of morbidity had yet to show, but her beauty wouldn't last much longer in the hot sun.

Cass depressed the talk key and spoke into her shoulder mic. "Unit 10 is on-scene at Camp Fork Beach. Requesting immediate dispatch of the Medical Examiner and a non-emergency response by County Ambulance Service for transport."

Despite the tragedy, Cass couldn't help but feel a twinge of excitement. This might be her first murder scene. She spied two deputies emerging from the forest trail onto the beach—backup at last.

Then she groaned. Even from this distance, there was no mistaking the florid, round face and protruding pot belly of fifty-five-year-old Tommy Reece, a twenty-five-year veteran of the department and the bane of her life ever since she joined the force. He was the more obnoxious of the last two deputies who still refused to accept the idea of a woman deputy.

Just last week she overheard him say, "Hey, she's a good-looking babe, built like a brick shithouse. But she ought to be somebody's secretary, or home taking care of her kid, not out driving a patrol car and carrying a 9mm Glock. No wonder that guy from down by Fayetteville divorced her."

What neither Reece nor the other deputies knew was that Orson Peters didn't divorce her. *She* divorced *him.* After graduating *Cum Laude* with a degree in criminal science from the University of West Virginia, Cass gathered up her degree and went to West Virginia's Police Officer Standards & Training course where she graduated at the top of her class, the first woman to ever do so.

She was a year and a half into her job as a UWV campus police officer, six months married, and three months pregnant, when she came home early one day in February, and found Orson in bed with a rail-thin, sallow fellow by the name of Stewart Kinross.

Cass somehow resisted the urge to shoot both of them where they lay. Instead, she ran them out of the second-story apartment at Taser-point as they clutched only a single white bed sheet between them. As they tried to hide outside, barefoot and bare-assed in the snow-covered bushes, Cass threw everything Orson owned out the bedroom window. It was with particular satisfaction that she watched Orson's TV make a spectacular crash landing on the sidewalk below.

Only after she'd decided that frostbite was a real danger did first their shoes, then underwear, pants and shirts come fluttering down. She watched with tearful amusement as the pair awkwardly tried to hold the sheet in place while trying to retrieve enough clothing to restore their decency.

The marriage was over. The day the divorce was final, Cass moved back to Summersville to have the baby—a baby she made damn sure carried the Rosier name, not Peters.

*

As Reece approached, his ungainly, wide-armed gait made him look more like a blow-up doll than a fit sheriff's deputy. Knowing him as she did, she knew he would be sweating profusely and likely cursing like a sailor by the time he arrived at the rock. *Why couldn't it be someone else?*

Then Cass recognized the other officer and felt a sense of relief. It was Hal Halverson, her friend and one of her strong supporters from the beginning. Reece wouldn't try any funny business with Halverson present. Maybe this wouldn't be as hard as she feared.

As the first officer on the scene she would be the Officer in Charge until the sheriff arrived. She asked Reece and Halverson to take charge of the crowd while she dealt with the body. The sheriff arrived ten minutes later and took over supervision of the crime scene. "Deputy Rosier, I'm assigning you to be lead investigator on this," he barked. "Deputy Halverson, you'll assist."

Halverson scowled. He was usually lead investigator on major crimes. Cass was elated at the assignment but at the same time concerned. With sixteen years on the force, Hal might not like being relegated to second place behind a college-educated upstart, and a woman to boot. She'd have to tread lightly.

She retrieved the department's high-res camera and object markers from the crime-scene kit the sheriff brought then approached Halverson and asked, "You okay with this, Hal?" At five-foot-eight, she was taller than most women, but Halverson towered over her by nearly a foot.

The man hesitated a moment then said with resignation, "Yeah, I guess so. It's about time you had your chance, kid. You're smart and better educated than the rest of us." He eyed Reece. "Any of the other deputies say anything, you just send them on over to me. Want me to put those out?" He pointed at the object markers used to identify anything at the scene that might be evidence.

"Would you? I'm going to start photographing the body."

"No problem. Let's get to work."

After shooting ground-level pictures of the rock and body from all angles, Cass climbed on the rock again and turned the camera straight down on the unfortunate woman. As she worked, the questions began piling up in her mind. *Who is this beautiful young girl? How old is she? Is she from around here? Who are her parents? Will I have to tell them, or will Sheriff Long take care of that?* Images of her own daughter flashed through her mind. *Dear God, don't let me have to be the one to tell the parents,* she thought.

Question after unanswered question flooded her mind, and as lead investigator, it would be her job to answer every one of them.

*

Dr. Gary Coleman, the county's young Medical Examiner, arrived, his hospital smock billowing behind him as he rushed across the beach with his ME jump kit in hand. "Who was the first officer on scene?" he asked after giving the body a quick preliminary examination.

"I was," Cass said.

"Anybody touch the body?"

"I took a neck pulse but that's all. I asked the bystanders if any of them had touched her. They all said they were afraid to."

"Deputy Rosier is lead investigator on this," Sheriff Long told Dr. Coleman. The doctor arched an eyebrow in surprise and nodded an acknowledgment.

"Deputy Rosier, would you help me bag her hands?" he requested. "If this is a murder, hopefully she got in a few scratches before she died."

Cass knew the routine, but this was her first chance to practice her skills on an actual dead body. "How long before you can give me a time of death?" she asked Coleman as she donned a fresh pair of latex gloves.

"Based on the temperatures out here and her state of rigor mortis, I can give you a preliminary estimate of six to eight hours, certainly no more than twelve. I won't be able to do any better until I can take a body-core temperature back at the morgue."

Dr. Coleman spent almost a half-hour giving the body a more thorough examination before saying he could find no obvious cause of death. "At first glance, she looks like she could have died of natural causes or perhaps overdosed on drugs or alcohol," he said. "But there's something very strange here. I tried to test her eyeballs for moisture depletion but they were sewn shut. I tried to swab her mouth but found the same with her jaw. Other than not being eviscerated and embalmed, it's like this body came straight out of a mortuary. It's like somebody carefully prepped and staged this body for us to find."

Chapter 2

Being lead investigator meant that Cass had to witness the autopsy. Not fully knowing what to expect, she entered the white, tile-covered, brightly fluorescent-lit room behind Dr. Coleman. It was a starkly sterile room, filled with cold, stainless steel fixtures and nose-wrinkling smells.

Cass caught her breath at the sight of the young woman's body laid out naked on the narrow autopsy table. More than one wager had been placed in the department as to how long she'd last before vomiting. As Dr. Coleman made the large 'Y' cut, she fought down her stomach with a steely resolve that she made sure none of those who bet against her won.

A microphone above the autopsy table recorded Dr. Coleman's running commentary as he worked. The autopsy revealed that the woman had been horribly abused. Only the parts of her body not covered by her dress were spared. There was evidence of savage beatings and brutal torture, right down to the soles of her feet. Three teeth were missing and she had four broken ribs.

The woman had no pubic hair, a feature not terribly unusual since shaven or waxed pubic areas became a fashion statement of sorts among trendy young women. But Dr. Coleman said this girl's hair had not been shaved, but rather the hair had been removed by plucking it out.

There was extensive bruising in and around the woman's vaginal and anal areas, but no third-party bodily fluids or hair was found on or inside the body nor on the woman's clothing. "This perp must have either used a condom or used objects to rape her with," Dr. Coleman said. He shook his head. "Whoever did this was an angry, sadistic bastard."

The cause of death was revealed only after removal of the girl's brain. "Ah, there it is," Dr. Coleman said as he held it up for examination. Pointing at the brain stem, he said, "There's your cause of death, Deputy Rosier."

It was easy to see even with Cass's medically untrained eye. While most of the stem was a uniform reddish pink, right in the middle was a dark, shriveled, damaged area that looked as if it had been burned. The doctor placed the brain in a stainless-steel bowl then turned the body on its side. He pulled back the hair at the nape of the woman's neck and looked closely. "I thought so," he muttered.

He invited Cass to come closer and look. He pointed at what looked to Cass like a tiny insect bite at the base of the skull. "That's where someone stuck something, probably a hypodermic needle, into this girl's medulla oblongata—the brain stem. The stab wound most likely killed her instantly, but this sick bastard injected something nasty, maybe some kind of acid, to make sure she died. We won't know what it was for sure until we get the tox report back."

"That's awful," Cass said, fighting the impulse to retch.

"She most likely died instantly from the brain stem puncture. Probably didn't feel the injection or tissue destruction at all. The killer chose this means of death very carefully."

*

Cass was relieved to leave the autopsy room. She followed Dr. Coleman to his office to discuss the findings. "This woman suffered a prolonged, agonizing ordeal that had to have taken place over weeks—maybe as long as a month," he said. "She was tortured just enough at any one time to keep her alive. Whoever did this knew what he was doing and was very good at it."

"You're assuming it was a man?"

"I'm not assuming anything; it's just a frame of reference. Odds would say it's more likely to be a man, but if the evidence takes us somewhere else, we'll go there without hesitation."

"So does the autopsy tell us anything at all about the killer?" Cass asked.

"There's no trace evidence that could lead us directly to someone's identity—no skin under her fingernails, no third-party body hair on either her or the clothing. But we have several hints.

"One of the first and most obvious is the woman's fingernails. They were elaborate, custom-designed acrylic nails that were put on after the torture.

"Then there's how her hair was all done up and the professional quality of her makeup. With her injuries she wouldn't have had the dexterity to do any of that. It's almost like someone took her to a beauty salon either just before or just after killing her. Since that's highly unlikely, I think we can presume the killer or killers have those kind of skills."

Dr. Coleman seemed perplexed. He stood and walked to the window scratching his head in thought. "Then there's the way the body was prepared," he said. "That old thing you see in the movies about someone closing a dead person's eyes after death is a myth. People don't close their eyes when they die, and even if someone else closes them, they don't stay shut. Same thing with the jaw. The jaw muscles relax, and the mouth naturally sags open. Mortuaries sew the eyelids and the jaw shut when they prepare the body so it can look like the person is peacefully asleep.

"The person who sewed this girl's eyelids and jaw used medical suture material better than most mortuaries use and made good, medical-grade surgical knots. I couldn't have made much better ones myself. Then it becomes bizarre. There's evidence that the killer broke and then reset some of her bones. Whoever did this to her was helping her heal at the same time he was killing her.

Cass scribbled furiously, trying to keep up. She couldn't tell if he was merely musing or giving her critical medical facts. She didn't dare miss a word.

"If this woman had sustained all of her injuries at once," Coleman continued, "it would have killed her outright. This killer kept his torture just under a lethal level. In my opinion, our killer is a person or persons with extensive medical skills and possibly experience as a mortician or morgue worker. Morticians use makeup in their job, but I've never seen one of them make a body look as good as this one."

"There's another possibility here," Cass said. "We could be dealing with a group of people, a 'murder club' if you will, who share all these skills among them."

"That certainly is a possibility, Dr. Coleman said. "Sorry I couldn't get you more on this girl's identity. Has the department had any missing person inquiries that fit her description?"

"Not as far as I know. And that's kind of strange considering how long you're saying she was in the hands of her torturer. That will probably change when her story hits the newspapers and the television news tonight."

Coleman leaned back in his chair and sighed tiredly. "Tell the sheriff I'll try to get a transcript of the preliminary autopsy report over to your office by tomorrow afternoon. Wish we knew more about what drugs she may have had on-board, but it takes at least three weeks to get a tox report back from the state lab. I'll see if I can hurry them up but I doubt it will make any difference.

"By the way, you did well in there today. Much better than most. You didn't make a single trip to the sink. Tell the sheriff you have my compliments."

Cass smiled. "It'd be better if you told him yourself, doc. There was apparently a lot of money riding on whether or not I would keep my stomach. I want the losers to get the bad news from someone other than me."

"I'll be happy to convey that news. For your information, there's more than one member of your department who didn't fare so well during previous autopsies."

"Glad to know that." Cass grinned wryly. "Care to share any names?"

"I'd better not, other than to say that one of them is the guy who wears the biggest star over there."

"Clint—our good sheriff?"

"You didn't hear it from me," Coleman laughed. "You better get out of here before my mouth gets me in trouble."

*

A thorough search of the beach and forest around the crime scene turned up no evidence Cass could tie to the murder. Fingerprints and the woman's DNA profile returned nothing.

Despite Cass's prediction otherwise, no one showed up to claim the body. Even with the crime being listed on the national NCIC (National Crime Information Center) registry and on every local police bulletin board and missing person's registry they could get access to, the case remained an utter mystery.

Nicholas County's evening gown clad victim bore only the anonymous name of Jane Doe.

Chapter 3

Murders were rare in Nicholas County. Prior to the evening gown murder, the only other one committed in the five years since Cass joined the department essentially solved itself. Nine months into her rookie year, a husband called in and confessed that he'd shot his wife. They'd been fighting over who got custody of the dog in their divorce.

It was early October, sixteen months after the discovery of the woman wearing the evening gown. Cass was just pulling out of her driveway on the way to take Katy to the dentist when the call came in.

"Unit 1, Dispatch."

Odd. Mary, the dispatcher, knew that Cass was taking her daughter to the dentist this morning." Unit 1," she responded a bit testily.

"Cass, they need you down at Mt. Nebo right away—mile post 79."

"Jeez, Mary, you know I'm busy with Katy this morning. What is it?"

Mary Donavan was a relatively new dispatcher. She sounded uncomfortable. "They've got another one, Cass. Remember that Jane Doe last year?"

A chill coursed through her. "Not again," Cass said under her breath.

Katy sensed the sudden change. "What's wrong, Mommy?"

"Nothing, baby. Just some police business. I've got to talk to this lady for a minute." Cass didn't want her eight-year-old daughter in on this conversation. "Use call signals, dispatch," Cass scolded. "Give me a 10-21." In moments, her cell phone rang.

"Thanks, Mary," Cass answered. "Sorry for barking at you. What's going on?"

"That's okay. I'm still getting used to this radio stuff. Deputy McKesson responded to a 911 call at Up-Yonder Road. He says he's got another body in an evening gown. He wants a 10-39 response."

10-39 meant drop everything but your pants, full sirens and lights and haul ass.

"10-4, Mary." Cass was so used to radio jargon that she sometimes unwittingly used it on the phone as well. "I'll call him right now."

It took five rings for Deputy McKesson to answer. "Go," was his terse, non-identifying greeting.

"It's Cass, Jerry. What's happening?"

"Got another one like we had over at Butt Beach. An old couple the body from up on the highway. She's lying in the bed of a farmer's hay wagon that was parked in a spot easy to see."

Cass wanted to curse but stifled the impulse before Katy could hear something out of her mother's mouth she ought not to hear.

"Mary said you want a 10-39. I've got my kid with me. Do I have time to drop her off at school?"

"Yeah, there's no perp on site. Just need you here fast to take charge of the scene."

"Will do. My 10-77's twelve to fifteen minutes depending on traffic. Keep that place clean, Jerry."

"10-4 Sheriff." He clicked off without a goodbye.

At times it was still a bit startling when someone called her sheriff. At the moment the title was actually 'Acting Sheriff.' As she raced toward Mt. Nebo, she couldn't help but reflect on the monumental changes that had given rise to her new job title.

*

It all started with an unexpected visit to her house by Jessie and Melinda Ginn around seven-thirty one night last May. The Ginns, a middle-aged couple, went to church with Cass's parents. She knew them, but not well. "Come in," Cass said, expecting a friendly chat. She seated them in the living room.

Jessie started the conversation in a shaky, hesitant voice. "We're sorry to intrude," he said, "but we just have to talk to someone. We've prayed about this and feel that if we can trust anybody down at the sheriff's office, it's got to be you."

The statement set off alarm bells in Cass's head. "Do you have reason to not trust the department?"

"Yes!" was the man's abrupt answer. "We understand you're the chief investigator down there. Is that right?"

"The department doesn't have an official chief investigator, but I guess you could say I've been filling that role. Why?"

"If we were to tell you that someone in your department was breaking the law, what would you do?"

"I'd investigate it, same as any other crime. Members of the sheriff's department aren't above the law. If anything, we have to be more circumspect than anyone else. If an allegation turned out to be true, I'd arrest them just like I would any other lawbreaker."

Cass watched a tear roll down Melinda's cheek. Her husband was actually trembling. Melinda reached into her purse, withdrew a sheaf of papers and handed them to her husband.

"Do you know our daughter, Jenny?" the man asked.

"I think so; fifteen-year-old, tall with long, sandy-blonde hair?" Cass knew the girl, by reputation, if nothing else. She was fifteen but looked and dressed much older. She ran with a rowdy bunch, several of whom had been arrested for various misdemeanors. She was a girl with a cocky attitude who defied authority and was suspected by the school resource officer of distributing prescription drugs around campus; a charge her parents would probably deny. After all, they made sure she was in church every Sunday.

"We..." Jessie's voice broke. He swallowed and began again. "Ahem—we lost control of Jenny over a year ago." The statement was too much for Melinda, who broke down and wept openly as her husband went on. "She won't listen to us or do what we say. And now she's in way over her head."

"I've got to tell you folks; Jenny's come up on the department's radar a couple of times. She's been mentioned as a source for prescription drugs at school. I hope it's not true but I'd watch your medicine cabinet very closely if I were you. Is that what you've come to tell me about?"

The man handed Cass the papers. "I wish that was all. We've warned her and warned her about drugs, but that's not the reason we're here. These are text messages I downloaded from her cell phone last night while she was sleeping. I printed them out this afternoon while she was at school."

Cass began to read. All were addressed to topstar@nctelco.com. The messages wove a trail of prurient, salacious, X-rated dialogues detailing a pattern of flirtations entirely inappropriate for a fifteen-year-old high-school sophomore. Mid-way through the stack Cass found a self-taken topless picture Jenny had sent to someone. The responding message was a corresponding photo of a man's erect penis.

The messages made it clear that a few days after the exchange of photos, the pair had met and had their first sexual encounter. Then there was another, and another. This girl was clearly on her way to an unwanted pregnancy—or worse.

24

Cass shook her head at the anguish of these poor parents. "This is a huge problem with high school kids," she said. "I'm sorry it's happening with Jenny. The kids consider this stuff no big deal, but what I'm seeing here is considered a felony; child pornography. Do you have any idea who the boy is?"

"It's not a boy," Jessie said venomously. His hands balled into fists. "It's a man!"

Melinda reached into her purse and this time produced what appeared to be a diary.

"We hated to do it," he said. "But we read her diary this afternoon. The man she's been seeing—the man whose penis is in that picture—is Sheriff Long."

The words struck like a thunder-clap. Cass was momentarily slack-jawed; unable to speak. Finally she stammered, "Sheriff Long?"

"It's all right here. Read it for yourself." He opened the book, handed it to Cass and pointed at what the girl had written. The damning evidence was, laid out in the girl's barely legible longhand.

I love it when my Clinty touches me down there…

Tonight I gave him a pair of my panties…

It's so kool doing it in his cop car…

Ain't nobody gonna mess with me and my sheriff…when that Durango's rockin', don't nobody come knockin'.

Cass felt sick. Tucked between the pages was a three-by-five photo of Clint in his dress uniform. Scrawled across the bottom was "This is my man!" The word 'my' was underlined three times.

"My God!" Cass whispered. She looked at Jessie and asked, "Where's Jenny right now?"

"We don't know. After we read her diary, we went looking for her. One of her friends said she saw the sheriff pick her up down at Dewey's Malt Shop around seven o'clock. We thought you might know where he is."

"I don't, but I'll find out. Can I keep these?" Cass indicated the messages and the diary.

"Yes. We don't want them in our house."

"You two go home." Cass instructed. "I'll look into this right now. If I find Jenny, I'll let you know. If she comes home first, you call my cell phone." She handed Jessie her business card and pointed out the number. "Don't worry; you've done the right thing."

*

Only a faint tincture of light remained above the mountains west of town when Cass drove back to the office. She couldn't use her radio for fear that Clint might hear. Once there, she asked the night dispatcher if she knew where the sheriff was. "Haven't heard from him," she said. "Do you want me to give him a call?"

That was the last thing Cass wanted. "No, no. It's nothing important. I'll run by his house."

Clint's house was actually one side of a small duplex he'd maintained since his rather nasty divorce from Nancy four years ago. She and the two kids still lived in the house he once called his own. As she drove past the duplex, Cass thought of the first time she met Sheriff Long.

It happened a year after Katy was born. Nick Hathaway, a long-time Nicholas County deputy sheriff, had suddenly passed away. A massive heart attack they said. Armed with her degree, her extra credits in crime-scene management, and her POST certification, Cass marched up the steps of the county courthouse and handed the surprisingly young Sheriff Long her application. She harbored no illusions about how slim her chances were of being hired on.

To her surprise, Long called the next day and asked her to come in for an interview. Young and progressive by Nicholas County standards, the then thirty-three-year-old sheriff said he considered himself a bit of a rebel. He said that, over the objections of some in his department, he'd been looking to hire a female deputy, but had so far been stopped by the fact that in conservative Nicholas

County, West Virginia, the very idea of hiring a woman deputy was unsettling to some, including two of the three County Commissioners, and downright offensive to others. He said that in light of her qualifications, he might be willing to buck the opposition.

Though she thought her interview went well, she was nonetheless somewhat surprised when Sheriff Long called three days later and asked her to come back for a follow-up interview.

She was happy to oblige, but was slightly offended by his first question. "It won't be easy doing this job, Ms. Rosier, are you certain you're ready to tackle this?"

"I wouldn't have applied if I weren't, Sheriff."

"You understand that some of my deputies are absolutely opposed to the idea of hiring a woman. If we do hire you, they'll probably give you a pretty rough time."

Cass bristled. She bit her tongue to keep too much of her redhead temper from showing. "Sheriff Long, I'm educated, I'm competent, and I'm qualified—far more qualified than a lot of your deputies."

"No question about that, Ms. Rosier. It's just that some of the guys are convinced that this department is no place for a woman."

"Do they mean can I keep up with the pace of the job? Am I smart enough? Can I shoot straight or handle a patrol car in a high-speed chase? What?"

"No, no. I've seen your POST scores. I'm sure you can do all that. They want to know what happens when you have to handle a drunk who's twice your size. What happens with an armed suspect? Will a perp take you seriously enough to believe you'll actually pull the trigger? Your fellow officers need to have confidence you'll be there to back them up in dicey situations."

Again Cass had to stifle an angry reply. Instead she said, "I was raised with five brothers; all a lot bigger than me. I know how to dish it out when I have to. I more than held my own in POST training against a class of forty-two other officers, most of them bigger than me. I'm five-eight and 159 lbs. I run at least five miles a day and bench press 220 lbs. I've seen your deputies, sheriff. Half of them are significantly overweight and out of shape. They couldn't run down a perp if their lives depended on it. Tell you what, you set up a 5K run and put up your best five deputies. If they all beat me, I'll withdraw my application."

A grin spread across Long's face. "You'd do that?"

"Damn right. I'll do it today, right now. And when we're done, we can take those same deputies down to the wrestling mat at the high-school gym, and I'll show them how this 'little woman' can plant them flat on their fat asses in at least ten different ways. I'd rather earn this job that way than have to start talking about things like sexual discrimination in hiring." It was a none-too-subtle hint that she'd better be considered solely on the basis of her qualifications and not disqualified because of her gender.

Two days later, as Cass crossed the finish line of the impromptu 5K, she looked back to find the second-place runner nearly two hundred yards behind her. By the time he came wheezing to the finish line, the sheriff had already offered her the job. He later told her he was going to give it to her anyway, but thought the race might be the perfect way to show his deputies what she was made of—and to shame them into getting into better shape themselves.

*

In the four years since his divorce, Clint had gained quite a reputation as a man about town. Cass didn't care who he slept with. Until now he'd been discrete. But this time he wasn't just screwing another woman, he was raping a child.

Failing to find him at the duplex, Cass took a swing through downtown. A fair number of high school kids hung out down at the Sonic, a drive-in hamburger joint just off Main Street. The business's large parking lot served as the pit stop where kids gathered to show off their cars and troll for attention from the opposite sex.

Cass spotted a gaggle of kids at the far end of the lot. They were standing around a nicely restored 75 blue Malibu Super Sport and a tricked out, impossibly tall, white Dodge pickup truck with rims that must have cost at least a thousand bucks.

The smell of burning Marijuana was unmistakable as Cass pulled up and rolled down her window. The source was nowhere in sight. "Hey guys," she greeted, "I'm looking for Jenny Ginn. She's not in trouble or anything, y'all seen her?"

A general snicker ran through the crowd. Piper Parker, a skinny blonde with a shock of pink hair on one side, looked around a little and responded with a smirk. "She was here a while ago but she left."

"Left? Was she with someone?"

"Ask your boss," a boy's voice from the back called out. The crowd laughed.

"Guess I'm a little behind," Cass smiled, trying to convey the message that she wasn't a threat. "I can't keep up with that girl's social calendar. Anybody care to enlighten me?"

"The Sheriff keeps pretty good tabs on it," another boy laughed. Cass heard someone whisper loudly behind him, "Shut up Kenny, you'll get her busted."

"Look guys, I've got to find her. It's kind of a family emergency. If you can't help me I'll just have to get out of my car and start investigating the burning rope I smelled when I pulled up. Make y'all empty your pockets, take a look inside those vehicles, that sort of stuff. I don't want to do that but it's up to you. Who owns the pickup? I'll start there."

A big gangly kid with hair to his shoulders and a half-finished tattoo on his left forearm pushed his way to the front. "Ahh come on deputy, you don't want to do that. We're just out here having a little fun. We ain't hurting nobody."

It was Nathan Caldwell, a nineteen-year-old who'd dropped out of school in the middle of eleventh grade but had never outgrown his immaturity. "You're right, Nathan," Cass said, trying to still sound friendly. I'm not here to hassle you guys, I just need to know where Jenny is."

"We don't know," Nathan said, looking around seeking confirmation. The sheriff came by here an hour ago and they took off."

"Anybody know where they went," Cass asked the crowd. There were a lot of shaking heads. A couple of girls in front twittered conspiratorially behind raised hands. Apparently Jenny's antics with the sheriff had become general knowledge.

"Look guys, give me something—anything," Cass pleaded. "Cause if I open this car door, a lot of you are going to be cited for possession and a couple of you might go to jail. I don't want to be a hard-ass, but that's just the way it is." She pulled the inside door lever and the door popped open slightly; just enough to let them know she was serious.

Nathan turned pasty faced. Obviously there was something in the pickup he didn't want her to see. He held up his hands defensively and said, "No, no, Deputy Rosier, no need for that. They could've gone almost anywhere. The sheriff usually drops her back off down here around ten."

"Where do they usually go?"

"I da'know. Nathan turned and asked, "Anybody else know?"

"Down to the city dump," someone shouted out. "Out to the Pit" another said. "She said something about the lake," revealed one of the girls who had twittered earlier.

It was all the information she was going to get. "Thanks guys," Cass called out as she closed her car door. "Just two things before I go. Nathan, I'm going to call for a vehicle check on the pickup in about two minutes. Same thing with the Malibu. If there's anything in there, you better get rid of it in a hurry. The other thing is that if any of you are entertaining ideas of calling Jenny before I find her, just remember this. We'll be checking her incoming calls. Any of you trying to warn her that I'm looking for her will end up in jail."

*

Cass caught the couple in the act in a dark corner of the marina parking lot. She crept up on the sheriff's Dodge Durango and peered cautiously through the windshield. What she saw sickened her—Jenny, wearing nothing but skimpy panties, kneeling on the passenger seat with her head bobbing up and down in Clint's crotch.

His head was thrown back and his eyes closed in the throes of ecstasy. Even with the vehicle running, air conditioner going full-blast, and the windows rolled up, she could hear his moans.

She wanted nothing more than to run away and erase the revolting vision from her mind's eye, but duty stopped her. Whatever else he was, Sheriff Clint Long was a child pornographer and a pedophile who was preying at this very moment on an underage girl.

She snapped a damning picture of the couple through the windshield then flung the vehicle door open and shouted a police warning to not move.

Arresting her boss—her friend, was the hardest thing Cass had ever done as a police officer. Trembling with anger, she actually had to pull her gun to get Clint to turn around so that she could get the handcuffs on. All the while she was thinking that if this was eight years from now, his victim could have been Katy. Friend or not, Clint Long was just another scumbag—and a child abuser to boot.

*

The arrest threw the department into complete disarray. Though she didn't feel like a hero, she was hailed as one in the press. In her mind she was just a police officer doing her duty. Cass struggled with the thought that she had betrayed a friend, but reconciled that dilemma with the knowledge that he was the one who had betrayed not just his badge and oath of office, but the trust of an impressionable, underage girl. She had to put duty before friend-ship, especially since there was a minor child involved.

The undersheriff was an aged, barely functional officer whom everyone liked, but knew wasn't qualified to be sheriff. To blunt any potential political fallout from the fiasco, the county commissioners came to Cass and requested that she serve as Acting Sheriff until a new one could be elected in November.

Whatever possessed the Republicans to nominate Deputy Cassandra Camille Rosier, a redheaded, attractive, thirty-one-year-old, divorced, female deputy with just less than seven years on the force, she couldn't imagine; she was the least political person she knew. But she was flattered and accepted the nomination more out of a desire to not hurt anyone's feelings than anything else. After all, she didn't think she stood a chance in the general election.

But the Democrats nominated a little-known, inarticulate candidate who was running a terrible campaign. His campaign ads made him look like a Nazi and he had already offended the League of Women Voters by telling them that he thought women were too tender-hearted to be police officers. He provoked outrage in most of the rest of the community by saying that he thought Sheriff Long's crime was more the girl's fault than Long's.

Now as she raced toward Mt. Zion and yet another encounter with a dead body apparently dressed in an evening gown, she was running the department and in the midst of a campaign to remove that 'acting' part from her title and change it to just plain Sheriff Cass Rosier. It appeared she was about to pull off what she and many in the county would regard as one of the most improbable wins in the history of Nicholas County politics.

The thought of being the honest-to-god sheriff would take some getting used to. Today, when people addressed her as Sheriff, she still felt like they were talking to someone else.

*

The crime scene was less than a half mile from Mt. Zion. The minute she arrived, Deputy McKesson escorted Cass to the wagon where a body of a young woman who looked to be in her mid to late twenties was again staged to look peacefully at rest. She looked strikingly similar to the first evening gown victim; long blonde hair, slender, fit body, perhaps a bit taller than the first woman.

She was dressed in a full-length, scarlet brocade evening gown. The soft, lustrous fabric seemed almost like a cloud around her. The dress's dramatic squared 'V' sweetheart-style neckline exposed the woman's considerable endowment. Cass shook her head. *This killer obviously likes boobs and low-cut gowns*, she thought.

Like the first victim, this woman had perfect makeup and elaborately done nails. Cass caught her breath when she saw an inch-wide scarlet and black lace ribbon festooned with embroidered daisies around her neck, fastened with a pearl pin.

Though the dresses were different, the color was the same. And the ribbon and pearl pin were identical to that found on the first evening gown victim.

"I'll take lead on this," Cass informed the other deputies. "Halvorson, you'll assist."

There was no scowl from Halverson this time. He'd come to respect Cass's investigative abilities, not to mention the fact that she was now his boss—at least until the election. Cass had heard through the grapevine that Halverson had already told people he was going to vote for her.

*

The ME's findings came back nearly identical to the first Jane Doe. Rape, prolonged brutal torture, and the same hideous cause of death; a syringe-full of acid delivered directly into the brain stem.

Again the killer covered his tracks well. Other than the body itself and the clothing the woman wore, there was a complete lack of physical evidence.

Six months later, a frustrated investigative team gathered to discuss whether to put the case on inactive status.

"How can someone show up and get themselves killed here with nobody knowing who they are, where they're from or why they're here?" Cass asked. "It's so damn strange."

"You're assuming it's a he," new deputy Eric Zeeman said. "Just as easily could be a woman." Zeeman was Cass's first new hire. He was sharp as a whip and loved being a cop.

"I thought about that, Eric, and I don't discount the possibility. But my gut tells me the killer is a man. That field we found her in was fairly muddy. We didn't find any heel drag marks or mud on her dress. Whoever put her in that wagon was strong enough to carry her there. Most women couldn't do that.

"Yeah you're probably right," Zeeman muttered, "and he's probably hiding in plain sight right under our noses"

"Anything new from the ME?" Deputy Halvorson asked.

"No," Cass said. "Dr. Coleman even called in the state ME and had her re-autopsy the body. As you all know, this body was prepped the same way as the first girl. Dr. Coleman is even more convinced that the killer has a medical background. I've been running checks on every medical professional in the county. So far they all look clean; same with morticians. I'm checking all their workers out as well."

"This may be a long shot, Halvorson said, "but how about military service records?"

"Good Call. We've got a lot of veterans in the county. It's anybody's guess as to how many of them served as medics. I'll put in a DOD information request and see what turns up."

"How about the other kind of vets—veterinarians?" Zeeman asked.

"I thought of that too," Halvorson said. "There are only two in the whole county. Doc Boynton here in town is nearly seventy years old. He's been here over forty-years. The other guy, Doctor Beasley over in Richwood, is nearly sixty years old and just lost a foot to diabetes. Both are married and neither has a criminal history. I ran criminal background checks on both and they each came back squeaky clean."

Cass sighed and leaned back in her chair. "I've been getting a lot of bad feedback lately. People are starting to lock their doors and pack guns. Concealed carry permit applications are up more than three hundred percent over the last three months, almost all of them for women. It might only be a matter of time before some nervous Nellie out there plugs some kid looking for his dog in her backyard."

"How's the county commission treating you?" Halverson asked.

It was a good question. She'd won the election and the 'acting' part of her title was gone. It was now just plain "Sheriff." That meant a lot of people were watching and judging her performance.

"Polite but nervous," she said. "Two nearly identical unsolved murders in less than two years don't do a lot to help their reelection chances any more than it does mine."

Zeeman shook his head, ran his fingers through his hair and said, "Sheriff, who'd have ever thought that Nicholas County would have its very own serial killer?"

Chapter 4

Damn you, Ricky Thornton, you stole seven years of my life! Sam's mind screamed the accusation for what had to be the thousandth time. She slammed the phone back down in its cradle and clasped her hands together to stop their shaking.

Why is this so hard? Cass has been through this herself. If anyone will understand, it's her.

But even as Sam questioned herself, she knew the answer. She'd been hiding the truth from Cass for more than two years. Cass might not count it as lying, but at a minimum she'd regard Sam's omissions as a serious breach of trust.

Sam, Samantha Louise Martin, and Cass Rosier had been spit-in-the-hand, cross-your-heart, double-pinky handshake best friends since the first day of second grade. Years ago, they'd promised to always tell each other everything. Easy to do when you're seven or eight, and even more so during the awkward teenage years. But today, 23 years later, Sam still considered the promise valid even though she was now a highly successful New York attorney and Cass was a successful cop back in good old Summersville. After all, a spit-in-the hand, cross-your-heart, double-pinky handshake promise had no expiration date.

Sam always intended to keep the promise, no matter what, and she had; at least up until the fairytale story of her perfect life with the perfect husband began to unravel. Whether from denial or embarrassment, Sam had falsely tried to maintain the façade of a happy marriage to her friend. "Ain't right to ask other people to carry your load," her intensely private father used to say. She shared the sentiment and hated other people knowing her intimate business. So even though she and Cass talked weekly, sometimes daily, Sam had never let a hint of the problems slip.

But now there was no way of avoiding it. There could be no more hiding; no more denial. Cass would learn the truth anyway. Far better that she learn it directly from Sam than in any other way.

I can do this, she resolved. *I'm a grown woman, a highly trained attorney, an associate partner at one of the most prestigious law firms in New York City. I've dealt with a lot tougher situations than this.*

The argument seemed valid except that, before now, all those 'tough situations' belonged to her clients and were by definition impersonal and distant. Never before had it been her at the eye of the storm.

Summersville was home—her sanctuary. To her mind, there was nowhere else she could ground herself and move the center of her world back to its proper place better than there. The artificial stony canyons of Manhattan wouldn't do. She needed the real canyons of West Virginia where regular people lived quiet, normal, real lives.

Her leave of absence started yesterday. This morning the car was loaded. The UPS man had already picked up the things she had to ship. All that remained was to let Cass know that she was coming. Cass was the only person Sam could hold on to as she stepped over the precipice to at least temporarily escape her frenetic life in New York and attempt a soft landing back in the mountains where she grew up.

But the more she thought about it, the more she realized she didn't have to fear telling Cass the truth—what she had to do instead was admit it to herself. Cass wasn't the enemy, she her savior. The fear retreated as she finally picked up the phone and dialed this time without putting it back down. Now all she had to do was control that sudden quiver that took over her lower lip every time she'd tried to dial before.

*

Katy answered the phone. "Rosier residence, Katy speaking."

"Hello, KK, this is Aunty Sam. How are you?"

"Aunty Sam!" nine-year-old Katy shouted in delight. "I'm fine. Guess what. Jackie Wooten got a new puppy, a little brown one. It's so cute. I asked Mom if I could have one too, but she says not till I'm twelve." The little girl's tone turned petulant. "That's a long time. I don't think that's fair, do you?"

"I don't know," Sam chuckled. "I'd have to think about it." Sam wasn't about to step into the middle of a dispute between mother and daughter. "Is your mom there?"

"Yes," Katy said with resignation. She obviously wasn't going to get her hoped-for ally in the puppy fight. "I'll get her." Without putting the phone down, she shouted into Sam's ear, "Mom! It's Aunty Sam. She won't let me have a puppy either." The phone went clattering to the counter.

"Sam!" Cass answered brightly a minute later. "How are you? Sorry about the 'Aunty Sam' bit. I keep trying to get her to call you Samantha."

"Don't worry. I like 'Aunty Sam' just fine. I'm sorry I haven't called much the past few weeks. There's been lot on my plate." *That's an understatement,* Sam thought as she eyed the final divorce decree lying on the coffee table.

Usually bright and upbeat, Sam knew she sounded down, but she couldn't help it. Her mood was not lost on her friend.

"Okay, who is this and what have you done with my Sammy?" Cass asked. "What's the matter, girl, did somebody run over your dog?"

"Darn you Cass Rosier, you read me faster than I sometimes read myself. Can't you at least wait until I'm finished saying hello?" She tried to put a smile in her voice, but the trembling lip was back.

Cass paused a moment then said, "Hello, Sammy. Glad you called. How's your gerbil? Now tell me what's going on."

Sam swallowed the lump in her throat. "I'm coming home Cassie. I'll be there tomorrow night." She said it with such indifference that it sounded more like a funeral announcement than a cause célèbre.

"Woohoo Sister," Cass shouted! Katy and I will be jumping up and down. But there's more, isn't there. What's the rest of the story darlin'?"

"I'm coming alone."

Again there was a pause. When Cass finally spoke her tone was more guarded. "Alone, as in driving by yourself, or alone, as in unattached, say-good-bye-to-Ricky, kind of alone?"

"As in all of the above. Ricky and I are over. The divorce was final last month. I'm coming home for a while because—just because I just need to come home, that's all. I'm pretty messed up."

Sam waited for Cass to speak for several long moments. She was obviously digesting the news. Finally she responded in typical Cass fashion. "Sammy I—I—oh shit Sammy girl, that really sucks. Are you okay?"

"I knew you'd have just the right words for it," Sam laughed softly. "No, I'm not okay. That's why I'm coming. Do I ever have stories to tell you."

"And I want to hear every one of them. What can I do to help?"

"I hate to ask, but could you go open up Daddy's house? I need to make sure the water's running and the lights are on, that sort of stuff."

"Of course. Want me to hook up the hot and cold running Chippendale Dancers while I'm at it?"

Sam laughed again, a real laugh this time. "I think I'll pass."

"Anything else you want me to do?"

"Just don't give up on me. I'm probably not going to be the best company for a while."

"Don't you worry, girl. Just get your skinny little ass down here. Do you need me to fly up and drive down with you?"

Sam shook her head. "No, no. I'll be okay."

"Well fine. Now that we both have exes, we can talk about them all we want while we're sticking the pins in our voodoo dolls."

Sam laughed again. It felt good. It was the first time in months she'd actually laughed out loud twice in the same day.

Chapter 5

You really shouldn't be doing this, Jennifer chided herself. *You only met him three hours ago.*

It was so kind of him to let her, a total stranger, drop in so unexpectedly; no appointment or anything. That could only happen in a little burg like this. It'd never happen in D.C.

Summersville was just another ignorable West Virginia mountain town among the many on the map that she'd never heard of. Simply another interesting little element in the milieu of places and things that would be part of her unscripted, meandering, three-week Appalachian vacation.

Strange how he didn't have a receptionist or other office staff. He said that was because he didn't want any barriers between himself and the client. Now that she thought about it—thought about him—it made perfect sense. He was so engaging and easy to talk too. In a matter of minutes she felt she could tell him anything. Then there was the fact that he was so damn good looking. And his hands—they seemed almost magical; gentle but undeniably strong; skilled but with a touch of intimacy that made the experience seem as much personal as professional.

Would she agree to go to his ranch for lunch? Of course. After all, she was on vacation. He was single—she was single—and it was, after all, only lunch.

He scribbled directions on the back of the folded receipt he printed off. He used a kind of cryptic shorthand that was easy to understand once he explained. The note said:

Arbk 5M, Cnvs, +2M, CR39/4 L1. 9M - RR.

He explained as he wrote. "Go out Arbuckle Road a little over 5 miles to the little town of Canvas. Continue a couple of miles farther to County Route 39/4. Turn left and go precisely 1.9 miles. Watch for the red ribbon around the big pine tree on the right side of the road. You can't miss it."

What an adventure! She was used to navigating the crowded, busy streets of Boston and Washington, D. C. This gravel road, County Road 39/4, was empty by comparison. *Piece of cake,* she thought.

His directions worked perfectly, right down to the ribbon on the tree. Even at that she nearly missed the turnoff where a small lane emerged from the left and met the main road—a barely noticeable break in the dense hardwood forest that bounded both sides of the road.

"Be sure to close the gate on the way in," he'd instructed, showing his beautiful, disarming smile. "I don't have a lot of cattle, but I need to hang on to those I've got."

Five-foot-four, pretty, and petite, Jennifer Oldroyd was intimidated by the heavy, black, iron gate. It was set back and nearly invisible from the road. But following his latching instructions, the gate swung easily on its well-oiled hinges.

As it opened, Jennifer suddenly shuddered. *Damn! This place is a little creepy,* she thought. The trees formed a dense, dark tunnel, with only an occasional shaft of sunlight penetrating through to the ground. This wasn't what she expected. With some apprehension, she decided to drive down the lane a little way just to see what was there. She remembered his admonition about the cows. She could always reopen the gate quickly enough if she decided to turn around and come out.

Jennifer drove slowly through the canopied trees for nearly a quarter of a mile. There was not a hint that anyone lived anywhere nearby. Then to her relief, the forest suddenly opened, revealing acres and acres of rich, pastoral, post-card perfect pasture land.

The little lane was actually a driveway that led right up to the front porch of a modest log cabin-style house a half-mile away where the pastures met the trees on the other side. A forested hill arose immediately behind the house.

A small herd of cattle grazed peacefully on either side of the drive. Jennifer smiled. How could she have doubted him? This was exactly how he said it would be.

The front door swung open as she mounted the steps. He'd obviously been watching for her. There he stood in his pressed flannel shirt and slender blue jeans that showed off his long, lean legs and perfect ass. *God! That smile could melt snow.*

"You made it. Come on in," he invited.

"Drove right to it." she said with a smile.

She stepped through the door into a Western motif living room—all leather and wood. This was certainly less than ordinary for a Boston-raised city girl on her first extended vacation since landing a terrific government job in D.C. just over a year ago.

Wonderful smells wafted from the kitchen. "You've been cooking," she said. "I thought we'd be eating Kentucky Fried Chicken or something."

"No. When it comes to someone really special, I prefer to cook for real."

She thought she might melt right alongside the butter.

The meal proved as delicious as it smelled. The red wine went perfectly with the Beef Bourguignon, the roasted baby potatoes, and tender asparagus spears.

Who would have ever thought I'd stumble across a single, attractive, obviously well-off gourmet cook in the middle of the mountains of West Virginia?

He was a perfect gentleman. The conversation was stimulating and comfortable. By the end of the meal, she felt as if they'd known each other forever. He informed her that their next task was to clean up the kitchen. She hated doing dishes, but the third glass of wine had disarmed her to the point that she would have agreed to almost anything.

"I'll wash, you dry," he volunteered.

During the dish washing, things became playful. "Give me that thing," she laughed as she lunged a little tipsily to get her hands on the plate he'd offered then snatched from her grasp.

"You're going to have to climb to get this one," he said with a chuckle.

Her five-foot-four against his six-foot-three made the task impossible.

"You're going to have to help."

"Help what?"

"Help me climb you."

"You want to climb me?"

"Yes. But I want that plate, too," she said with an impish grin.

"Would this help?" He bent, still holding the plate high out of her grasp. "Come and get it." His soft, husky tone clearly conveyed the message that he wasn't just talking about the plate.

She came fully against him, reaching high for the plate, but found his lips instead. The gentle kiss quickly turned into one of such savage intensity that it surprised her. This was not how she acted, especially with a total stranger. Was it the wine? Was it the man's incredible sensuality? Maybe it was the intoxicating sense of freedom of her first vacation in over a year. Maybe it was all of them. She didn't care. She was overwhelmed by the desire to simply devour this man.

They left a trail of clothing from the kitchen, through the living room and all the way to the bedroom. *My God, he's beautiful—and big!* Bigger than any man she'd ever been with. The man's size gave her pause. She was a small woman. Would she be able to accommodate him?

She had to collect herself a little. She stepped back and held him at arm's-length. "Whew, better slow down and take a deep breath here, cowboy. Now that we're both naked as J-birds, I know it's a little late to be saying, but I fear you've swept me off my feet. You probably won't believe me, but I'm a pretty straight-laced gal who's never done anything like this"

He chuckled and unleashed one of his devastating smiles. "I think it's fair to say that you've done the same to me, Miss Oldroyd. I certainly don't make a habit of treating a lovely new patient in the morning and making love to her that afternoon. If you're at all uncomfortable, we could put our clothes back on and continue the rest of our afternoon in the living room. It's completely up to you. However, I must say that having to cover such an incredibly beautiful body as yours at a time like this ought to be a crime." He reached out and gently caressed the slope of her right breast then pulled her against him and found her mouth again.

Her resistance vanished. She pushed him back on the bed and brazenly climbed on top. She had to have him inside her. Her earlier worry about his size disappeared as she guided him with her hand and wetly lowered herself on him. He filled her like no man ever had.

Suddenly, before she could move, he tensed and convulsed, painfully gripping her arms. His whole body stiffened as he writhed and gave out a loud, "Arghhhhhhhhhh!" She felt his warmth flow into her, and almost immediately felt his rock-hard erection begin to wilt. In a matter of seconds she could barely feel him inside her at all.

"Did you just—come?" she asked in disbelief.

He didn't answer but lay motionless for what seemed an eternity, his eyes turned to the wall. When he did finally look up at her, it was not with a look of shame or embarrassment, but of absolute rage.

Alarmed, she tried to soothe him. "Don't worry about it, buddy. I know it happens to men sometimes. Maybe things got a little too intense. Coulda been the wine. You know we hit that bottle pretty hard. Let's just relax, and try again in a little…"

"Get off me, you stupid bitch!" he screamed. His right fist suddenly shot out, connecting solidly with her jaw. He bucked and threw her off.

Half-conscious, she went flying off the bed and onto the wooden floor, landing awkwardly on her right arm. Had she been fully aware, she would have heard one of the bones break with a loud crack. She rolled over on her back as a sea of blackness engulfed her.

When consciousness returned, Jennifer felt the crescendo of throbbing, agonizing pain in her arm. But more terrifying was the sight of the man kneeling over her, his flaccid penis dangling uselessly in front of her face.

"Look what you've done!" he screamed at her. "You fucking women are all the same." Once again his fist lashed out, this time catching her squarely in the left temple and ear. Again a gaping whirlpool of pain and darkness reached out and this time pulled her completely in.

Chapter 6

At seven the next morning, while it was still cool, Cass went by the old Martin house to make sure everything was ready for Sam. She peeled sheets off the furniture, ran the faucets to get the old, stagnant water out, and checked that the fridge was working. She opened windows upstairs and down but avoided Sam's younger brother Kendall's bedroom. The Afghanistan war hero had been laid to rest just a few months ago. That room was still sacred ground as far as Cass was concerned.

She couldn't help but remember the hundreds of happy hours Sam and she had spent in this house. The slumber parties, the countless hours in Sam's bedroom looking through teen magazines, doing each other's hair, and talking and talking and talking about anything and everything—mostly boys.

Their one and only job then was to grow up. As simple as that task seemed from her adult perspective today, for two budding teenagers, it felt so difficult. Like that day when they were thirteen when Sam got her first period and thought she was going to die. Sam's shy, prudish mother had put off having that all important mother/daughter talk until it was too late. It was a good thing Cass was there. Her mother had explained what periods were and how to deal with them. She already carried her just-in-case tampon in her purse. It saved the day as Cass educated her friend on that particular inconvenient aspect of being a woman.

Then there was the day Cass broke up with Eldon Tollison in eighth grade and came here to cry and cry. Sam said she never thought Eldon was very cute anyway. That helped.

Then came college, Cass's own divorce, Katy's birth, and Cass's unpredictable rise in the sheriff's department—all while juggling the challenge of being a single parent.

Again she thanked God that her parents were still alive. She couldn't imagine life without them being here for her. It was such a blessing that Katy could go to Grandma's each day after school and that Dad was around to fix the little things that broke around that house. But most important, he filled the role of primary male figure in Katy's life. No one could have done a better job.

The house was ready for Sam. The question was, was Cass? She'd never given a moment's thought to the fact that she might have to nurse her friend through a heartbreak. Sam's life had always seemed so charmed; perfect job—perfect husband—that's how it looked. But Sam had seen some rough spots too. She'd lost her entire family. First her mother a few years back, then last year, her war-hero brother and her dad just two weeks apart. Cass shook her head. *I don't know how she survived it.*

Chapter 7

It was Sam's first time back in her family home since she and Ricky had closed it up right after Daddy's funeral. It seemed so eerie, so foreign to open the front door to nothing. No sound, no warmth, no smells of recently cooked meals, no sense of household; just a dark, empty space. It felt as if all life had been sucked out of the place. A tear slipped down her cheek as she was overcome by an overwhelming sense of loss.

Maybe this is a mistake, she thought. *Maybe I should have gone to Florida or the Caribbean—or perhaps just taken a few days off and stayed in New York.*

But New York was killing her soul—robbing her of her humanity. She needed to get it back. She decided that no matter how empty the house was tonight, coming back here was the right decision. This place was hers now. It would be up to her to put life back in it again.

This boxy, white clapboard 1930s-era house, where she'd grown up on McKee's Creek Road was her refuge from the world. This was the place with the dormer window upstairs that she used to sit in to do her homework or just gaze out of and daydream. This was the house with the huge covered front porch with Momma and

Daddy's tall rocking chairs. Here the vines climbed the brick columns on each side of the porch every summer and snaked all the way across the rain gutter, reaching out to touch each other by fall.

She remembered the smell of fresh cookies that greeted her after school. It was where Momma always was—where one of the most predictable things in the world was Daddy coming home at five thirty to sweep her up in a huge bear hug then tickle her ribs while she laughed and squirmed, trying to get away. Dear God, how much she would give to feel that same thing today.

That was when she felt like nothing ever changed here. The big trees always shaded the same places, the neighbors never moved away; even the dogs and cats seemed to live forever. Life on McKee's Creek Road was steady, constant, utterly predictable—and safe.

Then she left to go north to Morgantown and the University of West Virginia. Daddy, who had started in the mines before finishing eighth grade, was so proud. She would be the first of the Martin family line with a college degree. While her world changed, McKee's Creek Road stayed the same. And that meant that all was still right with the world.

But two years into her studies, McKee's Creek Road did change. Momma died—a stroke, they said. Kendall, Sam's younger brother, then a senior in high school, found Momma crumpled on the kitchen floor. That day shattered Sam's illusion of permanence. Her world had tilted, and she felt she no longer had control over it. Momma was gone, and with her went the smell of cookies and supper cooking on the old family stove. She who was always there was no longer there. But still, Daddy was, and Kendall was, and the dormer window, and the vines, and the trees up the road. McKee's Creek Road would survive this.

Sam had gone off to college naive in her expectation that she would never change. But in her senior year, just as she was about to matriculate to the prestigious Washington and Lee School of

Law at Lexington, Virginia, she met Richard James Thornton, a football player, baseball player, and the most lusted after man on campus.

Ricky was struggling through his fifth year of trying to secure a degree in architecture. He was easily the most gorgeous, charming, sensuous man Sam had ever met. Though she knew in her heart that he came with flaws, she had to have him.

Her strict Born-Again Christian upbringing dictated that she would only surrender her virginity to her lawfully wedded husband on their wedding night. Though Ricky attempted every way he could short of rape to thwart her determination, Sam won that battle—barely. They married six-months after graduation, and not a minute too soon. Sam sincerely doubted she could have maintained her vow of virginity even one day longer.

Now, halfway through their seventh year together, the marriage was over. Ricky Thornton had betrayed everything: Sam, his career, his integrity, his marriage vows, everything.

As Sam stood in the middle of Daddy and Momma's living room and contemplated the wreckage of the last six months of her life, she understood why it was so important for her to come home.

In New York, Ricky was her foundation, her focus. He was everything her life was built around. There was no part of Samantha Marie that didn't have a huge part of Richard James Thornton attached. Now he was gone, and all that remained of her was pieces. She had to gather them up and build a new foundation. She needed to start a life built around her, not someone else.

Samantha Marie Thornton was gone. It was time to put Samantha Marie Martin back together again, only better, stronger this time. It would be a daunting construction project.

*

Dear, sweet, Cass, Sam thought as she spotted the sheets that had covered the furniture, now all carefully folded and set by the door next to the stairwell closet. She surveyed the dust that had settled on the window sills, the fireplace mantle and the hardwood floor margins around the area carpets and told herself, *I've got a lot of work to do around here.*

In the kitchen, she found a note from Cass: "*Sam, everything works. There's milk, orange juice, and a little food in the refrigerator, plus some hot-chocolate mix, a can of coffee, and creamer in the cabinet above the fridge. I rinsed out the coffee maker, changed the linens, and opened a lot of windows. You may want to close them before you go to bed. Call me when you get in.*"

The note made her smile. It felt like the house had already warmed just a little.

Chapter 8

Jennifer awoke slowly to the sound of a running fan. Someone had covered her with a thin woolen blanket. When her eyes could focus well enough to see, she found herself lying in a narrow cot-like bed in a small, dim, windowless room.

Her first instinct was to sit up. "Ahhhhhh!" she screamed as she tried to push off. The action sent shocks of pain through her right arm. She lay back and raised the arm. To her surprise, it had been casted. *How long have I been here,* she wondered.

The left side of her face ached. She flinched and cried out again as she touched it. It was badly swollen and her ear throbbed unmercifully. Then she remembered. That was where the man hit her. She tried working her jaw. It moved but shot lightning bolts of pain through her temple and all the way to the top of her head. Damaged but not broken.

She had to get up. She cautiously swung her legs over the side of the narrow bed, being careful not to put pressure on her casted arm. She looked around in vain for her clothes. *That Freak's still got them,* she concluded. How easily her mind changed the man's status from gorgeous hunk to Freak.

Holy cow, this place is small. There was just enough light to reveal the room's details. She raised her tender right arm to touch one wall and found that her left arm could touch the other with room to spare. The walls appeared to be covered with metal. The only break in them other than the door was a small, empty niche a couple of feet above the pillow.

It took her only three steps to cover the entire length of the room. The bed was built into the wall leaving only a narrow walk space. There was a one-piece stainless-steel toilet at the far end like she'd seen in pictures of jails. Above it was a simple push-button water faucet.

The door had no knob. Light came from a single, bare, low-watt bulb housed in a fixture recessed into the ceiling which also apparently contained the fan.

She cast her gaze again toward the ceiling, praying to discover something, anything that would give her hope for escape. There was nothing. Then she spotted a tiny glint reflecting off what seemed to be a small piece of glass. She moved to get a better view. Whatever it was, it was tucked away high up out of reach in the left-hand corner.

Recognition struck her like a slap in the face. Staring down was a small camera; one that moved with her as she moved. She frantically tried to cover herself but couldn't adequately do so. She snatched the blanket from the bed and hid behind it. Was the Freak watching her at this very moment?

It was too much. She collapsed on the bed and dissolved into hysterical sobs. This was not a place of recovery, but of slavery. This was a cell. She was kidnapped. The thought came to her for the first time that she might never leave this place alive.

Chapter 9

The first rays of the early morning sun streamed through Sam's bedroom window and worked their way across the crumpled sheet, warming first her legs then the rest of her. She peacefully ascended to consciousness from a deep, dreamless sleep—her first truly restful night in months. She was home, and that simple fact worked to warm her soul just as surely as the sun's rays warmed her bed.

For the first time in forever she awakened not to the sounds of trash cans banging and horns blaring, and the choking smell of diesel smoke belched out by a steady procession of New York City busses, but rather to sweet-smelling mountain air and the sound of birds singing through her open window. A dog barked in the distance. Joe Peterson's rooster crowed two houses down. It made her smile.

Then old Mister Palmer next door, fired up his lawn mower. The smell of pine trees and magnolias wafting down the mountainside would soon be joined by the aroma of freshly mown grass.

She ignored the sound and tried to doze while Mr. Palmer was on the other side of his house, but when he made it to this side, he and his noisy machine passed directly beneath her open window. Further attempts at sleep were useless.

A full bladder forced Sam out of bed and compelled a short dash to the bathroom for relief. Then she threw her flowery silk robe over her sleeping tee and headed downstairs on a quest to find the coffee pot.

Sitting cross-legged in Mamma's kitchen chair, her eyes closed and her hands wrapped around a steaming mug of fresh coffee, she let the sunlight streaming through the kitchen window once again work its magic.

A knock came at the front door. She set her cup down and was about to get up when she heard a key slide into the lock and the door open. In New York such sounds would have been cause for alarm, but here they caused only a smile. She heard Cass's voice shout, "Everybody decent? Hope not, because I'm coming in anyway." It was the same brash, uninhibited, bull-in-the-china-shop girlfriend Cass had always been and whom Sam had missed so much.

"In the kitchen!" she called. She rose and caught Cass at the kitchen entry, threw her arms around her and said, "Cassie, I'm *so* glad to see you. Thanks for getting the house ready."

"Welcome home, girlfriend," Cass said gently. "Glad you're here."

Sam looked her friend up and down. "My, don't you look spiffy in that uniform, Sheriff Rosier! There's stars on that collar you didn't have the last time I was here."

"Yeah," Cass smiled. "Kinda crazy, isn't it?"

"Come sit down and tell me all about it." Sam retrieved a large coffee mug from the cupboard, filled it, dropped in Cass's usual one cube of sugar and two tablespoons of creamer and handed it to her.

Cass told her story of having to arrest him Sheriff Long. "He was my friend but turned out to be a damned pervert," she said. "Somehow the Republicans thought I'd make a good candidate, and the Democrat candidate had a serious case of foot-in-mouth disease. I won the election by three points and here I am, a female sheriff in Nicholas County! Who'd-a-ever-thunk-it?"

"How are people handling that idea?" Sam asked as she set down her mug.

"The public seems fine with it. A couple of my older deputies are having a bit of a hard time with the idea, but I can handle them okay. My biggest worry is the County Commissioners. Every now and then I have to go up there and remind them that I'm a pretty tough cookie."

"So is it exciting? Have you had to use your gun or anything?" "I've never had to use my gun, thank God. It's more interesting than exciting, but you wouldn't believe the paperwork. What time did you get in, anyway?"

"Just after ten. Sorry I didn't call. I was a bit overwhelmed with opening up Daddy's house again and getting my stuff in. What you did really helped. How's Katy?"

Cass smiled. "Fine. Growing like a weed. She can't wait to see you."

"It feels a little weird to be here without Ricky," Sam said quietly, knowing the statement would open the conversation that had to be faced.

"Feels weird to me too, Sammy. You ready to talk about it?"

"Yeah. I am, but I have no idea where to start."

"How about at the beginning."

"How much time you got?"

"KK's with mom and the office knows where I am." Cass pointed at her shoulder mic. "You can have all the time you need unless this thing tears me away."

"Okay, but I better do this first." Sam rose and stepped over to the counter to retrieve a tissue, thought better of it and grabbed the whole box. She placed it between them—just in case. Then she took a deep breath and began. "This is going to sound strange, but what killed my marriage was my own success. Things started to blow-up between Ricky and me about two years ago on the day I

57

was promoted to associate partner. I know I should have told you back then, Cassie, but at first I was in denial. After things really got bad, I was just too embarrassed.

Cass smiled. "You're right, sister, you should have told me. But we can beat you up over that later."

Sam took another deep breath and said, "Okay, here goes. My new promotion came with a big pay raise plus some pretty amazing bonuses. I would be earning over three hundred thousand a year."

Cass gasped. "Three-hundred-grand?"

"I know it sounds like a lot, but remember, we're talking about New York. We paid thirty-two hundred a month for a tiny four-hundred-square-foot apartment."

Cass shook her head. "I only pay seven-hundred-forty a month for my three-bedroom, fifteen-hundred square-foot house—and I own the joint."

"New York's a different world. That's why my promotion was such a big deal. We'd be able to move to a bigger, nicer place where we could start a family."

"Ricky must have been jazzed."

"You'd have thought so. But he was still working for the same forty-five thousand-dollar salary he started at years before. He had a dead-end job and knew it. My promotion was a huge blow to his ego. When I told him about it, all he did was shrug and say, 'That's nice,' then he slammed down his second shot of tequila and acted like he really didn't care."

"Tequila? I thought you guys were teetotalers."

"Ricky started drinking about a year before all this happened. Not a lot at first, just a drink or two before he came home. I was working so many hours that I didn't notice at first. But then the bottles started showing up at home."

Cass shook her head. "Sounds like the old Ricky back before you met him. He used to booze it up pretty good in college."

Sam sighed. "It was all because of this job thing. I didn't understand how badly it was affecting him."

"Still, a promotion and a hell of a raise? The money all went into the same pot, right? He should have been celebrating."

"That's what I thought. I tried to cheer him up. I told him the promotion meant we could finally get a bigger apartment. We'd been putting off having children. I told him it was time for us to start our family then I gave him my best 'come-hither' look and started taking off my shirt."

Cass grinned. "I hope he grabbed you and started tearing off the rest of your clothes."

"I wish so too, but all he said was, "Not now. I'm really not in the mood." He grabbed his shot-glass and the Tequila bottle and went in and sat on the couch. He poured himself a third shot, turned on the TV and ignored me.

"You're kidding! So you used a baseball bat on him right after you removed your knee from his groin, right?"

Sam's lip trembled and her voice caught. She swallowed hard and started over. "I never felt so ugly, so humiliated in my life. I started to say something but he cut me off and said, 'You can't treat me like your kept man, Sam. I'm not going to jump up and provide stud service on demand!'" Sam tried to staunch a flood of tears that suddenly spilled down her cheeks.

Cass caught her breath. "Oh Sammy, I can't imagine..." She reached for a tissue of her own.

Sam blew her nose and wiped her cheeks then said, "I was devastated. I told him that I had never, ever regarded him as a kept man. That he was my husband, we were a team, all for one and one for all—that sort of stuff. But he was so angry. He said he felt like a little kid who had to go to his mommy to borrow a nickel. He said it like he hated me, Cassie. He said 'It's really your money, Sam, and both of us know it.' Then to spite me he grabbed the tequila bottle, raised it to me and said, 'Yup! That Jose Cuervo—

he sure is a friend of mine.' He upended the bottle and guzzled it down."

Cass was speechless. She finally managed to ask quietly, "What did you do?"

"I tried to reason with him, but by then, he was drunk. He said we'd never been equal; that I was the great Samantha Martin, with the scholarships and the mega-bucks job, while all he did was draw meaningless pictures all day for a lousy, third-rate company where he'd never make partner.

Sam's voice trembled. "He called me *Martin* instead of Thornton. In all our married life, Ricky had never called me by my maiden name. He said I didn't need him; that I could have any one of those millionaire, fancy-ass, high-power Howell, Bernstein & Mancowitz lawyers any time I wanted. How'd he put it—oh yes—that he was as useful to me as 'tits on a boar hog'."

"That son-of-a-bitch," Cass said.

"That's when I realized there was more than just anger going on. Ricky was jealous. I told him I loved him and never had and never would want another man. I told him that any success I had belonged to both of us. I even said that if it meant saving our marriage, I'd quit and move anywhere he wanted. All he had to do was tell me where and when."

Cass shook her head. "You're a far better woman than I am. We'd have been on the way to the hospital to have my boot surgically removed from his ass."

"As drunk as he was, I think he realized he'd gone too far. He broke down and started to cry. He called himself—oh I hate this word—a 'F'-ing failure.

"I told him, 'Ricky Thornton, you are not a failure! "By then the alcohol had killed any possibility of romance. He kept drinking until he passed out. I was worried he might throw up and drown in his own vomit or something, so I sat next to him, crying and thinking. Apparently all this had been building up right under my nose but I didn't see it."

"Wow," Cass said. "Did he expect you were just going to walk away from your career?"

"I don't think he knew what he wanted. However, later we did make a huge decision about starting our family. Of course I must admit that he was coerced into it."

"Coerced?"

"Oh. I probably shouldn't tell you this,"

Cass leaned forward. "Samantha Martin, you're blushing. You seduced him into it, didn't you? Do I have to remind you that I'm the one who taught you what the word *sex* means, not to mention the word *orgasm*? No secrets here, girl. I might need to know how to use such coercion someday myself."

"Well—okay. But if you ever tell anyone about this I'll—oh—I don't know what I'll do, but it will be bad, real bad."

"I'll take my chances, girlfriend. Give me every juicy detail."

Sam paused, trying to master her life-long reluctance to discuss intimate matters. Finally she said, "When Ricky got home the next night, I met him at the door in a low-cut, very short and hot red dress. I gave him a huge kiss and asked him if he was ready to play a game. Ricky loved game-playing. He looked me up and down and said, 'Sure.'"

I led him straight to the bathtub which I'd filled with hot water and bubble bath just before he got home. I told him he was to remain there for one-half-hour. I even set a timer and told him that when it rang I'd bring him hot towels. I told him not to dress after the bath but to go straight to the bedroom where he was to lay on the bed on his stomach. When he tried to speak I shushed him and said he had to have permission to speak. He grinned and nodded and climbed into the tub."

"Don't stop now," Cass said as she stood and slurped the last drops of coffee from her mug then went for a refill.

"Between the hot water, the bubble bath and the hot towels, Ricky was so relaxed on that bed that he started drifting off to sleep. When I came in he started to turn over but I spanked his butt and told him no. I climbed onto the bed and gave him the best back massage I ever gave."

"Wait a minute. I thought you were dressed in some kind of hot dress."

"That was when he came home." Sam blushed. "Now all I was wearing was a smile."

"Whew girl, something tells me this is about to get X rated."

Sam laughed. "Not yet. I never let him turn over or touch me through the whole massage. It drove him crazy—and that's just what I wanted. After the massage he was so relaxed he started to drift off to sleep again. I put a towel over him and whispered in his ear to not move until I came to get him.

"While he slept I laid out a loose-fitting coordinated pair of pajamas, slippers and a brand new, chocolate-colored silk smoking jacket.

"When I woke him up I was wearing this low-cut, Champagne-colored chiffon dress and looked for all the world like a bosomy June Cleaver. I told him to put his new stuff on and meet me in the living room.

"You should have seen the look on his face when he came in. I had hired a catering company to turn the place into a one-table four-star restaurant. I had two liveried waiters standing by. The older one stepped forward and lifted one of the silver domed lids on the table and showed him two magnificent Maine lobsters and asked, 'Does Master find these acceptable?' He had a very proper English accent that fit the occasion perfectly."

Cass chuckled. "You're now my new dating consultant. Except that I'd have to take out a new mortgage for a date like this."

"Cassie, it was so romantic. After the waiters were gone and everything was put back together, we talked. When the time was right I snagged a glass from the kitchen and the last bottle of faux Champagne. I put them on the coffee table and told Ricky to take his clothes off. Of course, you never had to ask him twice to do that. Then I took off that chiffon dress. Underneath I was wearing this red lace, see-through teddy and a tiny 'G'-string thong. I thought Ricky was going to pant."

"Whoo. Getting hot here, girl." Cass fanned her face with her hand.

"It is getting a little warm, isn't it," Sam agreed. "I said to him, 'Last night you said you wanted to think about us trying to get pregnant.' Ricky apologized and blamed it on being drunk. He said he didn't really mean it. I'm sure he thought we were about to get into another fight. I asked him point-blank if he wanted us to have children or not. He said 'Sure I do Sam,' but that he just wanted to make sure it was the right time.

"I told him, 'Ricky, It's time!' I said I wanted to show him how much I meant it, but that if he went along with this he had to promise he'd never go back on the deal."

Cass looked skeptical. "After the night before did you honestly think you could trust him to keep a deal?"

"I hoped he would, but at that moment what I cared about most was having a baby. Based on how I was dressed, and how the night had gone so far, I think he would have agreed to just about anything."

"You called me a hussy once," Cass laughed, "but this is hussy-ness in the highest form of the art."

"A girl's got to do what she's got to do—right?"

"You know it, sister," Cass agreed. "I just never imagined my little old straight-laced, naive girlfriend being able to do it so well."

Sam laughed. "I told him to pour the Champagne into the glass. I went to the bedroom and came back with my birth control pills. I handed them to him and showed him how to punch them out through the foil on the back. I said that if he really wasn't ready to have a baby he needed to speak now or forever hold his peace. He didn't say a word so I told him to start dropping those pills into the Champagne. Twenty minutes later my birth control pills were dissolving away in the living room while we were in the bedroom consummating our agreement—and we did that all night long."

Chapter 10

Shortly after Jennifer spotted the camera, the Freak's voice suddenly seemed to come from the very walls: "I trust you're comfortable, Miss Oldroyd."

She nearly jumped out of her skin. If the man was expecting her to reply that meant he could not only see her but could converse with her as well. "You can hear me?" she blurted.

"Most assuredly. I can hear you. I can see you. You've nothing whatsoever you can hide from me."

Jennifer's anger welled up. She screamed at the camera, "Let me out of here, you freak! You're never going to get away with this." She decided that 'Freak' would be his name, henceforth and forever.

The Freak spoke with maddening calmness. "Oh, but I already have. Do you think you're the first guest to visit my little hotel? Not on your life." He chuckled as if laughing at his own joke. "Indeed Jennifer, not on your life. You told me you have no family and aren't expected at your job for the better part of a month. You're traveling by yourself. Didn't your mother ever warn you about the dangers of traveling alone?"

He's right! Jennifer thought with horror. No one would miss her for weeks. People at work would probably assume she'd taken a job somewhere else. That kind of thing happened all the time in her department. "You don't think I told you everything, do you," she retorted. "There are people expecting to hear from me. They'll have the police out looking very soon."

"I'll just have to take my chances on that, won't I. Where will they start looking? In Virginia? North Carolina? Surely not tiny Summersville, West Virginia. I think we're perfectly safe here—perfectly alone. So why don't we just make the best of it these next few weeks? I'm sure we'll become much better friends. You haven't eaten in two days, so once again I'm preparing us a rather sumptuous dinner. I'll be there to escort you to the table in ten minutes. I know there's not much you can do to get yourself ready, but please do what you can."

Two days? I've been here for two days? That Bastard must have drugged me. What did he do to me for two days? Then she registered on what else he had said. 'These next few *weeks?*' Panic seized her and she began to tremble. Then the panic transformed into anger.

"You expect me to sit down to another meal with you after all this? You can take your food and shove it straight up your ass, you pervert! Just bring me my clothes and I'm out of here. You and Summersville will never hear from me again. And turn off that god-damned camera, you limp-dicked sorry excuse for a man."

Several ominous moments of silence passed. When he spoke again, it was in the same madding, calm, oily-smooth voice. "I'm sorry, but you're not excused. You are the guest of honor. Did I forget to mention that this is a 'come dressed as you are' party?"

*

It might be her only chance. She was small and muscular but possessed no martial art skills. *I don't even have a usable right arm*, she thought. But what she did have was a timeline—ten-minutes.

If he's picking me up, he won't be watching that damned camera, she thought. Her only hope was to turn surprise into her one and only weapon. But what then? She had no idea, only the realization that she had to do something.

She paced the cell for what seemed an eternity, trying to formulate a plan of action. Then for the first time since she awakened to this nightmare. Someone was at the door—and she still didn't have a plan. She'd just have to wing it.

The instant the door cracked open she charged and hit it with all her might. The Freak wasn't ready. The door hit him sharply in the shoulder and knocked him off his feet. Jennifer ran past and took a quick glance around to get her bearings. She perceived that this place was a basement. She bolted for a flight of stairs against the wall to her left that seemed the only way out.

She was fast. By the time the Freak scrambled to his feet, holding a painfully bruised shoulder, she was already at the top of the stairs in a short hallway lined with shelves of bottled fruit and other food stores.

"NO!" she heard him shout as he tore off after her. She shot through an open door at the end of the fruit room, turned left down another short hall and found herself in the ante-room just off the kitchen.

Now she knew exactly where she was. Sure enough, the Freak was cooking again but she wasn't about to hang around for dinner. She dashed through the archway between the kitchen and the living room. The front door would be her escape route.

"Aaahhhhhhhh!" she screamed as she impotently turned the knob and shook the door. It was locked by a deadbolt that required a key to open—a key in the possession of the Freak. The door she'd counted on as her portal to safety became instead an impenetrable barrier.

Chapter 11

Sam smiled reluctantly. She'd never discussed the intimate details of her married life with anyone. It felt good to unburden herself. But the reluctance of the smile was not due to embarrassment, it was because she knew what came next. She pushed herself back from the table and asked, "You want a Coke or some orange juice or something? I've had about all the coffee I can take."

"Naw. I'll stick with the java," Cass replied. "Us cops bleed coffee. So obviously there was still a problem since I don't see you packing a baby around."

"Things did get a little better. We practiced that let's-make-a-baby stuff a lot over the next few months. We came to an agreement on the alcohol too. A social drink or two for Ricky when we went out was fine. But I drew the line at alcohol in the house."

"So he wasn't an alcoholic? He could control his drinking?"

"Let's just say that at this point he was trying. But there were other problems. Without either of us being really aware of it, we had been leading separate lives. For instance, I never realized how much Ricky hated taking the subway to work. With my new promotion money coming in, we decided he would take the Camry to work and I'd take a cab. A larger apartment came available next door. It was seven-hundred-fifty-dollars more than we were paying, but I thought it would be worth it if it helped our marriage.

We agreed to each pay half the rent despite my paychecks being a lot bigger than his. I never wanted him to feel like a kept man again."

During their conversation Sam was occasionally distracted when Cass's portable police radio squawked to life. Most calls Cass ignored, but a couple of times she had to respond briefly. Sam was amazed at how Cass could both listen to her radio and be fully engaged in their conversation at the same time. The radio seemed so much a part of Cass's life, she didn't seem to even think about it.

"So when did things start going south again?" Cass asked.

Sam paused and mulled something over in her mind. Finally she spoke in a very quiet voice. "Cassie, I'm going to tell you something only Ricky and I know. It's a little embarrassing, and you're going to be surprised. Please don't be offended that I've not told you before. This information has to be kept just between you and me."

"That's no problem. We've been keeping each other's secrets since second grade."

"This is a big one—one that could put me in danger. But what I'm most afraid of is that I don't want the people to look at me differently or treat me differently than they always have, especially you and Katy. This has already cost me my marriage."

Cass was alarmed. "Are you in some kind of trouble?" she asked.

"No, no. It's not that kind of secret. In fact, most people would love to have this kind of problem."

"Well, for pity's sake, girl, tell me what it is."

"Okay, here goes…I'm rich!"

"Say what?" Cass looked quizzical—as if she hadn't heard correctly.

"I'm rich, Cassie. So rich you wouldn't believe it. So rich I hardly believe it myself."

Sam could tell Cass was struggling to try and wrap her mind around the concept. When Cass spoke she revealed her great skepticism. "So you're not saying you have a few bucks in the old savings account, or that you paid off your house and have enough left over to buy a new car or something? What you're saying is—is—Samantha Martin, just what the hell are you saying?"

"All that and more. I'm saying that I'm really, really rich. And that's what finally killed my marriage to Ricky."

"So how'd all this happen?" Cass asked, still hesitant to believe.

"As you know, last year was a really bad year for me, what with Kendall getting killed in Afghanistan and Daddy dying. I ended up as the sole heir to Daddy's estate. No big deal, right? The only things he had worth anything were this old house, Momma's 1965 Ford Fairlane which hasn't been driven more than fifty miles in almost twenty years, and Daddy's old 1975 green Ford pickup.

"Daddy never ever told any of us about his finances. I thought that at best I'd inherit a few dollars to help offset the funeral costs and pay off the estate's bills. I thought there was just as much chance that I'd have to take some money out of my own pocket to settle everything. It hardly seemed worth going to the lawyer's office to hear the reading of the will.

"Daddy's lawyer was Judge Willis William McCormick—Uncle Willie?"

"I know him," Cass said. "Everybody around here does. Big, bushy silver hair, always wears a black, three-piece suit and those crazy bow ties."

Sam laughed. "That's him. Uncle Willie was Daddy's best friend as long as I can remember. He sat Ricky and I down and asked me how much I knew about Daddy's business? I told him that all I knew was that he used to be a coal miner up at the big mine up by Gilboa until he retired. I think that was when I was in third grade."

"Yeah. I remember that year," Cass said with an impish grin. "We both spent half the school year without any front teeth."

"Uncle Willie gave me the biggest shock of my life when he told me that Daddy didn't just work there, he actually *owned* that mine. He hadn't retired—he'd sold the mine to Expedition Mining Company. He got thirty-five million dollars cash plus a stack of fifty thousand dollar, ten-year maturity, Expedition Mining Corporation bearer bonds worth another ninety-five million."

Cass looked dumbfounded. Sam could tell she was doing the math in her head. "Wow!" she blurted. "Off the top of my head I say that qualifies as 'rich'."

"You know how humble Daddy was and how simple he lived. Nobody ever knew he had that kind of money. In addition to that, he was a great believer in life insurance. He had a five-million dollar, fully-paid whole-life insurance policy on himself and was living off a million-dollar policy he had on Momma. He was saving everything for Kendall and me. I worried all through law school that he might be sending me money he couldn't afford to spend. I used to check his house every time I came home to make sure there was enough food.

"I inherited just over a hundred and thirty-five million dollars. Uncle Willey gave me the key to Daddy's safe-deposit box over at the bank. It's full of all those bearer bonds and dozens of certificates of deposit from the insurance proceeds."

Cass was slack-jawed. "You have a hundred and thirty-five million bucks sitting over at that little old bank?"

"Believe it or not."

"Well glory be. You don't have to worry about the old light bill for a while. I'll bet that feels good."

"I won't have to worry about money ever again. But I was just fine before I got all that money. It only made things a lot worse between Ricky and me. In ways I wish Daddy had never left me a dime. I never understood how awful greed could be until I watched it sink its fangs into my husband."

Just then Cass's radio squawked to life. "Unit 1, Dispatch."
She picked up the radio and replied. "Unit 1."

"Sheriff, sorry to bother you, but Sheriff Dalton from Webster County is here. He said he needs to talk to you about housing some prisoners down here while they're upgrading his jail next month."

"Damn," Cass cursed. "Sorry Sam, I'm going to have to deal with this one." She keyed the mic and said, "10-4. I'm just around the corner. Tell him I'll be there in ten minutes."

"10-4, Sheriff."

Cass looked at Sam and shrugged.

"Don't you worry," Sam said. "You scoot along and do what you need to do. I've got a ton of work to do to whip this house back into shape. Have you seen all the dust?"

Cass laughed. "Yeah, up close and personal yesterday. Better take those cover sheets outside and shake them out real good. I'll be back sometime after five. Promise we'll pick this up right where we're leaving off. I don't want to miss a single word. This is better than a dime-store novel."

"I promise."

As Sam closed the door behind her friend she realized with some amusement that her West Virginia accent had returned. Her friends in New York would chuckle. Less than twenty-four hours, and already the mountain girl in her was making a comeback. It felt good.

Chapter 12

The Freak pounded into the living room, breathing heavily. Jennifer spun to meet him. He stopped across the room and grinned. "Told you there was no escape," he mocked. "It was a nice try, though. The others just cowered at the back of the cell and waited."

Others? Her eyes darted about the room looking for anything that might give her an advantage. "How many others, Freak?"

"That's not a very polite thing to call someone, young lady. I'm afraid I must insist that you use my real name."

"I'll never say your name again, Freak," she spat back. "You've earned your title."

He dismissed her statement and spoke in a calm, solicitous tone. "You're my third guest here. It's been months since the last one checked out. Remember that old Eagles song—Hotel California? I'm sure you've heard it. It goes 'You can check out anytime you want, but you can never leave'."

"Why are you doing this?"

There was venom in his answer. "You women think you're so superior—so much better. No matter how well we treat you, your kind always ends up humiliating us—just like you did me, you little slut."

She could tell his anger was escalating. His left hand began to shake. She had to defuse this, but how? Perhaps if she ratcheted down the rhetoric some; appeared more compliant and cooperative. At some point he would have to make a move, and when he did, she'd have to move faster.

She softened her tone. "Listen, we've both made mistakes on this date. I'm sorry if I upset you. I'm sure that little problem in the bedroom was because we both were a little over excited and maybe a little drunk. I'm sorry, okay? You're a great guy. Maybe you could... "

"What? Get a little help?" the man exploded." Is that what you were going to say? I don't need any help," he screamed. "The problem's not me, lady; it's you—you and all your kind." He took a threatening step forward and said, "Time to come to supper, honey. You're dressed perfectly for the party."

He leapt across the room at her. The man was tall and lanky but not terribly agile. She ducked under his grasp and ran for the kitchen. All she could think was *weapons, weapons*. She found what she wanted on the stove, hot and ready.

The Freak ran back into the kitchen. The veal cutlets went flying as one-handed, Jennifer smashed the hot cast-iron frying pan squarely into his face. He went down screaming, writhing on the floor and holding his face in his hands. She maneuvered around him to improve the angle, and then swung the frying pan hard against the side of his head. His body went limp. She hit him again just as hard just to make sure he was out cold—or worse.

Then she backed warily against the refrigerator, clutching the frying pan in her good hand, watching to see if he moved. She wouldn't even allow herself to think about her right arm, now screaming with pain.

The adrenalin coursing through her began to subside and she started to shake uncontrollably. Her knees turned wobbly. She slid down the front of the refrigerator to the floor and began to scream. The ordeal was over, and impossibly, she was still alive.

Chapter 13

It was almost six-thirty when Cass came scurrying back up the sidewalk, a pizza box precariously balanced in one hand and two bottles of beer in the other. Sam smiled. Her friend knew there would be no such "devil spirits" in her teetotaler house.

"Sorry I'm so late," Cass apologized as Sam swung the door open for her. "I couldn't get away from the office."

"You should have brought Katy."

"No way. This conversation's far too adult for her. If she were here you'd have to leave out all the juicy parts; and we can't have that."

"Sam laughed. No worries, girlfriend. I probably smell like an old workhorse. I've been sweating my guts out trying to get this house cleaned up. You'd think with all the money Daddy had, he would have bought Momma an air conditioner."

"Order one up, girl. No excuse not to. While you're at it, order me one for my office. That courthouse is like an oven. I've been thinking about instituting a new summer dress code."

"Which would be?"

"Clothing optional."

"Ha, ha. That would set tongues a wagging around here, not to mention making for some interesting campaign posters." She pointed at the beer. "That what you're drinking with your pizza?"

Cass nodded. "I know you don't approve. But with this heat, it's just what the doctor ordered. I know I don't need to ask, but do you want one?"

"Nope. It's milk for me."

"You're bound for heaven, girl. You and a few million Mormons to boot. I guess you'll just have to sneak me in the back door up there."

Sam retrieved glasses from the cupboard while Cass deposited the pizza box in the middle of the table. Midway through her first slice, Cass steered the conversation back to where they'd left it in the morning. "So you were saying that Ricky got greedy."

Sam nodded. "It was like Dr. Jekyll and Mr. Hyde. The instant the money appeared, the man I married disappeared. Coming out of Uncle Willie's office Ricky was literally jumping up and down. He said over and over, 'My God, Sam, My God.' He pulled our rental car onto Main Street then suddenly slammed on the brakes right beside that billboard down by the bank. It was advertising the Cadillac dealership over in Charleston. He pointed at the sign and said that he was sick and tired of our old Camry. He wanted to go over to Charleston and get an Escalade today, right then. I thought he was kidding and laughed, but he was serious. Then he decided we should get two—one for him and one for me. He said we could get a great deal if we paid cash."

"I'll bet your answer sounded an awful lot like 'No'."

"That's exactly what I said. I told him that what we needed was sound investment advice, not two new cars.

"He screamed at me. He asked, if the richest G.D. women in Summersville was still going to squeeze nickels till the Buffalo—you know—poops?" Sam blushed.

Cass shook her head. "Didn't he realize it was *your* money, not his?"

"I don't think he did. Against my better judgment, I let Ricky get his Escalade, but I kept the Camry. That was just the opening salvo in a never ending battle over what to do with Daddy's money. A month after I got the inheritance, Ricky quit his job. He said he quit to become my investment manager."

"Say what?" Cass said, "I thought he was an architect."

"He was and should have stayed one. I told him I was perfectly satisfied with the investment advisor we had, but Ricky said he'd double our money it in no time. 'No risk, no reward,' he always said. I told him over and over that I didn't like risk.

"I spent the next few months turning down one harebrained, get-rich-quick scheme after another. One night he came home all excited, trying to convince me to buy a restaurant and bar called the Tuscan Hills over by where he used to work. Apparently he used to stop there quite often. 'Only four-point-nine-million—a real steal,' he said.

"I told him that was a lot of money and asked if he'd seen their books? He said he hadn't, but that Maria told him she was clearing better than three-hundred-grand a month."

"Who's Maria?" Cass asked.

"That's what I asked him. She was supposedly the owner. It was the first time Ricky ever mentioned her name. He assured me they were just friends. 'No big deal, okay?' he said."

"I think I see where this is going," Cass said disdainfully as she took the empty pizza box off the table and put it on the counter.

"That's why you're a good cop," Sam said. "You're always ahead of the story. I asked him why she was selling and he said, 'I don't know, just wants to get out of the restaurant business or something.' The more I pressed him for a reason the more he avoided giving me a straight answer. He started to get irritated so I backed off. I did tell him that I suspected this business wasn't doing as well as she said and that she might be trying to cut her losses."

"What did he say?"

"He said the place was full every time he went in. He was convinced the business was making a ton of money. I told him I had to have a lot more information before I'd put five-million-dollars at risk. I told him he had to get hold of the woman's books. I said that if our accountant said was a good deal, I'd consider it."

"Sounds fair enough," Cass said.

"He said he'd go right over and ask her for her books. It was like he was bi-polar; one minute he was angry and the next he was jumping up and down with excitement. On the way out the door he said that if we didn't snap the place up, somebody else would. I said that at least we'd still have our money."

Sam stood and stretched. "I'm probably boring you to tears."

"Are you kidding me?" Cass replied. "This is better than reality TV. I'm just sorry you're the one it's happening to." She pushed back her chair and stood to stretch her legs as well. "Time for a potty break girl, save my place for me.

When they resettled, Cass said, "I always thought Ricky was smarter than this. Sounds to me like you were becoming as much the man's baby sitter as his wife."

"That's true. And all during this time we were trying to get pregnant but it just wasn't happening. The doctors ran all kinds of tests on me but couldn't figure out why I wasn't conceiving. They wanted to test Ricky, but he refused to go in."

"Why?"

"At first I thought it was embarrassment. But after we separated, I found out that he couldn't have children, and had known that since he was a teenager." A tear slipped down Sam's cheek. "In all the years we were together he never told me that."

Cass was shocked. "That bastard!" she said.

Sam dabbed at more tears. "The worst part of all was that by this time I was questioning whether I even wanted to have a baby with him anymore."

Chapter 14

Jennifer couldn't tell whether the Freak was alive or dead. Then his right leg jerked. His head tossed and he moaned. She raised the pan to strike again, but all he did was roll from his side to his back.

He was alive but there was no telling how badly hurt he was. She spied a butcher knife the man had been using lying on the counter. She grabbed it and knelt beside his head. "Say goodbye, Freak," she whispered as she pressed the point of the knife against his throat.

But try as she might, she just couldn't bring herself to start the cut. Knocking the Freak out was one thing, but killing him in cold blood was another.

It was time to leave. As much as she detested touching the man, she fished in his pockets hoping to find his keys. They were in his right front pocket.

The prospect of having him out of her sight was frightening, but there was no other way. She hurried to the living room. The third key on the ring opened the front door. She scurried back to check on him. He was still unconscious but was showing signs of coming around. She took the chance of letting him out of her sight again while she quickly searched for something with which to cover herself and for some protection for her feet. A quick search of the living room closet turned up only a long duster that came past her ankles and a pair of rubber boots far too big for her petite feet. They'd have to do.

When she returned to the kitchen, the Freak was definitely coming around. He was still on his back but his knees were drawn up. His right hand clutched his head. She crossed from the doorway to the stove again and picked up the still hot frying pan to give him another whack. He sensed her coming and tried to roll out of the way but was too late. When she delivered yet another blow to his head, his legs jerked back out straight and his hand flopped limply to the floor. Maybe she'd killed him this time—maybe not. She grabbed the butcher knife from the counter, shoved it into the deep pocket of the duster and fled out the front door. If he caught up to her again, she'd use it.

The sun had set behind the hill in back of the house; it would be dark soon. Jennifer looked around, hoping to see her car or some other vehicle she could use. The only one present was the Freak's pickup truck, and she'd left the Freak's key ring lying on the kitchen counter. No way was she going back to retrieve it.

How long would it take her to find her own car? And what about the key to start it? She knew instinctively there was no time for such a search. She had to get to the county road and flag down a car as fast as she could, and she'd have to get there on foot.

She tried a full-out run but in just three steps the duster tangled her feet and spilled her painfully to the ground. She stood and gathered it higher. The best she could do in the awkward rubber boots was the equivalent of a fast jog.

She was nearly three-quarters of the way across the pastures when she heard a vehicle rev back at the cabin. Somehow she had to run faster! She kicked off the boots and let the duster fly away behind her. *Should have done that in the first place!* she thought. Though she was completely naked again, and her feet would take a beating, she could finally move.

Darkness was falling fast. The vehicle coming from behind was catching up—fast! She was less than a hundred yards from where the road entered the trees when, to her amazement, she heard the vehicle stop. Would she actually get away? Despite her feet being cut and stone-bruised, she willed them to run faster.

Then something touched her left calf. Just a tap. It didn't hurt at all. But with her next step, her leg buckled and she went down. It was only then that the '*crack*' from the rifle registered in her mind.

Then the pain came in agonizing, sickening, paralyzing waves so overwhelming that she momentarily passed out. When she came to, the Freak was standing over her, rifle in hand. Angry, painful-looking red bruises covered the left side of his face.

"You know, it's rude to run out on dinner," he roared down at her. "I said you could check out any time you want." He raised the rifle and pointed it at her face. "But you can never leave!"

She perceived his finger tightening on the trigger but was too exhausted, pain-ridden and discouraged to care. As a blessed wave of black oblivion swept over her she actually felt a sense of relief. At least her horrible ordeal would be over.

Chapter 15

Sam had switched from milk to Dr. Pepper. Her half-full can was now warm. Cass was nearly finished with her second beer.

"Just thinking about the past seven or eight months makes my stomach hurt," Sam said. "Ricky and I were in all-out war mode over that stupid restaurant. I couldn't figure out what in the world had him so myopic about the place. It took him weeks to get that Maria person to produce her books. When she did, they were a disaster. The restaurant was losing money hand over fist."

"And couldn't he see that?" Cass asked incredulously.

"He tried to convince me that the books didn't mean a thing. He said they were being deliberately juggled to make it appear like the restaurant was losing money. Supposedly, the receipts on the restaurant side were almost all from credit cards that had to be run through a bank account while the bar's income was almost all cash. He said Maria ran all of the expenses from both sides of the business through the restaurant account to make it look like it was losing money while she was supposedly pocketing hundreds of thousands of dollars in cash from the bar operations. He said the profits were all off the books, as if that were a good thing."

Cass scowled. "That sounds like go-to-jail time."

"It was an IRS raid waiting to happen. I yelled at Ricky for the first time in our marriage. I told him I would never consider investing in a business that earned its profits through tax evasion. I told him I would lose my law license if we were caught. But more importantly, I asked him if he wanted us to go to prison."

"Did he care?"

"Apparently not, because he kept pressing me to do this. I was livid. I told him that after seven years of marriage, he should have known that I'd never get involved with anything like this. "His response was, 'But Sam, I'm doing this all for you'."

"Some favor," Cass muttered.

"I couldn't believe he was asking me to betray the very principles I thought we both believed in. I told him he used to be a man of honor and integrity; a man I could respect, but that I didn't know who he was anymore. I said he certainly wasn't the man I married."

"Wow," Cass shook her head

"I said I wouldn't give him one dime to invest in that restaurant. Not then, not ever, and that I never wanted him to mention it again."

Sam realized she was trembling. She leaned back and took a deep breath to calm herself.

"You okay, sister?" Cass asked with concern.

Sam sucked in another deep breath and said, "Yeah, I'm fine. It's just tough to tell you all this. I feel like such a failure."

"The failure isn't yours," Cass said gently. "It's a failure in the character of that asshole husband of yours."

"Intellectually I know that. I just wish my mind could convince my heart."

"That's why you're back here girl. The first step is to get it all out. So what happened?"

"Things got out of control. Ricky took a step toward me and said he was sick and tired of me disrespecting him. He said that he was done asking—that now he was telling me. 'You *are* going to give me this money,' he shouted. Sam shuddered at the memory.

"You know me, Cass." she continued, "if someone tells me I *have* to do something, I'll do just the opposite every time. I shouted back at him, 'Or what Ricky? You're going to spank me or make me go to bed without supper? Are you going to hit me?' I stepped right into his face and said, "Go ahead buster, give it your best shot because it will be the only chance you ever get."

"He knew about your black belt in *Taekwondo*, right?"

Sam nodded. "Yes," she said. "But I don't think he believed I'd ever try to use it on him. I raised my right hand into his face and said, 'See this hand, Ricky? It's the hand that writes the checks. You're never going to see it write a check for that restaurant or any of the rest of your harebrained schemes!' I told him he was fired as my so-called investment manager and that tomorrow morning he better go out and start looking for an honest-to-goodness job."

"Good for you, girl!" Cass clapped her hands.

"You should have seen his face. He looked like I'd slapped him. Then he lost it. He backhanded me across the face and called me an 'f'-ing bitch.

I went down, more from surprise than hurt. He bent over me and yelled that Maria was twice the woman I was and twice as smart, too. He said he was going over to tell her she'd have her check in the morning and that I'd better have it ready. He slammed out the door, leaving me lying there on the floor."

"Rotten bastard," Cass said again quietly.

Sam took a deep breath. "The instant he hit me, our marriage was over. I also knew there had to be more going on between him and Maria than he was saying. I called 911 and the cops were there within five minutes. I pressed charges for assault then called a locksmith.

"Ricky came home blind drunk after three in the morning. I'd left a note on the door telling him there was a warrant out for him. When his key didn't work, he pounded and pounded on the door until a neighbor came out and told him she was calling the cops. I filed for divorce the next day and took out a restraining order."

Cass glowered and asked, "So I'm guessing that he was sleeping with this Maria woman?"

Sam nodded. "Yep. Turns out they were planning to run off to Florida as soon as I bought the restaurant. Maria threw him out when she realized he couldn't come up with the money. Ricky was homeless and broke in the most expensive city in America."

"How about the trial, did he show up?"

"There never was a trial, Cassie. I gave him a one-time, take-it-or-leave-it offer—a million-dollars on the condition that he never contact me or try to see me again.

"I was able to get medical records that proved he had known since he was a teenager that he was infertile. I could have had the marriage annulled and he would have walked away with nothing, but that would have taken a huge court fight. The divorce settlement was quicker and cleaner. It was worth a million dollars to get him out of my life. That was two months ago. Where he is now, I have no idea."

"You gave him a million bucks?" Cass asked in disbelief.

A tear slid down Sam's cheek. "Yes. And I don't regret a dime of it. I hate the man Ricky Thornton has become. The trouble is, I don't think I'll ever stop loving the Ricky Thornton I thought I married. That's what has me turned completely inside out.

"After the settlement I became the insufferable bitch Ricky said I was. I took my troubles out on everyone around me. I was constantly being approached by men when they were the last thing in the world I wanted. One really bad day, I screamed at this guy. I told him to leave me alone or I'd slap him with a sexual harassment complaint."

"Whoa," Cass looked surprised. "I can picture me saying something like that, but it certainly doesn't sound like you."

Sam smiled. "The difference is that you'd kick the guy in the groin and pull your gun on him before telling him that."

"Yeah, you're probably right," Cass chuckled. "I never have been very good at subtlety."

"The sad part is that he was a really nice guy. All he did was ask me if I wanted to go to lunch. I was sinking into an abyss. Two of my law clerks quit because of how badly I treated them. It got to the point that I couldn't even stand myself."

"That's not you," Cass said sympathetically. "But I know what you were going through. I was the same way after my divorce. Of course, I didn't have seven years of marriage invested like you. My ex doesn't bother me. He knows I have a gun."

"It's a good thing I don't have one," Sam said. "The truth is that I think I'm in mourning, first because of Kendall and Daddy, and then over the loss of a life-long dream of love and commitment and the pitter-patter of children's feet. I'm mourning the loss of my great fantasy of how my marriage was supposed to be—a fantasy utterly killed by the reality of how life turned out with Ricky."

Sam blew her nose loudly into a tissue. "That's why I had to come home. I lost the real Samantha Martin somewhere in New York, and I've got to find her again."

Sam saw that Cass was having a hard time hiding tears of her own. "Oh, Cassie, I'm sorry," she said, "I shouldn't be laying all my troubles off on you."

Cass shook her head. "Don't you even think about apologizing. You're the one who helped me get over Eldon Tollison, remember?"

Sam laughed. "Eighth-grade! I never could figure out what you saw in him."

"He was the first boy my age who had hair on his chest. I thought it was sexy. Mind if I give you some advice?"

"Can't guarantee I'll follow it, but fire away."

"Your best friend right now is time. They say that time heals everything, and it's true. After my divorce, I thought I was going to die. I thought I was the ugliest thing that ever walked the earth—that I was so lousy in bed I'd actually turned my husband gay. It took me a long time to stop blaming myself."

"At least you had Katy."

"In a lot of ways, being a mom made it worse. I thought I was a bad mother for not being able to keep my child's father in the house. I thought no man would ever want me because I came with somebody else's kid attached. It took forever before I started liking myself again, and in that time, I was the biggest bitch to ever walk this valley. You've made it through the toughest part, Sammy, the first two months. You're halfway through the swamp. All you've got to do now is slog the rest of the way out."

"How? I still feel like I'm drowning—like I'll never be able to trust a man ever again."

Cass stood and stretched. "We've got to keep you so busy you can't think. It won't be long until you turn around one day and realize, 'Hey, this isn't so bad. I can do this'."

"Maybe you're right. Right now I'm going to have my hands full whipping this house into shape. I *am* going to get that air conditioning installed. By the way, I probably shouldn't ask, but is anyone blowing *your* skirts up lately?"

Cass looked suddenly embarrassed. "Well—uh—uh…" She gave Sam a sheepish grin.

"Out with it!" Sam scolded. You know you can't keep secrets from me."

"There is this one guy. We're not dating or anything, but I think we're both interested."

"Who is it?"

"His name's Gary. Dr. Gary Coleman. He's a physician over at the hospital and the county's Medical Examiner. I like him a lot."

"My, my, a doctor! I'm impressed."

"Don't get your hopes up. He's on the rebound, and between having Katy and being Sheriff, I barely have time to tie my shoes, let alone handle a boyfriend. We're just friends for now."

"Friends with benefits?" Sam asked impishly.

"Not those kind of benefits. It's been so long now, I'm sure I could qualify to be a virgin again if I applied."

"No need to worry," Sam chuckled. "They say it's a lot like riding a bicycle."

Chapter 16

Two months earlier

Ricky was ecstatic. Nine-hundred-eighty-five-thousand-dollars the check said. It was drawn on his lawyer's trust account. The fifteen-grand his attorney withheld seemed puny. Still, it would have been nice to see that full million-dollar cashiers' check Sam had sent.

His first call was to Maria. Maybe—just maybe he could pull some apples out of the fire on their deal.

As they lay spent after the longest and best lovemaking of his life, Ricky made his proposal. "So I don't have the five-million we started out looking for, but what I do have is still a lot of money. What would you think about letting me buy in? Say a fifty/fifty partnership for five-hundred grand? We can run the place together until we can sell out and go to Florida like we planned."

Ricky could see the hunger in Maria's eyes. He didn't know that the restaurant was deeply in debt and that Maria's restaurant and liquor suppliers were pressing harder for payments she couldn't make. The infusion of so much cash would be a godsend.

"That's a generous offer," Maria said, "but it's not enough for a 50/50 deal on both the restaurant *and* the bar. Tell you what, Ricky, I'll give you fifty percent of the restaurant side for five-hundred thousand. You can be the managing partner. For another two-hundred-fifty-thousand I'll cut you in on a third of the take from the bar. I'll give it to you under the table, just like it comes to me."

It was less than he'd hoped for. "Jeez, I don't know," he said. "I'll probably never get my hands on this much money again. I'd better keep a little in reserve, just in case."

Maria petulantly rolled away from him. "If you don't want a hundred-thousand cash out of the three-hundred-thousand I put away every month, that's fine with me. I'm sure someone else would be happy for me to love them that much." She moved further out of Ricky's reach.

In the end they agreed to seven-hundred-thousand-dollars, but only after Maria promised that she would put all of the money back into the business. True to her word, Maria put his name as managing partner on their supplier accounts. When the suppliers asked him to sign a personal guarantee, she explained that it was common practice for business owners to personally guarantee their business accounts. "I had to sign the same things," she said.

Ricky wished he could talk to Sam about it before signing, but of course, that was impossible, and he wasn't about to spend a big chunk of what money he had left on some unknown shyster.

While Maria's books showed the restaurant was just breaking even, the reality was that it was losing thousands every month. The first month its income fell short of expenses by nearly eighteen thousand.

No problem, Ricky told himself. *I'll make it up with this month's bar receipts.* But when Maria handed him only forty-two-hundred-dollars from the safe, Ricky was appalled. "What's this?" he asked.

"Sorry, but that's all I can spare this month. The bar receipts have been really down. You understand, don't you?"

"Hell, no, I don't understand. You promised me a hundred thousand a month. I'm going to have to come up with over thirteen grand out of my own pocket to pay the restaurant's bills."

"Like I said, that's all there is. I'll make it up to you next month, baby. Is that okay?" She said it in such a sexy, vulnerable way that it melted Ricky's anger.

"Okay, but I expect a hundred and ninety-five-grand next month. Don't do this to me again."

Maria turned petulant. "If you're going to have that kind of attitude *Mister Thornton*, forget about coming over tonight. Not until you can treat me with a little respect. I have problems too, you know."

Ricky left the building with a sense of unease. The bar traffic seemed normal to him. Maybe even up a little compared to other months. What was down was the restaurant traffic. It was only about half of what she'd told him to expect.

"It's the season," Maria said when he asked her about it. "Kids are getting out of school. People are taking vacations. Just wait. It'll be better next month."

Then the first food bills with his name on the top came in. "Holy hell!" he exclaimed, "This can't be!"

He decided to do a complete menu cost analysis. What he found shocked him. The restaurant's food cost averaged more than sixty percent of revenue. Normal for restaurants of the type was thirty-three percent By the time he factored in labor, expenses, and overhead, the place was losing an average of three dollars per plate.

"We've got to raise prices," he told Maria.

"You can't do that," she said. "When I tried it business fell off to almost nothing."

"Then let's cut back the menu. Maybe lay off a couple of wait staff. This can't go on, Maria. I can't subsidize this place out of my own pocket every month."

"How about we spend a little money on advertising to get the customer count up? That should help."

Ricky was dumbfounded. "And where is the money going to come from for that? We can't afford to pay the bills we have now."

Maria cast him a seductive eye. "You've got some bucks left from the divorce settlement. Think of it as an investment to protect your investment. What would a measly ten or twenty thousand be if it brought in five hundred to a thousand new customers? You'd make it back in a week. It wouldn't hurt the bar traffic, either. And you know how important the bar side is to both of us."

Reluctantly, Ricky reached into his own pocket again, paid the deficit, and put ten thousand into radio ads and a few TV spots. The advertising brought in a total of sixty-three new customers. The cost amounted to one-hundred-fifty-eight-dollars per new customer—customers on whom they were already losing around three dollars a plate. The operating deficit the second month was twenty-two thousand, eight hundred dollars.

"What do you mean, that's all you've got?" Ricky screamed. "A lousy eleven grand? You promised me a hundred and ninety-five this month. What am I supposed to do with a measly eleven grand?"

"I'm sorry!" Maria screamed back. "I can't help it if you're a lousy businessman."

Ricky was stunned. 'A lousy businessman?' "Look Maria," he shouted, "I took your word on everything. You told me the restaurant was breaking even. You said the bar was raking in a profit of three-hundred-grand a month. Don't try and pin this on me."

"I ain't no Harvard MBA, buster," Maria said. "It's your fault for not knowing what you were getting into."

"My fault? *My fault?*" Ricky wanted to smash her in the mouth but stepped back from the brink. Too much was at stake. He took a deep breath and said a little less stridently, "Maria, this isn't working out. I think it's best if we go back to square one. I want to dissolve our partnership. Just give me my money back, and I'll walk away. No harm, no foul. I won't even make you pay back the money I've put into this place the past two months. I want my original investment back, and I want it now."

Maria's tone turned caustic. "Well that's a problem, lover boy. I don't have it."

Ricky was staggered. "*What?* I gave you nearly three-quarters of a million dollars. You said you were putting all of it into the business. What do you mean you don't have it?"

"I spent it."

"On what? You told me you'd put all that money back into the business."

"I don't have to tell you how I spent that money. The only thing I have to tell you is that it's gone."

Ricky's mind reeled. He felt sick to his stomach. "You'd better be kidding me. You can't have spent all that money in less than two months."

"Believe it, buster. I got bills too, ya know."

"That money's everything I've got," Ricky screamed. "You get that money back, or I'll…" He took a threatening step forward.

"You'll what, sucker?" Maria reached into a side drawer of her desk, jerked out a silver-plated .25 caliber semi-auto pistol and pointed it at him. "You gonna beat me up—force me to give you what ain't here? You want the bottom line, lover boy? The money's gone, and you ain't ever getting it back. What's that old saying—buyer beware? Look at it this way; you're going to have a hell of a tax year cause you can write off all seven-hundred 'G's as a bad investment. Now get out of this office before I have to shoot my partner; you know, that cocksucker who attacked me and was trying to rob me. Catch my drift?"

Ricky recoiled. "You'll never get away with this, Maria," he said. "I'll be back. And when I do, I'll have the cops with me." He turned and walked out the door, half-expecting her to shoot him in the back. What he got instead was the sound of derisive laughter echoing behind him.

He returned three days later, escorted by a sheriff's deputy and a court-appointed receiver. The place was abandoned. The doors were chained and signs were taped to the windows that said "Out of Business." Maria was nowhere to be found.

*

God, how humiliating it was, having to slink back to West Virginia with his tail between his legs, creditors nipping at his heels, and having to ask his folks for help.

"Not this time, son," his dad said. "Not in the condition you're in. I thought that little girl from Summersville would keep you straightened out but you weren't smart enough to hang on to her. I'm sorry but your mother and I can't have a drunk lying around the house." He handed Ricky the keys to the family cabin down on Plum Orchard Lake just outside Oak Hill in Fayette County and said, "You go on down there and get yourself sobered up. When you've been clean and sober for three months straight, I'll talk to my friend in the hardware business down there. He might have a job for you—but I don't."

Chapter 17

Consciousness returned to Jennifer slowly. How long she'd lain in that stupor between asleep and awake, she had no idea. As her mind slowly came back, she was mildly surprised that she was awakening at all. Her last conscious thought was of the Freak pointing the rifle at her face. She'd thought there would be no tomorrow.

She was back in the cell. She groaned at the realization, then remembered—she'd been shot. She tore back the thin blanket. Her relief was palpable when she saw that she still had a left leg. The leg looked professionally bandaged by someone with considerable medical expertise. First a hospital quality cast on her right arm, then this? Could the Freak actually possess such skills, or was he in league with someone else who did so?

Suddenly her mouth was so dry she couldn't even make spit. She carefully sat up and looked at the little alcove above her head. That was where the Freak sometimes left things for her. Sure enough, there was a full water glass, a tooth brush and a small travel-size tube of toothpaste.

She grabbed the water, and gulped it down. It was a small effort but it exhausted her. She lay back to gather her wits and her strength then raised her head again to survey her situation.

She could tell there were new bruises. The left side of her face still ached. She tenderly touched it and jerked away. *"Yeouch!"* she said. She remembered her dentist telling her not long ago that if you could feel the pain, you knew you were still alive. He meant the statement to be humorous. It was then—not so now.

She tried to lift her bandaged leg. It didn't actually feel too bad. She swung both her legs over the side of the bed and attempted to stand. A flood of pain took her to the floor. The door suddenly burst open and the Freak rushed into the cell. "No, no, no," he said. "You'll burst your stitches. You can't put pressure on it for at least two more days." He picked her up and deposited her back on the bed. His hands on her bare skin reminded her that she was still naked.

Jennifer took wry satisfaction in seeing the damage she'd administered with the fry pan. The left side of the Freak's face was a mass of multicolored bruising.

She knew how volatile and unpredictable he was. She also knew that all hope of escape was gone, at least until she could heal. Confrontation was futile. She tried a different tack. "Thank you for taking care of my leg. What did the doctor say about it?"

"It was a clean wound. The bullet just nicked the bone. It'll heal." He gave no hint of any doctor's participation.

"Can I have my clothes back? It gets cold in here," she lied.

"No."

"But—"

The Freak shot his right hand out, grabbed her lower face, and squeezed, painfully puckering her lips and making it impossible to speak. "I said No! Don't argue with me. Don't ever argue with me. I like looking at you. The day I stop liking it is the day you'll be dead meat. Understand?" He pushed her head sharply into the wall—hard enough to make her see stars. "Understand?" he almost screamed.

Terrified, she nodded rapidly—the only response she could give.

With a final painful push, he released her. "That's better," he said.

"I—I'm sorry. I didn't mean to upset you."

"I'm not upset. Just don't argue with me."

"I won't, I promise. You make the rules. I just need to know what they are."

"You just learned the first one."

"Are there others?"

The Freak thought for a moment. "Yeah. You do what I say, when I say it. I don't want to have to say anything twice."

"I can do that. Can I ask questions?"

"You just did."

"Is there anything I can't ask?"

He scowled. "I don't want to hear anything about my so-called 'problem'." He held up the first two fingers of each hand and twitched them as if enclosing the statement in imaginary quotation marks.

"I understand. I can do that. How long have I been here?"

"Three and a half days."

Her mind absorbed this information. Then she said, "I'm very hungry. Are you going to feed me?" One of her great fears from childhood had been of slowly starving to death.

"I tried the other day, Remember? But you tried to run away." "That was before I learned my place. Now I know. You're the master and I'm the slave."

The Freak nodded. "Damn right. You're my sex slave, and any other kind of slave I want."

"But I can't be for long if I don't eat."

"You'll get food. But understand this—the only reason you're still alive is because I like you. The others never once tried to help themselves. You tried and I respect that. Just don't do it again. From now on, I'll have this with me." He reached behind him and pulled something off his belt. Jennifer knew instantly what it was.

"This here's a Taser," he said, "sixty-thousand volts of pure, living hell. Try anything again, and you'll get a full charge. They tell me it's excruciating."

Jennifer looked fearfully at the device. "I understand," She said again, her voice quailing.

The freak stepped toward her and said, "I'm going to carry you to the other room and introduce you to Bertha. You struggle or do anything I don't like, and I drop your bony little ass on the floor and Tase the shit out of you."

She recoiled at the thought of his hands on her again but she had no choice. He picked her up with ease and carried her out of the cell.

When she'd fled through this room before, there was no time to pay attention to the amenities. To her surprise, the place looked like a very modern, complete beauty salon. *What an odd thing to have here.* The center of the room was dominated by a huge, old-style leather barber's chair. He put her in it. "This is Bertha," he said. "You'll be spending a lot of time with her."

He activated a control button on the floor and the chair reclined until it was nearly flat. The foot rest rose until she found herself lying on a nearly horizontal bed. Then she noticed the heavy leather restraints.

"Give me your arm," the Freak commanded.

"What are you going to do?" she asked, her voice trembling.

"Whatever I want. Are you going to give it to me, or do I have to take it?" He raised the Taser ominously.

She timidly extended her casted right arm. He guided it to the arm restraint, and strapped it down. "Now the other one." Then he repeated the process with each leg, leaving her embarrassingly exposed and vulnerable.

He looked down at her and said, "I like to see all of my women—every square inch of them. He looked at her pubic area. "There's entirely too much down there covering up that beautiful little vagina of yours, But I think this should take care of that." He raised the first of many instruments of torture he would use on her—a pair of tweezers.

Chapter 18

Cass was right; time was magic. Just over a month back in Summersville, and Sam was already feeling time's healing influence. The events in New York were slowly but surely receding from the paralytic dominance they'd once had over her mind.

The house became her overwhelming passion. First came the air conditioning. Daddy was probably turning over in his grave over it. One thing Sam had never given much thought to was the fact that Momma never had a dishwasher. It always seemed perfectly natural to see her at the kitchen sink washing the dishes. That was one of Sam's least favorite chores as a teenager. Her mother made her use water so hot she could barely stand it. "Gotta be hot to get em' clean," her mother had always said.

Once Sam said something about getting a dishwasher, but her mother shook her head and said, "Foolish to spend a bunch of money on something you can do for free. Now get your hands back in that water, Sammy girl. These dishes aren't going to wash themselves."

But getting a dishwasher into the kitchen was a problem. The old cabinets had no provision for such an appliance. Sam briefly thought about getting a portable unit but there was scant room in the small kitchen for that. So right after the air conditioner came new kitchen cabinets and plumbing that would accommodate the kitchen's first step toward modernity.

"Momma, no disrespect," Sam whispered as the appliance store delivery men stripped the box off the dishwasher, "but these hands are just not made for scalding-hot dishwater."

Not living here for years had given Sam the ability to see the place with an entirely new eye. Daddy had been a busy man when he was in good health, always working on something around the house. But the years had robbed his ability to keep up. It was little things, a leaky faucet here, a cracked baluster there, the old back porch light switch that wouldn't work. Sam made a list and started on the projects one at a time. When she got to the old light switch, she hit a major roadblock.

"The wiring in this house goes back to the late twenties or early thirties," the electrician told her. "Up in the attic is what they call knob-and-tube wiring. It's in the walls, too. The insulation around those wires is so old and fragile that just a little squirrel bump could make it break off and expose the wire. With all due respect, ma'am you're living in a fire box. You don't even have a smoke alarm in here to warn you."

Sam immediately bought a smoke alarm and contracted with the man to replace the wiring. Then she decided to check the plumbing as well.

"Well, ma'am," the plumber said. "Some of these pipes are good copper that will last another hundred years, but they soldered them with lead solder. Dangerous stuff—kills your brain. It should be silver solder. There's some old galvanized steel pipe in here too. Normal lifespan for that is around fifty years. Your pipes are a lot older. I'm seeing rust where there shouldn't be none. Never know one of them galvanized pipe's bad till it breaks. Then you got a flood on your hands. If you want the truth, ma'am, if you can afford it, I'd replace it all."

With that, Sam decided to rehabilitate the entire house. Within days an army of contractors descended on the place. The dirt and sawdust mess was awful. No one in town knew how to fix the old lath and plaster walls anymore, so modern gypsum drywall went up in their place. But she had the new walls textured to look just like the old ones. She didn't want the house to lose the aura, flavor and charm she had grown up with.

She was able to save most of the light fixtures. Those she couldn't, she replaced with replicas. A month in and the remodeling was nearly complete. Just last week the floors, baseboards, door frames and stair rails had been stripped and refinished. The painters would start tomorrow. Within days, she'd have the skillfully renovated old house to herself again.

She didn't dare total the bills up to see what it had all cost—certainly more than the old house was worth. But it was home, and always would be whether she decided to go back to New York or not. Daddy and Momma's old house still felt like Daddy and Momma's old house, and it would for at least the rest of her life. That made everything worth it, no matter the price.

Chapter 19

How long has it been? Jennifer wondered. Weeks certainly. Probably a month if the coming of her period was still any sort of reliable indicator. Getting her period was the best part of her time here. The Freak put a box of tampons in the alcove and didn't touch her for days.

Her wounded leg now seemed to be fully healed. The Freak had removed the cast from her arm several days ago.

She could tell his routine. When he was here she could faintly hear him moving around upstairs. She could tell when the weekends occurred. He was here for two or three days at a time. The other days he spent somewhere else—at work, she assumed. She wondered if he spent his time at his office charming other women the same way he had her.

When she heard him come in at night she knew she'd soon have food. She began to think of herself as his Pavlovian dog. She took what small comfort she could in the fact that for all the horrible things he did to her, he fed her well.

Some days her food was served through the little door at the back of the alcove above the bed. On those days, she didn't have to see or deal with him. Other days, the cell door opened, and the Freak invited her to eat with him at a small table in the outside room. He always dressed the same; slippers and a terry-cloth robe that sagged open—nothing underneath.

But the taste of fear tainted these meals. The pattern of the bad days was always the same: a delicious meal at the table then his 'invitation' for her to sit in Bertha. She tried to refuse once and was painfully Tased for her disobedience.

Once she was in the chair, he'd strap her in then sit down and they'd talk. He was an engaging, highly intelligent conversationalist. Sometimes, the Freak would stand and gave her a gentle kiss on the forehead then say he was tired and that she could go back to the cell. Then there were the other nights—the nights the conversation turned sexual—the nights that she endured unspeakable things.

He compensated for his inability to prolong his sexual performance with a variety of objects; dildos, bottles, phallic-shaped food items. Sometimes he used a speculum to agonizingly stretch her vagina. It all turned him on.

He got huge erections that would last only until the instant he tried to use them. Then it would be over for him in seconds, and the anger would boil to the surface and her punishments would begin. Sometimes they came as simple beatings. Other times he employed agonizing exotic torture rituals. He broke four of her fingers and delighted in extinguishing cigarettes on her thighs. Improvised waterboarding was one of his particular favorites: Not for information extraction but simply for his sick, demented amusement.

A week ago, he'd turned to cutting as his torture of preference. He was expert at it. He inflicted dozens of thin, shallow cuts that stung horribly and bled profusely. The worst were to the bottom of her feet. After the cuts he applied an excruciating red liquid analgesic from a dropper bottle. The liquid burned like fire and made the actual cutting seem mild by comparison.

She'd been unable to walk ever since he started cutting her feet. He had to carry her where ever she went. During the hours he was gone, she had to crawl back and forth between the toilet and the bed. On those occasions she was thankful the cell was a small as it was.

Her pubic hair was growing back. Two days ago he again subjected her to the torturous tweezers. But for all the torture, after that first night here he never again assaulted her torso, back or face. After a month or more of brutal torture, incongruously those places appeared almost normal.

But today was different; today everything changed.

Every few days she'd been permitted only a brief shower in a tiny stall next to the cell. But this morning the Freak carried her upstairs to a bathtub where he treated her to what amounted to almost a spa treatment.

At first she was fearful. Was he setting her up for a new and different kind of torture? Drowning perhaps? Everything about him was different today. He was deferential and solicitous. He allowed her a deliciously long, hot bubble bath complete with luxurious shampoo and a rich conditioner for her hair. He let her decide when she was done.

Then he took her back downstairs and placed her atop a massage table she hadn't seen before. There he administered a long and relaxing full body massage. Normally such touching was the precursor to savagery, but for the first time, his hands on her was not sexual. He was even gentle around her injuries, telling her, "If this hurts, you let me know." He seemed to mean it. What was going on? Why this sudden change? She didn't trust for a moment that such treatment would last.

"Your nails are so beautiful," the Freak said. Indeed, it had taken him more than two hours to create and apply the intricate, lace-like design to the acrylic nails that he'd put over her own nails, now damaged beyond repair by his torture.

Jennifer knew better than to respond. She raised her head and lifted her fingers as high as the arm restraint would allow and looked down at them. The nails were impressive. Where did he get these skills?

"Now for your toes, my dear. They won't take long. Then we'll get started on your makeup and hair. But first let's sit you up. I have something I want to show you. You're going to love it."

The chair moved her into a seated position. The Freak walked to a closet at the far end of the salon table. He reached in and pulled out a new dress still in its clear plastic bag. He unzipped it and took out a gorgeous, empire waist, sequined, scarlet satin gown with yards and yards of full-length skirt. It had slender, full-length sleeves that flared at the ends. The shoulders were each gathered with a gold metallic ring. The front had a daringly attractive deep 'V' neckline, and behind was a scoop back that plunged to what surely would be her waist. It was one of the most beautiful gowns Jennifer had ever seen.

Is he getting ready to let me go? She didn't dare hope such a thing. She knew too much. She knew who he was, what he looked like, where he worked, and how to get to this place.

"Why are you doing this?" she asked suspiciously.

"Tonight is your night, my dear. Everything is going to be in your honor. Tomorrow we'll show you to the world. You've got to look your very best."

"Are you saying you're going to let me go?"

"In a manner of speaking. But now let's get those toes done and get started on your makeup. Everything has to be just perfect." He hung the dress on a hook on the front of the closet door.

He seems happy, almost jovial, she thought.

"Oh, yes," he said almost as an afterthought. "There's one other quick thing." He reached into a drawer and withdrew a roll of lacy scarlet and black ribbon with delicate embroidered daisies. "Let's try this around your neck. He pulled ribbon from the roll and placed it around her neck, measuring just the right amount to fit her like a choker necklace. "There, my dear. Wait till you see the beautiful pearl pin we'll use to fasten this together."

She couldn't help but notice that all the time he worked he was humming, "Hotel California." She remembered his words from the night he shot her—and realized with finality that indeed, she would be checking out tonight—but she would never leave. *I should have cut his throat when I had the chance,* she thought.

Chapter 20

"Wow. It looks the same but it's not. It's so much better," Cass said as Sam walked her through the nearly finished house. Over the past month Sam had let the renovations push all other considerations aside—including brooding over her divorce. When Cass and Katy visited, all talk was about the house—not about New York, and not about the fact that she was now single. The longer those subjects were pushed aside, the easier they would be to deal with when she finally gave herself time to do so.

"Come look at what I've done with Momma and Daddy's bedroom." Sam said as she led the way upstairs.

"Wow!" Cass said again. The old double bed with its thin, threadbare mattress was gone. In its place was a deep, queen-size pillow-top mattress housed in an Early American-style shelved cannon-ball headboard and matching footboard. The bed was covered with a fluffy, white, down comforter. A number of pillows with colorful shams were arranged against the headboard. Matching side tables each had an antique brass lamp with a Tiffany-style shade.

A new archway where the old clothes closet had been led into what was once Kendall's bedroom. It was now a lovely master-bath suite with twin walk-in closets. The mirrored doors made the room look twice the size it actually was.

"This isn't a restoration project; it's a *resurrection* project," Cass said as she and Sam returned to the newly remodeled kitchen.

"How about a Coke or something," Sam offered.

"Got a Dr. Pepper?"

"Sure do. You want a glass and some ice?"

"Nah."

Sam fetched the Dr. Pepper and a Diet Coke for herself then settled at the kitchen table. "You've done an awesome job with this place," Cass said, "but I think you've remodeled more than just this house. You're a far different person than the sad, depressed woman I sat here and cried with a month ago."

"I feel so much better. Fixing the house has been really good for my soul. I feel like I've had Momma and Daddy right beside me all the way. And Katy's had so much fun helping out. Thanks for letting her be my second-in-command. You should have seen her face when I sat her at the new dressing table upstairs and let her turn on the lights for the first time."

Cass smiled. "That's big stuff for her. There's nothing like that at our house. I can't even imagine how much this must have cost."

Sam shook her head. "I haven't dared total up all the bills. And I've still got the exterior to do." Sam looked at the kitchen window. "I think I'll put a bay window right there to give this room more of a breakfast nook feel. I may do the same in the living room. I've always wanted a bench-seat bay window."

Cass nodded her approval. "I have a question for you. How long do you think you're going to be around?"

"Originally I thought just two or three weeks. But I'm not ready to go back. The last place I need to be right now is New York. I took a six-month leave of absence and may use all of it."

"Remember how I said you could volunteer down at the hospital or the library or something?"

"Yes. I've been giving it some thought."

"How'd you like to volunteer for *me*?"

Sam was surprised. "You mean at the sheriff's office?"

"Yeah, sort of."

Sam shook her head. "I'm the furthest thing from being a cop. What could I possibly help you with?"

"Actually it wouldn't be for me, I want you to be a special investigator for the prosecutor's office. You wouldn't be actually prosecuting cases, but you'd carry a badge and have the full investigative authority of the prosecutor's office. I've already talked to the county prosecutor and he thinks it's a great idea."

"Oh, I don't know, Cassie. There's a huge difference between civil and criminal law. My experience is strictly on the civil side. I doubt I'd do you much good."

"After I tell you why we want you, maybe you'll change your mind. Have you heard of what people around here are calling the evening gown murders?"

"No."

"I'm not surprised. Murders aren't big news in New York, but they're huge here."

Sam's interest was piqued. "This sounds interesting," she said, leaning forward. "Fire away."

Cass set her Dr. Pepper aside. "We've had two recent murders we can't solve. The first was about two years ago, the second eight months ago. Both victims were attractive young women between twenty and thirty. We can't identify who they are or where they're from. We think they came from outside the area because no one around here has been reported missing and nobody's come forward to claim them."

"That's strange," Sam said.

"The killer leaves them laid out in beautiful evening gowns looking like they've just stepped out of a beauty salon. We don't have a hint as to who the killer might be. All we know is that the bodies have turned up here in Nicholas County. We're all holding our breath wondering when it's going to happen again. The FBI says if it's a serial killer, the time between killings will likely get shorter. The next body could show up anytime."

"I assume you want me to work on these cases, and of course I'll help if I can, but I'm not trained in criminal investigations."

"Don't worry. I know you're smart enough to do this. Keeping with my policy of distracting you as much as I can from that asshole ex-husband of yours, this could occupy a lot of your time while you're here. I won't ask you to work on anything else. I've created what I call the 'war room' at the courthouse. It's actually the spare jury room and it's dedicated to nothing but solving these murders. It would become your office."

Sam shook her head. Cass's proposal was outside the realm of anything she'd contemplated. "When do you want me to start?" she asked.

"Tomorrow would be soon enough."

Sam laughed. "Nothing like giving a girl a little time to think it over."

"Think about it as long as you want, Sammy Girl, but I want you to start tomorrow. That is, unless you're afraid to do it."

It was the ultimate challenge—a characteristic of their relationship that went all the way back to their childhoods. Whenever Cass had a hard time talking Sam into something, all she had to say was, "You're just an old scaredy-cat."

Sam always got mad and said, "I am not!" and in that moment Cass knew she had her.

Characteristically Sam spat back, "You know better than that."

"Yes I do. So are you going to do it?"

Sam hesitated a moment then sighed deeply. "If that's what you need me to do, I'll give it a try."

Cass couldn't suppress a grin." I knew you would."

"But I want you to know that this makes me really mad at you, Cass Rosier."

"Why?"

"For telling me about those poor girls." With a shudder, she thought about all of the house's creaks and groans as it settled around the new construction each night. "I live here alone, you know. Now I won't be able to sleep at night."

Cass laughed. "Just keep your doors locked. There's no evidence that whoever is doing this picks on locals. But even at that, I keep my house locked and my gun on my night stand. You ever learn how to shoot?"

"My dad and brother taught me how to shoot Daddy's old .22 pistol years ago. I inherited it but it's put away somewhere."

"Well you're going to learn all over again, and with a real weapon this time, not that little .22 popgun. You and I are going to the range a couple of times a week, starting tomorrow night."

Chapter 21

"Mary, this is my best friend, Samantha Martin. Sam, meet my right arm, Mary Stilson. She's our dispatcher"

"Happy to meet you," Mary said politely. "I knew your folks. They were fine people."

"Thank you," Sam said sincerely.

"I heard about your little brother. It was so sad. He made all of us here in Summersville very proud. I just want to tell you thank you for your family's sacrifice for our freedom."

Sam suddenly found herself having to fight back tears. "That's so kind of you to say. I'm very proud of Kendall. I'm glad others appreciate his sacrifice as well."

Cass found herself fighting a lump in her own throat. "Okay, enough of that," she said. "What would people think if they came in here and found all three of us bawling? The first thing we need to do is show Sam the department's most important piece of equipment."

Cass led Sam to a small nook between the reception area and Cass's office where the coffee machine that was located. She handed Sam a large mug—pink and festooned with pastel flowers. "I brought this in for you," she said. "None of my deputies would dare drink from a pink coffee mug."

A box of assorted fresh donuts sat on a side table. Cass pointed at them and said, "What they say about cops and donuts is true. Without them, we'd starve. Fill your mug, grab a donut and follow me."

Sam complied. Cass led her out of the sheriff's office and down the hall to a small corridor just outside the district courtroom. At the end of the corridor was a door that said 'Judge's Chamber.' To the left was another door with a sign on it that said, 'Jury Room.' Cass pointed and said, "That's the War Room, but we're going in here first. She knocked on the Judge's Chamber door.

Sam was surprised to find that Judge Aaron Luke and County Prosecutor, Doyal Stewart, were waiting inside. After introductions all around, Judge Luke swore Sam in as Special Investigator. She emerged from the room as an official public servant and carrying something she never imagined having—a badge!

Then Cass ushered her to the room across the hall. Sam surveyed the War Room with both consternation and curiosity. To the right on the far wall, centered above a wide whiteboard, was an 8x10 picture that had a small sign above it saying "First Victim." On the whiteboard below the picture were other pictures and various sheets and writings all connected by lines that appeared to be a timeline representation of sorts. A similar configuration took up the wall on the left side of the room under a picture of the second victim.

Cass walked Sam through each of the timelines. Sam was sickened by the horrible revelations of the medical examiner's photos juxtaposed with the surreal illusion of beauty the dead women presented, posed as they were in the places of their discovery.

Cass invited Deputy Eric Zeeman in. Together they gave Sam an hour-long evidentiary briefing. "This is terrifying," Sam said as they concluded. "What do you want me to do?"

Cass slid two fat case-file folders across the table. "I want you to be our fresh set of eyes. Read through all this stuff without me or Deputy Zeeman here coaching you. Then we'll compare your impressions with ours. Pay particularly close attention to the conclusions of the FBI profiler and the ME. Then let's get back together when you're done and compare notes. Are you up for that?"

Sam took a deep breath, nodded her head and said, "Where do I start?"

"At the beginning; with Jane Doe number one."

*

Sam had slogged her way through hundreds of ugly divorce cases, but thankfully none of them resembled anything like this. As she read, she scribbled notes about each of the women on a yellow legal pad. It was a habit that helped her retain details. Later she'd transcribe the notes into her computer and index and organize them.

The hardest to read were the medical examiner's reports. The medical language was sterile, straightforward, and dispassionate, much like the legalese she was used to in her own profession. But the trauma described was unlike anything Sam had ever imagined. Midway through the second report, she laid her head on the table and sobbed. How could any human being do such terrible things? No way would she sleep tonight—and probably not for many nights to come.

When she closed the last file and reviewed her notes, she resolved to do anything and everything necessary to see that this brutal, merciless killer was stopped.

*

Just before noon, Sam tapped lightly beside the open door to Cass's office. She stuck her head in and said, "I've finished the files."

"Come in." Cass invited.

Sam knew she'd never hide the trauma of her reading assignment. Her eyes were puffy and her runny nose was red.

"Those reports are the most awful things I've ever had to read," she said.

"Sorry to put you through that. You ready to talk about it?"

"As ready as I'll ever be."

"Here or in the War Room?"

"Let's do it in the War Room where we can look at evidence as we go."

"Want Deputy Zeeman with us?"

"I'd rather not—not yet. I can cry in front of you, but I'm not sure I'm ready to show that side of me to a total stranger just yet."

"You got it," Cass said gently. "I'll let him..." Cass stopped midsentence and listened to the radio unit on her desk. She monitored radio calls in her office the same way she had in her patrol car for years. It was second nature. Something in the deputy's tone made her stop and listen.

"Unit 21, dispatch." Unit 21 was Jess Dixon, her oldest and most experienced deputy.

"Dispatch. Go ahead, 21." the radio squawked

"Dispatch, I have a 10-35. Requesting 10-78 and a 10-79 to the ME at my location."

The instant Cass heard 10-79, the call for a medical examiner, she jumped into the radio conversation. "Stand by," she said. "21, is this an emergency?"

"Not anymore. This looks like another one of those two top jobs you've been working on."

Cass looked sharply at Sam and interpreted what was happening. "The deputy just gave us a major crime alert and requested assistance from other officers. He also requested that the medical examiner come to the scene. It sounds like we may have another evening gown murder." She re-keyed her mic and asked, "Unit 21, can you go 10-21?" Cass reached to take out her cell phone but the deputy's response arrested her movement. "Not at the moment. I've got no service here. I'll have to get back up on the ridge."

"Anyone there who can secure the scene while you do that?"

"The only other ones here are the kids who found the bo—"

"Not over the air, deputy," Cass barked, cutting him off. "Big ears, remember?" She had no idea how many civilians had police scanners in the county, any one of which could be listening. But one that was almost sure to be on was the unit owned by the local newspaper—and they understood the '10' codes. "What's your 10-20?" Cass asked?

"About six miles northeast of Richwood on Public Route 76, right were the bridge crosses the Cranberry River."

"I'll get the nearest squad to your 20 and get some other help on the way. I'm leaving right now."

"10-4."

Cass looked at Sam and said, "Saddle up and get ready to haul ass, girl. Stay with me." She grabbed her service cap and bolted for the door.

Cass paused at the reception area where Deputy Zeeman was the Duty Officer. She shouted around the wall to Mary in dispatch. "I'm 10-76 to Unit 21's location. Get that 10-79 out to the ME immediately. Use the phone, not the radio."

"On it," Mary shouted back.

"Send any available units on the east side of the county to 21's location. Assign one to get to high ground and act as radio relay in case we lose signal down in that canyon. Better call out Richwood EMS. Have them get to the scene and stand by for transport."

Though it would leave the office without a uniformed officer present, she looked at Zeeman and said, "Eric, you're with me! Grab the crime scene kit, and let's roll. I want your squad right on my bumper."

*

Sam's heart was pounding. She'd never ridden in a police car, let alone one rushing to a crime scene. In no time at all, Cass's SUV and Zeeman's squad car were racing through town, making for Arbuckle Road and State Route 39.

As they cleared the Gauley River Bridge Cass finally had a moment to explain what was going on. "We've got another dead body, Sam. You won't have to worry about reading up on this one. You'll see everything up close and personal."

"Oh no!" Sam's eyes widened. "What do you want me to do?"

"Just look, learn, and listen. Stay close, but out of the way. Don't touch anything—and I mean *anything*. You got a note pad or something?"

"It all happened so fast. I didn't grab anything to write with."

"No worries. I've got stuff in here. I want you to take notes on everything, even if you don't think it's important. Let your mind take pictures. Be aware of where you are at all times and don't disturb anything that could be evidence. If in doubt, don't touch it, just show it to me."

Public Route 76 out of Richwood was a dirt road leading to as remote an area as one could find in Nicholas County. Cass felt sorry for Zeeman, following behind in an old, worn-out Ford Crown Vic cruiser that used to be her patrol car. With no recent rainstorms, he'd be eating a full serving of her dust all the way.

She was lead investigator on the first murder and acting sheriff on the second, but she owned this one all by herself. The whole county would be watching. She suddenly caught a case of nerves.

How did a single, five-foot-eight, curvaceous redhead who some of her deputies wanted to sleep with more than listen to, get taken seriously as their boss? She wasn't just that woman the feds made the department hire, damn it! She was as tough and professional at this job as anyone.

If this third body turned out to mirror the other two killings, as the newly elected sheriff, she'd inherit responsibility for all three in the eyes of the public.

"Better not screw this up," she muttered as the road dropped off the ridge and into the Cranberry River gorge.

*

Cass brought the SUV to a sliding stop twenty feet in front of the bridge which was now blocked at both ends by highway patrol cars with blue lights flashing. A Richwood City ambulance was parked off the road on the flat area near the west side of the bridge.

Yellow crime-scene tape blocked public access to large areas on either side. Other than making sure outsiders didn't contaminate the scene, officers present were taking no purposeful actions. Not until she and ME arrived.

Cass turned to Sam and said, "You're about to witness my first murder investigation as sheriff. We're both on trial here, Sam. A whole lot of people will be watching. Let's put our big-girl panties on and go and show the people of Nicholas County they elected themselves a kick-ass sheriff."

Chapter 22

"Over here, sheriff," Deputy Dixon called. He was waiting in front of the ambulance.

"Eric, get the video camera ready," Cass instructed as Deputy Zeeman exited his vehicle. Then she introduced Sam to Dixon. "Deputy, this is Samantha Martin, a special investigator attached to the county prosecutor's office. She has full access to this crime scene."

"Yes, ma'am," Dixon responded. He tipped his hat to Sam. Cass could tell the deputy was uncomfortable with another woman's presence. "Don't worry, Jess," Cass said, "she's a tough bird. She doesn't bite, and you can still cuss just like you do around me. Now show us what you've got."

Dixon broke into a grin. "Yes, ma'am," he said. He led them to a well-worn path leading off the road and down the embankment to the underside of the bridge. It was a pathway fishermen frequently used to reach the river.

The path led under the west bridge abutment where the footing formed a four-foot-wide concrete shelf extending laterally all the way across the underside of the bridge. It was the perfect spot for fishermen to sit and eat lunch in the shade or seek shelter from a passing thunderstorm.

During spring runoff, or after prolonged rains, water sometimes reached a few inches up the vertical face of the footing. But now, in early summer, the river was ten or fifteen feet away.

Under the bridge the path became lost in an expanse of large river boulders one had to negotiate in order to walk along the front of the shelf.

"It's a hell of a lot easier up here," Deputy Dixon said. Some enterprising soul had placed a large rock against the abutment wall as a helpful step up. The deputy went first then turned to lend a hand to Cass and Sam.

Cass saw the body lying on the concrete about mid-way across the shelf. "Damn," she cursed. The body was clad in what appeared to be an expensive evening gown. "Oh my," she heard Sam gasp. Sam hung a little behind as Cass walked to where the body lay.

The young woman appeared to be in her mid-twenties and looked so peacefully at rest that it seemed like all one had to do was speak loudly, and she'd awaken. Cass's gut ached for the poor girl. She wanted to take her in her arms and tell her everything would be alright. But it wasn't, and for her, it never would be.

"Same type of woman, same M.O." Cass muttered. The woman had long, salon-perfect blonde hair carefully arranged to frame her face. The makeup was perfect. "See this ribbon?" Cass pointed to an identical scarlet and black lace ribbon as the other two bodies had worn. "Remember the pictures, Sam? This is the work of the same killer."

Cass looked at the nails, knowing beforehand what she would see. Indeed they were masterfully done. The shimmering scarlet satin gown was long, gorgeous and daring. Its skirt was perfectly arranged to show the girl's figure at its best advantage. Again the body was laid out in a classic death pose—hands folded one atop the other beneath her breasts. One held a small bouquet of what appeared to be fresh, hand-picked daisies with a sprig of baby's breath. Her legs were straight and close together. The matching scarlet patent-leather pumps she wore must have cost a small fortune.

Based on the other murders, Cass knew the beauty would turn out to be an illusion that would only be revealed after they peeled away the façade the killer had so misleadingly created.

"Who found her?" Cass asked the deputy.

"Couple of sixteen-year-old kids from Richwood who came down here to go fishing this morning."

"They here?"

"Yeah. I got em both in the back of the ambulance. One of the troopers riding herd on em."

"Bring them down here but not too close to the body. Tell them not to touch anything."

While the deputy retrieved the two young men, Cass inspected the area near the body, giving Sam dictation as she went. Against the wall forming the bridge abutment, were a couple of gum wrappers, several cigarette butts, and a Campbell's soup can that someone had used to carry worms. Cass knew this killer as much by what he didn't do as what he did. "I doubt any of these are evidence," she said. "Our guy's far too careful to leave gum wrappers or a cigarette butt lying around. We'll process them anyway."

Cass peered over the shelf to the river bed below. Several sets of fresh footprints were in the sand and mud between the rocks, some probably from the boys who found the body and others from officers who were first on the scene. She pointed them out to Sam. "We'll cast those then boot-print everyone here at the scene to exclude them from the investigation. A couple are a lot deeper than the others, like somebody was carrying something heavy. Maybe we'll get lucky and come up with a print that leads us somewhere."

Deputy Dixon showed up with two gangly, nervous teenage boys in tow. He brought them to a halt about fifteen feet from the body.

Cass walked over and eyed them. "What's your names, boys?"

Both were hesitant to speak. Finally the tall, sandy-haired kid on the left said, "Jerry Sanderson, ma'am."

"And you?"

"The shorter, freckle-faced redhead swallowed hard and said, "Danny Lovett, ma'am."

"I'm Sheriff Rosier. Either of you ever been in trouble with the law?"

Danny shook his head. The other boy's eyes dropped. "I got a ticket right after I got my license."

Cass nodded in response. "Which one of you found the body?"

"We both did," Jerry volunteered. "We was just coming down to the river, and there she was. We thought she was sleeping, but she didn't wake up. We figured out she was dead."

"So you touched the body?"

"Danny suddenly became noticeably nervous. "No, ma'am. We didn't touch nothing."

"How'd you figure she was dead?"

"We yelled at her?" It was a question more than a statement.

Jerry too seemed more nervous. They were hiding something.

"You didn't try to shake her awake?"

"Well—yes, ma'am," Jerry admitted. "I guess I coulda' done that. I shook her shoulder but she didn't wake up. I thought maybe she was drunk or drugged up or something."

"You touch her anywhere else?"

The boys quickly cast guilty looks at each other. Neither responded.

"Boys, if you touched her anywhere else we're going to be able to tell. You ever heard of DNA? If you left a single flake of your own dead skin on that body, we're going to know it. If you don't tell the truth, and we find your prints or DNA on her, you'll go to jail for lying to a police officer and obstructing justice. Then again, maybe you two killed her. We'd be able to know that and you'd go to prison. Might even be executed. Tell me the truth, boys. Did you kill her?"

"Noooo!" they both wailed.

"Listen to me, boys. You only get one chance at this. Where else did you touch her?"

Danny's voice quavered. He was on the verge of bawling. "We didn't mean nothin'. She was just lying there, her boobs nearly falling out of that dress. I never touched one before. With her asleep and all, I didn't think it would hurt anything. Danny's head dropped in shame. "Sorry Sheriff,' he said. "I touched one of her boobs."

"How? With your finger or your whole hand?"

"My hand, ma'am. That's really how we figured she was dead. She was so cold, like a piece of meat right out of the refrigerator."

"You touch her the same way?" Cass asked Jerry, who now trembled with fright.

"Y-Yes, ma'am. As soon as Danny touched her, he said he thought she was dead. He asked me to feel how cold she was, and I did. We listened for a long time to see if she was breathing, but she wasn't. We got scared and went up on the road to try to call somebody, but my cell phone wouldn't work down here in the canyon, so we jumped in my truck and went to the top of the ridge and called 911."

"You touch her anywhere else?"

"No, ma'am!" they chorused.

"Once we figured out she was dead, it freaked us out," Danny said. "She looked like a real nice lady and we was real sorry she was dead. But we didn't come back down here till the deputy came."

"Ok, boys, *now* I think you're telling the truth. I'm going to send you back up to where the police cars are parked. One of my deputies is going to write down your statements and take your fingerprints. Then you're going home."

"You gonna tell our folks what we done?" Danny asked fearfully.

"What would happen if I did?"

"My pa, he'd probably razor-strap me real good." Jerry nodded in silent agreement.

"Tell you what. For now, how about we only tell your parents that you boys found the body? I think we can keep the rest to ourselves. I'm willing to do that as long as you two stay out of trouble. Deal?"

"Oh, yes, ma'am," they said in unison, heads nodding so vigorously they risked whiplash.

"Turn em loose, Jess," Cass said. But get their shoe prints first.

*

Nothing could be done with the body until the ME arrived. Sam helped Cass mark the crime-scene artifacts—the cigarette butts, the bait can, and numerous other bits and pieces. Cass retrieved the camera from the SUV and took dozens of photos. Deputy Zeeman videoed the scene and marked every footprint in and around the base of the bridge. Two other deputies set about making plaster casts.

Nearly two hours after their arrival, a frazzled-looking Dr. Coleman rushed up. "Sorry I took so long," he said. "You know how these small-town hospitals are. The doctors need to do a little of everything. "I was in the middle of delivering a baby."

"We understand," Cass said. "Dr. Coleman, this is my friend, Samantha Martin. She'll be observing. She's a special investigator helping the prosecutor."

"Happy to meet you, Ms. Martin," Coleman said.

So this is Dr. Coleman, Sam thought as she appraised the man. *Not bad, Cassie.* He was long and lean. Not ruggedly handsome, but handsome nonetheless. "Glad to meet you as well," Sam said, extending her hand.

"What have we got here Cass–er—Sheriff?"

Cass nodded toward the body.

"Another pretty one." the doctor said as he walked carefully around the body. "Same ribbon around the neck, perfect makeup

125

and hair. I'm not looking forward to seeing what's under that dress."

"Neither am I," Cass said sadly. "Let me know when you can give me a time of death."

The ME took pictures of his own, then he bagged the woman's hands. Perhaps this time there was DNA evidence under her nails.

Cass and her deputies searched the area between the bridge and the road for useful evidence while Dr. Coleman carefully went over the body with a large magnifying glass and tweezers, stopping from time to time to pick up a piece of lint, thread, or other object that might contribute to unraveling of the mystery of who killed her.

"Given the body temperature and the state of rigor mortis, I'd say she's been dead ten to twelve hours," the ME finally estimated.

"I've done everything I can here. I'll release the body for transport directly to the hospital's morgue. I don't want her sitting in a refrigerator overnight. I'll autopsy her this afternoon, if that's alright."

"Fine by me, Gary—a—I—I'm sorry—Dr. Coleman," she corrected herself.

Sam was amused. Cass and the good doctor were obviously having a hard time keeping the personal side of their association from showing.

Chapter 23

"You sure you're up to this?" Cass asked as she and Sam walked toward the morgue.

"Not sure at all. I could barely stand dissecting a frog in biology. That's a far cry from watching a real autopsy."

Cass nodded. "Just ignore the fact that it's a person on the table, otherwise, you'll cry your eyes out. Disconnect your brain from your heart. The big incision is the toughest part. Lots of people throw up watching that. It's no shame. Just go on over to the sink and pitch your cookies if you have to.

*

Cass was prepared for their first view of the body, but Sam was not. Out at the river, the young woman looked beautiful, like a dress-up doll. Here, all such illusion was gone. "This is awful," Sam muttered.

From memories of her first autopsy, Cass knew what Sam was going through. She remembered how she felt embarrassment for the woman, lying there naked and utterly exposed before complete strangers—how she actually felt goose bumps rise on her back as if she was feeling the woman's nudity against the cold stainless steel of the table herself.

She and Sam stood back listening to Dr. Coleman. Sam scribbled furiously, trying to keep up. Dr. Coleman saw what she was doing and said, "Don't worry about catching every word. It'll all be in my report.

Coleman talked into a microphone describing his examination of the girl's body. "This guy's getting off on cutting now," he said.

He rolled the body and showed them where the killer had flayed the backs and sides of the woman's thighs and buttocks.

"Damn near skinned her alive," Cass muttered.

Long, thin cuts created a waffle pattern on the soles of the poor girl's feet. Some were nearly healed while others appeared to be fresh. "That had to be excruciating," Dr. Coleman said. "I can't understand how he kept her free of infection."

Something stopped Dr. Coleman. He looked at the woman's left calf then rolled the body slightly so he could look at the back of the leg. "Here's something new," he said as he pointed to a prominent circular scar on the front of the woman's leg.

"What is it?" Cass asked.

"The scaring is fresh. It looks to me like a bullet wound. There's a small entry wound on the back of her leg. What you're seeing is the exit wound." He walked to a table stacked with large envelopes of x-ray films. He thumbed through them until he found the one he wanted, then stuck it into a backlighted viewer. He looked at it for a moment then said, "That's what it is, all right. The bullet nicked the tibia. See this?" Dr. Coleman pointed to a bright spot in the x-ray a few millimeters from a similar sized deformity in the bone. "That's a bone fragment. The bullet knocked it off and missed the fibula by about three millimeters. Had to be a relatively small caliber, low-velocity round, perhaps a .22 or something of that order. Anything else and we'd be seeing much more tissue loss around the exit wound. If it had been high-powered like a .308 or .30-06, it would have nearly blown her leg off. Looks to me like this wound is four or five weeks old."

"First time we've see bullet wounds," Cass remarked. Wonder why he just didn't use the gun to kill her."

"My guess is that he thought it would ruin her looks. There's something else I want to show you." Coleman took down the x-ray film, returned it to the desk and shuffled through the stack again until he came up with another which he put up on the viewer. It showed the woman's right forearm. "I found a fresh oblique fracture of this woman's right radius bone. Appears to have happened around the same time as the bullet wound." He pointed out the jagged fracture line. "This is a serious break." He said. "The ulna was the only thing holding this arm together. If it had broken at the same time, this would have become a compound fracture and likely would have required surgery. Here's what's interesting. This bone would have had to be reset and properly immobilized for it to heal this way."

"How strange," Sam said. It was the first time she'd spoken during the autopsy.

"The broken arm doesn't surprise me," Cass said. "But the bullet wound does. Why now and not on the others?"

"No idea," Dr. Coleman said, "unless our perp is upping the ante on torture levels."

"How about the rest of her?" Cass asked.

"Much the same as the other two—ritualized, prolonged torture, including sexual torture. As you can see, she went through the same pubic-hair treatment. There was more mutilation on her thighs, buttocks and sides of her ribs than with the others, though he was careful to keep her face, breasts and back whole."

"Dear God," Sam said with a shudder. "How can a human being do this to another?"

"I'm no psychiatrist," Dr. Coleman said, "but I'd say you're dealing with one very angry, very psychotic person."

Cass nodded in agreement. "The FBI says it's likely a white male with a huge sexual problem. It's likely that he either can't perform, or has a deformity or physical disability that makes it difficult or impossible for him to function sexually. They said he almost certainly hates women and blames them for his problem. They think he gets his sexual gratification from hurting them."

Cass looked at Sam. "We've got to find this guy. Every time I see a high-school girl in a prom dress or watch our local girls compete in a beauty pageant, I can't help but think it could be any one of them on this autopsy table next."

Chapter 24

Entering the War Room the next morning, Sam found Deputy Zeeman making the final adjustments to a newly installed white board on the left wall. She was surprised that the picture of the third victim was already up. She and Deputy Zeeman would work together to create the timeline.

"Good morning." Sam said as she deposited her things.

"Good morning, ma'am, Zeeman said with a shy smile. Just getting things ready in here. Sheriff says she wants a meeting at nine."

"That will be fine, but may I ask you a favor?"

Zeeman looked her in the eye only briefly then quickly cast his gaze down at his shoes. Cass had warned her that the man was unusually shy around women. "Yes, ma'am?" he mumbled.

"Could you please call me Sam? We're going to be working together a lot and I don't want to feel like I'm your mother."

"Aaa—yes, ma'am. I can do that." "Aaa—I mean, yes, Sam, I can do that," he quickly corrected himself.

Zeemen was a nice looking young man; in his early twenties, solidly built, and just under six-feet tall. He had a shock of thick, sandy-colored hair and a baby-face that made him look like a teenager. Cass said he looked so young that sometimes people wouldn't take him seriously as a police officer. He was the youngest deputy on the force, both in age and tenure.

Sam had to make him more comfortable around her. She chose her next words very carefully. "You know, Eric, I was raised around here just like you. People taught us to be polite; saying 'yes ma'am' and 'no ma'am' or 'yes sir' and 'no sir.' That still works in public or with children speaking to their parents, but we're co-workers, and I hope, friends. So why don't we make a deal. When we're working together, let's make it Sam and Eric. In public, we can be more formal. Does that work for you?"

"Yes, ma'am—Sam." He grinned. "That kinda rhymes, doesn't it?"

"Indeed it does. It sounds like Dr. Seuss. I guess you could say I'm Sam I Am."

They both grinned and the deal was struck.

*

County prosecutor, Doyle Stewart, joined Cass, Eric, and Sam for the meeting. After discussing the latest murder, Sam had the chance to present her thoughts from the reading she'd done the previous day. "One thing that strikes me about the first two victims is their apparent lack of any connection to Nicholas County," she said. "It's like these young women appeared out of thin air and ended up dying here. No parents, husbands, boyfriends or anyone else has attempted to claim the bodies. Dr. Coleman says our latest victim was tortured over a month or more and as far as we know she's not been reported missing. Odds are that she'll turn out to be another Jane Doe."

Zeeman shook his head and said, "It's as if the killer knows nobody's going to claim them."

"But how could the killer know that?" Cass asked.

Prosecutor Stewart spoke for the first time. "He has to be in a position to pick up that kind of information. The question is, does he do it through some type of formal information gathering process, or is he getting the information by doing something as simple as talking with strangers at a diner or chatting these women up over drinks down at Maloney's?"

"Call it a hunch," Cass remarked, "but I don't think it's completely casual. We have three blonde girls spaced out over a couple of years, all with the same basic profile. That's a pattern, not a coincidence."

Sam spoke up. "Don't forget that the ME said he thought that whoever's doing this likely has a strong medical background. Every time you go into a doctor's office you have to fill out a ton of personal information.

"Plus he said the guy probably has training as a mortician *and* as a beautician," Cass's exasperation showed. "We made a list of everybody in the county that fits any part of that profile—over eighty people by the time we include hospital staff, doctors, dentists, licensed beauticians, and all the rest. We even included veterinarians.

"We eliminated more than sixty of them based on their alibis around the approximate times of death."

"How many are left?" Sam asked.

"Sixteen," Cass replied, "The list is where your investigation should start."

Sam turned to the prosecutor. "When I get the list down to my top few candidates, can I have Cass bring them in for questioning? 'Sweat them,' is what I think they call it in the movies."

Stewart smiled. "Most of them will cooperate but some we'll have to come up with probable cause on or name them as a Person of Interest. For the rest, I keep an old water board in the back of my closet."

Sam chuckled along with everyone else, then asked hesitantly, "Do you mind if I make a suggestion?" She was reluctant to tell these professionals how to do their job.

"Fire away," Cass said.

"Working that list is good, but there's something else we can do. If we knew who these girls were, that might lead us straight to the killer. As a civilian lawyer, I used a lot of other mediums to obtain information about our clients and our opponents. Top among them was the Internet. Somebody out there knows who these girls are. Let's create a website for them. Let's give them a Facebook page. We can get their faces on YouTube. If their video goes viral, we could have literally millions of people looking at these girls in no time at all."

Cass's eyes lit up. "Doyle, is there any reason we can't do that?"

"None whatsoever. It's a great idea. The question is, who's going to do it and what is it going to cost?"

"Not much," Sam said. "Facebook, YouTube, and Twitter are free and we can get a web page up for under a hundred bucks, including hosting. Does the county have an IT department?"

"Such as it is," Zeeman quipped. "Me and deputy Wellman are sort of the in-house unofficial geeks and we have a guy from one of the local computer companies who's sort of on-call if it gets deeper than what we can handle."

Sam looked at Stewart and asked, "I know you and Cass have budget constraints. Can I pay for this out of my own pocket?"

"There's certainly no law against it so long as you're not paying money directly or indirectly to a county official. You'll have to fully disclose any expenses paid in the county's benefit."

"Then let's do this," she said. "I'll start organizing it today. If we can just get names under each of those pictures, a whole lot of other information will come as a result—maybe even the name of our killer."

Chapter 25

The lawn around the house seemed larger than usual tonight. "Probably the heat," Cass told herself. The sun had dropped below the horizon, but it had yet to make much difference in the temperature.

Cass was dressed as far down as she could get away with in the neighborhood: a thin, light-blue cotton shirt held in place by two buttons and tied at her midriff, no bra, and a short, ragged pair of cutoffs. Even at that she was dripping with sweat. Her shirt clung and was becoming more see-through by the minute.

"Damn humidity," she cursed as she maneuvered the heavy mower to reach under the shrubbery at the corner of the house. She knew her shirt was pushing the limits of public decency, but it was past sundown, none of her neighbors were close about, and the lawn was nearly finished.

Cass was proud of her modest, three-bedroom brick home on the cul-de-sac around the corner from her parents. It sure beat the second-story two-bedroom apartment she and Katy had lived in before she got this place. It wasn't fancy, but it was hers.

She just got started on the front lawn when a white Volvo station wagon pulled up and parked in front of her house. Dr. Coleman—Gary.

She panicked. *I'm a mess! Sweaty, no bra, flat hair.* She wanted to run and hide as he stepped from his car but he'd already seen her. She killed the lawnmower, swiped her forehead with her sweaty arm and pulled the nearly useless shirt away from her chest, hoping that would make it a little less diaphanous. She put on the best, most radiant smile she could contrive and said, "Gary! What a surprise. I'm not very presentable but come on in."

This wasn't the first time he'd shown up, but it didn't happen often. What was unusual this time was that he'd come unannounced, with none of his children in tow.

"Sit down," she said, indicating the couch. The air conditioning felt glorious. "Can I get you something to drink?"

"No. I just stopped by to make sure you're all right. That was a pretty rough autopsy yesterday."

Cass was touched. "Thanks for caring. I had a bit of a rough time sleeping last night, but I'm fine today. I've got to have something to drink. Could I interest you in a wine cooler?"

"Since you put it that way—sure."

Cass retrieved two bottles of Bartles & James from the refrigerator. She quickly ran hers over her forehead to slow the sweat. Out of sight, she ran her fingers through her hair and pulled her shirt away again. She didn't want him thinking she regularly pranced through the neighborhood half-naked.

"Here you go," she said as she handed him his bottle. She was momentarily tempted to sit beside him on the couch but feared she was slightly too pungent to be that close. Rather, she sat across the room in an overstuffed chair.

"Do they ever bother you?" she asked. "The autopsies, I mean?"
"Some more than others. I'd much rather be just a general practitioner and have a pathologist do the autopsies. But small counties like ours don't have the luxury of a full-time ME.

"That's true," she said.

Gary took a sip of his cooler and said, "Doctors have to deal with dead bodies all the time. The ones that kill you are children.

The worst thing about my job is having to tell two frantic parents that their child has died. But I have to admit, that autopsy yesterday got to me more than usual. Such a young, beautiful girl, and it seems like the killer's torture level is escalating. I just came over to make sure you're okay, that's all."

"Glad to hear you're human," Cass said. "Of course, I've suspected that all along. The one I worried about was Sam. I worked with her most of the day today and she seems okay. In fact, she came up with a really good idea. We're going to do an Internet blitz to see if someone out there can identify any of the bodies. She's paying for it out of her own pocket."

"If I can help, let me know."

"How soon will we see your report?"

"Soon. I have it about finished. We're three weeks out from a full tox report." Gary hesitated a moment as if he had something else to say. "Ahmm ... Cass, I have to admit there's another reason I came over. There's something I think we need to talk about. I— I'm not quite sure how to say it, but I think it's time. He looked down at the floor and quietly asked, "I want to know what you think of me."

The question caught her utterly by surprise. Cass searched a moment for the right words then said, "I think you're a nice man, Gary, a good, decent guy. You're a good friend, and I'm grateful to know you. Why?"

"Because I feel the same way about you." Gary suddenly fumbled for words. "I, uh—this may sound a bit old fashioned, but ..." Beads of perspiration appeared on his brow. He had a hard time looking her in the eye. He swallowed hard and said, "At the risk of possibly changing our friendship, I want you to know that I think you're a beautiful woman and that I'm attracted to you. I'm telling you this because I'd like to start seeing you on more than just a professional basis. I need you to tell me whether you think that's a good idea, or should I just tuck my tail between my legs and go on back home? In medical terms, I think it's time to take our temperature, so to speak."

Cass was flattered, and charmed. Was this the way thirty-something's did it? Maybe she *should* have sat on the couch.

"Thank you," she said cautiously. "You sure picked a lousy day to call me beautiful—I'm a mess." She pulled at a strand of sweat-soaked hair to prove her point. "I'd be lying if I said I hadn't thought about you the same way. I've got to admit that you've made my little ole heart go pitty-pat more than once."

Gary looked relieved. "So I guess the question is where to go from here? We're not teenagers. We don't have to beat around the bush. We also both have kids that figure into the equation, plus we still have to work together professionally."

Cass didn't know quite what to say. "Hell, Gary, I don't know. I think we need to just take it low and slow until we find out if this airplane's going to fly. I think the first thing would be to have an honest-to-goodness date—all by ourselves and out in public."

Gary grinned. "Great idea! Where should we go?"

"I hate to sound sexist, but you're the guy, you're supposed to tell me that. However, there's an old fashioned drive-in theatre in Fayetteville. I've been craving movie candy, a greasy old hamburger wrapped in wax paper, and a sack of overcooked fries for weeks. Or we could picnic it. What do you think?"

"Sounds like a cholesterol-filled great time to me. How about Saturday night?"

"I'll have to make sure my folks can tend Katy, but that shouldn't be a problem. By the way, do the seats in that Volvo recline?"

"Yes they do, why?"

"Cause if they didn't, I was going to volunteer to take mine." Cass started to give him a wicked wink then thought better. She covered her mouth and said, "Oh, I can't believe I just said that."

"Too late," Gary chuckled as he stood to leave. "Now I'll lie awake tonight thinking about it."

"Forget the car, maybe we should take motorcycles instead," Cass chuckled nervously, trying to redeem herself as she escorted him to the door.

Gary hesitated in the doorway and said, "I've got to warn you, it's been close to fifteen-years since I actually dated someone. I may not remember how."

Cass put her hand on his forearm, gave it a little squeeze and said, "It's been a long time for me as well. But don't worry, Doc. I'm sure we'll get the hang of it. A good friend recently told me that this stuff's probably a lot like riding a bicycle."

Chapter 26

Nine-year-old Katy clapped excitedly as she watched Sam and her mother lift the evening gown over the head of the third mannequin. Sam had persuaded the owners of the old Chatworth's Department Store to allow the place to be transformed into a temporary photo studio. Twenty-years ago Chatworth's was the anchor of Summersville's business district. Then the Big-Box store came. It was a bonanza for the community but an event that spelled doom for many downtown businesses. More than half closed, including Chatworth's.

Several fashion mannequins were left behind. When Sam approached the family with her plan, they were more than happy to allow her to use both the store and the mannequins.

"I think that's got it," Sam said as she and Cass finish putting the dress on and smoothing it out. "All that's left are the shoes. Do you want to help me with them, Katy?"

Katy nodded and bounced over to the evidence boxes where she picked up the plastic bag containing a pair of scarlet pumps. "Careful KK," Sam warned. "Remember, only touch the plastic bag." *She certainly loves helping her mother,* Sam thought. It tugged at her heart a little. She couldn't help wishing she had a child of her own.

As Sam and Cass worked, Mr. Jenkins, the photographer, was busy setting up cameras, umbrella-type bounce flashes and background drapes.

Cass had told Sam that she'd spent two years searching Internet websites and women's catalogues trying to identify the source of the dresses and shoes. It was a fruitless search.

Sam did much the same the previous week, with identical results. Apparently the dresses were custom made, one-of-a-kind creations.

Perhaps casting a wide net across the Internet would turn up one or more of the dresses' makers.

After placing the three pairs of expensive pumps on the feet of each mannequin wearing the matching dress, Sam and Cass stood back to view their handiwork. The mannequins were eerily complete, right down to the distinctive neck ribbons and pearl clasps the victims had worn when they were found.

Sam couldn't help but feel a chill, but eight-year-old Katy viewed the dresses through far different eyes. "Those are so pretty," she bubbled. "I saw Brianna's big sister wear one like that. Some boy came to the house and pinned a big flower on the front. I thought he was going to stick the pin right into her boobie." Katy giggled as if she'd revealed a naughty secret.

Cass gave her daughter a playful, modestly disapproving look and said, "She was going to a dance they call Junior Prom. It's a very big deal when you're sixteen."

Katy gave her mother a quizzical look. "The boy was dressed up in a funny-looking suit; not like the ones the men wear to church."

"It's called a tuxedo," Sam said. "It's something boys wear for special occasions like dances and weddings and stuff."

Katy wrinkled her nose. "Why would a dance be special? They made us do that at school last year. The boys had to come over and bow and ask the girls to dance. Jackie Wooten asked me and I told him no." She lowered her voice almost to a whisper. "I think he likes me. He's always chasing me around the playground and stuff.

The other boys tease him about it." Then her voice returned to normal. "When I said no, the teacher said I wasn't polite. She made me dance with him anyway. We had to put our arms out like this." Katy held her arms in a dancing position, frowned and said, "He stepped on my foot."

Sam snickered behind her hand as Cass responded. "Sometimes the boys do that, honey, but not on purpose. Did you know that I like to dance?"

"You do? With a boy?" She looked incredulous, then the look turned skeptical. "Did you and Daddy ever dance?"
Sam caught her breath. She knew Cass had never hidden information from Katy about her dad, but answering questions like this had to be awkward—maybe even painful. She was amazed when Cass didn't miss a beat. "We sure did Sweetie. Your daddy was a good dancer. He used to be quite dashing."

Katy looked puzzled. "What's dashing?"
"It means charming, fun to be with."

"Oh!" Katy said brightly. "Like cool."

Cass laughed. "That's right, like cool."

"Yeah," Katy said thoughtfully." I guess sometimes Jackie Wooten can be cool too, except when I don't want him to chase me. But I'm not going to let him kiss me like Sarah Henrie let Andy Jacobs kiss her. That's gross."

"You hang on to that thought," Sam called from across the room. "There'll be plenty of time for kissing boys when you're older.

"Don't worry, Aunty Sam, I'm never going to kiss a boy."
Maybe I won't either, Sam thought.

"Pardon me folks, I think I'm about ready," Mr. Jenkins interrupted. Jasper Jenkins was a short, round, bald man with thick, wire-rim glasses without which he was totally blind. No matter the temperature or time of year, Jasper always seemed to sweat. On this hot summer day in a store whose air conditioning had been turned off years ago, he was sopping wet; constantly mopping his brow with a soaked handkerchief. It was mildly disgusting, but he'd been the Martin family photographer for years and was one of the best Sam had ever seen.

The mannequins were set up in front of a white drop cloth Jasper had rigged. "What do you think, Jasper?" Sam asked.
"With those dresses on, I'm tempted to ask one of them out," he said with a chuckle. Neither woman found the comment humorous.

*

With the photography shoot done, Sam went to work on the Internet blitz. Working with the county's part-time webmaster, she created Jane Doe pages that would appear on the county's website.

She paid for an optimization service that would help move the pages far up the list on search engines. They created Facebook and Linked-in pages that featured profiles on the three women and linked them to the county's website. They also set up Twitter accounts for each of women. Sam began a fusillade of tweets. She trolled incessantly for 'friends' willing to share photos.

The same day Mr. Jasper did the photo shoot Sam had the videographer, the same one who did the law firm's work in New York, do a video shoot. The YouTube video he produced was a masterpiece. The videography of the crime scene photos made it look as if the women were actually alive. How the man was able to create the disturbing part of the video that made it appear the viewer was witnessing a murder, she had no idea, but the video got over 30,000 hits in the first two days.

Last of all, Sam placed ads on Craig's List inviting people to visit the Jane Doe sites. If there was any way to communicate the dead women's stories via the web, she tried it.

Now came the hard part—waiting.

Chapter 27

Boom! Boom! Boom! The loud reports made by the .9mm Glock automatic pistol split the Sunday afternoon air. After Sam and Cass's hectic week spent presenting their murder victims to the world, the shooting excursion was a much needed break.

This was their third trip to the county firing range north of town. As promised, Cass was teaching Sam to use a handgun. Katy was with them this time.

"Nice grouping," Cass said, looking down-range at Sam's target through a spotting scope. "You're still a bit high and to the right. Move your rear sight two clicks right and line up the front blade so it just touches the bottom of the bull's-eye instead of holding it right in the middle."

Sam used the adjustment tool Cass had given her to move the U-shaped rear sight. "Katy still there with you? Sam asked.

"Right here."

Sam slipped the protective ear muffs back on, turned down-range, and fired off three more rounds.

"Right there, sister," Cass said, looking up from the spotting scope. You got two in the bull's eye and one an inch to the left. That little Glock likes you."

"I like it," Sam said with some satisfaction. "It fits my grip well, and the recoil isn't as bad as I expected."

Katy tugged at Cass's sleeve. "I want to shoot too, Mommy."

"Ok, sweetie, it's your turn. Tell me the rules again."

"Always know where the gun's pointing. Never point it at people. Don't put my finger on the trigger until I'm ready to shoot, and keep the safety on until just before I shoot. Did I get them all?"

"You got them. Now let me get a target out there for you. Cass pulled in the rope attached to Sam's target, took it off, and put up a fresh one for Katy. Then she ran the target out to the 30-foot mark. When it was in place, she pulled a nickel-plated, pearl-handled .25 automatic and a loaded magazine out of the gun bag. She handed the empty pistol to Katy. "What do you do first?" she asked.

"Always check the chamber yourself even if someone says it's empty, and keep the gun pointed downrange."

"Good job, little lady. Do it."

Sam watched Katy follow her mother's instructions precisely. When she indicated to her mother she was ready, Cass called out the standard firing range warnings. "Ready on the right! Ready on the left! Ready on the firing line! Commence fire!

Katy swung the gun up into a classic two-handed stance, bent her knees and pulled the trigger. *Crack* went the little .25. *Crack! Crack!*

"I'm impressed," Sam said with an amused smile. "She's a little pro."

"Sure is," Cass said proudly. "If she shoots like she normally does, that target will have less than a four-inch grouping."

"She's only nine. Why'd you start her so early?"

"She'll be ten next month. I'm Sheriff. That means I've always got a big old target on my back. If some puke I've busted comes after me at home and I go down, I want her to have a chance. Besides that, she loves it. I'm going to start her in the West Virginia junior target-shooting championship circuit next year."

*

"So just remember; center mass, center mass," Cass instructed as they rode back to town. It was dusk. Katy leaned against her seatbelt in the back seat of the Durango, already asleep. "If you were using that little .22 of yours, a center mass shot might not put an assailant down. But the .9 mm has enough stopping power to make center mass shots the best option."

Sam shook her head. "The hardest part would be knowing when to shoot and when not to," Sam said. "It's such an irreversible decision."

"That's why you have to make up your mind before you're ever confronted with it. You mentally run through scenarios to the point that your actions become automatic. If you stop to think about it, you may end up dead—or worse—she inclined her head toward the back seat—somebody you love could end up dead. What do you say we pick up some Chinese? Our little Sleeping Beauty back there would like that, and I could do with somebody else doing the cooking tonight."

*

"Good night, Aunty Sam." Katy, now dressed in her PJs, wrapped her arms around Sam's neck and gave her a big kiss.

"Good night, KK. You sleep tight, sweetheart."

"Ok," she said as she went to her mother and repeated the process. "Mommy, come tuck me in."

As Sam sat on the sofa waiting for Cass's return, she couldn't help but reflect on her New York life which now seemed so sterile, distant, and almost pointless. It was more than the problems with Ricky that made it seem so. It was the fact that in the middle of a densely crowded city of over eight million people, Sam almost always felt alone.

Here, she hardly could go to the grocery store without bumping into at least one person she knew. Here people waved as they drove by just in case they knew you. Every day she spent in Summersville restored more of her soul and healed more of her emotions.

"All tucked in," Cass said when she returned. "She was asleep the minute her head hit the pillow,"

"She's such a doll. I want one just like her," Sam said wistfully.

"She's a good one, all right. I'm sure proud of that little girl."
Sam asked a question that had been lurking all day. "So what's going on with you? You've been humming and smiling and bouncing around all day with a big smile on your face. You smoking something we need to talk about?"

"You could tell, huh?" Cass responded sheepishly.

"Hard not to. Whatever you're on, I want some."
"You're going to have to get your own." Cass hesitated then confessed. "I had a date last night."

"Say what? When—who? And you've waited all day to tell me this? Shame on you Cassandra Rosier! Who is it?"

"Gary—Dr. Coleman."

"Ok, I'm not moving off this couch until I hear every juicy detail. And don't think you can hide anything. I'll know. You know I will."

"Okay, okay." Cass laughed. "I've been dying to tell you anyway."

*

Cass had stewed for more an hour over what to wear. Her usual fashion choice was easy; either her uniform or jeans and a t-shirt. She wasn't used to the thought of dressing for someone else.

She settled on her best pair of relatively new, relatively tight-fitting jeans; the only pair she owned with a rhinestone design on the back pockets. For a top she chose a loose-fitting, wide-sleeved yellow cotton pullover with a bit of a daring neckline crisscrossed by a leather drawstring. The clever design gave a peek-a-boo effect that both revealed and concealed at the same time. Without a belt, the top fit like a potato sack. She dug out an old multiple-strand leather fringe belt with dangly ends decorated with large turquoise-colored beads. The belt tied rather than buckled.

That did the trick. The belt matched the leather look of the top's drawstring and brought out her shape very nicely.

"Not bad for thirty-two," she said as she inspected her profile in the full-length mirror.

Her hair was another matter. She kept it short, the kind of hair you could wash in less than a minute, towel off, run your fingers through a few times and were good to go. It also worked well with her uniform service cap.

This was the first time in years she felt she had to worry more about style than function. The best she could do was try to give it some sort of shape. She battled it into a kind of swept-back tomboy look and for the first time in months applied a generous helping of hair spray.

Makeup was tough. Cass hardly ever used it. But tonight when she opened the door, her foundation would be in place, with blush highlighting her prominent cheekbones. She'd do her eyes and powder her nose—and he probably wouldn't even notice. But damn it, she'd look good for her first date in well—forever.

*

"Your chariot awaits, madam," Gary said when Cass opened the front door. He smiled and made a deep bow, sweeping his hand toward the car.

He was such a cornball, such a throwback to a more chivalrous time. Cass loved it. "Why thank you, kind sir," she responded. She'd never ridden in a Volvo, not even an older model station wagon like this one. As she slid in, she viewed the center console with mild disappointment. *How's a girl supposed to snuggle up to the driver?*

Gary solved the problem when he pulled into the drive-in. Instead of parking facing the screen, he backed into their space. "I've got the back fixed so we can open the hatchback, and lean against the seats," he explained. I've got TV pillows and a blanket back there if you get cold."

Fat chance in this heat. She thought. She chuckled to herself. Years ago her mother had warned her about getting into the backseat with a boy. Now she couldn't wait. She did worry about appearances though, at least until she looked around and saw that virtually every other SUV and station wagon had pulled in the same way. *Been too long since I've been to a drive-in,* she told herself.

The movie was a complete bore, but it didn't matter. The hamburger and fries were glorious—greasy and messy. After a particularly big bite, barbecue sauce and ketchup laced with mustard dripped down Gary's chin. It was a problem because he held his Diet Coke in the other hand.

"I'll take care of that for you," she said with a laugh as she wiped his chin with her napkin then gave him a peck on the cheek.

"Why thank you," he chuckled. "Remind me to hire you as my napkin-bearer." Then he set his drink down, changed hands with his burger, reached out a greasy, sauce-covered finger and deposited some of it on her cheek.

She flinched and said, "Oh, you…"

"Let me get that for you," he volunteered, and returned her gesture in kind except that he ended at her lips with a gentle, lingering kiss.

The food and drink were discarded. Cass's arms were around his neck, pulling him in as kiss after hot, probing kiss carried her away. *My God, how long has it been?* She caught her breath as his hand found the open bottom of her shirt and touched the bare skin of her back. She tugged a shirttail out of his jeans and went seeking the same thing.

This feels sooooo good. She felt more like a teenager than when she really was one. Then she momentarily panicked. Were other people watching? She was, after all, Sheriff of Nicholas County. She pushed him away and looked around. The couple on the left seemed engrossed in the blood and gore of the supremely bad movie. She couldn't see the people in the SUV on the right, but by the sounds coming from the window and the motion of the vehicle, they were at least as engrossed in each other as she and Gary were.

"Whew!" she said, fanning her face. "Guess you can tell it's been a while for me. I forgot how good this feels."

"Me too," he said. "I feel like I'm a kid back in high school."

"Gary?" she said hesitantly, "You've got me real hungry tonight, and I'm not talking about food. I haven't felt this way in years. I love it, but you've got to promise me something. No matter how far we go, we won't go all the way tonight. I'm not ready for that. I'm not a do-it-on-the-first-date kind of girl. Maybe not even the fifth or tenth time or whatever. For right now, we can be friends with benefits, just not full benefits. Deal?"

"I promise. Your honor's safe with me, dear lady. We're making out, not making babies. Just to be on safe ground, exactly how far do you want this to go? It's a little late for just handholding."

"As far as we can without going all the way. Right up to the very edge, but not over it. I fear you've awakened a monster." She began untying the belt that earlier limited his explorations and said, "This damn thing's killing me. And if I'm not mistaken, I think there's something under here you were looking for."

*

"You're kidding," Sam exclaimed, covering her mouth. "You made out with him at the drive-in?"

"Boy howdy, did I ever, and it wasn't just at the drive-in. We continued right here in the driveway. We didn't break it up until around four this morning. He found buttons on me that haven't been pushed in a long, long time. It's a good thing he had better control than I did. For a while there, I would have let him off the hook to do anything he wanted. But he was a man of his word. I got inside the house *virgo intacto*."

"Cassandra Rosier!" Sam scolded. "You better keep those panties of yours on. I need someone to share this celibacy thing with. Where's our solidarity?"

Cass laughed. "I love you to death, Sammy girl, and you know that. But you had someone in your bed a lot more years than I did. Maybe it's my turn. She leaned back with a big sigh and said, "There are times that you just gotta have a man."

Chapter 28

Three months! Ricky felt like banging his head against a wall. Three months since the divorce was final. Three months since the biggest paycheck of his whole life. *How could I have been so stupid?*

Sam had tried to warn him. It still pissed him off that she was always so right. *This is all her fault,* Ricky thought. If she'd have just gone ahead and bought that damned restaurant like he wanted, none of this would be happening. She was so tight that a fart couldn't get out sideways. Oh sure, there was the Escalade, but outside that—nothing. Back then things were so tense at home that he stayed away as much as possible anyway. Sam didn't care; she was working eighty-hours a week.

His favorite hang-out was the Tuscan Hills Restaurant and Bar where he got to know that bitch, Maria. Maria was a friendly face and a listening ear. He told her how tough it was being married to a mega-rich wife who never showed him any respect. Man was that ever a mistake.

Maria not only cost him seven-hundred-'G's', but now the bill collectors were hounding him for more. Two food suppliers had already filed lawsuits. How the hell were these people finding him? His name wasn't on anything—not on this house, not on the telephone bill or electricity bill, nothing. And the Escalade was still registered in New York. The only people who knew where he was were a couple of buddies down at the bar. Of course, there was Charlene, good old Charlene. She stayed over a couple of nights a week. And that other girl, her best friend. *What was her name? Oh yeah, Karen something? That's it. Big tits.* What a night that was when she and Charlene came over together. But none of them would rat him out.

Then he knew—his parents up in Charleston. Frickin straight arrows. They wouldn't lie if their lives depended on it. If somebody convinced them that giving him up was the right thing to do, they'd do it for sure.

Ricky could dispose of most of the creditors with a simple, cheap bankruptcy. But there was one for whom that wouldn't work. It was the company that had been the restaurant and bar's primary liquor supplier. Ricky found out they were actually the New York mob.

He learned that just a week ago. That was the day the goon showed up on his doorstep. He was a big guy, huge, with a heavy Bronx accent and dressed in a thousand-dollar silk suit. He said his employers weren't the type of businessmen who took a screwing and laughed it off. "If they can't get money from ya, they take other things, like body parts and such." the man said. "You're going to pay us our two-hundred-thirty-grand, Mr. Ricky fucking Thornton. The only question is whether you'll have one hand left or two when you do."

"Wait a minute," Ricky said. "The restaurant only owes you a hundred-thirty-thousand."

The man shook his head. "Nope! You forgot the interest. Fifty-grand a month. Next month it'll go up another fifty-thou. After that, there won't be another next month, if you catch my drift."

When the man stood to leave, he extended his hand to Ricky as if this had been just another business meeting. Ricky reluctantly gave him his. The man gave Ricky's hand a crushing grip that made his wince. He said, "I'll be back a month from today. I'll have a couple of friends with me. If you can't pay up, I'll introduce you to them. You think you got a problem with me? Wait till you meet them, Mr. Thornton. They're real charmers, those two."

Ricky was so scared he hadn't touched a drop of alcohol since. He had to have his head clear. For a couple of days he was incapacitated with the shakes, but considered that insignificant compared to what the man had threatened

After sobering up, he decided to call his parents, eat crow, grovel a little, and tell them about the jam he was in. Maybe they'd loan him the money.

"Oh that man was just trying to scare you, Ricky," his mother cooed.

"We don't have that kind of money," his dad said with disgust. "We'd have to mortgage the house and the business, and even then, I don't think the bank would loan us that kind of money without us telling them what it's for. You think they're going to regard bailing out a drunken son from mobsters as being a good use of their money? What happens if you can't pay us back? Your mother and I would be ruined. We'd have no inheritance left for you or your brothers and sisters. I'm sorry, son, but the answer is no. You have to find your way out of this yourself."

So much for dear old Dad! That left only one answer—Sam. Yeah, yeah, she had that damned restraining order, and yes, he'd agreed to never see or contact her again. But a New York order didn't mean a damn thing as long as he was in West Virginia. And this was an emergency.

*

"What do you mean, she's not there?" Ricky shouted into the phone.

"I'm sorry, sir, but Ms. Martin has taken a leave of absence." Ricky was incensed. "Her name's not Martin, damn it. It's Thornton!" What an insult for her to use her maiden name—as if the past seven years never happened. "When will she be back?"

"I'm sorry, sir. We don't have that information." The sickly sweet, overly patient voice of the law firm receptionist only heightened Ricky's anger.

"Well where the hell did she go? How can I contact her?"

"I'm sorry sir, but I don't have that information either."

Ricky tried another tack. "Let me speak with Harold Howell."

When Howell answered, Ricky didn't get three words out of his mouth before the man cut him off and told him to go straight to hell. "Never call me again," Howell said as he hung up.

Ricky was so angry he picked the telephone book up from the coffee table and threw it across the room. It took him several minutes to calm down. Then a thought panicked him. *Maybe she's sick. Maybe she's got cancer or something and doesn't want anyone to know. God-damn you, Sam, don't you die on me; you're the only hope I've got!*

Where would Sam go on a leave of absence? She wasn't the type to go traipsing around the world, but maybe after the divorce she decided she liked world cruises or something. Not likely. He'd had a hard time just getting her to take a day off to slip down to Atlantic City.

Maybe she went home. Maybe she's over there in Summersville right now. He tried her dad's old phone number. Disconnected— no forwarding number. He punched the speed dial number on his cell phone to try and call hers. The call wouldn't go through no matter how many times he tried.

"Sam, where the hell are you?" he shouted to the empty house. He had to find her. He just had to.

Then a moment of reality struck: What would he say if he did? *Hey Sam, you know that million bucks you gave me a couple of months ago? It's gone. You were right. The restaurant was a terrible investment. Oh, and by the way, that Maria woman, she took almost all of my money—your money—and disappeared. I'm calling cause I need more. Maria left me holding the bag on Tuscany Hill's bills. Look, I know I really screwed up our marriage. I drank too much and never should have screwed Maria, but hey, I'm sorry, all right? You wouldn't mind parting with another million or so, would you? After all, we have history. We used to have the same last name. We're family, right?*

He recognized how ridiculous the narrative was. Sam had far more reasons to say no than to say yes. Getting her to pony up more money would require a different approach; one to which she couldn't say no.

He knew what the solution was. It was that stack of $50,000 bearer bonds she had sitting in that safe-deposit box over at Summersville National Bank. Nineteen-hundred of them. *Nineteen-hundred!* He only needed a few; fifteen, maybe twenty. Was that so much to ask? Surely he could convince Sam of the sense of it.

He was down to less than fifty-thousand. If he couldn't convince Sam to help, his only option would be to use what money he had left to disappear, maybe leave the country.

But in order to talk to her he had to find her. "Sam, where the hell are you?" he shouted again to no one. And that's exactly who answered him.

Chapter 29

"What's your plan of attack today, girlfriend?" Cass asked as Sam set her things in the war room on Monday morning. The Internet project had so totally dominated Sam's time that it had been nearly a week since she'd last stepped foot in here.

"I'm going to school today," she said. "I need to learn about serial killers."

Sam began searching websites; first the FBI then several universities and finally the American Psychiatric Association. She successfully resisted indulging in one of the office's ever-present donuts until 10:49 a.m. "Darn things," she said just before biting into a Bavarian crème. *I'll quit these tomorrow,* she promised herself.

According to the FBI, in order to officially classify someone as a serial killer, a person had to commit three separate murders spaced by a time they called 'the cooling off period' which could vary from a few days to years. One writer's article said that it was typical for a serial killer to favor a particular method of killing. Check! All three evening gown women were killed exactly the same way.

Sam's search proved informative but confusing. She found that 88% of serial killers were male and 85% of those were Caucasian. Average age when they killed their first victim was 28.5. In terms of victim selection, 62% of killers targeted strangers exclusively, while another 22% killed at least one stranger. One resource said that 71% of the killers operated in a specific area rather than traveling widely to commit their crimes. That fit with Cass's theory that the evening-gown killer was likely a local.

She learned that the more serial killers killed, the more their need to kill increased and the more they believed they could never be caught. Most thought they were invincible and were caught because they got sloppy and careless. "Hope our guy's the same way," Sam whispered.

*

With her head full of images of Ted Bundy, John Gacy, Dennis Radner—BTK killer, and a long list of others, her house, which had been a safe refuge the night before, became a house of terror tonight. Even with her 9 mm tucked under her pillow, sleep was impossible. She heard every creak and bump the house made as it cooled in the night air. Late-night summer breezes rubbed a tree branch against the eve outside her bedroom window. She'd heard that sound all her life, but tonight it sounded like footsteps coming up the stair.

She'd just drifted off to sleep around midnight when two tom cats erupted in a flurry of banshee-like screams right below her window. She screamed herself and leapt from the bed in a panic, her heart pounding. She found herself sitting on the floor between the bed and the wall, her sweaty hands gripping her pistol which she pointed shakily at the bedroom door.

Slowly she sorted out what had happened. This was the one night since her divorce she would have welcomed Ricky back in her bed—but only for protection.

The next morning, bleary-eyed and trying to fight off the medicine head that was the result of her taking a Tylenol PM shortly after the cat fight. Sam clutched her coffee mug and stood over the list Cass had given her. As she contemplated the things she'd learned yesterday, she wondered how to best distill all that information down to the names of the people before her?

There were sixteen of them. The first task was to move the least likely people to the bottom. *88% of serial killers are male.* Only two of her names were women. They went to the bottom. *Average age at first killing, 28.5.* Anyone who had been under twenty or over fifty on the date of the first killing she moved down. That took care of four more. Ten people left.

Now let's start moving people up, Sam thought.

She and Mary spent the next three days pulling criminal records on all sixteen people. They decided that sex offenders should go to the top.

There were two. Jimmy Judkins, a thirty-six-year-old EMT, was convicted of lewd and lascivious behavior when he was a senior at Summersville High. His crime was streaking a high-school football game on a dare. He only got thirty days, twenty-five of which were suspended, but it was enough to land him on the state's Sex Offender list.

Poor kid. He was married now, had held the same job for thirteen years and had three kids. Judkins was Sam's first exception. She moved him down instead of up.

Not so the second sex offender; forty-four-year-old Lester Gibbons, a physical therapy technician at one of the local nursing homes. He was busted fourteen years ago with over two-hundred child-porn pictures on his home computer. He did five years in the state penitentiary. Sam didn't know if some pedophiles were also attracted to grown-up women, but for the moment, she placed him at the top of the list just in case.

Sam's next criteria was domestic violence offenders. There was only one. The name jumped out at her; thirty-three-year-old Colton Farnsworth, son of Elvin Farnsworth, patriarch of the family who owned several funeral homes in Central West Virginia. Sam remembered going through grade school and junior high a year behind Colton. But as she thought back, she couldn't remember him being in high school. The family was still around—they'd lived here forever. *He must have dropped out,* she decided.

Farnsworth had tried and nearly succeeded in choking his wife to death during an argument. He spent two years in prison over it.

The big, fancy, white-brick Farnsworth Funeral Home with a large covered portico that had a brass outdoor chandelier hanging from the center was only a couple of blocks away from Daddy's house. She'd walked past it several times a week as a child.

Colton had been out of prison long enough to be off parole. His parole reports revealed that he worked for his dad as an embalmer. He also drove hearses and performed other odd jobs.

Farnsworth's handled both Kendall and her father's funeral. She wracked her brain trying to remember if she and seen or dealt with Colton. Then it struck her. He had helped her when she picked out Daddy's casket. He was a tall, craggy-faced, not unattractive man with shoulder-length brown hair and penetrating dark eyes. He'd worn a suit that day, with his hair drawn back in a ponytail. His heavy after-shave lotion couldn't conceal the strong smell of cigarettes that pursued him.

He must have known who she was but didn't give any indication of that. He seemed nice enough at the time, but she remembered how he wouldn't look her directly in the eye. His furtiveness left a vague, unnerving impression that he was trying to hide something.

Certainly this man wasn't bothered by dead bodies. He worked with them every day. The question was whether it was only dead ones he worked with. Might this man enjoy the macabre sport of torturing women to death?

Colton Farnsworth went straight to the top of the list, leaving seven people to be prioritized. Those left on the list were ordinary, everyday doctors, nurse practitioners, chiropractors, dentists, physical therapists and the like. *Where in the heck do I put normal guys?* she wondered.

She remembered the maxim Cass had told her about suspects. "Motive and opportunity, motive and opportunity." The motive for the evening gown murders she could only speculate about, but opportunity was determinable. *Let's find out where all these gentlemen were when the murders were committed.*

She took a sip of what was left of the now warm can of Diet Coke she'd nursed for the past two hours and then picked up the phone. Time to start doing some old-fashioned detective work. *Who knows,* she thought, *I just might have my first conversation with a serial killer.*

Chapter 30

"Sam. Sam!" Mary said excitedly. Pick up line two. It's that television program, America's Most Wanted. They want to talk to you."

"America's Most Wanted? You're kidding!"

"He *says* he's John Walsh. I don't know if he's kidding or not."

Sam picked up the phone. "This is Samantha Martin. How may I help you?"

Indeed, it was the real John Walsh. "We've been watching your efforts online in behalf of the three young women who were killed in your area," he said. "We'd like to help. Would the Sheriff's Department have any objection to our coming down there and taping a show segment?"

National television coverage—it would be a dream come true. "Not at all," Sam said without hesitation. She could barely contain her excitement. "When do you think you'd be here?"

"We're wrapping up a taping in Pittsburg this afternoon. Would Friday work? I can have a couple of my advance people in town tomorrow, if that's okay."

Friday? That's only two days away! Sam could scarcely keep the excitement out of her voice. "That would be fine, Mr. Walsh. What do you need us to do?"

"We'll email you an instruction sheet this afternoon. You need to be there to help out with information and give us access to your photos and to the crime scenes. We'll need a couple of you to do taped interviews. What's your position there?"

"I'm a temporary special investigator helping the county prosecutor's office. The best person for you to talk to would be our sheriff, Cassandra Rosier."

"Could I talk to her now?"

"I believe she's out of her office for an hour or so. Can I have her call you?"

"Certainly. Let me give you my personal cell phone number." Sam scribbled it down. "Thank you, Mr. Walsh," she said. "You've no idea how much we appreciate this."

*

"You're kidding," Cass said. "How'd they pick us?"

"They monitor the Internet for this sort of stuff."

"America's Most Wanted. I can't believe it. When are they coming?"

"They'll have people here tomorrow. He said they want to film on Friday. They sent us an instruction sheet." Sam handed Cass the two-page email.

Cass read it quickly, then said, "We'll have to take them to all the body discovery locations and setup security for the shoots. We'll need to get witnesses back together and decide which photos we can give them access to." Cass looked panic-stricken. "Friday! How will we ever get ready that fast?"

"We'll just do it, that's all."

Cass sighed and said, "You're going to do the talking, right?"

Sam held her hands up defensively. "Whoa! They'll get a little bit from me I'm sure, but these are your cases. You're about to be a TV star. This should really help your next election campaign."

"Oh, no, Sammy. What will I say? I'll be too nervous. I can't do this; really I can't!" The thought of a TV camera pointed in her direction had Cass in a panic.

"Don't worry," Sam reassured her friend. "You'll say all the right things. We've been trying to find wider exposure for these cases and now we've got it. Congratulations, Sheriff Rosier. You're about to put Nicholas County on the map."

*

It took three weeks for the program to air. They had an America's Most Wanted party at Sam's house the night it did.

Gary, Cass's parents, Zeeman and two other deputies were there. Katy bounced all over the place, excited at the prospect of seeing her mother on television. When the program ended, everyone sat as if mesmerized. Finally Cass said quietly, "That's that. Now we wait for the phones to ring."

And ring they did. The first night, over two-hundred-fifty calls came in to the program's call center. Many were hoaxes, others were from people who said they might have known one of the women but they really weren't sure, and thirteen seemed to have some credibility and would be followed up.

*

By the end of the week. Cass's voice was almost gone from fielding so many calls. She was just gathering her things to go home when Mary buzzed. "I think you better take the call on line one," she said.

"Who is it?"

"A woman who says she knows one of the girls."

Cass wearily sat back down. Several callers had said much the same, but the calls led nowhere. When Mary transferred the call, Cass checked the caller ID. "Nicolo Basso." She didn't recognize the name or the area code. She sighed wearily and answered. "This is Sheriff Rosier."

"Are you the one that was on television?" a timid-sounding woman asked.

"Yes, ma'am. How may I help you?" Cass thought she heard the woman sob. "Ma'am, is something wrong? Do you need help? I can barely hear you."

"No," came a slightly stronger reply. "I'm okay. I know one of those girls you're looking for." Another sob. The woman was crying—softly to be sure, but crying nonetheless.

"Which girl are you referring to?" Cass asked gently, holding her breath against the hope the woman might be telling the truth.

"The first one they showed. The one they found on that beach. She's my daughter." The woman broke down and wept.

Cass waived wildly at Mary to get her attention. When Mary looked over, Cass pointed to the phone and mouthed "Recorder." She waived a finger in a circle to ask if it was running. Mary nodded.

Cass allowed the woman time to regain control. When she did, Cass asked, "Can you tell me your name, ma'am?"

"Basso. Mrs. Millicent Basso."

"Where are you calling from, Mrs. Basso?"

"Pittsburg. I live in Pittsburg."

Cass scribbled the information on a notepad then waved at Mary to come into her office. "Is there a Mr. Basso?" she asked.

"He passed away about a year after Angelina left us, poor man. He always said it was all his fault she was gone."

"Angelina. Is that the name of your daughter?" Cass wrote a big #1 and scrawled the name boldly across her pad so Mary could see.

"Yes. She's my youngest," the woman replied.

"And you believe the person you saw on the program was Angelina?"

"It *was* my Angelina. I've been looking for her all this time. The night she left she told us that she never wanted to speak to us again. It broke her father's heart. We always thought she'd come home someday. But now my Nicolo's gone and my baby's never coming home." Once again she broke down.

Cass waited patiently. Finally she said, "Mrs. Basso. Mrs. Basso?" I know this is difficult. But I need you to calm down for me. Can you prove the young woman you saw on television was Angelina?"

"Oh yes," she said, stifling one last sob. "I've got dozens of pictures of her from the time she was a little baby."

"Did you take her to the dentist regularly?"

"Yes, when we could afford to. She had braces when she was fourteen. Didn't get them off till she was almost seventeen."

"Did you keep locks of hair, or anything like that?"

"Yes, from all my kids."

Cass paused thoughtfully then asked, "Are you going to be home tomorrow?"

"Yes. I've got to tell all my kids their sister is dead."

"I know this is a terribly difficult time, but I need to come up and see you. It's very important. I'm going to need you to help us make a positive ID."

"The television program said she was murdered; that she was raped and tortured. Is that what happened?"

Cass had to fight down a lump in her throat. "I'm afraid it is."

"Dear God, my poor baby girl. Sheriff Rosier, can you tell me where my daughter is now?"

"She's buried here in Summersville. We didn't know what else to do."

"Would it be possible to bring my Angelina back home?

The question broke Cass's heart. "Yes, Mrs. Basso, she said tenderly, "you can take her back home. It will take some doing, but I'll help."

"Thank you. At least we can have a funeral now. My address is 4988 East Turnbury Circle. You come up here and see me, and then I'm coming down there to bring my baby girl back home."

Cass didn't relish the prospect of a 180-mile weekend drive to Pittsburg, but if it helped identify one of the two evening-gown murder victims, it would be worth it. She thought briefly of taking Katy with her but thought better of it. She damn sure didn't want her eight-year-old daughter sitting in on a morbid meeting with the Basso family.

I'll take Sam instead, she decided.

*

Three days later, as Cass watched Sam tape the name under Angelina Basso's picture in the War Room, she couldn't help but feel that the case had taken a giant leap forward. But a week later the elation had subsided as reality once more settled in. While the family was getting their beloved Angelina back, the identification led the investigators no closer to finding her killer.

She, Sam, and Eric had been huddled for over two hours, pouring over the case files, trying to find something, anything they'd missed. Cass was pleased she'd assigned Zeeman to the case. He was young, energetic, and loved being a cop. A lot of people wanted the job but weren't that excited about having to do the cop part.

Zeeman had his Police Science and Procedure AA degree and was working on his bachelor's through a correspondence course. The only thing that tripped him up on his way to a full bachelor's degree the traditional way was the baby he and his girlfriend found out they were having. It was a mistake, but Zeeman immediately did two things. He got a job with the department to support his kid, and he married the cute redhead as fast as he could. He reinforced Cass's sense that there were still a few young men with a sense of honor in the world.

"This is so damn frustrating," Cass said. "The only thing we know is that Angelina likely came here by car. She owned a red Pontiac Grand Am. Where is it? If she was abducted in Nicholas County, her car should be around here somewhere."

"Not to point out the obvious," Sam said, "but she could have been abducted somewhere else and transported to Nicholas County."

Cass shook her head. "My gut doesn't tell me that's how it went down. If the killer was doing them somewhere else, why not scatter the bodies around the state or even out of state? It would make it a lot harder to connect the dots. I think the killer's dropping the bodies here because he lives here and wants us to see his handiwork. They're his trophies."

"So what do you think we should do next?" Eric asked.

"Find Angelina's car. Go out and pound some pavement, Eric. Take that picture of Angelina standing by the car and show it to every new and used car dealer. Start right here in Summersville then work your way outward for a hundred miles around if you have to. Check the records of every junk yard and car dealership. Get that picture blown up to an 8x10 and give them all a copy. I want that car fresh on their minds."

"What about me?" Sam asked.

"Keep answering the phone and working on our list. You never know when one small bit of information will break a case wide open. I call it the magic bullet. Once you find it, everything comes together so fast you can't believe it. But until then, you have to just keep slogging."

Chapter 31

Spectacular was the only way to describe the early August morning. The temperature and humidity were both down. A gentle breeze riffled the glass-like surface of Summersville Lake and sent diamonds of light dancing toward the beach.

At the dock, boaters were loading their ropes and skis and wakeboards, along with coolers laden with snacks and sandwiches, and, of course, the obligatory case or two of beer on ice. Other boaters were bringing aboard fishing tackle boxes and poles; and coolers laden with snacks and sandwiches, and, of course, their own obligatory case or two of beer on ice.

As the air warmed, some of the young men doffed their tee-shirts, revealing fit young bodies that would be clad for the rest of the day only in baggy, colorful swimwear.

Not to be outdone, girls and a number of older women cast aside their wraps, revealing tiny colorful triangles of cloth held in place with thin fabric cords. The sole purpose of the attire was to conceal only those few square inches of flesh not deemed socially acceptable for public exposure and not a millimeter more.

The Freak watched the show with equal amounts of lust and disdain as he walked the beach above the dock. It was excruciatingly delicious how the disgraceful women flaunted themselves, silently taunting and tempting the men around them, daring the men to act. They had to know the torment they were causing, knowing that in public they were out of reach to all but those they condescended to allow to touch. Damn them! They knew exactly what they were doing.

How long since Jennifer? Two and a half months since he first took her to the ranch? *Oh how I loved you, Jennifer.* What spirit she had. And how pretty she looked in her special gown.

The Freak reflected that life was easier for a time after each of his guests left. The monster was safely fed and could be put to sleep again. Once more it became easy to attend church, even sing in the choir. "Yes Jesus Loves Me," he would sing with gusto.

With his first guest's departure, the monster had lain quiet for nearly a year. After the second, the monster went away for almost eight months. When the monster slept, the Freak would not even look upon a woman with a lustful eye.

But inevitably, the monster would stir and he'd feel the rise of his manly needs. At first he denied them, then fought against them, but eventually the monster would win and the hunt would begin.

Already the monster was raging, stronger than ever this time. Day by day, almost hour by hour, the monster conquered a little more of his sense of reason; his sense of caution.

On days like this, the monster made him come down and watch the brazen, wanton little bitches at play; almost naked, completely shameless, and totally unconcerned about the sins they made men want to commit. It was their fault—all their fault! How he hated those lovely, alluring, vile creatures.

He passed a friend strolling down the beach. "Hello, Evan," he called, giving the man a smile and a quick, friendly wave. "I see you're following my advice about walking."

"Sure am." The man responded. "Are you going to be in your office this afternoon?"

"I open at nine and will be there all day."

"Good. I'll swing by. Damn, those girls down there sure bring out the best in a man, don't they?" Evan gave the Freak a lascivious wink.

If you only knew, the Freak thought. The monster was almost fully awake now—already hunting. The selection rules were very exact. Not just any woman from off the street would do. She had to look just right—like Jennifer did. She had to be feisty—like Jennifer was. She had to be able to carry on an interesting, intelligent conversation. There could be no extended connections to the area that could cause problems. But most of all she had to be healthy enough and strong enough to play for a long, long time— just like Jennifer.

The monster was much stronger this time. If he didn't find someone soon, they might have to amend the rules. But he could afford that. No one suspected him. No one knew who he really was. No one knew about the house in the woods, and most of all, no one knew that the monster moved within him.

Chapter 32

"Come on in, chicken!" Freddy Hunsaker shouted. "Get a run and jump way out—and don't belly-flop."

It was Lanny's first trip to the pit, and he was honored by the invitation. Last year, Lanny had watched this exclusive clique of a dozen or so football players and cheerleaders pile into two or three cars almost every night after summer practice and take off for who knew where. To be included required a rare, highly valued invitation. One had to be deemed worthy.

Just an hour ago Lanny got his invitation. As they were leaving the practice field, Freddy caught up with him and whispered, "We're going out to Franklin's Pit. Why don't you jump in and come with us?"

Lanny had never heard of Franklin's Pit, but agreed immediately. The tiny, seldom-traveled dirt road followed a shallow canyon bottom deep in the woods about five miles east of town. Suddenly the trees gave way to a half-mile-long, 200-yard-wide body of water that Lanny didn't know existed. It was an abandoned gravel pit, now filled with crystal-clear water.

"Welcome to the pit!" Freddy shouted as the three vehicles slid to a stop only a few yards away from the twenty-foot high sheer cliff that dropped off into the water. Everyone tumbled out and to Lanny's astonishment, began discarding their clothes, even the girls. He was shocked! He was looking at real, live, naked female bodies for the first time. Life was good!

Clothes cast aside, the others raced away to leap far out over the edge of the cliff, followed a second later by the sound of the splash they made as they hit the water below.

What should I do? Lanny fretted. *People are watching.* What would his mother say if she ever found out? But he had to do something. He stripped to his boxers then walked to the edge of the cliff to get a look at what he would be jumping into. It was a sheer drop into the dark blue-green water. The place was deep—very deep.

He was still struggling with the idea of whether or not to remove his last vestige of modesty when Hal Okelberry shouted up at him, "Hey rookie, unless you're dressed like the rest of us, you're not allowed in.

"That's right," some others, including Serena Jenkins, chorused. Lanny would have gladly died for Serena upon request.

He swallowed hard. Lee Hudson had the longest schlong in the school, and he was one of the ones in the water calling for him to lose the shorts. He could never measure up to Hudson, but how would he measure up to the other guys? Would the girls laugh at him? Would Serena?

He made up his mind. The trick here was to make sure everybody got as short a look at him as possible. He stepped back where no one could see him and dropped the shorts. He threw them on the trunk of the car, turned and shouted, "I'm coming down!" then he raced for the edge of the cliff and his reluctant debut as a naked man.

He leapt as far out as he could and hit the water arrow-straight with his arms raised above his head, just like the rock divers on TV. He went down and down, farther into the crystal clear water than he ever thought possible.

Suddenly as his descent was ending he encountered something hard but slick. His feet went out from under him and he found himself sitting on whatever it was. He opened his eyes and to his surprise found that he was sitting on the roof of a white car. He couldn't tell what make it was but it looked new, not wrecked or anything. As his natural buoyancy lifted him up, he kicked off the roof toward the surface. What was a car doing down here? He had to ask Freddy about it.

"There's a car down there?" Freddy was clearly surprised. "I've never seen anything like that."

"Come on, I'll show you." They swam out to where Lanny judged the car to be. They each gulped a lungful of air and made for the bottom of the lake. Lanny was first to spot the white blob off to Freddy's left. He tapped Freddy on the shoulder and pointed.

The car sat on the lakebed at about a twenty-degree angle. Freddy pointed excitedly at the Lexus emblem on the trunk then gave Lanny the OK sign. Neither was used to holding their breaths for long periods of time. Freddy pointed up and held his other hand around his neck as if choking. It was time to catch some air.

"Holy shit," Lanny sputtered as he wiped the hair out of his eyes when they broke the surface, "it's a Lexus. Looks practically brand new."

"I know. It's weird. Who would drive a car like that off into a lake?"

"I don't know. I wonder if somebody's still in it."

"Wazup?" Hal asked as he swam over to see what was going on.

"There's a car down there." Freddy responded. "A white Lexus. Looks pretty new."

"Anybody in it?"

"We're going back down and see."

"I'll come with you," Hal volunteered.

All three dove back down. Lanny looked through the windshield while Freddy and Hal tried to peer through the glass on each side.

They looked at each other and shook their heads. Hal, his air spent, pointed toward the surface and kicked himself upward.

Several other swimmers were waiting, treading water and wondering what was going on. Lanny didn't want to swim the last ten feet to the surface too fast. The water was crystal-clear and three of the bodies treading water above him were girls. Was Serena was one of them?

"It's a car," Hal sputtered between gasps. "It's a freakin' Lexus just sitting on the bottom of the lake."

"We gotta go talk about this," Lanny said. We have to figure out what to do." As one, they all paddled back to the little spit of sand that once served as a vehicle access to the gravel pit. Today it was a ramp that provided the only walking access to the water on the otherwise completely sheer-walled lake.

Lanny was amazed how quickly his concern about his lack of clothing vanished. Serena sat down right beside him as if it was no big deal. He too tried to act as if her missing clothes were a perfectly normal state of being, though he couldn't help but steal a number of quick glances, hoping she wouldn't notice. He prayed she wouldn't touch him. That could cause a real problem.

"I say we keep our mouths shut, go get my dad's wrecker, pull that thing out of there, and fix it," Davy West said.

"What if it was used by gangsters to commit a crime?" Kathleen O'Neill asked. "The police might be looking for that car right now. They see you driving it and you could land up in jail."

"You know what I think?" Les Faden, Summersville's huge all-state center asked. "I think somebody couldn't make their payments, so they dumped it here to collect on the insurance."

As the invited guest, Lanny spoke hesitantly. "I think we have to tell the sheriff about it," he said quietly. "If somebody shows up driving that thing around and it's stolen or something, they could get in a lot of trouble. If it was used by crooks, that could mean more trouble. They might even think one of us dumped that car. But if we turn it in to the cops—no trouble. We could even be heroes. Who knows? If nobody claims the car, they might even give it to us."

Silence prevailed for several seconds as young minds digested what Lanny said. Serena finally broke the silence. "Lanny's right. But we can't tell them we were skinny-dipping. Everybody was wearing a swimsuit today, right?"

"Right," they all chorused, nodding their heads vigorously.

"We all have to go in together. If only one of us shows up, the sheriff might think one of the rest of us did it."

Again they chorused their assent.

"Alright, that's the way it is," Freddy said with finality. "Lanny, since you found that thing, you speak for the rest of us. Let's get our bare asses out of here and over to the courthouse."

*

Mary poked her nose into Cass's office and said, "There's a delegation of young people here to see you."

Cass looked at her quizzically. "What do they want?"

"Beats me. They said the only one they want to talk to is you."

"How many?"

"Thirteen, I think; all Summersville High students."

"Must want a donation for some fund raiser. Send them down to the commission chambers. I'll be there in a minute."

Cass took a moment to primp her hair and adjust her uniform. *Have to keep up appearances for impressionable young minds,* she thought.

"Y'all are telling me there's a new Lexus at the bottom of Franklin Pit?" Cass was as incredulous as the kids were when they found the car. She knew Franklin's Pit from her own high-school days." You guys been skinny-dipping out there, huh?"

"Noooo," came the chorused reply.

"It's ok. I used to go out there myself. I won't tell your parents. But some of them will know the minute they hear where you were. Tell you what. I'll round up a tow truck and our police diver. I want you to show me exactly where that car is."

She walked to the War Room on her way out, stuck her head in, and said to Sam with a grin, "Come on girl, we're going skinny-dipping."

*

"You think this might be linked to the evening-gown murders?" Sam asked as Cass guided the SUV along the narrow road to the Pit.

"There's an outside chance, but better not get your hopes up. When was the last time you were out to Franklin's Pit?"

Sam blushed. "Just that one time when we were seniors—and you told me you'd never tell anybody about that."

"Don't worry, sister, your secret's still safe."

The wrecker and Deputy Ed Hollis, the department's certified diver, arrived a few minutes after Sam and Cass. Hollis had a man with him that Cass didn't recognize. "Needed to bring my dive-buddy," Hollis said. "This is Andrew Warner. He works as a commercial diver down at Summersville Lake."

"Glad to meet you, Mr. Warner," Cass said. "We appreciate you coming out on such short notice."

"No problem. It's always fun to dive somewhere new. Let's get ready, Buckshot," Warner said, giving Hollis a playful elbow shove.

"Buckshot?" Cass looked curiously at Deputy Hollis, whose given name was Edwin.

He looked at Warner and pleaded, "Don't tell her, Andy. It'll be all over the department by tomorrow morning."

Warner laughed and continued to tattle. "This guy may be a great shot with a pistol, but with a shotgun? He couldn't hit a turkey in the ass if it landed on his shoulder. Worst shot I've ever seen with a twelve-gauge. That's why we call him Buckshot. Bugs him to death."

"Ahh shit, why'd you have to…?"

"Don't worry, Hollis," Cass said, trying to suppress a grin. "The secret's safe with me."

Once the divers were in the water, the wait seemed interminable, but in reality was only about thirty minutes. Finally, first one, then the other masked head broke the surface. Cass walked to the water's edge as the men came to shore. "Is the Lexus down there?" she asked the instant Hollis doffed his dive mask.

"Sure is—pretty new—just like the kids said."

Cass was hesitant to ask for fear she might not like the answer. "Anyone inside?"

"Not in the front or back seat. Can't say about the trunk till we get it out of there and pop the lid."

"Are the plates on it?"

"Yeah, they're there. Shouldn't be a problem ID-ing the registered owner. That is unless the plates are stolen. There's one other thing."

"What's that?"

"There's two more down there."

*

Cass's cop instincts practically jumped through her skin as she watched the third car being pulled from the lake. The white 2012 Lexus and a blue 2008 Dodge Neon sat side by side nearby, their trunks popped open but otherwise untouched. A deputy stood guard over them. The vehicle emerging from the water was an older red Pontiac Grand Am.

Cass pulled out her cell phone and called Mary. "Pull the file on Angelina Basso," she instructed. I need the license plate number of her car." She tapped her toe impatiently as she waited.

"Got it," Mary finally answered. "It's Pennsylvania license number WJF-399."

Cass was staring at Pennsylvania license number WJF-399. "Well I'll be damned," she muttered.

"What's that, sheriff?"

Cass realized she was still talking into her phone. "Oh, sorry Mary. Thanks. Thanks a ton!" She turned to Sam and said, "That's the Basso girl's car." She glanced at her watch. 7:18 p.m. She had to call Deputy Zeeman. He'd been out of radio range all day, spending time up in Charleston checking car lots and salvage yards for the very car she'd just pulled from Franklin's Pit. He answered on the second ring. "Deputy Zeeman, what's your 20?" she asked.

"Just pulling into my driveway. Didn't turn up anything in Charleston."

"No problem, I just did." She told him about the kids finding a car at the bottom of Franklin's Pit and the divers finding two more. "They just pulled Angelina Basso's car out of the lake. I'm standing beside it right now."

"I'll be right there," Zeeman said. She could hear excitement in his voice as he clicked off.

Cass looked at Sam. "I think we just hit the jackpot," she said. What do you bet those other two cars belong to our other evening gown victims? The state police are running the plates for us right now. Sammy girl, we may be within minutes of knowing the names of all our victims. I think those kids stumbled across our perp's first big mistake."

Chapter 33

It was after midnight before the three tow trucks finished depositing the cars inside a small warehouse which normally housed the county's snow-removal vehicles; now evicted to parking places outside. The doors to the building were quickly draped with yellow crime-scene tape to keep tomorrow morning's curious county workers away until the forensic examination of the vehicles was complete.

Sam arrived at the War Room shortly before 9:00 a. m. and was mildly surprised to find things even more crowded due to the addition of a large new table. *Does that woman ever sleep?* she wondered. The table was shoved against the far wall and had a sign Scotch-taped to the front that read, *Evidence! Do not disturb!*

"Good morning," Sam said as Cass walked through the door carrying her coffee mug. "What's this?" She pointed to the new table

"It's for the things we'll recover from inside the three cars." Indeed, the tabletop was divided into three segments, with a sign designating which car belonged to which segment. "Sammy, you're going to have company in here for a few days. The state lab guy will start processing the cars today. He'll be in and out."

"That's fine. I'll be on the phone most of the time anyway. I'm starting what I'm calling my perp survey."

"Perp survey?"

"I'm calling each person on our suspects list to answer some survey questions. They're subtlety designed to do one thing—find out where each person was on the dates of our three killings. Then I'll want to sit down with you and Eric to go over the list. I should be finished by tomorrow afternoon. Could we do it then?"

"Sure thing. How's three o'clock?"

"That works."

Cass set her coffee mug down, looked at Sam and asked, "Can you break away for a couple of hours this afternoon?"

"I think so, why?"

"Because you have a date tomorrow night."

Sam was startled. "Saturday night? A date?"

"Yeah; with me. You need some social life. I'm hauling your butt to the hospital's Women's Auxiliary Ball. It's the social event of the season in Summersville, and you need a dress."

"Me—go to a dance? Oh Cassie, I don't think so. I'm not ready for that."

"Yes you are. I'm not telling you that you have to tackle every guy in sight, but you're becoming a hermit, and we can't have that. You can be a wallflower if you want, but you and I need to go, if for no other reason than the fact that I have to go and don't have a date either."

"Gary didn't ask you?"

"No, and I'm a little pissed about that. He's got late clinic, plus he's on call. Said he didn't want to leave me standing high and dry in the middle of the dance floor if he got called in."

"You two okay?"

Cass sighed. "Yeah, I think so. I think our make-out session at the drive-in scared him a little, so I'm not going to push it."

Sam could see her friend's disappointment. Perhaps she needed Sam's support as much as Cass thought Sam needed hers. "Okay, I'll go; but only as long as I'm not a fifth-wheel. What's the dress?"

"Formal, believe it or not."

Sam was appalled. "How in the world will I ever come up with a formal and have it fitted by tomorrow night?"

"Not to worry. First, we're going to the mall down at Fayetteville this afternoon. And second, I have a secret weapon."

"Which is?"

"My mother. She can sew anything. We can pick a dress you like, take it to Mom tonight and by tomorrow night she'll have it fitting you like it came from Sac's Fifth Avenue, guaranteed. And Sam, we're not going just to play, it will be work-related too. I have a plan."

Sam was puzzled. "A plan?"

"Yeah, let me tell you about it."

Chapter 34

All three cars had their windows rolled up tight, just the way they had come out of the lake. Even after sitting all night, they still dripped water. Cass had allowed only the trunk lids to be opened at the lake just to make sure there were no bodies inside. Then they were immediately closed.

Cass led Jack Tucker, the forensic investigator the state had sent down, on an inspection tour of the vehicles. Tucker was a small, bespectacled, inquisitive man with dark hair that had grayed halfway up his temples

"We've touched nothing inside," she explained. "One of my deputies tried to open the passenger door of the Neon at the lake, but I stopped him. It would have been hell picking through the mud out there trying to find what evidence may have washed out. We've allowed the water to drain out naturally. Whatever was inside the cars is still there. You'll be the first person to open those doors."

"Have they been dusted?" Jack asked.

"The outsides have. I did that myself. There's a few prints that I suspect are from people who handled the cars getting them here, but I didn't find any on the door handles except the one my deputy touched. Either the cars were wiped down, or lake water washed away all the print evidence."

"I'll be surprised if we find any. Body oils naturally emulsify and assimilate into water over time. Same thing with blood. Cold water dissolves blood well, especially if the blood is fresh. Makes DNA evidence hard to find. Best we can probably hope for is some hair with mitochondrial material intact. "I'll have to hand-dry any paper evidence in place before I try moving it. I'll need a couple of extension cords for my dryers and I'll need a place to put stuff."

"I've set up a table for you in what we call the War Room. There's space for each of the cars. Will that work?"

"That should do nicely. I understand you have identities of the victims, is that correct?"

It was a relief for Cass to be able to answer yes. "The red car belongs to Angelina Basso from Pittsburg. We already knew who she was. The blue Neon was registered in New Jersey to a Naomi Quinn. She's the right age and her driver's license photo looks remarkably like victim number two.

She walked to the white Lexus and said, "This one belongs to Jennifer Lorraine Oldroyd. Her car was registered in Washington, D. C. She has a Facebook page. We found out she worked for the government. I spoke with her supervisor and a couple of people she worked with. They said she went on vacation and never showed back up. One of her co-workers said she bought the car in anticipation of an Appalachian vacation. Some vacation, poor girl.

"We've got positive ID on the Basso girl, but not on the other two. We're trying to track down next of kin on Quinn and Oldroyd, but so far no luck."

Jack ran his fingers through his hair. "Maybe we'll find something here that will help, some gas receipts or something. Were the doors and windows closed when you got the cars out?"

"Yes."

"Good. As long as the water action inside the vehicles hasn't been strong and the water's not too acidic, we'll probably find some recoverable paper evidence.

Cass sighed deeply. "I hope you're right. These cars could be an evidence bonanza compared to what we've had.

Chapter 35

"Come in, Pastor," the Freak said. "Sister Clarisse, how nice to see you tonight. I'm so glad you could come." Pastor Paul Bennion and his wife, Clarisse, were an odd couple. Pastor Paul was tall and rail thin, possessed of a stern, severe look that belied his gentle, friendly nature. Sister Clarisse was short and plump. The Freak suspected that no one had ever seen her without a smile. She was a chatterbox, a matchmaker, and the congregation's not-too-secret central source of gossip, much to her husband's chagrin.

"Thank you," Pastor Paul answered for both of them. "Your dinners are always such a treat."

"Could I ask you to sit in the living room for a bit? Dinner's nearly ready." The Freak escorted the couple to the living room of his three-bedroom, slightly upscale home in the slightly upscale neighborhood on the northwest side of town. "Can I get you something to drink while I get the food on the table? I have just about any soft drink you'd care for, or perhaps some sparkling apple juice?" There was a nice bottle of Burgundy in the refrigerator, but the good pastor was a notorious teetotaler who had preached many a fiery sermon railing against the evils of 'demon rum.' The Freak knew better than to even ask.

"Nothing for me, thanks," Pastor Paul said.

"I'll have a Diet Coke, if you don't mind," Clarisse responded. "Got to watch my girlish figure, you know." She laughed. She always laughed. Sister Clarisse was one of those women of ample girth who laughed at the end of almost every sentence. But her kind heart and open smile allowed one to overlook the nervous habit. "Your home is always so neat and clean," Clarisse commented. "I don't know how you do it."

It was true. The Freak obsessed over his home's cleanliness. Every object was placed just so and never moved. The woodwork was fastidiously oiled and dusted, the carpets meticulously vacuumed in exactly the same pattern every time. The same compulsion was evident at the office—including even the magazines there. When a patient left, he quickly retrieved any reading material they'd used and restored it exactly to its place. Any that showed a torn cover or wrinkled page were immediately replaced.

"I hope you're in the mood for fish tonight," the Freak called as he retreated to the kitchen. "We may as well keep up the old Friday night Catholic tradition. I'm grilling some wonderful mahi-mahi served in a lemon teriyaki sauce. We'll have cashew rice pilaf and grilled pineapple on the side."

*

"That was wonderful," Clarisse said as she pushed herself back from the table at the Freak's invitation to adjourn their social visit to the living room. "Every meal you cook is like eating at a five-star New York restaurant."

"That's true, my boy," Pastor Paul affirmed as he settled into his seat on the living room couch. "Where did you get your training? Surely not at your mother's knee; otherwise you'd weigh three hundred pounds."

The Freak chuckled. "No, my parents were of quite humble means. After I left home for college, I discovered fine dining. Since I couldn't afford to buy such meals, I learned to cook. It's a hobby I quite enjoy."

"You know, young man, several sisters in our congregation have expressed interest in you. Not many of us can understand why you're not married. I certainly don't wish to offend, so please tell me if you think it's none of my business." He paused nervously as if considering what to say next, then plowed carefully forward. "Is there possibly a gender-preference issue we should perhaps talk about?"

"Oh no, no, Pastor," the Freak said with a chuckle as he held up his hands in denial. "Believe me, my gender attractions are absolutely limited to the opposite sex. In fact, I was married once, before I moved here." He gestured toward a large portrait that hung over the fireplace. It was of a striking, sandy-haired woman in a lovely scarlet gown. "That's Susan. She was the love of my life until she was taken away. I've never quite gotten over her. I painted that portrait myself after she was gone."

"Oh I'm so sorry, dear," Clarisse, said. "Did the Lord take her?"

The Freak looked down at the floor and his countenance darkened. "I'm sorry to say that the devil took her—him and my best friend, Jim. I caught Jim and Susan engaged in the vilest sin just nine months into our marriage. She and Jim went away. It broke my heart and I'm afraid it's never fully healed. But the Lord watches over each of us in his own way. I have women friends, but they're usually not from around here. When the time and person is right, perhaps I'll consider remarrying."

"Clarisse shook her head without losing her smile. "You certainly are handsome enough, and a fine professional. Any woman would be lucky to be your wife."

"Why thank you, Sister Clarisse. That's very kind of you to say."

Clarisse eyed the portrait more closely. "That certainly is a distinctive looking necklace she's wearing. I've never seen one quite like it."

The Freak was suddenly nervous, but made sure it didn't show. "Yes, uh—yes, it is. I made that for her myself, just before she left. I expect she's wearing it to this day."

*

Long after his company was gone, the Freak stood before the portrait. Tears welled up in his eyes. *Why did you do it, Susan?* his mind cried. *Why did you choose Jim after all I did for you?* The vision of her betrayal flooded back.

He heard them long before he saw them. He stood outside the bedroom door listening, and then opened it to see them in his own bed, coupled like sweating pigs. How they laughed at him. How she ridiculed him in front of Jim, saying things like "It's not the length of the wand, sweetie, but the magic in it." She said "Doesn't matter how long the train ride is if you run out of gas before you leave the station."

They both laughed so hard and made no attempt to cover themselves as they heaped scorn upon scorn, trying to convince him to leave his own bedroom. But he didn't leave. Instead he went to his dresser, reached into the top drawer and took out his pistol—the one he'd so carefully taught Susan to use.

As Susan screamed, he raised the gun and pointed it directly at Jim's head. Jim, his best friend. Jim, who was screwing his wife. Suddenly there was no more Jim.

"Don't! Oh please don't," Susan begged hysterically. She held her hands in front of her as if they could somehow shield her from his vengeance.

"Ok, Susan, I won't shoot you," he said in an absolutely calm voice. He rolled Jim's body onto the floor. ""Lie down on the bed," he commanded. She instantly complied. "Now spread eagle and don't move." He went to the closet and retrieved four neckties. He carefully tied each of her limbs to the corners of the bed, cinching each bond tightly. Then he retrieved yet a fifth tie and a sock. He rolled the sock into a ball and stuffed it into her mouth then used the tie to make sure it wouldn't come out. Her look of wild-eyed terror gave him a sense of empowerment; a sense of superiority he'd never experienced in the nearly nine months of their marriage. It felt good. It felt right.

Satisfied she was fully immobilized, he asked, "Does anyone else know he was here?" She fearfully shook her head no.

He left her and Jim in the bedroom while he drove his car into the city. He carefully picked a spot to dump Jim's body on the edge of one of the worst neighborhoods. He parked his car a block away from the spot then took the subway as far as it would go then hired a cab for the rest of the journey home.

He loaded Jim into his own car, covered him with his own overcoat, and drove back to the city. He moved the body into the driver's seat, took out Jim's wallet, pocketed the cash, and dumped the rest of the contents on the street beside the driver's door.

Discarding the wallet a few feet away, he hoofed it back to his own car and drove home. The next day, Jim was just another mugging victim in a bad part of town. The news mentioned that he might have been killed somewhere else, but nothing ever came of it.

Before coming to the Freak's house, Jim had told his wife that he was going down to a favorite bar with a couple of his friends. The police questioned the friends and everyone at the bar and finally gave up after they turned up no evidence or witnesses.

With Susan under his complete control, The Freak got rid of the carpet, the mattress and bed clothing. He covered the new mattress with plastic. He wasn't near as good at being a torturer back then, but he became addicted to the feeling of absolute power it gave him. The power was far better than the sex, because it was all on his terms—his way. Anything he wanted her to do, she'd do, not willingly at first, but she'd do it, nevertheless.

He kept her with him as long as he could. When neighbors asked about her, he said she was visiting her parents for a month or two. He told them that sadly, they were having problems with their marriage.

She was a stay-at-home spouse, so he didn't have to worry about someone at work missing her. No one questioned him. No one suspected.

A quite good amateur artist, he wanted her to see how much he loved her, so he set an easel up in the bedroom where he could continually update her on how beautiful she was in his eyes. He painted her in her college senior ball gown, the dress she'd worn the night they met.

She was four years his junior; inexperienced and naive to a fault. She had 'saved herself' for him. Somehow they got through the barely consummated wedding night with his excuse that she was so beautiful he just couldn't contain himself. But the problem persisted. Her sympathy for his plight eventually turned into humiliating ridicule. He came to love her and hate her in equal measure.

During the third week of her captivity, her health took a downhill slide. First it was bed sores that smelled and weren't fun to treat. Then she developed a persistent cough, which got worse and worse. A few days later, a fever showed up, and the cough became nearly constant. She had difficulty breathing.

He fed her every antibiotic they had in the house, along with Ibuprofen to fight the fever. None of it worked. In less than twenty-four hours she became delirious then lapsed in and out of consciousness. Taking her to a hospital was out of the question. It was time to let her go.

He studied all the fast and certain possible causes of death and settled on a hypodermic needle to the medulla oblongata, laced with a lethal dose of something to assure an instantaneous result. He settled on a common household hydrochloric acid-based cleaner. She would never feel a thing.

The neighbors were shocked to hear the pleasant young couple at the far end of the cul-de-sac were divorcing. The poor man was heartbroken. The woman told him she was going home to visit her parents, then dumped him without so much as a fare-thee-well.

They didn't know that Susan was an only child whose parents had been killed in a boating accident years earlier.

The nice young man sold the house and moved away. That was four years ago.

"Look at me now Susan," he said to the portrait. "Successfully settled in Summersville, West Virginia, of all places. You would be so proud. Oh, how I miss you."

Chapter 36

"Thank you, Mr. Watkins. Your information has been very helpful." Sam hung up, leaned back and stretched hard. Six straight hours of phone calls had left her with a sore ear and a stiff back, not to mention mentally exhausted. However, her innocuous sounding survey "in behalf of the county" enabled her to glean much information. Time to take the list to Cass and Deputy Zeeman.

Sam handed Cass and Eric a sheet listing the sixteen names she'd started with. Cass scanned the list, looked up sharply and said, "You've got Gary Coleman here. Why?"

Sam expected her reaction. "I don't think he's the one, but he fit the profile. You told me not to exclude anyone. Here's how I come up with the order I did." Sam explained her methodology and concluded by saying, "I've divided the list into three categories: those with violent criminal records, those who have no clear-cut alibi for all three murder dates, and everybody else. That's why Dr. Coleman is on the list—he matches the second profile. When I called him, he couldn't come up with a clear-cut alibi for one of the murder dates."

"I can verify his whereabouts on the days we found each of those poor girls. He was with me conducting the investigations. I'm sure he'll just have to check the hospital records for the murder dates. I promise you—it isn't him." Cass's tone was testy. Sam knew Cass would have a hard time being objective in regard to Dr. Coleman.

"There are two people I haven't been able to reach: Martin Betts is a radiologist at the hospital who lives down at Mt. Zion. I talked to his girlfriend. They've been together for twelve years and have two kids. She said he's at a convention in Orlando. I verified that with the hospital. The other is Dr. Barlow, a chiropractor and massage therapist here in Summersville. No criminal record, but he's single and the right age. All I got was an answering machine. I left a message."

"Doc Barlow's pretty well known around here," Cass said, clearly eager to discuss someone other than Dr. Coleman. "He's a nice guy. I doubt there's any fire behind that smoke."

Zeeman, who to that point had sat quietly listening, finally broke his silence. "One of the most important things a cop learns is to trust hunches. After going through all of this information, Sam, do you have any hunches about any of these guys?"

"Actually, I do have a hunch. The person at the top of my list is Colton Farnsworth, son of Elvin Farnsworth, the man who owns most of the funeral homes in this part of the state. Colton works for his dad as an embalmer. Obviously dead bodies don't bother him.

"He has problems with women too. He nearly choked his ex to death and went to prison for it. He's single, the right age, and according to parole reports, was right here in Summersville when all three murders took place. He got out of prison two months before Angelina Basso turned up out at the lake."

"I know Farnsworth," Cass said. "He's pretty quiet, kind of a loaner. But he does have a temper. We've had to roll on him a couple of times over bar fights. Nothing serious. The first time, they were going to revoke his parole, but his dad talked the parole officer out of it."

"Have any other women complained about him?" Zeeman asked.

"No. He's been clean. There have been some rumors about drug use but nothing we've been able to pin on him. I think he's been seeing a woman from over at Ansted for quite a while. He lives in an apartment his dad built on the back of the mortuary. It's close to your place, Sam."

"Maybe his wife deserved the choking," Zeeman said quietly.

Both women were shocked. "What a sexist thing to say," Cass said sourly at the same moment Sam said, "Deputy Zeeman, that's totally out of line!"

"Oh, no, no, I didn't mean it that way," Zeeman held up his hands defensively. "What I meant was that maybe he was provoked, and went overboard. Real abusers don't usually quit. They reoffend. If the original object of abuse is no longer around, they find someone else to abuse."

"He has a point," Cass said. "It's the same way with a lot of second and third-degree murderers. Most of them are the result of a domestic problem. They do it one time and never offend again. Maybe it was the same with Farnsworth."

"Maybe it wasn't," Sam replied. "Maybe he became more careful. Dead women don't tell tales. The question is, how do we find out?"

"We watch him, Cass said. We find out who he's seeing, or, perhaps more important, who he's been seen with. He hangs out down at The Rusty Barrel. Eric, ask around. Talk to the bartenders. Find out who he's pals with, especially women. We'll just lie back easy and watch for a while and see if he reveals himself. Who's next on your list, Sam?"

"Marvin Lieblong, a physical therapist. He's a child abuser. I don't know if that proclivity translates upward into becoming a woman killer or not, but my thought was that if he hurts children, he has a sick kind of violence built in. I put him second on the list because I think he's a rotten SOB who deserves it."

"Is he married?" Cass asked.

"Not as far as I can tell. His first wife divorced him shortly after the child-abuse charges were brought.

"Is she still around?" Zeeman asked.

"I don't know."

"Eric, see if you can track her down," Cass instructed. "If she's still in the area, she may give us a good insight into this guy. Who's next?"

It took two hours for Sam to brief them on the balance of the sixteen names. It was after 6:00 p.m. when they finished.

"Great job, Sammy," Cass said, apparently now over her pique at seeing Dr. Coleman's name on the list. "Now we need to get over to my mother's place and try that dress on you. How about you, Eric? Are you and Melanie coming to the ball tonight?"

"I don't think so," Eric said, a little embarrassed. "Melanie's nearly eight months along and refuses to even try on a dress for that thing."

"Too bad," Sam replied with a disappointed smile. "I was going to ask you to dance."

For some reason, Eric's face turned bright red.

Chapter 37

"The basketball arena was transformed from a sporting venue into an elaborate dance hall with miles of crepe paper, subdued lighting, and a giant disco ball suspended from the scoreboard that shot random flashes of reflected light into every corner of the room.

The Freak did his best to be a gracious host. After all, that was what was expected of this year's Hospital Board Vice-chairman. Unless he was run over by a freight train or something equally catastrophic, next year he'd ascend to the chairmanship.

For now, it was all he could do to maintain decorum. The monster made it nearly impossible for him to concentrate.

My God, Just look at all the evening gowns. Some were full and flowing—he liked those, and others were short and form-fitting, which he didn't care for as much. Most were revealing to one degree or another, but some of the women were fairly falling out of their low-cut, spaghetti-strap or strapless satiny creations, especially one thirtyish beauty whose deep V-neckline plunged all the way to her navel. The Freak had no idea how she managed to keep vital parts of herself within the confines of the luxurious black fabric.

It was an excruciating, tortuous, ecstatic visual feast. The band began to play. Couples swirled onto the dance floor amid acres of billowing skirts. As the Freak watched, he began, unbidden, to respond. Thank goodness he'd anticipated this problem. He'd worn his tightest, most constraining underwear, hoping it was enough to contain his uncontrollable reactions. Boxer shorts would have been an unmitigated disaster.

His job tonight was to greet patrons with a smile and hearty handshake, and to do so looking happy, healthy and—normal. Now if only the monster cooperates.

*

Cass and Sam were engaged in their grand conspiracy. Sam was dressed in a deep scarlet satin gown with a tasteful, multi-level squared neckline that revealed enough décolletage to leave no doubt as to her femininity. The ruffles of her widely spaced shoulder straps made one want to reach out and tug them in just a bit—just in case.

The tight-fitting layered bodice was arranged in two-inch wide chevron pleats that met across her middle and descended all the way to her waist. The full skirt began its voluminous cascade from there and tumbled gracefully to within inches of the floor.

Cass looked nothing like a sheriff tonight. Her black satin gown featured mid-length tight sleeves that opened to a bias-cut bell shape just below the elbow. Descending from an open scalloped bodice that accented her gender were vertical pleats of black satin that gave way at the waist to a sleek, semi-full skirt that hugged her hips then split on the right at mid-thigh to allow her leg to peek-a-boo in and out and permit freedom of movement. The skirt ended in a bias-cut flourish mid-calf in almost a flamenco look. The swag back scooped to a mere four inches above her waist, revealing her taut, muscular back to great advantage. She looked drop-dead gorgeous. Most people wouldn't recognize her.

But something else they wore might prove more provocative than their gowns. Around each of their necks was an inch-wide, scarlet and black lace ribbon adorned with embroidered daises and pinned together with a pretty pearl fastener. The ribbons came from evidence boxes in the War Room. They were the ones Angelina Basso and Jennifer Oldroyd wore. "If anyone reacts unusually to them, we may have our killer," Cass reasoned. It was with considerable emotion that they helped each other place the ribbons around the other's neck.

*

"See anyone you recognize?" Cass asked.

"I thought I'd recognize nearly everyone, but it's been long enough that the faces have changed and new people outnumber the old," Sam lamented.

"I know what you mean. I sometimes wonder if I'd recognize some of the people we went to school with if they came up and slapped me in the face. But I've seen at least three people on the list."

"Who?" Sam asked.

"I spotted your old friend, Colton Farnsworth." She inclined her head over her shoulder toward the bar. "At the far end of the bar with Harris Crenshaw."

Sam looked without appearing to do so. Farnsworth stood next to a ruddy-complexioned man with long, sun-bleached hair which fell over the collar of his light-green suit. Colton's hair was in the same ponytail style he'd worn while helping Sam pick out Daddy's casket. Both men held drinks and were engaged in intense conversation. While she watched, they moved to a nearby table.

"Do you want him, or should I?" Sam asked.

"I'll take him. Colton knows I'm nobody to mess around with."

"Who else?" Sam asked.

Cass looked around the room. "That guy over there, standing in the corner near the souvenir table wearing a dark suit."

Sam followed her gaze. "Bald with black fringe, thick -rimmed glasses, kind of round?"

"That's him. Hyrum Payne. He was fourth or fifth on the list. You said he was an inhalation therapist at the hospital."

"I remember talking with him. Practically couldn't get rid of the guy."

"Barlow, the chiropractor and massage therapist, is the tall guy in the tuxedo next to the podium. He's number seven, I think."

It took a moment for Sam to spot who she thought Cass meant. "Tall, medium-dark hair, kind of a combed back wet-look, white boutonniere?"

"That's him."

Someone spoke from behind. "Hey, lady, I have something for you."

Both turned to see Dr. Gary Coleman dressed in a tuxedo, holding a rum and coke in one hand and a vodka gimlet in the other. "I owe you an apology," he said to Cass. "I didn't think I'd make it tonight, but I was able to get someone to cover my shift at the last minute. All I have to worry about now is being on-call."

"I see," Cass said with frost in her voice—not completely over her offence at his failure to ask her to the dance.

Gary was clearly trying to make amends. "Sam, I'm not sure what your drink preference is, but I know this lady is partial to these." As he handed the vodka gimlet to Cass he nearly spilled the drink down her front when he recognized what was fastened around her neck. "Is that...?" He nodded to the ribbon. "Is that that what I think it is?" Sam could tell he was genuinely shocked.

"What do you think it is?" Cass asked coolly.

"Last time I saw one of those I was taking it off a dead body," he said quietly, looking around to make sure no one else heard.

Despite the fact that his name was on the list, Sam realized that this test was unfair in regards to Gary. What would have been most suspicious on his part would have been if he saw the ribbons and *hadn't* reacted.

"Isn't that a bit gruesome?" he scolded.

Sam leaned over and whispered in Cass's ear. "Right reaction. I think your fella's okay. We've got to tell him."

Cass nodded her agreement. "We didn't mean to shock you," she said, "but then in another way we did. We wore these to see if anyone would recognize them and reveal themselves by their reaction. We have a list of possible suspects. Until right now, your name was on it because you fit the profile. We knew it was improbable that you were the killer, but your reaction was exactly what we needed out of you. It moved you to the bottom of the list."

"I was a suspect?" Gary looked at Cass in disbelief. "How could you even think such a thing?"

"It wasn't Cass," Sam said quickly, "it was me. You have to admit that as a medical professional, you lie within the broad profile of possible suspects. You also meet two or three other characteristics of the FBI's profile. Cass defended you from the instant she saw you on the list. If you want to blame someone, blame me. You have absolutely no reason to think badly of her at all."

"I should hope not. I love Cass" he said. "The thought of her thinking such a thing of me..." He caught himself and realized what he'd just said, but it was too late to take it back. Cass was already looking at him wide-eyed, with tears threatening to spill. He quickly backpedaled a little. "The truth is, Cass is my best friend. The thought that she could think of me as such a vile person is heartbreaking; that's all."

Cass reached out and turned his face to hers. "Gary Coleman, I don't think that! I never did for a single second. You got caught up in the broad strokes of the investigation, that's all. And as for that other thing. If we weren't standing in the middle of half the population of Summersville right now, I'd kiss you so hard it would curl your toes. We need to talk about this a whole lot more. For now, Sam and I are here working the evening-gown cases. We could use your help if you're interested?"

Gary thought only a moment before nodding.

"There are several people here who are on our list," Cass said. "We're going to be circulating among them. You could help us read their reactions to the ribbons. If anyone seems to react unusually we want to know it. Just one question though..."

"Yes?"

"Do you forgive me for your being on the list?"

Gary didn't hesitate. "Of course I do."

"How about me?" Sam asked.

This time he did hesitate. Finally he said, "Okay, you too, Sam. I forgive both of you."

"Thank you," Sam said.

Cass put her arm around his waist, pulled him close and gave him a chaste kiss on the cheek.

*

My God, it's Susan! the monster shouted. *That scarlet gown, the long blonde hair. And my ribbon! The special one I made just for you. Susan, my darling, my love! I've missed you so much.*

Go after her! the monster screamed. *Susan. It's Susan! Remember how it felt? She was our first. Now we can have her all over again.*

The monster's voice was so compelling, so overpowering that the Freak took several steps in the woman's direction before the intrusion of cold reason seeped into his brain. He halted.

This can't be Susan, he reasoned with the monster. *We know where Susan is. This isn't her.*

Lately it was all he could do to keep the monster from taking over. The Freak was barely hanging on to control. He'd broken out in a heavy sweat the instant he spied the woman in the scarlet gown and the special ribbon. Even in death, Susan was always the monster's real prey. The others were simply substitutes—dalliances along the way.

I don't care what you say. It's Susan! the monster shouted. *She's back. This is the one I want. Feed me. You've got to feed me.*

202

Slowly, the Freak counseled the monster. *We mustn't frighten her. We have to think this through. There's something strange going on here.*

The Freak backed up and maneuvered himself to where he could better observe. Who was this woman? Could she possibly know about Susan? Was she mocking him, taunting him? Or was this just an enormous coincidence? Granted, she looked as if she'd walked out of Susan's portrait, blonde hair, scarlet evening gown, scarlet shoes and all, but now, even through the fog of his shock, he could see subtle differences.

The woman's blonde hair was long and flowing, like Susan's. It cascaded gracefully over her practically bare shoulders—just like Susan's. But this deep yellow hair was natural. It had color and highlights that didn't come from a bottle. He knew because he'd helped Susan color her hair a number of times.

Susan stood only five-foot four, while this woman appeared to be several inches taller. Susan was petite, almost delicate. This woman was slender but lean, far more muscular than Susan was.

The woman was too far away for him to see if she had Susan's deep-blue eyes, but she had the same high cheekbones and angular face. They looked enough alike to have been sisters, but he could tell even from here that close up, they could never be confused.

Suddenly alarms went off in the Freak's head as he recognized the woman standing next to Susan's look alike. "Sheriff Rosier," he muttered under his breath. She certainly looked different in a dress rather than a uniform. She and the other woman were talking. He made his way closer. *What's this?* Rosier wore what looked to be an identical ribbon.

He worked his way unobtrusively to within a few feet of the pair. They were talking with a tall gentleman who looked familiar—Dr. Coleman. Rumors about him and Sheriff Rosier had circulated for some time.

How could this be? Both ribbons appeared to be fastened by a pearl fastener—*his* pearl fastener! "Impossible," the Freak muttered. Those pins were custom made. How could these women be wearing that unique, handmade accessory only four other women had ever worn? Impossible, just impossible!

But wait! The sheriff had seen the ribbons before—around all three of his guest's necks. And Dr. Coleman, the medical examiner likely had also. Why would the sheriff and this woman ...? Ahh... The Susan lookalike had to be working with the sheriff. *This is a sting! Clever, Sheriff Rosier, very clever.*

We must avoid those two tonight, he told the monster. *There is much danger here.* But despite the recognition and warning, the monster still shouted. *I want her! She's the only one I want. Damn the rules. Damn everything! We must have the woman in the scarlet gown.*

*

Cass made her way behind the table where Colton Farnsworth sat and casually hovered there, hoping to pick up threads of his conversation with Harris Crenshaw. The drinks on their table were obviously not their first. Cutler Crenshaw, Harris's father, owned a sizable timber operation north of town. Other than the mines, the sawmill was Nicholas County's largest employer. Harris was known as more of a beach bum at Summersville Lake than anything else.

The conversation Cass overheard was innocuous, something about repairs done to Harris's ski boat. Their man-radar appeared to be working well, as neither let any shapely female pass unnoticed. She had to laugh. *Boys must be boys.*

Cass glanced at Gary standing nearby. He stood where he had full view of Farnsworth's face. He nodded slightly, letting Cass know he was ready. She moved behind the pair without saying anything. Harris was the first to notice. He gave her a double-take then a quick glance up and down then turned his attention back to the conversation.

Humph, she thought. *So much for my nice rack. He must not have recognized me.* She moved to within Colton's peripheral

204

vision. He glanced up, then back, then did a strong double-take. His eyes widened and roved over her.

That's better. Cass thought, but immediately repented of the thought. The man giving her the lustful look might be their serial killer.

Cass couldn't tell if he was looking at her face, neck, or chest. Did his eyes linger on the necklace for a moment?

"Don't I know you?" Colton asked with a suspicious, inebriated smile.

"You should. Colton. I know you."

"Thought so." He smiled and stood with his drink in hand. "You're looking fine tonight." This time his eyes roamed directly to her chest and lingered a moment before returning to her eyes.

"Love the dress," he said. "It brings out the very best in you. I know that I know you from somewhere but can't place it. What's your name?"

"Perhaps you'd remember better if I were in uniform. My name's Cassandra. But you know me better as Sheriff Rosier."

Farnsworth's eyes widened. "Damn, Sheriff, you're right. I didn't recognize you. I gotta say, I like this uniform better the other one. You shouldn't sneak up on a guy like that."

"I wasn't sneaking. I'm attending the dance, same as you are. I haven't seen you around lately. You staying out of trouble?"

"You know me," he said, "Trouble ain't my middle name anymore."

"Heard you were seeing some woman from over at Ansted." *Did his eyes just go to the ribbon?* It was hard to tell. Men who served prison time had a hard time looking police officers in the eye. Then again, she did have some attractive feminine assets exposed.

"You mean Carly Jasperson? Yeah, I been seeing her. She wanted to come tonight but couldn't get a baby sitter. Why?"

"No reason, just heard you were seeing her, that's all. You been around town the past month or so?"

"Yeah," he answered hesitantly, suspiciously. "Why all the questions? You and me, we get along okay, but we ain't exactly bosom buddies, ya know? Why you all of a sudden have such an interest in my life?"

"Just curious. That's all."

Colton suddenly connected the dots." Hey, this isn't about that woman they found out at Cranberry River a few weeks ago, is it? You trying to pin that on me?" Colton held his hands up in defense. "Look, I been clean ever since I got out, especially as far as women are concerned. Sure, I got in a couple of beefs at the bar, but I didn't start them. I don't even cuss at women no more. Ask Carly. I treat her real good. Ask any of the other women I've seen since I got out."

Cass backed off. This was neither the time nor the place. "I'm not trying to pin anything on you, Colton. I just gotta cover all the bases."

Cass heard a sudden loud BEEP, BEEP, BEEP—Gary's pager. She watched him pull back his tux coat and retrieve the pager from his waistband. He looked at it then at her. He nodded in the direction of the door. "Gotta go," she said. "You boys enjoy the dance."

She barely caught up with Gary on his way to the door. She took his arm and turned him around. "Thanks," she said. "I'll talk to you about what we saw back there tomorrow. Just so you know, Gary, I know you're one of the good guys."

"I try to be. If there's anything more I can do to help you with your investigation, just ask."

"The investigation will be fine, but there's one more thing you can do for me."

"What's that?" he said as he glanced at the pager one more time.

"Kiss me."

Gary's departure was delayed several moments as he fulfilled that urgent demand.

*

Upon returning to the dance floor, Cass spotted Sam. She was walking away from Hyrum Payne. Cass caught her elbow and asked, "How are you doing?"

"Not bad," Sam answered in a hushed tone. "When he's not on the phone, Mr. Payne is very reticent. His wife was none too pleased that another woman was talking to her husband."

"Ex-husband," Cass corrected. "They divorced a couple of years ago. Fought like cats and dogs when they were married. We used to get domestic calls on those two about once a week. We could never figure out who was the instigator. They yelled and hollered and broke things, including windows, but we never saw any evidence of assault."

"Strange that they showed up here together."

"Happens all the time. You'd be amazed at the number of people who get along far better after they divorce than they ever did living in the same house. You get any reaction out of him?"

Sam shook her head. "Not that I could tell. I couldn't get his eyes off the floor. I think he was afraid his ex might catch him looking at something she thought he shouldn't be looking at. How'd you do with Colton?"

"He's still at the top of the list as far as I'm concerned. Hard to read his reactions. I want to interview his current girlfriend. He claims he's never touched her but I want to hear it from her before I believe him."

Sam looked around and asked, "Where's Gary?"

"Got called out. I didn't even get a chance to dance with the bum. But we did get a chance to suck face for a minute before he ran out the door."

"Oh, what an awful term." Sam scrunched her face in mild disgust.

Cass laughed. "Ok then, I kissed him. Is that better, Miss Prissy? You stick around the department long enough, and you'll hear a lot worse than that."

"In that case, I'm glad I'm an attorney," Sam said. "How do you want to handle this next guy, the chiropractor?"

"May as well deal with him directly. I know him fairly well. I'll introduce you."

*

Dr. Barlow was seated next to the podium on the low-standing dais, talking with a matronly looking woman with graying, big hair and wearing a fluffy, sky-blue gown. She was Cora Thorson, President of the Women's Auxiliary. He looked up, saw Cass approaching, and smiled without interrupting the older woman's chatter. Cass and Sam stood quietly by until he was free to turn his attention toward them.

Cora spied the two younger women waiting their turn with the Doctor. "Why, Sheriff Rosier, how nice to see you tonight." She said as she rose. "Thank you for supporting the Women's Auxiliary. You look so beautiful."

"Thank you, Mrs. Thorson. You're lovely yourself. How's your husband?"

The woman shook her head. "He's being an old poop tonight, as usual. He'd rather stay home and play with his silly old horses than have to come here and dance with me."

Cass shook her head. Knowing that the woman thrived on compliments, she said, "I'm sure he's the loser in that proposition."

"Oh how nice of you to say," Mrs. Thorson twittered. "I'm trying to snag at least one dance with our handsome young doctor here." She gave Dr. Barlow a sideward glance.

"Don't you worry, Cora," Barlow said. He reached out and took her hand. "I'll catch up with you at least once before the night's out." Cass had no doubt he meant it. Cora Thorson was one of the hospital's most generous contributors.

"Well, I'll run along and leave you young people to yourselves," Cora said. She took a second look at Sam. "Say, aren't you Frank Martin's daughter?"

"Yes, ma'am. I'm Samantha."

"I thought I recognized you. I haven't seen you in years, child. You probably don't even remember me. We're so sorry about your brother. Your father was a wonderful man. You may not know it, but he was our biggest contributor for many years. He never would let us tell people about that."

"You can count on me to see that his donations continue," Sam said—meaning it.

Cora's face lit up. "Oh that's wonderful, just wonderful."

"Just one condition," Sam cautioned. "I want my donations kept as confidential as they were when my father was alive."

"Oh, we're happy to honor that, Samantha. You Martins sure don't like publicity, do you."

"No, ma'am."

"I'll trundle along. Enjoy the dance you young people."

"Now that that's settled," Dr. Barlow said, turning back to Cass, "How are you tonight? I must say your lovely dress will leave a much longer impression with people than the uniform you usually wear."

"Why thank you, Tom. I admit it feels good to be looked at as a woman and not a police officer. I'd like to introduce you to my friend Samantha Martin. Sam, this is our most prominent local chiropractor and massage therapist, Dr. Thomas Barlow."

"Oh, my, that's far too formal, Ms. Martin," Barlow said as he extended his hand. "Please call me Tom."

Sam returned the handshake and said, "I will so long as you call me Sam."

"Deal," Barlow said. He held her hand just a little longer than necessary then dropped it and turned his attention back to Cass. He gestured to the crowd. "Quite a turnout tonight. This may be the best attended Ladies Auxiliary Ball we've ever had."

Cass agreed. "You and the board should be proud."

"Not to be impertinent," Barlow said with a sly smile, "but I saw you earlier with Dr. Coleman. Rumor has it that you two have been seeing each other outside the call-of-duty, so to speak. Care to confirm the rumors?" He cast her a playful eye.

She smiled. She could tell her face was starting to turn red. "No, I won't confirm the rumors. I'll confirm that Gary's a wonderful friend, a wonderful father, a good doctor and a terrific Medical Examiner. Beyond that, everybody will just have to keep guessing." Her face, now fully flushed, spoke volumes more than her cautiously chosen words.

Barlow turned his attention to Sam. "Apparently your family is old Summersville stock," he said. "I haven't been here that long, but I know your father was well thought of. Speaking for the Hospital Board, let me say how much we appreciate what your family has meant to this community."

"Thank you Doc…Tom. How long have you been here?"

"Not quite four years. I moved my practice here from upstate New York. I couldn't help but notice that you're both wearing lovely ribbons and matching pins tonight. That's quite a striking look. Is this some sort of occasion?"

"No, not at all." Cass laughed. "We made these for a high-school Sweetheart Ball more years ago than I'll confess too. We thought it would be a hoot to wear them again."

"Well, you'd better be careful. You'll start a whole new fashion trend." Dr. Barlow turned to Sam. "Miss, Martin, I haven't danced all night. Would you care to honor me?"

"Why certainly, sir." She accepted his extended hand and followed him to the dance floor. As she did, she gave Cass a lingering backward look.

Cass nodded her approval. *So much for him,* she thought as the couple was swallowed by the dancing crowd, *No way would he have asked about the ribbons like that if he'd had anything to do with the murders.*

*

He certainly is a handsome man, Sam thought. He reminded her vaguely of Richard Gere. The song was a smooth, easy, slow one.

"Why haven't I bumped into you before, Samantha?" Dr. Barlow asked as he held her in the classic dance position and took the lead.

"I just returned to town. My law practice is in New York. I haven't lived in Summersville since college. I took a fairly lengthy leave of absence after a nasty divorce."

"I'm sorry to hear that. It certainly is hard to keep marriages together sometimes, isn't it? I'm afraid I've had that experience myself. Any children?"

"No, I'm sorry to say. The marriage ended before any blessed events. It's probably a good thing—although I certainly do want children someday. How about you?"

"Same with me. My marriage lasted only nine months. I haven't yet had the courage to try again."

Sam wanted to steer the conversation to more pleasant things. "Tell me about your practice," she said.

"Not much to tell. Chiropractic services and therapeutic massage. Small town, small practice I guess you could say. But Summersville has been very good to me. I have a very loyal clientele."

Sam was lulled by the music as they continued their small talk. It was the first time any man had touched her since Ricky. It felt strange but it also felt good. The doctor was an excellent dancer.

She looked at the other couples on the floor. A few, like them, were locked at arm's length in a chaste dancer's position. Others had modified the pose to hold each other more tightly. She suddenly wanted to get closer herself. She wasn't ready for full body contact, but a little closer would be nice. She moved her arm up his shoulder and extended the other a little, drawing him in.

There, that was better. She allowed her leg to go between his just a little. The conversation waned a bit and they silently danced.

This was wonderful, but was he shaking? She allowed him to pull her in a little more tightly—or did she do that? Her thigh rubbed against his. Then her tummy encountered something hard.

"Oh," he gasped as he instinctively tried to pull back, but found no graceful way to fully do so. She caught her breath a little as well as the reality of what had just touched her registered. She eased back herself so that the touch became just a soft, occasional brush that was less embarrassing for both of them. *Good that I can still have that effect on a man,* she thought.

The music stopped, and the dance ended. When she looked up, she was surprised to find Barlow sweating profusely. *My God, he's trembling.* "Dr. —Tom—are you alright?" Could he be having a heart attack?

He extracted a handkerchief, mopped his brow, and apologized. "I'm sorry. I've been fighting the flu and a fever all week. Guess I'm not fully over it yet. Let me get you back to Sheriff Rosier before I expose you to something."

"I can find Cass myself. Let's get you to a chair. Can I get you a drink of water or something?"

"No, no. I'll be fine," he stammered. "You and the sheriff go on and have a good time. Thank you for supporting the Auxiliary." He turned and rushed away, leaving her standing in the middle of the dance floor.

What a strange man, Sam thought. She spotted Cass sitting with her parents in the bar area. She couldn't help but smile as she thought about the doctor's obvious ardor. While it was a bit off-putting, it was also a huge stroke to an ego badly shattered by Ricky.

The whole episode made her realize how long she'd been without a man. A suppressed, ignored ache suddenly sprang to life. It pleased her to know that the longing was still there. *All in good time girl,* she chided herself as she joined Cass and her parents. *All in good time.*

*

Midnight was approaching. After finishing their drinks, Cass's parents excused themselves, her father saying, "We old folks can't take much of this night life. We'll check on your babysitter on the way home. You young folks have a nice time."

After they left, Cass asked, "So what did you think of Barlow?" "The guy was real happy to see me," Sam chuckled. She told her of the man's very male reaction to their dance. "He was sweating like a pig by the end. I think he was embarrassed. He dropped me like a hot potato in the middle of the floor."

"You're kidding." Cass laughed. "At least we know he likes women. Some people around town are starting to think he's gay."

"I doubt that, Sam said, blushing a little. Actually, I found him charming and gracious."

"He didn't seem to react to the ribbons," Cass said. "If anything, his comments about them seemed perfectly natural and innocent. Either he's a very good actor, or they meant nothing to him."

"What do you think we should do with him?"

"I think we move him down the list. Not off it, but down."

Sam nodded. "I agree. We'll put him down there with Gary."

"I'd take Gary off and leave Dr. Barlow just barely on at the bottom."

"Sounds right to me," Sam agreed.

Chapter 38

"Sam, where the hell are you?" Ricky pled into his bathroom mirror. Five days! Just five days before the return of the goon, and still no sign of her. The thought popped beads of sweat on his brow. He had to find her before Monday morning; otherwise he'd have no choice but to disappear.

Yesterday, he'd withdrawn all the money he had left in the bank. His passport and forty-six-thousand-seven-hundred-twenty-three-dollars were locked in his briefcase—enough to get him started in Mexico. It wouldn't take but a half-hour to pack what clothes and other stuff he'd need and be on his way. But all that could all be avoided if he could just find Sam.

Twice in the past month, he'd driven to Summersville to see if she was there. He went to her parents' old place and was surprised to see it fixed up real nice. He gathered his courage and knocked on the door both times, but nobody ever answered. He looked through the front windows. The inside was all different, especially the kitchen.

The way Sam talked about the ratty old house after her dad died, he doubted she'd ever change a thing. It was like a sacred shrine or something. *I wonder if Sam sold the place?*

He ventured into the side yard to see if he could spot her car. No such luck. The driveway was empty and the white 1930's style clapboard garage with no windows had a padlock securing the door.

Who else would know if she was in town? The only name he would think of was that old girlfriend of hers, Cass something or other. Good-looking, but she was a cop. *Be careful with that,* he thought. Probably best not to ask her. With few other options, he'd driven around for a while on the chance he'd spot her. It was a fruitless effort.

Today was different: Today, he was desperate. If she was in Summersville he *had* to find her. He'd search Wal-Mart and other shopping centers. He'd search all the parking lots in town to try to spot her car. Undoubtedly she still drove that ratty old Camry. Hell, that car meant more to her than he did. He'd stake out the old house until he knew for sure who lived there. If Sam was in Summersville, he'd find her.

Then what? he wondered. He had to come up with a pitch—a story that would convince her she had to help. *Maybe I could tell her I'm sick.* He rejected the idea. She'd want information about the doctor and what hospital he was going to, all kinds of stuff.

He thought and thought but couldn't come up with a plausible lie. He decided to simply tell the truth. *Look Sam, they're going to hurt me real bad, maybe even kill me.* She'd probably believe him. No need to fake being scared. He was scared shitless.

He looked around the cabin and realized that Monday might be the last time he ever saw this place. Too bad. He'd grown quite fond of it.

But time was a wasting. He jumped into the shower, then shaved for the first time in weeks. He even thought about getting a haircut to make himself look as good as possible, but rejected the idea. It would take too much time—time he could spend searching. Sam always liked him in tight, clean jeans and a fresh western-style shirt, preferably blue or dark brown. He combed his hair back into a rakish style and splashed on an extra dose of cologne. She always liked Polo—so Polo it was. When everything was just right, he jumped into the Escalade and pointed it toward Summersville.

Chapter 39

"Aunty Sam! Katy shouted as she burst through Cass's front door and rushed up to collect a big hug, nearly knocking Sam over in the process. She was ready for their weekly Friday morning outing, all dressed up in her new black fighting pants and white Karate gee, a gift from Sam for her 10th birthday last month.

Cass came out on the porch dressed in her uniform and closed and locked the door behind her. She smiled. "You two have a good time," she said. "Don't break anything except a few boards, okay?"

With Cass's permission, Sam had enrolled Katy in a beginning *Taekwondo* program. This would be Katy's seventh class—only three more to go before school started. After that Katy's classes would be at night.

"Hey, little girl." Sam laughed as she hugged her gangly, precocious, carrot-topped unofficial niece.

"Watch who you're calling little," Katy said in mock dismay. She stepped into a martial arts stance. "I'll have to hurt you, lady." She moved her arms about and let loose a "Whaaaaah!" indicating she was ready for battle.

"Oh, you're far too fearsome for me," Sam said, trying to look serious.

"You two better not start fighting; I'll have to arrest you both," Cass chuckled as she stepped into her SUV.

After dropping Katy off at her class, Sam watched for a few minutes as the Sensei took the young children through their warm-up routine. She couldn't help but smile. *That girl's going to be a good one,* she thought as she watched Katy square her stance and snap kicks and punches.

Sam slipped into the dressing room and changed into her own fighting gear, then ventured into the practice room next door. No sense in letting her skills, acquired by years of hard work and determination, deteriorate.

It felt good to work up a sweat. The sedentary hours spent in the War Room gave her little opportunity to limber up and get her blood pumping. Eight or ten others were in the room, some going through solitary floor exercises while others worked with a sparring partner. After warming up, Sam sought a sparring partner of her own. A high-school-age boy, a blue-belt, was delighted for the chance to work out with a black belt, who also just happened to be a very attractive older woman.

"What's your name?" Sam asked as the two maneuvered for their first aggressive moves. He was a nice looking kid. Probably a touch over six-feet, thick, medium-length sandy blonde hair and blue eyes. He still had the slender body of youth that was just beginning to put on some muscle. Judging by the level of his warm-up exercises, Sam judged that he wasn't far from becoming a second-level brown belt.

"Lanny Johnson, ma'am," the boy replied in a heavy West Virginia accent. "I haven't seen you in here before. You new?" He feigned a leg sweep take down which Sam quickly countered. He drew back and kept circling.

Sam smiled at the boy's polite reply. *Yes, ma'am* and *Yes, sir* were honorifics rarely heard out of the mouths of young men and women in New York City. It was refreshing to realize that kids in this part of the country were still taught manners and respect for their elders.

"I grew up here," she replied, "but I live in New York now. My name's Samantha Martin."

"Glad ta meetcha, Mrs. Martin. We don't get many black-belt women here. You're the first I've seen."

The 'Mrs.' stung a bit but also confirmed her status in the boy's eyes as an older woman. "I'd like it if you just called me Sam," she said. "How old are you?"

"Seventeen, ma'am." Something about the boy's name was familiar, but she couldn't put her finger on it.

Lanny feigned the same leg sweep move, but this time Sam stepped inside the sweep, shot out one of her own that caught his balance leg, and took it from under him. At the same time, she gave him a flat-hand thrust to the center of his chest, sending him sprawling on his back to the mat. In a flash, she was over the top of him, giving him two lightning-fast closed fist punches that came within millimeters of landing on his throat. Lanny stared up at her; wide-eyed and breathless at the blinding speed with which he'd been defeated. Sam extended a hand to help him up.

"Wow! You're real good," he said in awe. "I've never seen a woman move that fast." He brushed himself off, put his hands together, and gave her a respectful martial arts bow.

As Sam returned the bow, it dawned on her where she'd heard his name. She was sparring with the kid who'd found the cars. Suddenly practicing became less important. She dropped her hands and asked, "Lanny, aren't you the young man who found those cars out at Franklin's Pit?"

He looked around quickly, suddenly seeming nervous and a little guilty. "Uh, yeah, I guess. Why?"

"Don't be nervous. I'm working with the sheriff's office on the murders of the women who owned those cars. I was there the day you kids came in and reported them. Do you mind if we chat for a couple of minutes?"

"You a cop?"

"No, I'm an attorney. You're not in any trouble or anything. I just want to see if you can help me out."

"Well, uh—sure, ma'am, why not. What do you want to know?"

"Let's go sit over there." Sam indicated a bench that ran all the way around the wall of the practice room. Once they were settled, Sam said, "I don't necessarily want you to tell me anything specific. Just tell me about what happened out there."

"It's weird," Lanny began hesitantly. "I mean, when I touched that car underwater, I couldn't believe it. Who in the world would throw away a good car like that?"

"How often do you go out there?"

"That was my first time."

"Do a lot of kids swim out there?"

"Not a lot. Some kids go necking out there. Not many. Too many good places closer to town. Some go out there to go neckin' and skinny dippin' at the same time."

"Can you tell me who?"

"Oh geez, ma'am—uh, Sam—I don't want to give names." Lanny again cast his eyes nervously around the room.

"Could you do me a favor? Would you ask your friends if they've ever seen anything suspicious out there, especially at night? If someone has, could you call me? It might help us solve those murders."

"I reckon I could," Lanny said nervously, "but I'll have to be real careful. Don't want people thinking I'm a snitch or something."

"I know this kind of puts you on the spot. If you don't call, I'll understand. You can reach me at the sheriff's office. By the way, you're doing real well with your *Taekwondo*. How long have you been studying?"

Delighted with the subject change, the Lanny brightened. "This is my third year. I'd have my second-degree brown by now but football takes up a lot of time."

"Let me guess something about you. I'll bet you're a good student. What's your GPA?"

Lanny turned shy. "3.8. It'd be 4.0, but I biffed English last year cause of the flu. Missed a pop-quiz and ended up with an A minus."

"For your information, *Taekwondo* students who continue the art more than two years are generally excellent students. The dedication and discipline you develop shows up in your character and your school work. Would you like to spar with me again sometime?"

"Uh—sure. You're good. I'll just have to get used to the idea of a woman beating me."

Sam gave him a secretive smile. "If you don't tell, neither will I," she said. "Shall we get out there and go a couple more rounds?"

"Yes ma'am. I'd like that."

Lanny and Sam continued their sparring for the better part of an hour before Katy came running up. "Watch this, Aunty Sam," the little girl said. She took her battle stance and let loose with a sideways waist kick. "Jackie Wooten can't do that without falling over," she bubbled. "He says he's going to get me cause I laughed when he did."

"Good job, young lady. You ready to go?"

"Yup! The only thing I need now is ice cream. Pleeeease!"

Sam nodded a 'yes'. "Let me get changed," she said, "I want you to meet my new friend, Lanny Johnson. He's been doing *Taekwondo* for three years."

"Really?" Katy's eyes got big as she gave the young man a look just short of hero worship.

"Lanny, meet Katy Rosier. She's Sheriff Rosier's daughter."
Katy precociously stuck out her hand. "Pleased to meetcha," she said.

Lanny smiled. "And you too, Miss Rosier." He winked at Sam. "Why don't you show me what else you learned in class?"

Sam returned in her street clothes ready to go to work and found Katy vigorously demonstrating all her best moves to her new-found friend.

Chapter 40

Sam was surprised when Cass met her in the courthouse foyer.

"I was coming out of Judge Renshaw's courtroom and I saw you coming in," Cass explained. "I have an interesting piece of news." She was not smiling. "Colton Farnsworth is sitting over at the jail right now. They brought him in last night."

"Why?" Sam asked, wide-eyed.

"Domestic assault. He punched Carly out down at the bar in Mt. Nebo. She had to go to the hospital for stitches. I sat in on her peace bond hearing against him. The judge granted it so he'll probably make bail this afternoon."

"Can we talk to him first?" Sam asked.

"We can try, but he's lawyered up already. I'd love to get a look inside his house. Since the fight took place at the bar, we won't have probable cause for a search warrant on the house. But I'll see if he'll give us permission anyway. Probably won't work, but I'll try.

"Too bad. Do you want me in there during the interview? I'm a lawyer too."

"He knows me. Probably better not throw someone new into the mix. I'll call if I need you."

"Fair enough. I'm off to the War Room." On her way past the office Sam called to Mary, "Many word on those credit-card reports?"

"No, but I'll call about them again right now. You know how the FBI is."

Sam didn't, but she was learning.

*

"Good morning, Jack," Sam said, greeting the state lab investigator. "You've been busy, haven't you?" The table the department had provided was beginning to fill with objects enclosed in various sizes of clear plastic bags, each carefully labeled in permanent marker.

"Yes I have," Jack replied. He was a humorless man. In the days he had been here, Sam had never once seen him crack a smile.

"The paper evidence is mostly dried and bagged." he said. "I've got just a few more items left to process. Fortunately, the windows on the cars were rolled up, so water seeped in rather than washed in abruptly. That left most of the paper evidence intact. The water in that gravel pit has a 6.9 pH which made it a wonderful preservative."

"How soon can I handle what's inside these?" Sam asked, holding up one of the bags.

"Right now, if you're careful. Anything in the bags will bear normal handling unless I mark it otherwise. I'd prefer that you try to read the contents through the bag if possible. If you have to take something out, ask Sheriff Rosier for evidence gloves."

"Have you spotted anything of interest yet?"

"Nothing with the killer's name written in bold print, if that's what you mean."

"What am I supposed to do when I handle this stuff?"

He picked up one of the bags. "See these two columns?" One was marked 'Out' with date and time and the other marked 'In' with date and time. "Every time you take a bag from the table, you sign it out and back in. It's called chain-of-possession. Courts are very strict about it. If you break the chain, evidence gets tossed.

Have Mary make you up your own evidence handling binder. Every time you handle one of these, you document its bag number and a write a detailed description of what you did with it. Your binder is your Bible. If you ever get called to court, you won't have to rely on your memory to give an accurate testimony."

Sam nodded. "I'll hold off on handling any of them until Mary gets me my binder. Do you have any other suggestions for me?"

"Write everything down, Ms. Martin; and I mean everything. What did you do on this case last week?"

"I mostly worked right here. I'd have to check my notes. Cass and I did have some contact with potential suspects at the Hospital's Ladies Auxiliary Ball."

"Did you talk to any of them?"

"Yes, several. Why?"

"If I asked you to recite, word-for-word each of those conversations six months from now, could you?"

"The general gist of them."

"Not good enough. Courts will rely on a contemporaneous written record much more than a vague recollection. Write it down, Ms. Martin. Write everything down."

*

"Looks like you're screwed again, Colton," Cass said. "I thought you'd learned your lesson." Farnsworth sat sullenly at the small table set in the middle of the interrogation room at the jail. His lawyer, Kenneth Downs, whose father was the attorney for Farnsworth Funeral Homes, Inc., was also present.

"Don't respond to that," Downs cautioned his client. "I don't know why you wanted this conference, sheriff. I've instructed my client to say nothing, and that's what you'll get."

Downs was young enough that it appeared he still felt the need to carve out a tough reputation. "You don't have to try and impress me," Cass said. "I'm trying to work to your client's advantage. I'm not interested in him on this little assault charge. She looked at Colton. "You remember our conversation at the dance the other night?"

Colton glared at her intently. "I told you. I didn't have anything to do with those."

"You also told me how well you treat women. But here you sit in an orange jumpsuit, and another woman is over at the courthouse getting a protective order against you."

"Those?" Downs practically shouted. "What are you two talking about?"

Cass answered for him." We've got someone in the county not treating women very well, Mr. Downs. He leaves dead bodies lying around dressed in some really nice evening gowns. Your boy Colton here has been somewhere around the top of our list of suspects. I thought that if he wants to cooperate a little, we may be interested in cutting him some slack. That's all."

"You're accusing him of murder?" Downs was nearly apoplectic. "Colton, don't you say another word, you hear me? Not one more word!"

"Shut up, Downs," Colton said, irritated at the man's antics. "What do you want from me, Sheriff?"

"I protest!" Downs screeched. "Mister Farnsworth, if you refuse to follow my advice, perhaps you need a new attor—"

"Shut up, Downs!" Colton said again, more vehemently this time. The attorney's jaw kept going up and down, but the sound stopped coming out.

"I want to talk to you off the record," Cass said. "What happened out there last night? I thought you had this hitting women thing whipped."

"I didn't start it. I swore I'd never hit a woman again, and I meant it. But she broke a pool cue across my back and was coming at me with the broken end. I had to hit her; otherwise I would have been a shish-kabob."

"You got witnesses?"

"A whole bar full. I wasn't drunk, but she was, real drunk—nasty—making a real ass out of herself. The bouncer was ready to throw her out, but she hit me first. It was pure self-defense, Sheriff, and I can prove it."

Cons were good liars, but this sounded like the truth. Colton was a man who truly didn't want to go back to prison. Time for a little good cop rather than bad. "Colton, I need your help. You told me you didn't have anything to do with these evening-gown murders. Other people in the department think you did. A couple of them want me to arrest you for those murders right now, but I've been putting them off. I need a sign of good faith from you. I need to take a look at your house. It would look a lot better for you and maybe get those other people off your back if you gave me permission."

Cass watched as Colton mulled the proposal. He looked as if something was bothering him. Finally he said, "I could do that. It's just that I've got a couple of little problems. Nothing big, and nothing to do with anything we're talking about, you know what I mean?"

"What and how much, Colton?"

"We're still off the record, right?"

"Unless we're talking felony stuff. Anything over an ounce and I can't ignore it."

"It's way under. I got about a fourth of a baggie in my desk drawer."

"Weed?"

"Yup."

"That's it?"

"There might be a joint in my car, but yeah, that's it." Colton obviously thought they'd find the stuff anyway. Better for him to cut a deal than spend thirty days in the county lockup for possession.

"You don't have to worry about that," Cass said. "I've got a lot bigger fish to fry than a misdemeanor possession bust."

"I got your word on that?"

"Yes, but only that. Everything else is fair game."

"I'll beat this assault charge for sure. If it'll get you and the department off my back about those evening-gown chicks, come on over. Bring all your friends. You can search my house, my car, anything. My dad would even let you search the mortuary if you want. I got nothin' to hide. Hell, you can even look down my shorts if you want to. That good enough? Only thing I ask is that me and my lawyer be there when you do it. Deal?"

Cass suppressed a smile. The last place in the world she wanted to look was down the man's shorts. "It's a deal. Your bail hearing is about a half hour from now. You should be on the street around one. We'll do it then."

*

"Farnsworth agreed!" Cass said jubilantly when she walked into the War Room.

"You're kidding," Sam said. "You must have kissed the Blarney Stone."

"Didn't kiss anything else this morning, damn it. We're going to search his place as soon as we can get over there. I've got a deputy escorting him. He's agreed not to go inside until we're there."

"Did he tell you what happened?"

"He did, and his story squares with the police report. Only reason they didn't arrest Carly last night was that she needed to go to the emergency room. She'll be arrested today." Cass took a breath and shrugged. "I doubt we'll get anything out of his house or car. He's practically begging us to come over. He wants off that suspect list. You turn up anything here?"

Sam shook her head. "Not yet. Jack says he's about done. I just started looking at some of the bags. Mary got me a pair of evidence gloves and is making me up an evidence-handling binder. As soon as she does, I'll start on the bags in earnest."

"Sounds good, Cass said. "Any luck on the next-of-kin notices?"

"Not yet. Mary may have a lead on the Quinn girl. I'll keep you posted. You want me here or with you?"

"Might as well hang in here. If we turn up anything interesting I'll call you.

*

It was just before 3:00 p. m. Sam had been examining evidence bags for over an hour when the phone rang. "Yes, Mary?" she answered.

"I've got a young kid on the line. He says he talked to you this morning. Says you asked him to call you."

"That would be Lanny. Which line's he on?"

"Line three."

Sam punched line three. "Lanny," she answered brightly. "I'm glad you called. What can I do for you?"

"You said to call if I learned anything. This one guy and his girlfriend were out to the pit a week ago Saturday, and they might have seen something. But I can't give you their names or anything like that. They made me promise."

"I understand. We'll keep everything confidential for now, okay?"

"Uh-huh."

Sam turned on the recorder Cass had set up on her phone. "Okay, tell me what you've got."

"These guys have a special place out there. McKala don't like anybody snooping around his car when they're—you know—making out and stuff. Oh, I probably shouldn't be telling you this much."

"No, you're fine," she said gently, trying to keep him comfortable. "We're not using names, remember?" She didn't remind him that he'd already used one.

"Yeah, okay. There's this place where there's an opening in the willows on the other side of the ramp. There's only room for one car. He says other people don't even notice ya there. Well him and McK—um, his girlfriend were parked there pretty late when somebody with pickup and a trailer drove up. There wasn't much moon, so he couldn't see what was on the trailer at first. The guy got out of the truck with a flashlight and started messing with it. Brad said—oh shit, I—oops, sorry. I didn't mean to cuss."

"You're fine," Sam reassured him. "I know you're nervous, but you don't have to be. We're friends. Tell you what. We can use names as long as we don't use last names. How's that?"

"That'd be okay, I guess. Anyway, they could tell when the flashlight shined on it that there was a car on the trailer. The guy unhitched the car and drove it off the trailer. Brad said he heard the car engine rev up real loud, then it sounded like the guy popped it into gear. Next thing they heard was the car hitting the water. He said the guy took his flashlight out to the edge of the cliff and watched the car float out a ways then sink. They could see cause the guy was shining the flashlight on the car until it went completely under. Brad said McKala and him was real scared that the guy would shine the flashlight on them so they ducked down until he was gone."

"This is important," Sam said. "Could they tell what kind of pickup the man was driving?"

"It was a new Dodge Ram, ma'am. Brad knows cause he wants one himself real bad. He's looked at em a hundred times. Said it was a silver or light gray Dodge Ram with tall tires and real nice rims."

"How about the man driving it? Did they get a look at him?"

"He said they never saw the guy's face."

"Did they get any general impressions of him—was he tall, small, how old he may have been, what he was wearing, that kind of stuff?"

"Geez, Sam, I have no idea. I didn't ask that kind of stuff."

"You know the easiest thing would be if they would agree to talk to me face to face. They don't have to worry about getting in trouble or anything, and I'd never tell their parents."

"I don't know; they're pretty scared. The only reason they talked to me was because of what the paper said about those women when the story came out about the cars. I'll ask them, but no promises, okay?"

"That's fine. I'm proud of you, Lanny. Are you going to be there when I take Katy to her next lesson?"

"I should be, but school's starting in a couple of weeks, so after that I'll have to go at night."

"Don't worry. We'll get plenty of sparring time together. Let's set a goal of you having your black belt by the end of the school year. I'll help."

"Yes, ma'am," Lanny said. "I'd like that."

Sam hung up and made a beeline for Mary's desk. "Run a DMV check on everyone on our suspect list. See if anyone has a late-model Dodge Ram pickup registered to them, silver or grey"

Mary caught the excitement in Sam's voice. "That kid give you something?"

"I think someone may have seen our killer dump one of the cars."

"How long ago?"

"Two weeks ago, tops. Must have been Jennifer Oldroyd's."

"I'll get right on it. Probably take an hour or so."

"That's OK. Just get it as fast as you can. We're getting closer, Mary. This guy's starting to step out of the shadows. I've got a feeling we're going to see his face very soon."

Chapter 41

"I'm happy we were able to be of service to you, Mary Ann," the Freak said. "I really appreciate the time we've spent beyond your appointment. Too bad you're only passing through. It would be nice to get to know each other better."

The Freak placed his hand gently over hers, which was resting on her bare knee several inches below the cuff of her medium-length bib overall-style shorts. His hand rested there only a moment. He had to be careful to not scare her off by seeming too forward. Seductions were such delicate things.

She's good. This one's good, the monster said hungrily. *But she's not who we want. The scarlet gown—the woman in the scarlet gown—Sam, Don't you remember? This girl would be delicious, but she's not Sam. We're safe. We can break the rules if we want to. We're the ones who made them, remember? We know where she lives. We could just go take her. Yes, I know, they'd start looking for her right away, but where would they look? No one knows about the ranch. Hell, it's not even in your name. We're safe there. We're safe!*

Then the monster proposed an entirely new thought. *"I know, let's have both! I'm so hungry. So hungry. You've got to feed me—now, damn it—Now!*

"I don't know if it fits your schedule," the Freak said solicitously. "But I'm about to take a break. Would you be interested in a cup of coffee? Better yet, I have to take the afternoon off anyway. How about lunch?"

"Why thank you, kind sir, I'd be delighted." Mary Ann said.

"There's just one other hitch." The Freak gave her his most charming smile. "The restaurant I'm thinking of is about 15 miles from here. I have a working ranch over by the little town of Canvas. I just sold a couple of bulls to a guy from Fayetteville. He's picking them up around two o'clock, and I have to be there. I have a reputation around town as a pretty fair gourmet cook—I can furnish references if you'd like. If it wouldn't seem too forward, could I interest you in homemade Beef Bourguignon? Dessert will be a fresh strawberry tort with warm crème de caramel sauce. I have a great bottle of 1996 Chateau Santa Margareta Reserve Pinion Noir I've been dying to open. I guarantee a meal terrible for your diet, but great for your soul. You're on vacation, right? What's that old saying—you only live once?"

"That sounds suspiciously like you're asking me on a date," Mary Ann said.

"You've found me out. It actually *is* an invitation for a date. After all, you're leaving tomorrow, and this is the only chance I'll ever get."

"Are there any horses on this here ranch of yours?" she asked.

"Yes, there are, several as a matter of fact. My favorite's the one I call Renegade. He's a big red roan quarter-horse stud that keeps all my mares very happy."

"We don't have many of those up in Boston."

"What, horses?"

"No. Studs who keep their mares very happy." She laughed at her own double-entendre with that high, tinkling laugh that made her so extraordinarily charming. "If I come out there can we ride the horses?"

"Why certainly. I've got a saddle that's just your size."

233

The prospect of riding horses seemed to settle the issue. "In that case, I'd be happy to join you," Mary Ann said. "Do you want me to follow you there, or what?"

"I have some errands to take care of here in town first. But here." He snatched a note pad off his desk. "Let's try this." He scribbled a note, and carefully explained the route as he annotated in his cryptic shorthand. When he was finished, he tore it off the pad and handed it to her.

Arbk 5M, Cnvs, +2M, CR39/4 L1. 9M - RR

With the Freak's explanation, the note was easy to read. "Shall we say about 4:00 o'clock?"

"Fine with me. Give me your phone number in case I get lost."

"There's no phone service to the ranch, but here's my cell number. Coverage is a bit spotty out there, but you can try." He took the note from her and added, 304. 555. 1229. "There, that should do it."

"Yes, it will! See you this afternoon, cowboy."

*

As she walked from his office to her car, Mary Ann wondered what Beef Bourguignon was and how it tasted. *It can taste like cardboard, for all I care,* she told herself. *That cowboy is what's on my menu. After all, I am on vacation.*

Chapter 42

Mary and Cass walked into the War Room at the same time to see Sam. "The FBI just faxed these over," Mary said, holding up several sheets of paper. She handed them to Sam. They were credit and debit-card records for Oldroyd and Quinn. "I'm still waiting on the Basso girl. Her records were archived so it's taking a little longer to dig them up. They'll probably be here tomorrow."

"Thanks," Sam said. "How's your vehicle registration search going?"

"Vehicle registration?" Cass asked.

"Yes," Sam said. "We may have stumbled across something big." Sam told Cass of her conversation with Lanny. "I've had Mary doing a vehicle registration check on everyone on our list."

"I'm about two-thirds done," Mary said. "I've got several pickup trucks, even a couple of Dodges, but one was black, and the other one dark green."

"Sounds like the same kind of luck I've had," Cass lamented. "Colton was very cooperative. We searched his house, his car, everything. With old man Farnsworth's permission, we even did a walkthrough of the mortuary, including the body-prep room. Nobody in there, thank God. We checked every closet and storage area, even the basement. If Colton's hiding anything, we sure couldn't find it.

"I sent Deputy Zeeman down to Mt. Nebo this morning to talk to the bar owner. He confirmed everything Colton said about the incident. We're going to arrest Carly as the aggressor." Cass looked at Sam and shrugged. "I don't think Colton's our guy. Let's keep him on the list, but move him way down."

"Done," Sam said. "Who do you think we should replace him with?"

"Hyrum Payne is next. Maybe it's time to bring him in and have a little chat. The interrogation room can be pretty intimidating."

"Sam nodded. "Works for me. When?"

"Tomorrow."

Sam held up the credit-card reports. "I'll keep slogging away here. I want to look these over before I go home. By the way, Jack says he's about done with the cars."

"That's right," Jack said as he walked through the door bearing several more plastic bags. "This is it except for the thick stuff I'm still drying—car manuals and stuff. There's something in this last batch I think you should see." He set the bags on Sam's desk and rifled through them until he found the one he wanted. He handed it to Cass and said, "This piece has a local connection."

The bag indicated the contents came from the Oldroyd vehicle. It contained a single sheet of paper. Cass signed and dated the 'Out' column on the bag, pulled her evidence gloves on and examined the sheet of paper inside. "I'll be damned," she whispered.

"What?" Sam asked.

"See for yourself."

It was an invoice for chiropractic services marked 'Paid' in blue ink. The name and address at the top of the invoice said.

Dr. Thomas R. Barlow, DC
266 West Main St
Summersville, WV 26651

It was dated five weeks prior to the discovery of Jennifer's body.

"I'll be darned," Sam responded.

As Cass read the rest of the invoice, Sam spotted something. "I think there's writing on the back," she said.

Cass turned the invoice over and found a handwritten note;

Arbk 5M, Cnvs, +2M, CR39/4 L1. 9M - RR.

"What do you make of that?" Sam asked.

Cass wrinkled her brow and shook her head. "Looks like Greek to me. What do you think?"

"Some kind of code or shorthand or something."

"We have a new name for the top of our list." Cass said. "Mary, I want a full background check on Dr. Barlow—a complete FBI workup, everything. Go to the recorder's office and get a list of every property this guy owns in the county. Sam, go through everything that came out of those cars and see if there's anything else we can tie to him. Mary, where's Eric?"

"Last time he checked in he was on his way back from Mt. Nebo."

"Have him come straight back here. He and I are going to pay the good doctor a visit."

*

Sam shuddered as she returned to her task of searching the evidence table. Had she actually danced with a serial killer? His decidedly male reaction certainly didn't give the impression that he hated women. But then she remembered how he was sweating at the end of the dance. Had he really not been feeling well—or was it something else?

She hadn't had a chance to write down her recollection of the night of the dance yet, but she reviewed every word of her conversations with Barlow in her mind, hoping for any hints that might be buried there. Try as she might, she couldn't pick anything out.

If he's the killer and recognized those ribbons, he must have been shocked. Yet he showed no obvious reaction to them at all. *Maybe this is just an unusual coincidence,* she concluded—then she read the credit card statements.

*

The sign on the door read *Closed until Monday.*

Cass rattled the glass door to Barlow's office. Locked. "Eric, can you see anything?"

Deputy Zeeman shook his head as used his hands to block the glare as he tried to peer through the dark glass of the front window. "Nothing moving inside. No lights on," he said.

The doctor shared the building with two other tenants. "Haven't seen him all day," the barber on the right said. "He was here yesterday morning but I didn't see him in the afternoon."

The barber's statements were confirmed by the family counselor on the left. "Let's try his house," Cass said.

*

There was no answer to her knock. She tried again, then again. She placed her ear to the door. Silence. She tried the door knob. Locked.

She adjusted her duty belt on her hips and unsnapped the strap that secured her pistol. "Let's walk around and see what we can see," she said. "Stay loose and alert."

The house sat at the back of the cul-de-sac where he lived. There was a house on each side. The narrow front yard gave way to an expansive, wedge-shaped backyard completely enclosed by a vinyl privacy fence. The driveway led to a separate garage set a short distance behind the house.

The back gate was unlocked. She cautiously opened it. The yard looked like something out of a magazine. The lawn was precisely mown, the shrubs perfectly trimmed. There wasn't a weed or errant scrap of paper or discarded soda can or any other type of litter. The flowers looked carefully chosen and meticulously placed.

"Check the windows," Cass said as she went onto the porch to check the back door. It too was locked.

"Windows all have blinds," Eric said as he returned from the side of the house. "I didn't try to open any of them, not without a warrant."

"Let's check the garage," Cass said.

The side garage door was unlocked and slightly ajar. "Get out your notebook and write this down, Eric," she commanded. "Two-car garage. Officers observed that the side door was open. You got that?"

"Got it sheriff," Zeeman said, scribbling quickly to catch up.

"Good, now take a look at the back fence and see if we missed anything."

"Huh?" Zeeman looked puzzled.

"Just do it, Eric," she said quietly.

Zeeman smiled as he finally caught the drift of her instruction. As he turned his head, Cass placed her foot against the base of the door and pushed gently. The door opened more than half-way, as much as she dared get away with. She couldn't go in without a warrant but at least they could see inside.

"Keep writing, Eric," she said as she resumed her recitation. "One car present—a white, late-model Acura, license number SJJ-222, registered in Nicholas County. Other car space empty but appears to be regularly used. Officers observed tire prints and several oil marks on the floor. Visible wall on left side of garage mostly covered by shelving. A lot of automotive stuff, yard-care chemicals, etc. Near wall and back wall not visible. Officers did not attempt to close door."

As they walked up the driveway to the front of the house, Cass asked, "Do you want the neighbors on the right side or the left?"

"Doesn't matter to me."

"You go right, I'll go left."

*

The story was the same from each of the neighbors. Neither knew where the doctor was. The neighbor Cass talked to thought she saw him earlier that morning around the time he usually went to work.

"When asked about the other vehicle he kept in the garage, both neighbors had the same answer, "A silver Ram pickup." When asked if they had ever seen the doctor accompanied by women they didn't recognize, both said they'd never seen him with any at all.

Both neighbors assured them that if they saw Barlow come home they'd call.

*

"That silver pickup is strike two on this guy," Cass told Eric as they compared notes. "I'd give you 90% odds the Doc is our guy." I want a stakeout on this place and at his office. But I don't want them sitting right on the guy's front steps. We can't afford to scare him off."

"10-4," Eric replied. "I'll set it up."

Cass pulled out her cell phone and dialed Sam. "Sammy girl, don't go home. Same for Mary. I've got some news."

"I wasn't going home till you got back anyway," Sam said. "I have big news for you as well."

*

It was just after five when Cass walked into the War Room. "I'm ninety-nine percent certain it's Dr. Barlow," Cass informed her friend.

"I'm ninety-nine percent certain it's him too," Sam replied.

"How do you know?" they both asked each other at the same time.

Sam laughed and said, "You first." Cass told her of the interviews with Barlow's neighbors and their confirmation that he owned a silver Dodge Ram pickup. "It's not enough for an arrest warrant," she said, "but my gut's telling me that this guy is our dirt bag."

"Maybe this will put us over the top," Sam said. "Look at these." She handed Cass two of the credit-card statements. "Top one's Oldroyd's, bottom one's Quinn's." She pointed to a charge she'd circled on the first statement—$49 to Barlow Chiropractic and Massage Clinic, Summersville, West Virginia.

Cass flipped to the second statement where Sam had circled an identical charge. Different women, different statements from different credit-card companies. The dates of the charges were eight months apart, but each charge occurred roughly a month prior to the discovery of each woman's body.

"Three strikes, you're out, doc," Cass said grimly. "Good job, Sammy. Three separate pieces of evidence from three different sources. In my book, that's more than enough to give us probable cause."

Cass glanced at the wall clock. It read 'Five forty-five.' The courts were closed. "Friday night, it's going to be tough finding a judge," she said. "Mary, track down Prosecutor Stewart and get him in here as fast as possible. Then find us a district court judge if you can. Eric, put out a 'be on the lookout' notice to our officers and an APB to all other agencies. Tell them to detain and hold this bastard on sight. I gotta call my parents to tell them they've got Katy tonight. It's going to be a late one, folks. Better put more coffee on and call Domino's."

Chapter 43

"I understand, judge, you're almost there." ... Yes Judge. I know Roanoke is two-hundred miles away. Prosecutor Stewart spoke so that everyone in the room could understand the conversation. ... "I don't know. Let me ask." Stewart covered the mouthpiece and said, "He wants to know if we can hold the hearing in his chambers at noon tomorrow."

Cass was frustrated, but nodded her assent. It would have to do. "That's fine Judge," Stewart confirmed. "But I think we'd better get search warrants on this guy from one of the magistrate court judges. That may give us more evidence for the arrest warrant hearing." Stewart listened then nodded to let everyone know the judge agreed. "Fine. Thank you, Judge. So sorry to interrupt your trip."

Stewart hung up, sighed deeply, and leaned back in his chair. "Well that's that. What do you want to do now?"

"I'll have Mary track down a magistrate judge" Cass said. "We won't execute the search warrants until tomorrow morning anyway. I want to hit Barlow's office and his home simultaneously. That will take practically the whole force."

It took over two hours to find a magistrate judge, make the evidentiary presentation, and get the search warrants signed. With warrants in hand, Cass wearily gave the group final instructions.

"Eric, be in here at six in the morning to organize the teams. You'll lead the team at his office. I'll lead at his house. We'll brief everyone at seven and plan on an eight o'clock execution time. Any questions?"

"Needless to say, I'm new at this," Sam said. "What do you need from me?"

"I want you and Mary to be here for the morning briefing. Then the two of you can set up an evidence table in my office and stand by to process and catalogue everything we bring in."

"Got it," Sam said. "Mary, how about we come in at six-thirty. You brew the coffee, and I'll bring the donuts."

"Works for me," Mary said, her eyes alight. "Oh, this is so exciting. I don't know if I'll be able to sleep tonight."

Cass nodded. "I don't think any of us will, but we better try. She tiredly ran her fingers through her hair. "Tomorrow's going to be a big day. I think we're about to catch our evening gown killer."

Chapter 44

Ricky watched in frustration as the sun sank behind Lonetree Mountain. *What a wasted day. Maybe she's really not here. Maybe she's—God knows where.* But he had little choice but to continue his search. If Sam wasn't in Summersville, the game was over. *Welcome to San Felipe, Mexico,* he thought.

The tiny resort town 150 miles south of Mexicali on the Gulf of California was his last-resort refuge of choice. It had a sizable American ex-patriot population and was close enough to San Diego that he could occasionally duck back across the border for a quick sanity break. Plus, it was far enough away that the goon would likely never be able to find him.

His remaining money would last two, maybe three years down there. Hell, if he went native, it might last him ten. But could he really live on a desert coast with no trees, nothing but rocks, sand, and 120-degree summertime temperatures? Hell, he didn't even speak Spanish. It was not a prospect he relished. All of that could be avoided if he could just talk to Sam.

For the last two hours he'd been fighting off the shakes. God, what he'd give for a drink. Trouble was that if he had one, he'd have a dozen—and he couldn't afford that.

But giving up alcohol didn't mean giving up everything. He drove slowly past Appleby's checking every car. Then he pulled into a space at the now near-empty south end of the shopping center parking lot. He looked quickly around to make sure no one was watching then reached into the center console and withdrew a small dark-amber vial and a small mirror. Alcohol might dull his senses, but a good shot of cocaine wouldn't.

Thus fortified, he thought, *Maybe I'll run up to Wal-Mart again. Then I'll run by the house and see if any lights are on.* If not, he'd park and wait. Maybe she really had sold the place to someone else, but he had to know. The only alternative was Mexico.

*

Ricky was parked in the same place he'd been ever since just after the sun went down—on the side of McKee's Creek Road a couple of hundred yards past the old Martin house. For the past hour, a full bladder and an empty stomach had urged him to abandon his vigil at least for a few minutes. He'd resisted the urge, but now his bladder was *demanding* his attention.

The Quik-go convenience store and gas station at the corner of Broad Street and Arbuckle Road was where he could solve both problems and still keep an eye out for anyone turning down McKee's Creek Road. Sam's house was just three blocks down. You could almost see it from the Quik-go.

As he stepped back into the Escalade with a cup of coffee and fried pie in hand, he looked up and saw Sam turning right off Broad Street onto McKee's Creek Road right in front of him. He only caught a glance of her, but he'd recognize that Camry anywhere. Oh how he hated that car.

Yes! He was about to start the Escalade and pull in behind her, but the driver in the vehicle directly behind her stopped him cold. Sam's friend Cass driving a sheriff's department SUV, turned and followed her. He watched as both vehicles braked in front of Sam's house. The Camry pulled in the driveway. The SUV parked out front

Had Sam seen him? She'd looked in his direction just as she turned. If she had spotted him, she'd tell Cass. Better move. No sense taking any chances.

He saw the light bar on the roof of the Durango come to life as he started his vehicle. He hurriedly pulled through the Quik-go parking lot and turned north on Broad Street. He went two blocks to Main St. As he turned left he saw the flashing police lights of the Durango pull into the Quik-go.

Damn it! Why'd she have to have her cop friend hanging around? He went two blocks then turned left again on Alderson Avenue. He drove a block and a half then parked well off the street and turned off his lights.

At least I know she's here, he thought. He'd wait long enough for her cop friend to go home then cautiously approach the house.

No matter what, he had to talk to her tonight.

*

Cass had followed Sam home to stash a birthday present for Gary. She was surprised when Sam came running to the SUV with a frightened look. She opened the passenger door and jumped in. "I think I just saw Ricky down at the Quik-go," she said.

"Are you sure?"

"Pretty sure. Whoever it was, he was getting into a white Escalade just like Ricky's.

"Don't you have a restraining order against him?"

"There's one in New York but not here. I don't know, Cassie, maybe it wasn't him. Maybe I'm just being paranoid."

"We'd better go check. Better safe than sorry. If it's Ricky, we can throw a little scare into him. Cass switched on the light bar and made a hasty three-point turn.

They pulled slowly through the Quik-go parking lot, but the Escalade Sam saw earlier was gone. Cass pulled directly in front of the convenience store's door, jumped out and said, "Stay here. Sam saw her walk up and down the aisles then speak to the cashier.

She watched Cass hand the woman her business card then come back out. "Clerk said that somebody matching his description was here all right. She said he bought a fried pie and a cup of coffee then left. She didn't see which direction."

"Ricky loves those fried pies," Sam said quietly. "I'm sure it was him."

"What do you want to do?"

Sam had calmed considerably. "I'll just go home. He never violated the restraining order in New York. No reason to think he'll do it here. But just in case, I'll get an order against him here too."

"I don't want to scare you," Cass said, "but Sammy, a restraining order is only as good as the people they're supposed to restrain. You want to sleep at my house?"

Sam considered it a moment then said, "No. I'll just make sure everything's locked up tight."

"How about I call the city cops and ask them to up their patrols past your house? I'll give my guys the word too."

"That would be fine, but I'm pretty sure he'll stay away."

Cass couldn't conceal her concern. "I want you to sleep with that Glock under your pillow."

"I will, for all the good that will do. I could never use it on Ricky anyway. He can be a bit foul-tempered, but he's actually not a violent man."

"Probably true, but remember, there's always our friend, Dr. Thomas Barlow, to worry about."

Sam shuttered. "Thanks for reminding me," she said with mock gratitude. "That'll help me sleep *soooo* much better tonight."

"You want me to walk through the house with you?"

Sam sighed. "No, I'll be fine. With what's happening tomorrow, you've got enough on your mind. Get out of here and I'll see you in the morning."

*

Sam had just changed into her long sleeping tee shirt when she heard a soft rap on the front door. It was ten thirty and it wasn't Cass. She would have used her key and just walked in.

Ricky. She threw on a pair of PJ bottoms and pulled a white hoodie over her tee-shirt. She debated briefly before taking her 9 mm off the dresser and shoving it into the pocket of the hoodie.

She padded down the stairs, turned on the porch light, pulled aside the door curtain and looked out. Indeed it was Ricky standing there. He was thinner, haggard, looking like he had aged years in just a few months. He had a hang-dog, morose, appearance that at once repulsed her and made her feel sorry for him.

She replaced the curtain, checked the door-chain and prayed, "Lord, help me through this." She cracked the door open and said the first words she'd spoken to him since the divorce. "What do you want, Ricky?"

"Hi, Sam," he said, shuffling his feet and backing away slightly. His eyes never left the floor. "Can I talk to you?"

"What about? You know you're not supposed to be here. That was our deal, remember?"

"I remember. It's just that I miss you and wanted to say hi. I know I screwed up big time. I don't blame you if you hate me. I was stupid. I just wanted to tell you I was sorry. That's all."

It wasn't all. Sam knew the speech was just the butter-up. She'd lived with him long enough to know another shoe would drop. But regardless, his words still tugged at her heart. For all the stupid things he'd done, she had loved him once. A sudden lump formed in her throat. But that wouldn't make her drop her guard. "There's more, isn't there?"

Ricky shuffled his feet. His head dropped lower. Sam thought she saw his lip quiver. "Yeah, there is. A lot more. I'm in trouble, Sam—big trouble. Can I come in?"

Against her better judgment, Sam's heart overruled her head. She slid the chain out of its slot, opened the door and said, "You look terrible."

Chapter 45

Where the hell was Sam? With eight of the twelve members of the department sitting in their chairs in the briefing room, the meeting was about to get underway. This wasn't like Sam at all. She was always prompt; always reliable. If something had come up she would have called. She pulled Deputy Dixon aside and whispered to him, "Jess, Sam's supposed to be here. Could you go over to her house and see if anything's wrong?"

"Sure, Dixon replied. "Be back in twenty-minutes."

"Cass briefed her team first, drawing a diagram of Dr. Barlow's yard. Now it was Deputy Zeeman's turn to brief the deputies going to Barlow's office. As she paced back and forth at the back of the room, Cass speed dialed Sam's number for the third time. Again her call went straight to voice mail.

Deputy Dixon walked back in. "What'd you find?" Cass whispered anxiously.

"Front and back doors were locked. Her car's in the driveway. I knocked but no one answered," Dixon whispered back

"Thanks, Jess," she said. *Something's definitely wrong.* Maybe she was sick. Maybe she fell down or something. Cass refused to let herself even think about the other awful possibility. Yet there it was, lurking, ever present—and there were three bodies to prove it.

Then there was Ricky. Was he really in town? Had Sam actually seen him last night? Was he so far gone that he'd harm Sam? Questions, questions, questions.

"Where are you Sam?" she mumbled to herself. "Where the hell are you?"

*

The instant the meeting broke up, Cass made the quick drive to Sam's house. As Dixon had said, her unlocked car was still in the driveway, her computer case was lying in the passenger seat. "Sam! Sam!" she called as she opened the front door and rushed through the house.

There were no apparent signs of a struggle. No overturned chairs, no broken glass. Just an unwashed dish on the counter and two glasses and a cereal bowl in the sink. She rushed upstairs to the bedroom. The bed was made. Had it been slept in or did she make it fresh this morning?" *Sam, where the hell are you?"*

She looked at her watch. Five minutes to eight. Time was up. She had the signed no-knock search warrant for Barlow's house in her pocket. Both teams were supposed to hit the buildings at the same time."

Where the hell are you, Sam? her mind screamed again as she cleared the stairs three at a time and bolted out the front door.

*

"Search warrant," Deputy Zeeman shouted while banging on the office door. Zeeman and the two officers accompanying him were intimidating, dressed in full SWAT team gear. There was no response. Zeeman expected none. Chiropractors didn't usually keep Saturday hours. "Okay Mr. Johnson," he said to the building's owner who accompanied the team, "go ahead and open it."

Zeeman and the two deputies accompanying him poured into the building, guns drawn, shouting "Sheriff's department, search warrant," as they went. No one was present in the reception area. Two doors presented themselves at the back of the room. One led

250

straight ahead, the other to a room on the left. The second deputy, Chuck Wellman, threw the front-facing door open, pulled down on the space with his AR-15 and swept the interior. It was a small bathroom/supply closet combination. "Clear!" he shouted. One door remained. Zeeman shouted the police warning then swung it open and stepped in, sweeping the interior with his gun as he went.

The only object in the room that someone could hide behind was a standard chiropractic table. He verified that no one was hiding there then shouted to his companions, "Clear!" The building was secure.

Zeeman keyed the radio mic on his shoulder and said, "Unit 9, Unit 1"

"Go ahead Unit 9," Cass's voice answered.

"We've executed on the office. Negative on the suspect. We're proceeding with site processing. Over."

"10-4, Unit 9, keep me posted."

The office was sparse, Spartan, even. A single medium-sized wood desk with an L-shaped return faced three waiting room chairs. A small table sat beside the last chair and had three magazines stacked precisely at its center.

The desk was home to an older CRT computer monitor. The tower, equally aged, resided in the foot well of the desk. A small laser printer sat on the desk return. All the items on the desk top were arranged in perfect order. A matching upright four-drawer filing cabinet, bereft of anything on its top, stood against the wall behind the desk. The drawers were neatly labeled; Patients, Accounts Payable, Accounts Receivable, and General Ledger/Misc.

There was nothing personal—no pictures on the walls, mementos on the desk, nothing. The only decoration of any kind was a framed medical-school diploma on the wall behind the desk which established the doctor's credentials.

"Wellman, you start on the computer," Zeeman instructed. "The invoice they found yesterday was computer generated, probably from here. We're looking for anything with our victims' names. Once you've given his computer files a good look, we'll take the machine over to the courthouse and have the IT guys go through the hard drive."

"Deputy Hansen, you process the treatment room. I'll start on the file cabinet."

*

Three sheriff's department squad cars and Cass's SUV were parked out of sight around the corner from Dr. Barlow's home. "We go on foot from here, quick and silent," Cass instructed. "Bradley, you go down the driveway and cover the right side and back of the house. Keep an eye on the garage. We'll clear that as soon as we clear the house. Hudson, cover the left side of the house from the front.

Also present was the local locksmith. "Mr. Pickett, you stay back until I wave you up to the porch. I want you to look at the locks and tell me how fast you can get them open. If it's more than just a few seconds, say so and we'll go ahead and use the door ram. Jamison, you're on the ram. I'll do the warrant announcement. We'll give him two shout-outs before we go in. Got it?"

All the officers nodded.

"And for the record, boys, let's try to not shoot each other, okay?" The officers laughed. If any were reluctant to follow a woman into this battle, they kept that fact to themselves.

Cass led the officers at a swift trot around the corner and up to Barlow's house. At the driveway they split to take their assigned positions. Cass and Jerry Jamison, who was toting the heavy battering ram, mounted the front steps. They stood on opposite sides of the front door and held their position for a few seconds until hearing Deputy Bradley whisper into his shoulder mic, "Unit 6."

Cass drew her weapon, banged loudly on the front door and shouted, "Sheriff's Department! Search Warrant!" She waited twenty seconds, banged the door again, and repeated the announcement, this time adding, "Open up, Dr. Barlow!"

No response. She tried the doorknob to confirm it was locked. She waived Pickett forward. The man looked at the locks and said, "The door latch is no problem, but the deadbolt is a good one. Might take me a couple of minutes."

"Too long," Cass said. Clear out of here, Mr. Pickett, and thanks for your help. "Go ahead, Jerry."

Deputy Jamison stepped in front of the door, heaved back on the heavy battering ram, and slammed it into the door beside the latch. The door jamb splintered and the door flew open.

"Sheriff's Department!" they all shouted as they rushed through the entry. Cass saw straight through a long hallway to the back of the house. To the right was what appeared to be the living room.

She pointed, telling Jamison to go there. On her left was an elegant dining area. She poked her head in quickly to get a snapshot of the place in her mind before entering. She saw no one. She crouched and stepped in, clearing the room with her weapon as she went. Her glance inside the room was confirmed. No one was present. "Clear!" she shouted.

"Clear!" she heard Jamison shout from the living room.

At the back of the dining area was a wide archway that led straight into the kitchen. And what a kitchen it was—large and well-equipped, with a commercial cooktop, and two commercial ovens. The refrigerator was huge. The center of the kitchen was taken up by a butcher block food-prep island. There was a rack above the island from which dangled a large assortment of pans and utensils. The counters held commercial-grade mixers and toaster ovens and other appliances, some of which Cass had never seen the likes of before. It all befitted the doctor's reputation as a gourmet chef.

"Clear!" she shouted as she went from the kitchen into a large family room that took up the entire back of the house. "Clear!" She shouted again in the family room. Almost simultaneously the same shout came from Jamison in another room. A few seconds later, he repeated his announcement as he cleared yet another room then entered the family room through the hallway entrance.

"First floor clear?" she asked. He nodded. "Secure the stairway. We'll both go up." She keyed her shoulder mic. "Units 6 and 11, first floor is secure. Secure the garage. Repeat, secure the garage. Then come into the house. Copy?"

"Copy," Hudson's call came back.

"Copy," Bradley responded.

She unlocked the back door for them then joined Jamison at the foot of the stairway leading off the foyer to the upstairs.

"Sheriff's Department. Show yourself!" Jamison shouted in a deep, booming voice.

Only silence from upstairs.

"Go ahead," Cass said quietly. They proceeded up the stairs, sweeping their guns to every possible place someone might emerge. Once on the second floor they quickly cleared the three bedrooms and the bathroom up there.

"Upstairs clear!" Cass shouted down to the two deputies who'd come in through the back door.

"Looks like we missed him," Cass said as they gathered in the family room. "Hudson, you and Brad move the vehicles in. Let's get the crime-scene stuff set up. Jerry, get the print kit. Let's dust this place down."

While the three officers hurried about their tasks, Cass wandered through the house. She walked up the hallway and stuck her head into the guest bathroom for a quick look-see then went to the den Jamison had cleared. It was a nicely-done man cave— heavy wood desk, walnut bookshelves, a couple of brown leather chairs. No computer, but there was a laptop docking port and keyboard. *Probably has the computer with him,* she surmised. This room would likely be the focus of their search.

She wandered to the foyer and turned left into the living room— and stopped dead in her tracks. *My God, it's Sam!*

On the back wall over the fireplace mantle was a portrait that could have been a photograph of Sam at the Ladies Auxiliary Ball. Cass had to take a couple of steps forward before she could see by the subtle differences in the eyes and facial structure that the picture was not of Sam. But the hair and dress were startling similar. "Gotcha," Cass said softly as she recognized the ribbon depicted around the woman's neck. She stepped closer.

The ribbon was identical in every detail to the ones on the victims, the one's she and Sam had worn to the ball, right down to the same pearl fasteners. *How the hell could he not have reacted when he saw what we were wearing?* "Barlow, you are one cold-hearted bastard," she whispered.

Now she knew Sam must be in the hands of Dr. Barlow. She ran out the door to grab her crime-scene camera from the SUV and passed Jamison on her way. "Set this place up as a crime scene," she said. "Get the tape out and make sure everyone handles evidence properly."

"What's up?" Jamison was puzzled by her sudden agitation.

"That picture in the living room is *prima facie* evidence that the doc's our perp. I think he has Sam.

Cass snapped several pictures of the portrait. She'd need them for the arrest warrant hearing. She found Jamison. "I'm leaving you in charge of this crime scene while I run over to Sam's." She jumped into the SUV and peeled out, lights flashing and siren wailing. "Damn you Samantha Martin. Don't you let this bastard kill you," she pled as she went. She picked up the radio mic. "Unit 1, Dispatch."

"Dispatch."

"Mary, I think Barlow's got Sam. I want you to upgrade the APB. Make it priority one for all agencies and alert them that he may have a victim with him. Notify the FBI and get them over here. We'll fax a description and picture to all police agencies in the state and the highway patrol. Pull out all the stops. I'm on my way to Sam's house. Pull Zeeman off the doctor's office search and put Wellman in charge over there. Have Zeeman meet me at Sam's. Call in every off-duty deputy we've got, even the night-shift. We need all hands on deck and we need them now!"

Chapter 46

Her first conscious thought this morning was of waking naked and disoriented in a tiny cell with metal-covered walls. She had a terrible headache. When she touched the side of her face, she yelped in pain. It was badly swollen.

She remembered shaking her head, trying to clear the fog of her clouded memory. She should know where she was, but it wouldn't come together in her head.

Then came the voice. It seemed to be coming right out of the walls "Good morning, my dear. My, you look lovely."

She jumped, screamed, and tried to cover herself. Could he really see her?

"There, there," the voice chided. "You've nothing to hide from me, Susan. It's going to be so wonderful getting to know each other again."

"You're crazy!" she screamed. "My name's not Susan. Leave me alone. I don't care what you've already seen, you're not seeing more. You'll never get away with this!"

"That's what my other guests said. But they were all wrong. They've all checked out now, and I'm still here. I've waited for you so long. I've missed you so much, Susan. More than you'll ever know."

"I said my name's not Susan, you pervert. People know me. They're already looking for me."

"Oh, I'm sure they are. But they'll never find you here. I'm afraid it's just you and me. I'm sorry about your face. I have some Tylenol out here, and breakfast's almost ready. There's a toothbrush and toothpaste in the little alcove above your bed. There's a water faucet above the toilet. I know it'll be hard to get used to dining without your clothing, but I do insist you join me. You really can't say no. The Eggs Benedict will be quite delicious, I assure you. Please be ready in ten minutes."

Her attempt at a leg sweep to take him down as she came out of the cell failed miserably. He moved deftly and clubbed her down as easily as one might swat a gnat. Now she lay fully exposed in this macabre barber's chair. What else did he have in store for her? Would anyone ever find her? Would anyone know where to even look? She didn't want to show her weakness, her vulnerability, but she couldn't help it. She broke down and wept.

"There, there, my dear. No need to cry. We're going to be great friends," Barlow said. You've just got to learn the house rules, that's all. The first rule is that I get whatever I want. The second rule is, well—uh, there is no second rule. Let me give you some guidelines. Never, and I mean never, argue with me. When I ask you to do something, you do it—now. And never ever be disrespectful.

"I expect you to participate fully in our little discussions. You can ask questions, state your opinions, tell me jokes, talk about your family, your likes, your dislikes—all that stuff. Just don't be disrespectful. And by the way, I'm the one who decides what's disrespectful.

"I'm sorry you had to learn the hard way. Why don't I just put this in the freezer?" He pointed at the stainless steel bowl on a side-table that now contained the bloody severed little toe from her left foot which he had removed using a pair of ordinary wire cutters. "I promise I'll put it back on before you leave," Dr. Barlow said, "and you won't feel a thing when I do."

At first she was awash in a sea of pain and shock, but after the fact, the man had administered a shot of pain killer. He must not have liked her screaming. At least she wouldn't bleed to death. Barlow had expertly staunched the blood flow and bandaged the foot. But she knew with certainty that any hope of leaving this place alive was as dead as her severed toe. *So much for martial arts.* She thought. *Damn it! I worked so hard on that leg sweep.*

Chapter 47

Cass was frantic. "I'm coming Sam, I'm coming," she said resolutely as she pulled into Sam's driveway for the second time this morning. Sam's car was still in the driveway, right where it had been earlier. Cass did a fast check of the yard to make sure Sam wasn't down somewhere outside. She put on latex gloves and crime scene booties over her shoes then opened the front door, trying to avoid smudging any latent prints. This time her look through the house was more deliberate, much more thorough.

She started upstairs in the master bath. Nothing seemed amiss. The towels were still slightly damp. She checked the soap dish in the shower. The underside of the soap bar was slightly moist and gooey. Sam had taken a shower this morning. That was good. It meant she hadn't been missing for all that long.

As Cass came back downstairs, her eyes misted over. This wasn't just another investigation. It was Sam, the closest thing she had to a sister. She began to question whether she could be objective enough to keep her emotions from getting in the way.

She shook off the doubt, telling herself that she was a professional and that no one in the world had more reason to see that everything was done right. She'd find time for crying later. Right now there was only Sam and the job of finding her before that monster could kill her best friend.

Downstairs looked the same as earlier—nothing broken or out of place—no struggle. In the sink was an unwashed cereal bowl, a plate, two glasses, a juice glass, a spoon and a fork and a coffee cup. The milk residue and a couple of corn flakes that remained in the bottom of the bowl hadn't dried out. Sam had eaten breakfast.

The plate had what looked like cake crumbs and dried traces of frosting on it. The two glasses appeared to have contained milk. One of them had what looked to Cass like chocolate cake crumbs remaining in it. The residue in the glasses was completely dried. *Last night*, she thought.

Although Dr. Barlow occupied most of her mind, she also thought of Ricky—tall, ruggedly handsome Ricky who could charm the fuzz off a peach. *Oh Sam, you didn't let him in, did you?* The more she thought about it, the more that seemed possible. Good old tenderhearted Sam. She always was a sucker for a sob story.

Barlow? Ricky? Barlow? Ricky? She weighed both possibilities then made up her mind. Barlow was the proven killer.

"What's up Sheriff?" Deputy Zeeman asked as he walked through the door.

"I'm pretty sure Barlow has Sam."

"Are you kidding? Think he's ballsy enough to do that?"

"It's not a question of balls; it's a question of crazy." She told him about the portrait. "I'm not kidding, when I walked into that living room, I thought it was Sam staring down from the wall. The ribbon around the neck of the woman in the portrait clinched it. Barlow's our evening gown murderer. The really creepy part is that on the night of the Ladies Auxiliary Ball, Sam was dressed in a gown nearly identical to the one in the portrait. She and I both wore the ribbons found on the victims that night specifically to see if we could provoke a reaction from anyone. Barlow didn't give us a clue. He even danced with Sam knowing she was practically a clone of the woman in the portrait. Want to know if he's ballsy enough? I think that's your answer. What'd you find in his office?"

"They're dusting and processing the place now. You know the writing on that back of that invoice?"

"Yeah."

"That's the way he writes everything. All his patient records are in that same weird shorthand. We figure how to read that, and we'll know a lot more than we know now."

Eric had to see the other side of the coin. "We have another possible perp," she said. "Last night, Sam thought she saw her ex at the Quik-go. I talked to the clerk and confirmed that a guy matching his description was there. We tried to spot him in town but couldn't. I dropped Sam off here just before ten. I think some of the dishes in the sink were from last night—two glasses and a plate. "Sam doesn't normally eat late at night. The ex could have shown up and talked her into letting him in. I want those dishes swabbed for DNA and dusted for prints.

"I'm pretty sure Sam was here this morning. The towels in her bathroom are still damp, and the soap's gooey. She probably got up early to come in just like she said she would." Cass pointed at the dishes in the sink. "She ate breakfast. Her cereal bowl has fresh residue. Those dishes may be our only physical evidence so be careful processing them.

"I've got to get to the courthouse for the arrest-warrant hearing. You stay here and set this place up as a crime scene. Nobody in or out except the investigating officers. I'll have Mary send help. Sorry to abandon you, Eric. I'll be back as soon as I can."

Chapter 48

The best word to describe Judge Crenshaw's chambers was *crowded*. His desk took up almost half the room. There was only knee space between the desk and the ancient-looking leather-bound, high-backed chairs that lined the wall. A court reporter sat at a steno machine to the side of and behind the judge. Cass listened as Prosecutor Stewart made the evidentiary presentation.

"Understandably, the evidence is circumstantial," Stewart said. "But the diversity of origin, the circumstances of its discovery, particularly of the invoice found in the dead woman's car, and the link between the portrait in Dr. Barlow's house and an item found on the bodies of the three victims, makes any other conclusion as to the identity of this dangerous killer highly improbable. Sheriff Rosier would like to explain that link."

The judge nodded toward Cass and said, "Go ahead, sheriff."

"Thank you, Your Honor. We obtained no-knock search warrants from the magistrate court last night which gave us the right to enter the residence of Dr. Thomas Barlow at 1125 West Huckleberry Circle, and his office located at 274 W. Main Street. Those warrants were executed this morning at 8:00 a.m. In the process of executing the warrant at the residence, I discovered a painting, a portrait of a woman, hanging on the living-room wall of Dr. Barlow's residence. I took pictures of the portrait. I also have pictures of the three young women whose bodies have turned up here in Nicholas County."

Cass spread the pictures in front of the judge. "Note the ribbons and pearl pins around the neck of each body. They are handmade necklaces, all three identical. I have the actual ribbons and pins we found on the bodies with me, judge." She removed three evidence bags from her briefcase and deposited them on the judge's desk. "These ribbons and pins are the one single thread that is common to all three murder victims."

Then she picked up her camera and set it on the desk with the back facing the judge so he could see the display screen. She turned the camera on and flicked through a number of pictures until she found the one she wanted. It was a headshot that showed the face and neck of the woman in the portrait. "I took this picture this morning at Dr. Barlow's house. Notice that the ribbon and pin depicted in the portrait is identical to the three ribbons and pins we found on the three murder victims. Since these are unique, handmade artifacts, we believe that either Dr. Barlow made them himself or had them made for him."

Stewart spoke. "Judge, we have a situation this morning. My assistant, Ms. Samantha Martin, and Sheriff Rosier each wore one of these ribbons to the Ladies' Auxiliary Ball last week. Ms. Martin bears a striking resemblance to the woman depicted in the portrait. This morning, both she and Dr. Barlow are missing. We suspect that Barlow may have kidnapped her. We believe it is imperative that the court issue an arrest warrant for Dr. Barlow immediately."

"Hmm," the judge said as he looked at the photos and rubbed his stubbly jaw. "Got any evidence that points to anybody else?"

"No." Stewart said. "Everything so far points to Mr. Barlow."

"You'd better pick him up then. I'm assuming you're going to want all of these exhibits marked and moved into evidence?"

"Yes, Judge." Stewart confirmed. "We'd ask that the picture in the camera be duplicated in digital media and printed, and that the print copies be admitted as evidence since the sheriff needs the camera in her further investigations."

"You've got the portrait don't you?"

"Yes Judge, we do."

"Under the rules of best evidence, we'll admit the portrait instead. Have your officers bring it to my office. Let the record show that the county prosecutor has presented sufficient evidence to show probable cause that Dr. Thomas Barlow should be arrested and held by the county until such time as he can be brought before the court to answer the accusation of murder committed by him against the persons of Angelina Jean Basso, Naomi Quinn, and Jennifer Oldroyd. Mr. Stewart, you'll prepare the warrant. Have it to me within thirty minutes, and I'll sign it. Otherwise you'll have to chase me all the way to Roanoke."

"I've got it right here." Stewart held up a prepared, unsigned warrant in his hand.

"That solves that." The judge signed the warrant and handed it back to Stewart. "Now you people get out of here. If I don't get on the road, you'll be swearing out one of those for my wife. She said if I wasn't back in Roanoke by five o'clock she'd kill me."

Chapter 49

Deputies were already showing up with boxes of evidence seized from Barlow's home and business when Cass got back to her office. But she was more concerned about what was happening at Sam's house. She picked up her phone and called Zeeman.

"How's it going, Eric?" she asked.

"Fine. I'm about wrapped up here. How do you want me to leave the place?"

"Leave the crime-scene tape up. We don't want some kid coming through and messing with the car or other stuff on the property."

"Will do."

She hung up and turned to Mary. "What's the status with the other two search teams?"

"Wellman and Hansen are done with Barlow's office. Jamison and his team should be getting pretty close to finishing up his house."

"Tell Jamison to leave Hudson in charge at the doc's house and come on in. I want a debriefing in my office in one hour. I'll need Zeeman, Jamison, Wellman, and you. Let the duty deputy handle calls while you're with us. We need to get the geeks going on the computer forensics."

"Already happening," Mary said. "I've got the county IT guy and one of his assistants setting Barton's computers up in the War Room."

"Like I said, what would I do without you, Mary? They'll need a deputy with them when they get the machines running. Use Wellman."

The chairs in her office had been haphazardly pushed aside to accommodate the new evidence table. But there was a problem—no room. *This isn't going to work,* she thought. She had to find another solution.

Cass walked to the War Room and found the table Sam had been using as a desk an utter mess. Sam's stuff was pushed into a pile in the middle while the geeks set up Barlow's computers on each end. New cables and power cords that crisscrossed the table looked like a mass of black spaghetti.

She's going to love that, Cass thought wryly. What she'd give to see Sam walk through the door and start screaming about the invasion of her space. Her eyes turned misty at the thought. Then she fought her emotions down. *No time for tears,* Cass scolded herself. Sam needed her. She could not let tears overwhelm her professionalism.

Cass had to reclaim the space in her office, and the war room was already full to overflowing.

The commission chambers, she thought. The commissioners might not like it, but there were two big tables in there and plenty of room to spread evidence boxes out. The next commission meeting wasn't until Thursday night. That gave her five days to make other arrangements.

She walked to the front office. "Mary, we're setting up a new temporary War Room. Assign a couple of deputies to transfer everything from the warrant searches to the commission chamber."

"That's going to make some people unhappy," Mary said.

"Screw 'em," Cass snapped. "Finding Sam is more important than the sanctity of that room."

*

The commission chamber was large enough to handle a couple of hundred people in theater-style seats. At the front was a raised dais where the three commissioners held forth behind pontifical raised benches as they conducted the business of the county. The well was an approximately 15 foot wide open area which separated the commission benches from two eight-foot-long witness tables, behind each of which were four upholstered leather chairs. Between the tables was a podium for citizens and witnesses bringing information before the commission.

This is our new War Room. Cass thought. *I'll fight it out with the Commissioners later.* The normal stately quiet of the chamber was quickly disrupted as evidence boxes were brought in and lined up along the south wall of the well. The debriefing group pulled one witness table back so everyone could sit around it.

"You go first, Eric," Cass said. "What did you find at Sam's house?"

"Not much, just what you saw when you were there. There were no signs of a struggle, no blood inside the house, nothing like that. I agree with your assessment that she was there this morning. The presence of her car would indicate she left the property by other means. We tried to get prints off the front doorknob but it was too smudged. We did dust the unwashed dishes and swabbed them for DNA. We found latent prints on all of them. Mary's already sent them off to the FBI."

"Mary, how soon can we expect results?" Cass asked.

"Their turnaround is anywhere from four hours to a day. I sent them in an hour ago."

Cass looked across the table at Jamison. "Jerry, how about the doc's house?"

"Hard to tell what we've got. We found a few prints. We're assuming they're the doc's. The guy's a real neat-nick. All his files were in meticulous order, mostly personal bills and stuff. Not much in the way of personal correspondence or family records.

"The guy writes real funny. You can hardly figure it out. It's like a code or something. You'll see it when you look at the files."

"I've seen it." Cass said. "It *is* weird. Chuck, it's your turn. What did you find at his office?"

"Same thing," deputy Wellman said. "Everything was neat as a pin. Not much in the way of prints. He must have wiped down his treatment table and all the chairs; they were clean as a whistle. We found a couple of prints on the desk and one on the file cabinet. His file cabinet had the usual business papers—receipts and bills, that kind of stuff. He doesn't keep the same kind of patient files a regular doctor does. When someone comes in for treatment, he drops a short handwritten note in the file. Keeps them all in order by the date. Like you said, the writing's weird. I mean you can pick out some of it, but the rest is some sort of gobbledygook."

"Did anyone turn up anything that could give us a hint of where he is this weekend? Cass asked."

The deputies looked at each other and all shook their heads.

"Okay, I want each of you to take the boxes from your searches and start reading," Cass said. Look for anything that tells us where he might be. If you've got credit-card records, let's have the FBI check to see where he's charging stuff. If you turn anything up about another property he owns or uses, we need to look at it. You guys know the drill. We aren't leaving this room until we've read every scrap of paper the man has. Anybody got a problem with that?"

No one voiced an objection.

"Can I help with anything?" Mary asked. "With all these officers stuck here in the office there's not going to be much dispatching going on."

"What would you like to do?"

"How about if I take some of those patient records and start reading. I can do that while I dispatch."

"Sounds good to me," Cass said, giving her a quick shoulder hug. Just make sure you keep everything in order and log each record in and out. Ok, people, let's get to it. I'm going to go canvas Sam's neighborhood. Maybe someone saw something."

*

Cass knocked on every door on both sides of McKee's Creek Road for more than two blocks in each direction. No one had noticed a thing this morning. *What good are neighbors if they don't keep an eye out for you?* she wondered.

The frustration and fear for her best friend were getting to her. It was mid-afternoon. She was about to knock on yet another door but the reality was that all she wanted to do was sit down on the curb, bury her head in her arms, and cry. It was getting harder by the minute to stave off that paralyzing instinct. Her radio suddenly crackled to life. "Dispatch, Unit 1."

"Unit 1," she answered despondently.

"Unit 1, could you come to the office?"

"Sure, Mary. Why?"

"Because I think I know where Barlow is."

"What?" Cass practically shouted. If Mary made such a claim it was with good reason.

"I'm not one-hundred-percent sure, but I think I've figured out that note on the back of the invoice they found in Jennifer's car."

"I'll be right there." Cass flew off the porch of the house she was at and sprinted the two blocks back to her SUV. She left the neighborhood with tires squealing and lights flashing. Rather than stop at the intersection by the Quik-go, she used her siren.

Chapter 50

Cass burst through the courthouse doors and ran straight to Mary's desk. "What have you got?" she asked breathlessly.

"Can we go to your office?" Mary asked.

"Yes, yes. Of course.

Mary followed her in, carrying a sheet of paper in one hand and a file folder in the other. She laid both on Cass's desk and explained. "While I was reading some of the doctor's stuff this afternoon, I started noticing a pattern. I watch Wheel of Fortune on TV, and I'm pretty good at it."

"Yes," Cass said, a little exasperated that talk of a television show was getting in the way of Mary's revelation.

"You know how they reveal words or phrases one letter at a time until someone guesses it?"

"I know how the game works."

"I swear I was beginning to read words into the doctor's notes. Here, I'll show you." Mary pointed to the cover of a patient file she'd brought with her. "He labels every file with the person's name and address. This file's for someone named Dennis Hatcher. The file jacket lists an address in Pittsburg. Must have been traveling through or something. The notes are all handwritten. Since there's only one note in this file, he must have treated Mr.

Hatcher just once." Mary extracted the note and pointed to the top of the page.

Nm: Hatcher, Dennis
Adr: Ptsbg, PA

"See how he abbreviated Pittsburg? He does that in nearly every note. If you read this one, knowing that most of the words are abbreviations, you can start figuring out what it says. Like here, he spells Summersville 'Sumvll.' And here I think he's talking about lumbar muscles which he spells 'lmbr.'

"When I started recognizing some of these words and seeing numbers with them, it reminded me of something." Mary pointed to the separate sheet of paper she'd brought in—a copy of the back of the invoice recovered from Jennifer Oldroyd's car. "Remember this?" She pointed to the cryptic note:

Arbk 5M, Cnvs, +2M, CR39/4 L1. 9M - RR.

"It's still Gobbledygook to me," Cass said.

"Not if you're a Wheel of Fortune player." Mary pointed to the Cnvs "Pronounce that, sheriff."

"Cavus, Can—something. Wait a minute. Without the vowels, I'd say that's *Canvas*; as in the town across the river?" Cass was getting excited.

"That's right. Now try this." Mary pointed to Arbk.

"Arbu, Arbuk?"

"Try Arbuckle."

Cass rose from her desk, her eyes wide with recognition. "I'll be damned. Arbuckle Road?"

"See the '5M' between those two words? I checked Google Earth for the mileage from Arbuckle Road in Summersville to Canvass—five miles, right on the button. Come to my office. I want to show you something."

Cass stood over Mary's shoulder as she brought up Google Earth on her computer and zoomed directly in on the Summersville area. She scrolled eastward until Canvas was centered on her screen. Mary said, "After I had that much figured out, the rest was easy," She zoomed in further and Cass could actually see individual houses.

"When Arbuckle crosses the river, it turns into Highway 39," Mary explained. The note then says +2M. I assumed that if 'M' meant miles in the first reference, it might mean that here too. Look where 2 miles east of Canvass puts us." Mary used the ruler tool to measure along highway 39 for exactly two miles then scrolled in and pointed to the screen.

Cass looked at Barton's note then back at the screen. "I'll be damned," she muttered. Even though he was just a few steps down the lobby, running to find him would take too long. Cass keyed her radio mic and shouted, "Zeeman, get in here!"

Eric came rushing in. "Yeah," he responded breathlessly.

"Mary's figured out the note on the back of the invoice we recovered from the Oldroyd woman's car." She explained what they had deciphered so far. "Ok Mary, keep going," Cass said.

Mary zoomed back out and selected the same measuring tool. She clicked on the intersection of Hwy. 39 and County Road 39/4 and moved the cursor up the county road until the ruler read 1. 9 miles, she stopped and zoomed out slightly. Where she stopped was in the middle of a heavily wooded area. But as she zoomed further out, a large cleared space appeared on the left. It appeared to be a farm. She centered the place on her screen and zoomed in again. As she did, at one end of the acreage the roof of a building became visible.

The further she zoomed in, the more apparent it was that they were looking at a ranch. The roof they first saw was a large barn. Though it was harder to see, there was what appeared to be a ranch house to the left set nearly against the trees at the end of the cleared space. There were two or three other smaller outbuildings and what appeared to be a sizable corral area. The picture showed cows and horses grazing in the pastures around the house.

"I have no idea what the RR means at the end," Mary said. "There aren't any railroads in the area. But I bet that note is what

Jennifer Oldroyd used to find this place." She pointed at the roof of the house.

"And if Jennifer was there, maybe that's were Sam is now," Cass said, suddenly animated. "Eric, you know anything about that property?"

"Not a thing. I've been out on that road a few times, but I didn't know that place was there. You darn sure can't see it from the road."

Cass picked up the phone on Mary's desk. "What's Reed Hathaway's home number?" Hathaway was the Nicholas County recorder.

Mary consulted her county directory and read off the number.

"Reed," Cass barked when the man answered, "This is the sheriff. I need you over here at the courthouse as fast as you can get here. I've got to know who owns a piece of property. She listened and nodded. "Yes, five minutes will be fine. Thanks."

As she hung up, she said, "If it turns out that the doc owns this property, we already have warrants. We can roll out there with full force. If he doesn't own it, we'll have to go in a lot softer—no probable cause. We can't be violating anyone's rights."

Cass took a deep breath and slowed herself down. Her instinct was to bolt out the door and head for the place right now. But this had to be done right. It had to be planned. And she had to keep her deputies safe.

She looked at Zeeman and said, "That's a big place with several buildings. It's going to take every deputy we've got. Mary, you notified the FBI didn't you?"

"Yes. They said they're not supposed to get involved until someone's been missing for 24 hours, but since there's a potential serial killer involved, they're making an exception and sending down a couple of agents from the Columbia office as observers. I don't know when they'll be here."

"We're not going to wait. Eric, looks like it's going to be just us. Mary, call the state police. They can handle access in and out of the area. She gave Zeeman a hard look. There's not a minute to waste. If this thing's a go, I want to hit that place before sundown, which doesn't give us much time. I'll meet Reed and be back as soon as I have the property ownership information. Any questions?"

Eric and Mary shook their heads.

On the way out the door, Cass said, "Great job, Mary. You're a Redwood among pine trees. We gotta find a way to get you a raise."

Mary beamed.

*

Cass could scarcely contain her impatience. Her foot tapped nervously as the Recorder unlocked his office door. Once inside, she had to wait more interminable minutes for his computer to boot up. Cass handed him a print-out Mary had made of the property and explained to him where it was. He walked over to a stack of large post-binders, sorted through them and selected one out of the middle of the stack. He plopped the book onto the counter and opened it. The maps inside didn't look like regular road maps; they were plot maps—far more difficult for a lay person to decipher.

Hathaway turned pages until he found what he wanted, and then used his finger to trace boundary lines. Finally he said, "Ah-ha, there it is: four-hundred-twenty-acres owned by OmniCom Associates, LLC. Says here they're based in Delaware. Let's see what the abstract says." Hathaway wrote the parcel number on a scratch pad and returned to his computer.

Cass's hopes dimmed. She needed the record to show that the property belonged to Barlow, not some anonymous, amorphous, obscure business entity. She waited far less eagerly for the rest of the information.

"Yup," Hathaway said. "That's it. OmniCom Associates, LLC. Doesn't show any mortgages or liens against the property. The only information we have is the address of their agent of record in Delaware and his phone number. It's clear of taxes and has no clouds on the title. That's the best I can do, Sheriff. Hope that gives you what you want." He printed a copy of the abstract and handed it to her.

Cass's disappointment was palpable. She could barely walk back to her office. They'd still go out to investigate, but all it would be was a friendly visit. If they encountered a locked gate, or if the people weren't home or they refused to let them enter, without a warrant they wouldn't be able to do a thing.

The clock was ticking—going on ten hours since Sam missed the morning meeting. In kidnap cases, every minute, every hour counts. The more time went by, the less chance Cass had of finding Sam unharmed.

No one had to ask about the results of her meeting with the Recorder; it was written all over Cass's face. "The place belongs to a Delaware LLC, some outfit called OmniCom Associates," she said. "I'm afraid all we're going to be able to do is make a social call."

Jerry Jamison raised his hand. "Sheriff, I know that name. It's in the stuff we brought in from the doc's house. It's on one of the files from his desk."

Cass brightened with hope. "Get it," She barked.

The lanky deputy returned a couple of minutes later with a file folder. He held it up and said, "There's a bunch of stuff in here— credit-card receipts with stuff charged at local building supply and feed stores. Gas receipts. Repair bills." Jamison laid the folder on the reception counter and thumbed through its contents. One item caught his attention. He picked it up and looked closer. "I think we got him," he said, looking up triumphantly. "This here's a copy of an application for an account at Stringham's Feed and Seed in the name of that OmniCom outfit. He signed it as the managing general partner."

Cass was jubilant. "That clinches it," she nearly shouted. "The warrant gives us access to all business properties in Barton's possession or under his control located in Nicholas County. She glanced at the wall clock—5:42 p.m. "We've got to hustle or it's going to get dark on us. Jamison, you're on the door-ram again.

Our rally point is 1.9 miles up CR 39/4. We have no idea what we'll find out there, so be on your toes. Who's got the outbuildings?" Four deputies raised their hands. "And who has the back of the house?" Two more raised their hands. One of them said, "We'll come through the back door."

"Hansen, I want you at the entrance to the property at the county road. Zeeman, you're with me and Jamison." To the rest she said, "If you haven't heard your name called, you're going through the front door with the rest of us. I'll take lead. I want everybody in flak-jackets and helmets. We'll use light bars on the road but no sirens. The lights go off once we're on that property. No sense announcing that we're coming. We'll use flash/bangs in the front and the back of the house. Nobody jump the gun. We go on my call. Everybody clear?"

There were nodding heads and a few "yeah's" around the room. "Alright boys, the Nicholas County sheriff's Posse is about to ride."

Chapter 51

Eleven patrol cars were parked on the side of the road behind Cass's SUV.

"There's your RR, sheriff," Zeeman said, pointing at a strip of red plastic flagging ribbon about six feet up the trunk of a sizable pine tree. Cass consulted the print-out of the property Mary had given her. They were gathered at the entrance to an unmarked lane leading to the left into the dense forest. The lane would have been nearly invisible had they been traveling past at normal speed, but Mary's GPS coordinates placed them within fifty feet. The lane was the only break in the forest for nearly a mile on either side.

Every officer had a copy of the print-out. Cass took several minutes to make sure everyone knew exactly where to go once they were on the property then said, "We want to roll in as quiet as possible. Make sure your lights are off, and for God's sake, don't anyone hit their siren. Any questions?"

None were raised so she said, "That's it then. Watch your back and don't shoot each other. Let's go!"

Cass's SUV led the way. She traveled only a short distance before the convoy's progress was halted by a heavy iron gate with a *No Trespassing* sign. "Damn it," she cursed.

Zeeman stopped behind her and together they walked to the gate. A heavy combination padlock with the dial turned away from them toward the ranch secured the latch.

"Whoever locked this is still inside," Cass said. "Otherwise that lock would be facing the other way. Get your bolt cutters, Eric."

Zeeman retrieved the heavy-jawed cutters from his trunk and made short work of the lock. With the latch undone, the gate swung freely. "You stay here," Cass said. "I'll pull down to the edge of the trees to see what I can see. If everything looks good, I'll give you a radio call and you and the other deputies pull up behind me. Then we'll go in hot and hit the place hard."

"You want me to pull down there with you?"

"No. If I have to get out fast, I don't want to have to back over your car."

"Gotcha."

Cass pulled slowly down the lane. The forest was thick, making the roadway like a tunnel. The approaching darkness worried her. It wasn't long until sundown. This thing had to happen while there was still light.

She cautiously approached where the forest ended and the fields began. She stopped her vehicle just short of the fields, grabbed her binoculars, and walked to where she could see across to the other side.

It was exactly as the place looked on Google—a wide expanse of cleared land bisected by the little road. The scene was pastoral. Against the trees on the far side was a cozy-looking, medium-sized log home. A large herringbone barn was on the right, with corrals attached. A number of smaller outbuildings were scattered about. A silver pickup truck was parked in front. Cass had no doubt it was a Dodge Ram, license # WJF-623. No other vehicles were visible.

The road led right up to the porch steps. She and her deputies would be completely exposed to view all the way across the fields. Anyone looking out from the house would see their approach. It was a risk they'd have to take. Given more time, she could have positioned everyone in the woods behind the house. But the sun was setting rapidly. Every passing minute was one the man she believed to be inside the house could use to harm Sam.

On the way back to her vehicle, she keyed her shoulder mic. "All units form up. We are proceeding. Repeat, we are proceeding." She deliberately kept location references out of the call in case anyone in the house had a scanner.

Back in her vehicle, Cass said a quick prayer: "Lord, let me find Sam and let her be safe." She looked in her rear-view mirror and saw Zeeman and the convoy pulled up behind her. She touched her mic and said, "Let's roll!"

The line of police cars barreled out of the woods and across the field. Time was critical. The raid had to go down as fast as possible. Cass bailed out of her vehicle, weapon drawn, and verified the license number on the pickup truck. It *was* the doc's. Behind her, Eric exited his vehicle carrying an AR-15 assault rifle. She dashed up the porch steps and stood to one side of the front door. Eric took the other. Jamison came up carrying the door ram. Behind him a fourth deputy carried another assault rifle and had four round objects dangling from his flak-jacket. They were the flash/bangs.

The fourth deputy joined Cass on her side of the door and set his assault rifle against the wall. He pulled two of the flash/bangs off his flak jacket. They looked like hand grenades and that's exactly what they were, only not the type intended to kill people. They were made of cellulose that shredded into harmless paper when they went off rather than spewing shrapnel. They produced blinding flashes and ear-splitting explosions of sound, but did little or no property damage. They were designed to distract, confuse and disorient, not maim or kill.

Cass's radio crackled. "In position," came the whispered report from the officers at the back of the house.

"Go, go, go," Cass answered back. The deputy with the grenades pulled the pins on two of them and hurled them through the window glass on the left. He quickly repeated the process on right, this time shattering a large plate-glass living room window.

All the officers covered their ears and closed their eyes.

The first two grenades went off with blinding flashes and deafening concussions. A couple of seconds later the next two grenades detonated with equal effect. Almost simultaneously they heard the sound of those thrown into the back of the house by the team entering the rear.

Cass tried the doorknob. Locked. "Now, Jamison," Cass commanded.

The big man stepped forward, drew the ram back and heaved it with a mighty blow against the door. The jamb splintered, and the door slammed open.

Chapter 52

What a nice cauliflower bisque, Dr. Barlow thought as he sliced the last floweret into the bubbling leek soup base. A soaring aria from The Barber of Seville filled the kitchen with sound. The savory liquid on the stove was flavored with finely chopped onions, a hit of garlic, and a small sprinkle of bacon bits. *Tonight's dinner is shaping up nicely,* he thought as he reached for the corn starch to thicken the concoction slightly.

Strange, he thought he heard a woman's voice, but it wasn't coming from the basement. He reached over and turned the music down. Suddenly he heard breaking glass. Panic gripped him. Who in the world could have done that? Then he heard the same from the rear of the house. Someone was breaking in. He dropped the knife and fled for the basement.

As he jerked open the door to the stairwell, bright flashes erupted, accompanied by jarring, deafening concussions. The first came from the front of the house followed by the same from the back. Even as protected as he was from direct exposure, the concussions still made his ears ring.

Through the din, he heard someone shout, "Sheriff's Department!"

Dr. Barlow slammed the door behind him, wishing it had a lock, then he leapt down the stairs. He rushed to where his latest victim laid waiting in the chair. He bent over, kissed her on the forehead and said, "I'm afraid I have to leave you, dear. It appears we have unwelcome company. What a shame we couldn't get to know each other better. Good-bye my dear Susan."

He sprang to the end of the salon counter, opened a drawer, and withdrew a silver .45-caliber automatic and a flashlight. Then he slipped around the corner and banged on the wall precisely at the point where a hidden magnetic latch was located. A cleverly designed, virtually invisible door sprang open just far enough for him to get his fingers around the edge. He swung it fully open.

He could hear shouts from up above and the sound of heavy boot steps—a lot of them. He stepped into a hidden space between the salon wall and the foundation and swung the secret door closed.

"Damn," he cursed, Light from the salon still spilled around the end of the door; the magnetic latch hadn't fully caught. He opened the door and pulled it closed again with the same result. The door was only open a crack, but it was enough for someone to detect its presence if they looked closely.

He heard louder voices and heavy footsteps coming down the stairs. He shined his flashlight down the stone foundation of the house, took three steps and ducked into an opening. The passage wasn't large. It was dark and dank and foreboding, but it was there. He always thought he might need it someday. Today was that day. He stepped into the passage and allowed the earth to swallow him.

Chapter 53

"Sheriff's Department! Do not move!" Cass shouted as she stepped through the door and cleared the room with her pistol. Eric and the other officers followed on her heels, each shouting the same warning.

Cass found herself in a western-style living room. She quickly looked behind the furniture to make sure no one was hiding there while Halverson checked out what appeared to be a clothes closet.

Clear!" she shouted as Halverson did the same. To the right was what appeared to be a bedroom. She held up one finger and pointed toward it, indicating that one of the deputies was to go there. The deputy behind Zeeman peeled off.

Directly in front of her an archway led into another room. She quickly moved to one side of it and poked her head around long enough to give the room a quick glance—a large kitchen. She nodded to Eric, who entered and swept the muzzle of his assault rifle all around.

"Clear!" he shouted.

"Clear!" they heard the officer shout from the bedroom.

Cass looked around the kitchen. Pans on the stove were steaming. The remains of a head of cauliflower lay on a cutting board along with a half-sliced eggplant. Someone had just been in here. The knife that had cut the vegetables lay on the floor. Whoever was using it left in a hurry.

Behind the kitchen was a hallway with a closed door at the far end. Cass could see side doors leading off the hall but not where they led.

The door at the end of the hall swung open. Cass and Eric instantly aimed their weapons. "Don't Move!" they shouted simultaneously. Then someone shouted from the back of the house, "Sheriff's Department. Do not move!"

"Police officers!" Cass shouted back. Two officers emerged through the door. Cass and Eric moved to the hall entrance at their end to back up the incoming officers as they cleared the two doorways leading off the hall. The first man threw open the door on the left. "Pantry!" he called. "Clear!"

The second deputy took the door on the right. Standing to the side, he turned the knob and pushed the door open. He shouted the sheriff's department warning. "Stairwell," he called as he pointed downward indicating to the others the presence of a stairway leading to a basement.

"Hold," Cass said.

Stairs were problematic. Going down, they'd be fully exposed with no idea where they were going or what they were getting into. She turned to the deputy who'd cleared the bedroom. "Wimmer, you and Jamison stay here and keep the upper floor secured. The rest of us will deal with the basement. Wellman, what could you see down there? Is it light or dark?"

"Looked like the lights were on."

"Good. I'll take lead. Wellman, you take second."

"Wait a minute," Eric complained. "You just took lead. Some of the rest of us need a chance to get shot."

Cass was touched by his concern. "Thanks, but this is personal. My best friend could be down there. What would she think if I let someone else rescue her?"

The first four feet into the space was actually a small room with fruit shelves lining the side. Then three steps descended to a lower landing. The stairs then turned left off the landing and descended against what appeared to be the home's stone foundation.

The view to the basement was blocked all the way to the landing. Cass moved to the bottom of the first set of stairs and peered quickly around the wall to see what she could see of the basement below.

The space appeared well lit, but her view was limited to the stairs leading down the stone wall and a small portion of the room below. She wouldn't be able to see the rest until she actually went down. They would be entering the space blind. Anyone down there with a firearm would have the advantage; they could fire on her and the other deputies before she would ever be able to see them. *God, I hate stairs. Be careful, girl, you don't want to leave Katy an orphan.*

She swallowed hard and shouted out. "Sheriff's Department. Do not move!" She clattered down the stairs, her deputies close behind, pointing her gun rapidly at every area of the space as the topography of the room revealed itself.

At the bottom of the stairway she stepped out of the way to allow her deputies to get down as quickly as possible. The room was anything but what she expected. It appeared to be a modern, fully-stocked beauty salon, complete with long mirrors, a hairwash station, a commercial helmet-style hairdryer—everything one might find in the finest hair establishment downtown.

But most surprising of all was the large, old-style leather barber's chair, with its back somehow reclined flat and the foot stool elevated, making it into a virtual bed.

Strapped in the chair was a blonde-haired woman, completely naked except for some kind of bandage around her left foot. Cass sprang to the chair. "Sam! Oh Sam!" she cried. But it wasn't Sam! The young woman in the chair was a complete stranger. She stared up at Cass wide-eyed. Tears streamed down her cheeks as she uncontrollably sobbed over and over, "Thank God you're here—Oh thank God you're here!"

As Cass stared at the woman, the room seemed to tilt. This couldn't be. Where the hell was Sam? It took a moment for the enormity of the situation to clarify itself in her mind. There wasn't one kidnapping going on, there were two!

It took a second for Cass to regain her focus. Her heart broke for the poor woman. Knowing that she must look fearsome, Cass threw her face protector up, reached out and touched the woman's shoulder. "You're ok now. You're safe," she reassured. She looked quickly around the room as the other deputies cleared the rest of the space. A rack at the end of the salon counter held a couple of haircutter's capes. "Get one of those and cover her," she barked at Eric.

The woman writhed, struggling to get her arms free. "You're ok, honey. We've got you. Try not to struggle." Cass removed the arm restraints. The instant the woman's right arm was freed she grabbed Cass's arm in a painful grip. "Thank you, thank you, oh thank you," she uttered between sobs. "I thought I was dead. I thought I was dead."

"You're going to live," Cass said gently. "You're going to be alright. We're not going to leave you. What's your name?"
The woman fought to regain control. "Mary Ann." Her voice came out a whisper. "Mary Ann Gilson."

"Mary Ann, I need your help. Was someone else in here with you?"

"He was cooking supper. I heard some real loud noises from upstairs, then he came running down here, told me good bye, and just disappeared."

"Disappeared?"

Mary Ann shrugged and pointed toward the end of the salon counter.

"Search this room!" Cass barked to her deputies. "He's either still here somewhere of there's another entrance." She turned her attention back to the girl. "We'll have an ambulance out here as fast as we can. The doctors will take care of you."

"He was a doctor," Mary Ann said fearfully.

"Over here sheriff," Deputy Wellman called out. Cass followed Wellman's voice. She went around where the salon counter ended and found herself in a six-foot alcove where the salon wall had been built back all the way to the stone foundation. Wellman pointed to where a section of the paneling stuck slightly out from the rest of the wall. It was a door designed to blend right in with the wall. Had it been fully closed, the wall would have looked solid. Another mistake by the good doctor.

"Hudson. Stay with the woman till the EMT's get here!" Cass shouted. "The rest of you with me."

Cass threw the door open, stepped to the side and pointed her pistol into a dark, empty space formed by the back of the salon on one side and the rough, unpainted stones of the house's foundation on the other. She shined her service flashlight in. The pitch dark place was empty. There was an opening in the foundation a few feet down. She stepped in and moved to the side of the opening.

Keeping the stone wall as cover, she pointed her flashlight into the void beyond, and stole a quick glance. "Rabbit hole," she said to the others behind her as she pulled her head back.

The house originally belonged to one of West Virginia's fabled moonshiners. These turn-of-the-century or older rural homes often housed stills in the basement and had secret escapes in case 'revenuers,' federal agents, showed up.

No wonder this house sits so close to the woods, Cass thought. She tried her shoulder mic. "Jamison, Wimmer, you got a copy on me, over?

There was no response. They were below ground far enough that the radio signal couldn't get out. "Zeeman. Go up and tell Jamison and Wimmer to get out behind the house and start looking for the entrance to this thing. Have them alert everyone outside that the perp may be in the woods behind the house. Then get your ass back down here."

The pursuit of Dr. Barlow was now tunnel warfare. There could be booby traps; there could be rats, spiders, snakes; or someone could simply wait out of sight around a bend and pick pursuers off one at a time. *This guy sure isn't making it easy,* she thought.

"We're going in!" she commanded as soon as Zeeman returned. Deputy Otten, stay with us.

Thoughts of Sam momentarily pushed to the forefront of her mind, but she pushed them aside. *One kidnapping at a time,"* she told herself. *One kidnapping at a time.*

Chapter 54

The previous evening

You shouldn't do this! Sam's mind screamed as she opened the door to the man she'd divorced months before. She pointed him to the kitchen. "You look terrible," she said. I have some cake left over from ladies auxiliary meeting at church." It struck her that devil's food cake was his favorite late-night snack. She preferred yellow cake. She didn't know why she kept making devil's food. Habit, she guessed.

"Uh, sure. That would be real good,"

Sam noticed his hand was shaking. *Bet he'd really prefer a stiff shot of Jack Daniels*, she thought, *but he won't find it in this house.*

Ricky looked around as he sat down. "The old place looks good," he said. "Don't know what you did, but it looks better than it did before."

Sam put a large slice of cake in front of him and plunked down a glass of milk. He liked to carve off a bite of cake with his fork and dunk it in cold milk, which he promptly did. He was so predictable.

Sam's mind was spinning. She didn't want to see or talk to this man. It was only for civility's sake and her own sense of confusion that led her to unconsciously pour a glass of milk for herself. When she realized what she'd just done she shook her head, scowled, set her glass on the counter and retreated a step. She would not sit down with him.

As Ricky shoveled in a second large bite, she got hold of her senses and coldly said, "You're not supposed to be here. I'm not interested in chit-chatting. We're not friends anymore, remember? The only reason you're in this house is that you said you were in trouble. Say what you have to say and get out!"

He was surprised by her tone. He looked at her with hurt, pleading eyes and said, "Ahh come on, girl. No need to be unfriendly." Then he gave her the grin that used to charm and disarm her. Now it brought only a sense of revulsion. "I just want to talk to you, Sammy," he said. "After all, we were married for seven years. That's got to mean something."

"That quit meaning anything the night you hit me; not to mention finding out you were sleeping with another woman at the very time we were supposedly trying to get pregnant. Or have you forgotten that?"

"No. I admit I was stupid." There was a hint of exasperation in his voice. Ricky was not a man who took criticism well.

"Your being sorry doesn't change anything." she said. "Let's not play games. This isn't a casual social visit and both of us know it. "I'm going to ask you for the last time, what's your trouble and why are you here?"

Ricky told her the story of Maria and the Tuscany Hills restaurant, of how he'd been duped and swindled out of nearly all of the money Sam had given him in the divorce. "So the bottom line is that you were right and I was wrong, he said." You could see through Maria, but I couldn't. I should have listened to you."

Sam was disgusted. "If you're here to cry on my shoulder about your girlfriend and your own foolishness, you came to the wrong place. You got what you deserved. But this isn't just about losing your money, or making bad business decisions. I know you, Ricky. There's always one more shoe to drop. Let's hear the rest of it."

Ricky swallowed hard. "Like I said, Maria left me holding the bag on all the restaurant debts. I can get rid of every bill but one with a bankruptcy. Trouble is, that one bill is owed to some mobsters in New York. I didn't know she was doing business with them before I came on the scene. But they can't find Maria and since I was her partner, they're looking to me for payment. They're going to hurt me real bad unless I come up with their money by Monday. They're not kidding, Sam. These are really bad people. You're my last hope. I'm here to ask you to help me."

Sam could see the fear in his eyes. He was telling the truth. "How much?" she asked.

"Six-hundred-fifty-thousand," he lied.

Sam gasped. "Over half a million dollars? I thought you were going to say five or ten thousand. But six-hundred-fifty thousand? How could you... ?"

"Because I'm not the business genius you are," Ricky snapped, then caught himself and apologized. "Sorry. I don't mean to be disrespectful. It's just that I'm under a lot of pressure. Please Sam; you've got to help me."

In that brief burst of anger Ricky revealed himself. Sam suddenly felt sick as her mind flashed through the history of their relationship—of the many days she spent trying to placate her husband's volatile temper and how she denied the real truth about who and what Ricky Thornton really was.

The old tension was back at the pit of her stomach. It was that familiar feeling of having to walk on eggshells wondering what he would blame her for next or what word would cause his anger to flash. She realized with finality that there was not an ounce of love left in her for this man. She could not allow him to suck her back into the vortex of his lies and manipulations.

"If I don't do this for you, what will you do?"

"I'll have to disappear," he said. "Otherwise these guys will kill me. I may not even be able to stay in the country."

"How much money do you have?"

Chapter 55

"That Bitch! That crazy fucking *bitch!*" Ricky raged. Who does she think she is, pulling a freaking gun on me like that?" He pounded the steering wheel with both hands, nearly throwing the Escalade off the highway as he sped back toward Oak Hill. The inequity of it all gnawed at his gut. She had all the money in the world and he so little. She was always right; he so infrequently so. It wasn't fair. She couldn't treat him this way. She owed him. Something had to be done—but what?

Ten miles out of Fayetteville, he called Charlene. "Hey, baby, I'm coming home. Meet me at the cabin. Yeah, I know it's almost midnight, but what the hell. You love me, right? Just be there. It's important."

When he arrived she was already in his bed, dressed just the way he liked—wearing nothing. He slipped his clothes off and climbed in beside her. But lovemaking was not on his agenda, at least, not yet. He had a plan, one that would take two people.

"Charlene, you love me, don't cha?"

"You know I do, baby." She turned languorously and ran her hand up the inside of his thigh.

Ricky stopped her. "We'll have time for that later. I gotta ask you some things."

It was rare that Ricky wasn't ready for sex. She sat up and pushed herself against the headboard. "Okay baby, ask away, she said"

"How much do you love me?"

"Baby, I'd do anything for ya. You know that. Why?"

"I love you too." He'd never told her that before. He watched her eyes get big and moist. "I have for a long time. Do you love me enough to want to be with me from now on?"

"Oh, Ricky," the woman said, getting weepy. "Are you asking me what I think you are? Of course I do. I'd move in here with you in a heartbeat. I'm a pretty good cook, you know."

"What if I was to ask you to go away with me—like a long ways away?"

"Like move somewhere else?"

"Yeah. Only we might not be able to come back here, ever. You wouldn't be able to call your mom or your sister or anything. It would be just you and me and nobody else."

Charlene looked at him quizzically. "I could do that if I had to. Are you in some kind of trouble or something?"

"Let's just say I have a problem. I told you how I got screwed over by that woman in New York. Well, we were business partners and she left me holding the bag on some huge bills. I got a handle on most of them, but there's this one she owed to some gangsters. Now she's disappeared and they're looking to me to pay up—two hundred and thirty grand by Monday. If I don't come up with the cash, they'll hurt me. They'll hurt me real bad, maybe even kill me."

"Oh, Ricky!" Charlene's hands covered her mouth. "Monday? What are we gonna do?"

"I've been making a plan to come up with a lot of money and then get out of here. It's going to take two people. Do you love me enough do something a little crazy, a little against the law?"

Charlene's eyes got big. She thought for a moment. "You want us to rob a bank or something? Maybe I would, long as nobody got hurt. But what then? Everybody would be looking for us."

"Naw—I don't want to do nothin' like that. My ex-old lady has money—millions. I thought she was still in New York but I found out she's in Summersville. I saw her tonight."

"You saw her?" A flash of jealousy lit Charlene's face.

"Nah, not like that. I just talked to her for a few minutes. She's still real pissed at me, real bitter. I asked her to help me out but she told me to go piss up a rope. I helped her get all that money, Charlene, so I deserve some of it. All we need to do is get her calmed down so she'll listen to me—hear me out. The trouble is, we'll probably have to force her to listen; maybe bring her back here a couple of days where I can work on her."

Charlene looked distressed. "Kidnap her? Oh Ricky, I don't know…"

"It's that, or you're going to be fishing my body out of some river," Ricky said sharply. Listen, here's the plan. There's these things called bearer bonds. They're just like cash. My ex old lady has over nineteen-hundred of them sitting over there in the bank at Summersville. They're worth fifty-grand apiece. All we have to do is convince her to let me have ten or twenty of them. Hell, she could lose that many and never miss them."

Charlene did the math in her head. Her eyes lit up. "That's a lot of money."

"Damn right it is, enough to set you and me up for the rest of our lives."

"But what if we get caught?"

"We put this to Sam the right way and she won't even call the cops. She doesn't want anybody knowing she's got all that money. If she goes to the cops and they make a big deal of it, the whole world's gonna know she's rich; and that's the last thing she wants.

"And you'd pay those mob guys off, right?"

297

"Maybe, maybe not. If we were to disappear, it'd be that much more money for us."

"Yeah, but if you pay them off, we wouldn't have to disappear. We could stay right here where I could call my mom sometime."

Her comment frustrated Ricky. Charlene just wasn't getting the big picture. But he couldn't afford to piss her off. "Maybe you're right, baby." He could deal with this issue later. "Let me think about it."

"So what do you want me to do?" Charlene asked.

"We need to go over to Summersville and bring Sam here. We need to do it right now—this morning—before she has any time to think about our conversation last night. I've got it all planned out. There's these trees between the street and her driveway. She parks her car right next to them. When she goes to get into her car, I can grab her and nobody will ever see. I need you to drive the Escalade. She's going to be pissed, so I'll have to keep her calmed down." He didn't mention that just over an hour ago, she'd pulled a gun on him nor the fact that Sam's best friend was sheriff of Nicholas County.

"So we'll bring her back here and have a couple of days to convince her before the bank opens on Monday, Ricky continued. "If it turns out I can't grab her, we drive off. No harm, no foul, right? I've already got a little place picked out in Mexico where we can live like kings on practically nothing. Nice beach, a lot of Americans. You'll love it."

Ricky could see the wheels turning. Finally Charlene spoke, "So you really do love me huh, Ricky? You ain't bullshitting me or asking me to do this just cause you need somebody to help you? If you were, I'd be really pissed."

"Nah, of course I love you. I trust you too. Look, if I didn't, do you think I'd tell you about all this?"

Charlene thought a moment longer. "No, I guess you wouldn't," she finally said. "It scares me though. I ain't never done anything like this."

"So you'll help me?"

She suddenly pushed him down on his back, straddled him and said, "I'll do it. But if you screw me over, it's the last time you'll ever get any more of this." She pushed her hips hard against him and started to move.

Chapter 56

Despite holding the gun in her hand, when Sam closed the door on Ricky, she was shaking so badly she could barely stand. She quickly went through the whole house checking the locks on every window and door. Still shaking, she sat at the kitchen table and wanted to cry. Instead she screamed in anger, "I will not let you do this to me, Ricky Thornton! It's my life, and I won't let you take it!"

She thought about calling Cass but decided not to. The crisis had passed. Ricky wouldn't be coming back. She'd let Cass get a good night's sleep. After all, she did have a serial killer to catch in the morning.

Sleep was impossible; her mind riled equally by Ricky's disconcerting visit and the prospect that today could spell the end of the evening-gown murders. As excited as that prospect was it kept getting pushed aside by thoughts of Ricky's sudden appearance. She couldn't believe she'd actually drawn a gun on him. She had no idea Ricky's eyes could open that wide.

When she finally did drift off to sleep it felt like only moments before her alarm clock jarred her awake. She awoke groggily and stumbled into the shower. A deluge of hot then cold water brought her back to a semblance of consciousness. Her coffee mug dragged her the rest of the way awake. She almost skipped breakfast, but settled on a quick bowl of corn flakes and a glass of orange juice. With today's agenda, who knew when she'd get a chance to eat again?

Six fifteen. The sun was just peeking over the eastern horizon. She'd promised Mary she'd be there by six thirty—and she still had to run by Wal-Mart for donuts.

She hurriedly threw the strap of the laptop case over her shoulder, grabbed her coffee mug and dashed for her car. She slung the laptop into the passenger seat then reached to retrieve the coffee mug from the top of the car when she heard something rustle behind her. She partially turned to look when suddenly her whole world exploded. She saw stars then a dark tunnel sucked her down, down, she could tell she was falling but there was nothing she could do. By the time she hit the ground there was nothing but darkness.

*

"I thought you said you wouldn't hurt her!" Charlene screamed.

"I didn't!" Ricky barked from the backseat as he bound Sam's feet with duct tape and put a blindfold over her eyes.

"Don't tell me you didn't hurt her," Charlene said. "She's getting blood all over the back seat."

"I gave her a little knock in the head, that's all. It's a small cut. You know how head cuts bleed. She'll be fine. Now shut up and drive." In truth, Ricky was worried too. *Had* he hit her too hard? She'd gone down like a sack of rocks.

As he struggled to tie her hands behind her, he felt something hard at the back of Sam's hip. "Oh ho!" he exalted as he pulled Sam's 9 mm Glock from its concealed-carry holster. "Look what we have here." He held the gun up so Charlene could see. Her eyes widened. "What the hell's she doing packing? Is she a cop?"

"Nah." Ricky held a handkerchief against Sam's head, trying to staunch the blood. "But her friend knows all about guns. She must be teaching Sam."

Sam stirred. She threw her head a little and spasmodically moved her legs. Ricky was relieved. "See, I told you she wasn't hurt," he said. "She's coming around already." He put his lips next to Sam's ear and whispered, "Don't struggle. You've got to stay calm till we get to where we're going."

"Ricky? Ricky? Is that you?" she asked groggily. She tossed her head then moaned. She tried to move her pinioned arms. "Oh, my head hurts. What happened? Where are w....?" Then her head lolled to the side. She stopped struggling and drifted into unconsciousness again.

Ricky felt her go limp and was alarmed. *Shit!* He felt her neck for a pulse. Good! It was there; strong and regular. Her breathing seemed normal. She must have passed out. He'd give her a few minutes. If she didn't come around, he'd do what he could to wake her.

*

"Sam. Sam!"

Ricky's voice pierced the fog of darkness. This time the journey back to consciousness was swifter but more painful. Her head hurt terribly. She tried to move her hands but they seemed stuck behind her.

I need to sit up, she thought as she tried to push off with her elbows but couldn't. *What in the world?* She tried to move her feet and couldn't do that either. She realized she was bound. Despite the ringing in her head, she opened her eyes but saw only a blur. She was blindfolded as well.

She could tell from the sound and vibration that she was in a moving vehicle. Whose? But more important, why? Then she remembered, or thought she did. "Ricky?" she asked quietly, almost whimpering. "Are you here?"

"Yes," she heard him say. "You're in my car. I've got to talk to you, but after last night, this was the only way to do it. You're tied up so don't struggle."

It took Sam's mind a moment to absorb what he had said.

Ricky was to her immediate right so someone else had to be driving. "Sit me up please," she requested.

She felt Ricky's strong hands lift her to a sitting position. The movement sent waves of pain through her head. "Oh—oh!" she cried. The waves slowly subsided. As her senses stabilized, she asked, "Who's driving?"

"My girlfriend, Charlene."

Sam addressed her. "Charlene, do you understand how much trouble you're in? Kidnapping is a federal offense—you'll get life in prison. Ricky isn't smart enough to let that stop him. I hope you're smarter."

"I told you this was a bad idea, Ricky," Charlene wailed.

"Shut up," Ricky growled. "I told you we needed to spend some time talking to her. Just keep driving. Sam, you shut up too or I'll hurt you. All I want you to do is listen to reason, that's all."

"You've already hurt me. I didn't just fall down and knock myself out."

Ricky hated her sarcasm. "That's not what I meant," he spat. "All we need to do is come to an agreement about what we talked about last night, that's all."

"Agreements made under the barrel of a gun aren't agreements. They're coercions."

Ricky's anger flared. "The only one packing a gun was you, Sam. Just like last night. Only I've got it now, not you. You better remember that."

Sam heard Charlene gasp. She got the impression the woman had turned to look at Ricky. *Sure hope she's keeping this thing headed in a straight line,* she thought.

"She pulled a gun on you last night?" Charlene asked. "You didn't tell me that, Ricky."

"It was no big deal. She wouldn't have used it."

If you believe that, why don't you give it back to me? Sam thought. "Where we going?" she asked.

"Someplace. Don't want you to see, that's all."

Sam made a guess. "You mean your folks' place up on Plum Orchard Lake? That place we spent a week at three years ago? Is that where you don't want me to see?"

"Ricky!" Charlene wailed. "She knows."

"Will you shut up?" Ricky barked, furious that Charlene had confirmed their destination. "You too, Sam! You're starting to piss me off." He cuffed the side of her head.

"We certainly wouldn't want to do that," Sam retorted, despite the wave of pain the blow set off. You're a real big man, hitting me while I'm all tied up. You must be real proud. Since I already know where we're going, would you please take this blindfold off?"

"If I do, will you keep your mouth shut the rest of the way?"
"Sounds like a good trade to me. I never wanted to talk to you again anyway."

Ricky removed the blindfold and the trio rode in silence the rest of the way to Plum Orchard Lake. By the time they arrived Sam had drifted off again. Ricky had to carry her into the cabin.

Chapter 57

The rabbit hole escape route was one of the deciding factors when he bought the old broken-down farm house; that and the fact that the property was isolated from the outside world. But the isolation was broken now. Dr. Barlow knew his little paradise would be lost forever the instant the police discovered Mary Ann.

The tunnel was low-ceilinged and narrow. One had to bend over and practically crawl through much of it. For the first twenty feet or so it went straight then the tunnel jogged to the left at a forty-five degree angle just far enough that it disappeared from view to anyone looking in from the entrance. Then it went straight for thirty or forty-feet then jogged right. There were two more such jogs before reaching the exit. He guessed that they were a safety feature to prevent someone from being able to shoot straight through the tunnel and hit whoever was inside. They also made a perfect place for an ambush in case one wanted to stand and fight.

Barlow stopped just past the first jog, out of sight from the entrance, and tried to collect his wits. There would be no standing and fighting today. For him the tunnel had but one purpose—escape!

The first time he'd explored this place it was so full of cobwebs that he had to go back for a board he could use to clear the way. God, how he hated spiders. The only thing that scared him worse was snakes. He normally carried a little Snake Charmer .410 gage single shot shotgun with him in here to deal with that contingency. He'd only had to use it once. But the little gun was now safely tucked away in his bedroom closet and he wasn't about to go ask the police for it.

He had been surprised at the length of the tunnel. Its exit was completely out of sight from the house, nearly two hundred feet into the woods. Back then the end of the tunnel was a leaky, soggy debris-filled space that reminded him of a rock walled sewer manhole more than anything else. When he looked up at the exit hole, he found that all that held back the foot or so of earth that camouflaged it from above were a few old rotted planks. The whole thing could have easily collapsed on top of him.

The exit was now concrete from top to bottom. He'd had a solid aluminum lid built that fit snuggly over the opening but was light enough that one could easily push it open from below. The lid had to be camouflaged. Barton painted it flat brown then sprayed adhesive over it and dumped dead leaves over the top and sides. Each successive year's leaf fall would cover the lid until now it looked like nothing more than the normal leaf litter of the forest floor.

The original rickety, rotted wooden ladder was replaced by a shiny new aluminum one, making climbing out of the exit far safer. After that first trip he'd faithfully inspected the tunnel at least once a month.

How long would it take for whoever was invading his house to find the rabbit hole? His question was answered a couple of minutes later, when he heard a woman's voice shout down the tunnel. "Sheriff's Department!" It was the unmistakable voice of Sheriff Rosier.

He knew several people were in the house and undoubtedly many more outside. The whole property was probably crawling with police. He had to get to the forest exit before they found it or he'd be trapped.

He ran for the back of the tunnel as fast as his hunched-over stride could take him. He scrambled up the ladder and carefully raised one edge of the lid, listening for anyone nearby. He heard nothing. He swallowed hard, pushed the lid up further and poked his head out. He could see light from the clearing through the trees, but here in the dense woods, it was almost dark.

Good, he thought. All he had to do was find a safe place to hide until it was fully dark, then he could make his escape. He heard voices in the tunnel. No time left. He scrambled out and put the lid over the exit. He found a nearby rock large enough he could barely lift it and placed it on the tunnel lid. He quickly got his bearings then headed to the right.

Moving as quietly as he could through the noisy leaves, he paralleled the tree line behind the house on a path that would take him behind the barn and on to an animal trail he knew about a few hundred yards away.

He'd traveled scarcely more than a hundred yards when voices came from near the house.

"Form a skirmish line," someone shouted. "Twenty feet apart!" A few seconds later the same voice said loudly, "Keep your eyes peeled. Move out." Then he heard the sound of boots crushing dried leaves as officers entered the forest.

He could tell from the sound that several people were spread out across the back side of the house. But the one that alarmed him most was whoever was coming straight at him. As far as he could tell, the man was at the end of the skirmish line. He had to move. Only a few more steps and whoever was coming toward him would be within sight.

It was impossible to move silently, but he would have to chance it. He angled away from the man's line of march. Barlow thought his every step sounded like thunder as dry leaves crackled and popped.

"Got something over this way!" the man at the end of the line yelled. He changed course and started in Barlow's direction.

Faster, move faster, the doctor urged himself. But how could he go faster? He was sprinting as it was. The man following was running himself now. This wasn't the answer. He had to hide. He took several more steps before he spotted a place where a rocky overhang created a sizable pile of leaves beneath it. It might be his only hope.

Oblivious of the fact that the place might be home to who knows what variety of snakes, centipedes, spiders, or other vermin, he dove into the pile and covered up, hoping he'd made himself invisible in the natural camouflage of the forest floor. His heart pounded, and his chest heaved. He willed himself to slow his loud breathing but could do nothing about his heart; it would have to calm down on its own. He lay silent and motionless. The only way the cop would find him now was if he stepped on him—and Barlow had in his hand a .45 caliber response to deal with that.

Chapter 58

Sam spent most of the day fighting off the effects of the blow to her head. She almost certainly had a concussion, which wasn't helped any by being tied to a living room chair. She had an overwhelming desire to sleep and was occasionally overtaken by alternating waves of dizziness and nausea. Charlene offered her Tylenol, which helped, but if she took more than a sip or two of water her stomach rebelled. But as the sun sank below the crest of the western mountains she started feeling a little better. The dizziness and nausea subsided and the headache was down to a dull throb. At last she felt hungry.

"Could I have a piece of toast or something?"

"Of course," Ricky said cheerfully. "You want anything else—a sandwich maybe?"

"Not now. My stomach can't take it. Just a piece of toast and maybe a little milk."

Charlene couldn't move fast enough to comply. When she sat the food on the side-table, her hands were shaking.

This chick's scared, Sam thought. *Maybe she's realizing what Ricky's gotten her into.*

Sam looked at Ricky. "I can't eat unless you untie my hands."

"I'm leaving your legs tied. I know how good you are with that *Taekuondo* shit. I don't want to have to hit you again."

"Fine. Do what you have to. Just let me eat."

The curtains were drawn, cutting off what was an otherwise spectacular view of Plum Blossom Lake and the hills just beyond. The sun was fully set, killing what light had filtered through the tall floor to ceiling windows that formed the back wall of the cabin.

Ricky and Charlene plopped themselves on opposite ends of the sofa that faced Sam. Sam's headache was at last under enough control that she could give them full attention.

Ricky began. "Look, Sam, I never wanted it this way. But when you pulled that gun on me you left me no choice."

"There's always a choice when it comes to kidnapping," Sam retorted. "You've obviously made the wrong one."

"Don't call it kidnapping. This is a negotiation, that's all."

The pain in her head and the ringing in her ears proved him a liar. "I know negotiation very well, Ricky. If all this is just a negotiation, untie me. Let's all sit at the kitchen table like civilized people and negotiate. If holding me hostage is your preferred negotiation technique, I've got to tell you, it really sucks."

"Don't pull that fancy lawyer shit on me," he said. "I lived with you too long. It won't work. I told you about the wise guys who'll be here Monday to start breaking my legs or tying chains around me and throwing me in the river. I can't let them do that. And you're the only one who can stop them."

"So tell me how all of this became my problem?" Sam asked. "I paid you a million dollars less than six months ago. I didn't have anything to do with you blowing your money, Ricky. Is it worth throwing away the rest of your life to try and drag me into the sewer with you?"

Ricky's look hardened. "The way I see it, you're a part of it the same way I am. If you'd have just bought that damned restaurant like I wanted you to, none of this would be happening. This is just as much your fault as it is mine."

It was crazy logic. He really *did* blame her. *Same old Ricky,* Sam thought. *He'll never change.* "Your logic is as fuzzy as your math," she said. "But I know you well enough to know that you've probably come up with some crazy plan to get yourself out of this. Let's hear it."

"Consider this an extension of our divorce negotiations," Ricky said. "If I told you back then that I wanted two million instead of one, you'd have taken it, right?"

Sam shook her head. "My offer wasn't a negotiation. It was a take-it-or-leave-it proffer of a million dollar one-time payment to make you go away. I had you nailed, and you know it—adultery—fraud—assault, and the fact that you hid from me that you're shooting blanks. Have you told Charlene that bit yet?" She looked at Charlene. "Did he tell you he can't have kids? That there's no lead in the pencil—no seed in the ole' bird feeder?"

"Shut up!" Ricky stood and took a threatening step forward.
"Or what? You'll hit me again? That's a real good way to get me to cooperate."

Charlene spoke up. "Stop it Ricky, she's right!"

Ricky backed off. Confrontation would get him nowhere. "I'm sorry Sam," he said. "People get pissed when they think they're going to die."

Sam's head was starting to spin again. She had to get him to the bottom line. "What do you want, Ricky? How much is all this supposed to cost me?"

"Nothing you can't afford. You've got over nineteen-hundred of those bearer bonds sitting over there in the bank. All I'm asking is for twenty of them, just enough to get these wise guys off my back and get me on my feet again. That's only about one percent of those bonds. Do that and you'll be rid of me for good."

Compliance was impossible. "There's only one problem with your little plan, Ricky," Sam said. "I don't have any bearer bonds.

They've all been converted to safer treasury bonds which are being held in my brokerage account in New York. All I keep in the Summersville bank is enough money to cover my day-to-day living expenses. It's Saturday night. All the banks and brokerage houses are closed. I couldn't get my hands on a million dollars by Monday even if I wanted to. You might as well let me go and start packing for Mexico."

Ricky's look hardened. "You better be kidding me," he growled.

"You know me well enough to know I don't lie. I swear to God I'm telling the truth. And I would never invoke God's name unless I was."

"God *damn* you, Sam," Ricky exploded. "God damn you to hell!" He leapt across the room and raised his hand to strike her.

Sam recoiled but could do nothing to pull away. At the last possible moment Ricky diverted the strike to the wall behind Sam's head, apparently forgetting that it was the thick solid-wood decking that formed the wall of the living room on this side and the cabin's roof on the other side. Aughhhhhh! he screamed as his fist crumpled against the unyielding surface. Sam thought she heard something snap. Ricky's face contorted with pain. He shook his damaged hand as if that would somehow make it feel better.

When the pain subsided to a more tolerable level, still trembling with rage he turned to Charlene and said, "That's it, baby, we're out of here. Mexico's our only choice now." He tried flexing his fingers and cried, "Ouch—Damn! I think I broke my hand." He looked venomously down at Sam and said again, "God damn you, Sam!"

Ricky looked at Charlene and was surprised to see that she was crying. "Now what?" he snapped.

"We should have just loaded up and gotten out of here, Ricky. Now we've got to decide what to do with her. We can't take her with us and I'm not a murderer. So don't you even think about that."

Ricky didn't answer for several seconds. When he did speak, she heard defeat in his voice. "We'll leave her here," he said. "We'll leave her tied up long enough for us to get out of the country; two, maybe three days. Then we call somebody and tell em where she is."

Sam panicked. *Two to three days?* What if something happened to them? What if they were killed in a car accident or something and couldn't call? "Look Ricky," she said "There's way too much danger that way. What if there was a fire here? What if something happens and you can't call. You'd be wanted for murder, not just kidnapping. But I can take the whole kidnapping thing off the table."

Ricky's head came up. "What are you saying, Sam?"

"I'm saying that if you let me go, take me back home right now, I'd be willing to walk away from this whole thing like it never happened. You and Charlene could get out of here without having to worry about the law."

"You'd do that?" Ricky asked skeptically. "How do I know I can trust you? You might go straight to the cops."

"I always tell the truth. Always! Remember? If you know anything about me at all, you know that if I swear to something before God I'll never break that oath.

Ricky looked at his girlfriend. "What do you think, Charlene? She's right. If she ever swears to something, she keeps her word."

Charlene didn't hesitate. "Oh Ricky, let's do it. I gotta be able to call my momma sometime, maybe sneak back into town once in a while so I can see my sis. Please, Ricky. We gotta do this!"

"Ricky sighed. "I'm no murderer either. I guess that's what we've got to do." He looked at Sam and said, "You've got to swear to this, Sam—just like you said. Swear it so good that if you ever break this oath you'll go straight to Hell."

Sam took a deep breath. "Ricky, I swear that if you release me and then take me home and never try to contact me again, I will never bring charges against you or Charlene for kidnapping and bringing me here—so help me God."

Ricky exhaled. "Good enough." He walked to her chair to untie her but his tortured hand refused to cooperate. "Charlene, you're going to have to help me," he said.

In a matter of moments Sam was free. It was all she could do to keep from crying with relief. Charlene, get your purse," Ricky barked. "We'll take her to Summersville then come back here to pack."

Sam's gun lay on the kitchen counter. "What about that?" She asked, "It doesn't belong to me, it belongs to Cass."

"You'll get it back when we drop you off, unloaded of course. Till then it stays with me." Ricky pulled his knit shirt out of his pants and shoved the .9 mm into his belt at the small of his back, then pulled the shirt over it.

Suddenly there was an unexpected knock at the door. "Who the hell... " Ricky turned on the outside light and looked out the kitchen window. It looked like a car was parked in the driveway on the other side of Charlene's, but he couldn't see any people. The knock came again. Ricky went to the door, slid the door chain in place, and then cracked it open just slightly.

The door exploded inward, the door chain ripped completely off its mount, propelling Ricky backward, nearly toppling him. A huge body filled the doorway. A man dressed in an expensive Italian silk suit held a gun in his hand. He strode brazenly in, followed closely by two others. Ricky staggered backward and moaned, "Oh God. Oh God!"

Chapter 59

There was room for only one person to stand at terminal end of the tunnel. Cass stood on the ladder leading up to the exit hole, trying to push the lid open. But try as she might, she couldn't budge it. Maybe someone with more brawn would have a shot.

"You give it a try, Eric," she said. She was slightly embarrassed as they worked themselves tightly past each other in a space only meant for one. Eric mounted the ladder and gave the lid a hard shove. It moved a little but wouldn't open.

"We're going back, Cass commanded." She turned to the other two officers who'd followed them in. "Turn around and get us out of here fast."

Cass emerged from the tunnel covered with dirt and grime. To her surprise, Mary Ann was sitting in a chair near the stairs. She was wearing both the barber's aprons, one in front and one behind.

The two officers Cass had left behind were standing watch over her. Also present were two strangers; a man and a woman, both dressed in dark suits. "Who the hell are you?" Cass asked none too gently.

At the same time, both reached into the inside pocket of their suit jackets and produced ID. The man, tall and several years older than the woman, answered. "FBI Special Agent Clayton Clinger.

This is Special Agent Ashley Holmes. Sorry we couldn't get here sooner but we were just notified about this kidnapping."

Cass understood. "No disrespect intended, Agent Clinger, but this is no longer just a kidnapping. We're trying to catch a killer. If you'll step back and observe, I'll brief you when I get a chance."

"I assume that's our victim?" Clinger nodded toward Mary Ann.

"One of them," Cass said. "We may have another kidnapping going on as we speak. She looked at her deputies and inquired, "Where's the ambulance?"

"On its way," the deputy standing next to the stairs said. "Wouldn't you rather be lying down? Cass asked Mary Ann gently.

"I'd rather be anywhere than in that chair," she said defiantly.

Cass didn't blame her. The woman's foot appeared to be freshly bandaged. She pointed to it and asked, "What happened?"

"He cut off my little toe," A tear spilled from her eye and left a wet trail down her cheek. "It's in a bowl over there in the fridge." She pointed.

Bastard! Cass cursed under her breath. She brushed a hair from Mary Ann's face and said, "Everything's going to be okay. We're not going to leave you until the EMT's get here. If you want anything, just tell someone? We'll do whatever we can to help."

She turned to Agent Holmes. "Agent, you're the only other woman here. Could you take care of her until the EMT's arrive?"

"Be happy to," Holmes said.

"Did you catch him?" Mary Ann asked.

"Not yet, honey, but I'm going upstairs to make that happen right now. We'll get him, I promise." Cass squeezed her hand reassuringly.

"When you catch him, would you do something for me?" Mary Ann asked.

"Sure. Just ask."

"Hold that big dick of his up and slowly cut off his balls. Then stuff both of them down his throat."

*

Cass and Eric emerged from the house on separate missions. Cass looked at the darkening sky and scowled. If they didn't find Barlow before dark the search would be immensely more difficult. Eric's job was to find out what was going on with the search and report back to her.

Cass now had time to think about what she was certain was another kidnapping. She checked with dispatch several times to see whether Sam had checked in. Each time Mary gave her a negative report, Cass's worry increased. She'd been fully prepared to find Sam in Barlow's hands but not Mary Ann Gilson. Though she was enormously relieved that this victim wasn't Sam, there was no doubt that something bad had happened. Where the hell was she?

After last night, the most obvious answer was Ricky. Cass knew the guy was flaky, erratic, and unpredictable, but was he crazy enough to kidnap his ex-wife? Stranger things had happened. They should have looked for him longer last night. If Ricky Thornton had hurt Sam, she'd follow Mary Ann Gilson's instructions precisely—but on a different man.

Chapter 60

Don't move! Don't make a sound! Barlow commanded himself. Easier said than done. Something—an ant, a centipede, a spider, who knew what—was happily munching on the back of his left thigh. *Please don't let it be a spider,* he prayed. It took every ounce of self-discipline he could muster to keep from erupting from his coffin of leaves to smash whatever was feasting on him.

More fearful than spiders at the moment was the fact that the person who'd followed the sound of his footsteps now stood only three feet away atop the rock overhang that created his leafy sanctuary. A couple of minutes before, that cop had been joined by another, who by the sound of his voice, also stood only a few feet away.

"What you got over here, Casey?" the second person asked.

"Don't know. I didn't see it. Thought I heard someone or something running this direction. Couldn't tell if it was man or animal."

"Lot of deer around here. As thick as this forest is, it's pretty tough to see anything."

"What do you think? Wanna keep looking?"

"Nah, whatever it was is gone now. Another ten minutes, and it'll be completely dark. We better get back and join up with the formation. Don't want one of our guys mistaking us for Barlow in the dark."

"10-4. I'll give them a radio shot and let them know we're rejoining."

"Unit 3, Unit 12," the second man said.

"Unit 3," came back the reply.

"Be advised that Units 12 and 7 will rejoin the formation from the northeast. ETA three minutes, over."

"Copy, Unit 12. What'd ya find over there?"

"Nothing. Could have been a deer or something."

"10-4. We'll hold the formation for you."

Barlow's relief was palpable as the two men moved off. He waited until he was sure they were safely away before he emerged from his hiding place as silently as possible and beat furiously at his pant leg.

As far as Barlow could tell, the police seemed to be concentrated behind the house, but he had no way of knowing for sure. He had to get further away. Then perhaps he could find a safe place where he could see more of what was going on before attempting to make his way out of the woods.

Slowly and cautiously he moved farther north and edged closer to the tree line, making frequent stops to listen as he went.

He reached the forest's edge a couple of hundred feet the other side of his barn. It was nearly dark. The barn blocked his view of the house. Seeing vehicles coming and going on the road gave him an overwhelming sense of sorrow. His beautiful, private, isolated property was now perhaps the busiest place in the county. By tomorrow the whole world would know where it was.

The flashing lights of an ambulance came rushing up the road, followed by a tow truck. The ambulance had to be for Mary Ann, sweet Mary Ann. An adequate substitute for Susan, but not as good as Sam would have been. He regretted he would likely never enjoy Sam's company. With the information he found on her on the Internet, he felt like he already knew her.

Undoubtedly the tow truck was there to take his truck away. Too bad. He liked that truck. There had to be a place to hide and get a better look at what was happening at the house, but where?

Then he looked up and smiled. He shoved the .45 into his belt and the flashlight into a pocket and began to climb. At the top of the tall oak tree he concealed himself in the thick foliage. He could see the house and yard perfectly over the top of the barn.

Well hidden in the leafy canopy, he felt secure. People rarely looked up when walking through the forest, especially at night.

Chapter 61

Charlene stared wide-eyed at the intruders, unable to utter a sound. Sam bolted for the sliding glass door set in a frame in the middle of the windows that formed the back wall of the living room. As she struggled to find her way through the closed curtains, a bullet exploded into the door frame right above her head. When the gun went off, Charlene began to scream. Through the screams, Sam heard a man's voice thunder, "Where do you think you're goin', lady? Get your ass over here and sit down on this couch. Sam's shoulders sagged. She had to comply. She wasn't about to take a bullet in the back for Ricky.

Then the man leveled his semi-auto pistol at Charlene's head and growled, "Shut up and sit down, Bitch. And quit bawling! Charlene silenced her screams but could not control her shaking hands or the flow of her tears. She collapsed onto the couch beside Sam.

"Watch em," the big man barked at a short, swarthy fireplug of a man with long, slicked back hair. He was dressed in dark slacks and a black silk shirt whose long sleeves were rolled nearly to his elbows. The top two buttons of his shirt were open, revealing a mat of dark chest hair that billowed over the open edges of the shirt and provided a hirsute nest for a half-dozen gold chains dangling from his neck.

The goon turned to Ricky, now cowering against the kitchen counter and being guarded by a tall, bald, rather round man whose thick, rimless glasses made his eyes look twice as big as they actually were. He too held a pistol loosely in his hand.

"How ya doin, Ricky," the big man greeted, "Forgive us for comin a little early. We didn't want ta miss ya in case you was planning on being on vacation or somethin' on Monday." The goon looked around. "Why don't you just take a seat in that chair over there?" He indicated the chair that Sam had vacated only a few minutes before.

Ricky walked like a drunken man. As he was about to collapse into the chair, the man escorting him said with surprising politeness, "Pardon me sir, but could I trouble you to not move? And would you please extend your arms straight out to the side?"

"What?" Ricky asked. The man laid his pistol against Ricky's ear. "I said don't move and put your arms out!" This time there was steel in his voice.

Ricky complied. The man raised the bottom of Ricky's shirt. "As I thought," he said. He confiscated the pistol concealed at Ricky's back. "All right sir, please take a chair."

"Well, well, Ricky, you're just full of surprises," the big man said. He turned to the women. "Sorry to barge in like this, ladies, but we're here to do a little business with our friend, Ricky. You can call me Tony, or anything else ya want." He nodded to the man standing at the end of the couch watching over the girls. "This here's Pauly. You'll love him. He's quite a lady's man. And we call Ricky's friend over there, the Professor. The Goon reached into his inside suit pocket and removed a long, gray, plastic cylinder. He opened it and took out a fat, black cigar. He reached into his pant pocket and withdrew an expensive-looking Guillotine-type cigar cutter. As he clipped the end of his cigar, he said, "Hey Ricky, why don't cha introduce us to the ladies here?

Ricky could scarcely speak. "A—a—sure," he stammered. He nodded toward Charlene. "This one's my girlfriend, Charlene. The other one's my ex-old lady."

Tony leered at Sam as he held a lighter to the cigar and puffed rapidly. "The ex-old lady got a name?" he asked between puffs. "A—Samantha. Sam."

With an acrid cloud of smoke billowing around him, Tony said, "Glad to meet cha, Sam. "You and Ricky must get along real good, being here with his girlfriend and all. He looked at Ricky. "You banging away at both ends of the stick, Ricky boy?"

Sam couldn't remain silent. "He certainly is not. He forced me to come here. If you don't mind I'll leave now and you and Ricky can go about your business." Sam stood to leave, but Pauly stepped in front of her and pushed her roughly back into her seat. "Sit-down, Bitch," he growled.

"Hey, hey," Tony said. "Pauly, take it easy on the broads. Let me explain what's happening' here. Ricky owes my boss some money, see? He was supposed to pay it back a while ago but we ain't never seen the money. So my boss sent me out here to collect. Ricky pays us the money and we go away." Tony turned to Ricky. "So how about it, Ricky boy? You got my money?"

Ricky trembled. He tried to speak but no sound came. When words finally did come, they were strangled and so high-pitched he sounded like a girl. "I—I—I've been working on it, but you said you were coming Monday. I don't have it today."

"Well that's a problem, Ricky," Tony said, shaking his head. "How much you got today?"

"Not much. But Monday I can probably have the whole thing."

"Monday huh? We might be willing to hang around that long. Especially with these nice lookin' ladies here to entertain us. Whadda ya think, Pauly? Wanna stay in this dump til Monday?"

Pauly looked down at Sam. "Whatever it takes Boss," he said in a heavy Brooklyn accent. He grabbed Sam's chin and turned her face up to his, then he slid his hand down to cup her breast.

"Hey!" Sam shouted, slapping his hand away.

Pauly grinned. "Don't worry, little dolly, sounds like we're gonna have a couple of days to really get to know each other, you and me."

"That one's mine," Tony said. "You and the professor can have the other one. I gotta say, Ricky, for being such a pussy, you have fine taste in women. So tell me more about Monday."

Ricky gave Sam a brief pleading look. "Well—a—it's just that I made arrangements to get the money on Monday. I can't get it sooner because the banks aren't open."

Tony looked skeptical. "You bullshitting me, Ricky? Cause if you are I'm gonna be real pissed—if you know what I mean?"

Ricky gave Sam another beseeching glance. She returned his look and almost imperceptivity nodded her head. His relief was enormous. He looked at Tony with confidence and said, "It's not bullshit, it's the truth."

"That's good, Ricky, real good." Tony stepped over and gave him a none-too-gentle double-pat on the cheek. "But just to let all of you's know we ain't kiddin' around, Ricky, come on over here." Tony stepped to the living room side of the kitchen counter.

Ricky rose and followed hesitantly.

"Put your hand up here," Tony patted the countertop.

"What—Why?"

"Remember our little conversation last month about hands and stuff? I just want to give you a little reminder." His tone turned ominous. "Now put your fuckin' hand up here." From behind, the Professor pressed the muzzle of his semi-auto .32 against the back of Ricky's head and said, "I'd strongly advise that you comply, Mr. Thornton."

Fearfully, Ricky stretched out his left hand and placed it on the counter. "Naw," Tony growled, "you ain't no southpaw. Put that other one up here. Ladies, you come over here too. I want you's to watch this."

"Move your asses," Pauly said as he waived Sam and Charlene off the couch. Then he moved to block their access to the door which Tony had nearly torn off its hinges.

Ricky placed his already damaged right hand on the counter. Tony addressed the women. "Now pay close attention cause there's a lesson here for you girls, too," He grabbed Ricky's pinky finger and bent it painfully back, prompting a howl. When he took the cigar clipper out of his pocket, Ricky's eyes bulged. He moaned and tried to flinch away but Tony bent the finger further back, causing Ricky to almost go to his knees. "Don't move that hand," Tony growled. He slipped the cigar cutter over Ricky's little finger and forced it past the second knuckle. "Ladies," he said. "This is what happens to anybody who screws us. I want you's to pretend that finger is your neck if either of you ever decide to tell anybody about this. Ricky, consider this the first installment on the money you owe us."

"No," Ricky screamed as Tony slammed his hand down on the plunger of the razor-sharp guillotine blade. Ricky's watched his finger roll across the counter in silent disbelief in the moment before the pain impulse reached his brain, then he screamed and snatched his hand away as blood fountained from the wound and hit him squarely in the face.

A squirt of blood traced a crimson line across Tony's shoulder and down his front. "God damn it," he cursed. "You're bleeding on a thousand dollar suit." He grabbed a kitchen towel from the handle of the refrigerator and tried to swipe the blood away.

Ricky squeezed what was left of his finger to staunch the flow of blood. Tony threw the towel at him and barked, "Cover that thing up! The towel fell uselessly to the floor. The big Italian looked at Sam. "You, Mrs. Ex-wife, help him!"

Sam's stomach rolled. While Ricky squeezed off the stump's blood flow, Sam draped the towel over his hand to prevent further spurting. It would have to do until she had access to first-aid supplies. Every time Ricky relaxed his grip, the bleeding would erupt again.

"All right, get back over here," Tony said to Sam. Then he picked up Ricky's severed finger, turned to Charlene and said, "Open your hand."

Charlene recoiled. "What are you going to do?" she whimpered.

"Give you a little present." His hand shot out and grabbed her painfully by the wrist. Then he squeezed until her hand opened. He dropped the severed finger into it and said, "This here's a souvenir to remind you to keep your mouth shut. Now you two broads get out of here. Our business is with Ricky, not you's. If he comes up with the money on Monday you'll get him back just fine. If he doesn't—well—see ya later, Ricky—Capish? Just you's remember that finger."

Sam and Charlene looked at each other, scarcely believing they were actually being let go. Pauly complained. "Boss you said we was gonna have em around for a little fun. Why you lettin' em go?"

"Cause I said so," Tony growled. "We're here to collect from Ricky, not dip our wicks into trouble."

To everyone's surprise, Ricky, who had been moaning in pain, suddenly said, "No, no, Tony, you can't do that! You can't let her go!"

"Why not?"

Ricky nodded toward Sam and said, "She's the one who's got the money! You let her go and we're all screwed."

Chapter 62

The ambulance had evacuated Mary Ann over two hours before. The tow truck had long since left the property with Barlow's pickup. Though they'd successfully rescued Barlow's latest victim, all efforts to find the man himself had failed.

It was near midnight. The mutual aid officers sent by the surrounding counties to help and all the state troopers had been released from the scene. Clinger and Holmes, the FBI agents, had returned to Summersville to rally a special FBI search team to search for Barlow in the morning. But they would get no sleep tonight. As soon at the search team was arranged for, they would turn their attention to finding Sam, starting with an evidence search of Sam's home.

Eight Nicholas County Sheriff's Department vehicles remained at the scene, most with their headlights shining on various parts of the night-shrouded property.

They found Barlow's laptop in his bedroom. Deputy Wellman discovered horrible documentation of every murder Barlow had committed. The sick bastard had photographed and videoed every girl and every step of the unspeakable torture. The question that remained was, why? Mary Ann Gilson could probably help with that. But for now the poor woman needed time to rest and heal.

Cass found Mary Ann's car parked in the barn. The state forensics officer would process it tomorrow, along with the thousands of other threads of evidence that would ultimately confirm this farmhouse as Nicholas County's most notorious crime scene ever.

As Cass stood with Eric in the barn, an idea niggled at the corners of her mind. "Eric, if you were facing the prospect of walking through these woods all night, how would you feel?"

"Depends. If I had a good flashlight and snake boots, I guess I could do it. Why?"

"I don't think Barlow would use a flashlight. Too easy to spot him. I've had this feeling all night that Barlow's not far away—that maybe he's somewhere close right now watching what's going on. If you were him watching all this, what would you do?"

"I'd wait until things quieted down then try to make my get away."

"I think so too. And I'd want to gather some things if I could, then try to find a way to make it back to civilization without walking." Cass patted the roof of Mary Ann's car.

Eric grinned. "Something's going on in your head. Spit it out."

"How do you feel about pulling an all-nighter?"

"I've done it before; I can do it again."

"Here's what I'm thinking." Cass laid out her plan. It made Eric smile. It was like a game of cowboys and Indians all over again.

Chapter 63

It was well after midnight. It had been over two hours since Barlow heard anyone in the woods. He watched from his perch as the remaining police cars surrounding his cabin began to leave. The last to go was Sheriff Rosier's white SUV. Earlier, searchers had passed right beneath him. But predictably, they never looked up. Not that he'd have been easy to spot if they had. He was quite well concealed.

He waited for nearly an hour after the last vehicle left before breaking cover and making his way carefully, quietly to the ground. He cautiously stepped from the tree line. It would be much quieter for him to walk in the pasture than in the trees.

Suddenly he heard movement in front of him and to his left. He froze and raised the .45 in that direction. Whatever or whoever it was seemed to be coming his way, but slowly. Out of the dim moonlight, a dark shape materialized as one of his cows grazed her way toward him. He chuckled under his breath and exhaled for the first time in many seconds. If she was here grazing, there probably weren't other people close by.

There was just enough moonlight that he could make his way across the pasture without the flashlight. He crept to the back of the barn. Even in the darkness he could tell that the barn doors were open on both ends. It offended him. "Good way to get the cows in here on the hay," he muttered.

As he peered through the barn, he detected a shape at the other end near the front door. Could it be? He didn't dare enter the barn until he was sure that there was no one around, but he took a chance and clicked his flashlight on and off for just a split second.

"Yes!" he whispered as he did a fist pump. Mary Ann's white Nissan Altima was still parked where he'd left it. The keys were under the floor mat on the driver's side. The car was his passport out of here. But first he had to make sure the place really was devoid of cops.

He made his way down the side of the barn and peered cautiously around the front. No one! It was fifty yards from the barn to the house. Between the two buildings was the tool shed he'd built to look like a miniature version of the barn. He dashed stealthily to the back side of it and stayed there long enough to catch his breath and listen. The noise he'd made running across gravel was appalling, but as he waited and listened, all remained silent.

He cautiously stepped from behind the tool shed, his .45 in a two-handed grip, sweeping the area in front of him. He made it to the side of the house and worked his way to the front. He cautiously leaned his head around and peered onto the porch. No one there.

He couldn't believe his luck. The place was abandoned. Undoubtedly they'd be back in force at first light to take up the search for him—this time with dogs. He'd be long gone by then.

He stepped into the front yard, held still for a moment—listening just in case—then cautiously ascended the porch steps.

Even in the dark, he could tell that the front door was crisscrossed with yellow crime-scene tape. That would prove no obstacle. He felt for the door knob. The damage from the battering ram was immediately obvious. The knob was canted at an odd angle and would not turn. But to his surprise, just the light pressure of his attempt caused the door to move. He pushed a little harder and was rewarded by the sound of tearing tape. Could sealing tape be all that was preventing the door from opening? He pushed a little harder and the tape gave way. The door swung open on hinges that had acquired a considerable creak not present before the forced police entry hours earlier.

He only needed to retrieve a few things. He shuffled in the dark to the bedroom, trying not to stub a toe or make any excess noise. Once there, he made his way to the closet where he pulled a small suitcase down from the shelf and threw it on the bed. He didn't dare turn on the light. Someone might spot it if they were manning the front gate or watching the house from across the pasture.

Fumbling in his dresser drawers, he gathered socks, underwear, and a couple of pairs of jeans. He went back to the closet and withdrew a couple of shirts and a pair of slacks. He couldn't see if they matched, but right now, fashion was the least of his worries. He stuffed everything into the suitcase.

He ducked into the bathroom, a windowless space, closed the door and turned on the light. He quickly gathered toiletries—his razor, hairbrush, and toothbrush. He placed everything in a pile on the counter. It would be a challenge, but if he had everything arranged just right, he could turn off the light, open the door, gather it all up with both hands, and make it to his suitcase.

He barely made it before the precariously-held stash came apart and landed with a clatter right in the suitcase, exactly where he intended it to go in the first place.

There was only one thing left. Something important. He returned to the closet and felt around the floor until he encountered what he was groping for—a single slightly raised floorboard. He ran his fingernails down the crack and slowly lifted. A small trap door opened. Now he had to use the flashlight. He held it low inside the opening and turned it on. The beam fell on a small metal box, which he carefully removed. He didn't have to open it to know what was inside: The picture he'd used to create Susan's portrait, a passport, and a two-inch tall stack of one-hundred-dollar bills. The box would be his only other piece of luggage.

Now let's get out of here, He thought. With the metal box under his arm and suitcase in his left hand, he made his way back to the front door and peered out. All remained quiet.

On his way to the barn, he thought seriously about how to handle the drive out of here. Of course he'd have to go slowly, quietly, without lights all the way to the road. The gate would be the most likely place he'd encounter police. He'd stop at the edge of the pasture and walk down to the gate. Granted, there was the chance of encountering a snake on the road, but it was an acceptable risk. A snake bite would be dangerous, but a cop's bullet would be fatal.

The interior of the barn was so dark, even knowing it was there he practically walked right into Mary Ann's Altima. He set the suitcase on the ground in front of the car and made his way to the driver's door. The dim overhead light came on as opened it. He quickly bent and felt under the floor mat for the keys. Sure enough, they were there, right where he'd left them.

Feeling quite triumphant. He straightened and allowed himself a satisfied smile. Now the only obstacle remaining was to get past the front gate.

What? Suddenly he was blinded by a light blazing from the darkness from across the other side of the car. He instinctively raised his arm to shield his eyes. From behind, where the horse stalls were, he heard a female voice shout, "Sheriff's Department! Don't move, Dr. Barlow, or we'll shoot! Place your hands on top of the car and spread your legs!"

The shock was immense. He froze in place, gripped with an overwhelming, horrible fear. Where had they come from? He heard movement from behind and felt his gun being snatched from his belt. Then he was slammed hard against the car as Cass repeated her command, "I said hands on top of the car, dirt bag! Spread your legs. Do it NOW!"

"Do it!" a deep male voice shouted from the direction of the light that was blinding him.

The fight drained out of him. In shocked slow motion, Barlow let out a frightened moan and complied. Cass placed her leg between his, reached out and caught his right arm. She roughly wrestled it behind him and snapped on a handcuff. "Now the other one!" she said. He put up no resistance.

Once Barlow was cuffed, Cass walked him to the front of the car, kicked his suitcase aside and sat him against the front bumper. "Turn on the lights, Eric," she said. She keyed the mic on her shoulder radio. "Unit 1, all units. Suspect is in custody. Repeat, suspect is in custody. Come on in."

The barn lights flared to life, revealing a shaking, pasty-faced prisoner. "Read him his rights," Cass said to Zeeman as the sound of approaching sirens came blasting up the road.

As police cars stormed back and once again shined their headlights on the scene, Cass's mind was already elsewhere. She turned to Eric and said, "One kidnapping down, one to go! Let's go find Sam."

Chapter 64

It was barely past five. The morning sun was only a hint on the eastern horizon. The overtime would kill her department's budget this month. *Screw it*, Cass thought as she, Zeeman, and agents Clinger and Holmes combed through Sam's house, searching for any clue as to her whereabouts. They'd been at it for over two hours without success.

In the pre-dawn darkness Cass went outside to take another look around Sam's car. She used her flashlight to search the ground for something, anything that might point her in a good direction. She made it all the way around the vehicle without results and was about to give up when her flashlight illuminated a small scrap of white paper lying at the base of one of the trees lining the left side of the drive. The trees separated Sam's property from the street.

She leaned closer and saw that the piece of paper was a gas receipt from the Quik-go. *Must have fallen out of her car*, Cass surmised. *Better bag it.* As she bent to pick it up, a tiny dark spot on the paper caught her eye. *Is that blood?* She held the paper closer and put her flashlight practically against it. She couldn't tell.

Then she held the flashlight behind the receipt to see what showed up in backlight. Though the center of the spot was dark, there was no mistaking the almost invisible filigrees of red that traced the veins in the paper for a short distance all around the spot.

"It is blood!" Cass gasped. She'd seen blood spatter too many times not to recognize it. "Oh, God, Sam, please don't let this be yours." She looked for more blood spatter. It didn't take long to find. Her flashlight, held so it shined sideways across the white roof of the car, revealed a thin spray of red. She found the same on the doorpost. "Eric! Grab the spatter kit," she shouted into her shoulder mic. "Meet me in the driveway!" She wanted to be sick but fought it down.

Spatter kit in hand, Eric ran up. "I spotted blood on this piece of paper," Cass explained, holding up the scrap. "Then I found spatter on the car." She held the beam of her flashlight so he could see too. "Let's use the Luminol on this to confirm that's what it is, then we need see if there's a trail." Eric grabbed the Luminol, a chemical that when sprayed on human blood, luminesced bright blue when exposed to a black light.

It was all Cass could do to keep herself from hysteria as Eric pumped the Luminol spray around the area and she wielded the black light. They found exactly what she feared most. A faint trail of scattered blood droplets leading to the rear of the car then away through the trees and onto the street right-of-way. The pavement began fifteen feet further on. The margin between the trees and the pavement was a place vehicles frequently parked.

The morning light was stronger now, making it more difficult to see the luminescence, but her flashlight and the increasing morning light made up for the lowered effectiveness of the black light.

"Look at this, Eric." She pointed to a cluster of blood droplets intermingled with several shoe prints. The blood trail ended at the spot.

"What do you make of it?" she asked.

Eric scratched his head. "I'd say somebody hit her back at the car, then carried her here. Must have been a vehicle waiting. I think whoever did it threw her into the vehicle right here and took off."

"I agree. Get Clinger and Holmes out here. Get some pictures of this blood, and then cast these footprints. These tire marks look pretty fresh. Let's cast them also. I'm going back to the office to make a couple of telephone calls. I think I know who's got her. I just pray the bastard hasn't killed her."

*

As the sun breached the eastern horizon, Cass leaned back in her office chair, ran her hand over her tired face, and moved the mouse on her computer, bringing the screen back to life. She typed in the URL of the local telephone company directory, then typed in Charleston, WV in the location box. She typed 'Richard James Thornton' in the name box and clicked on the search button. In a matter of seconds she had the name and address of Ricky's parents.

"Hello," answered a groggy-sounding older man.

"Hello, Mr. Thornton? Richard Thornton, Senior?"

"This is Richard Thornton. Who's this?" He was clearly not happy about being awakened at six in the morning.

"Mr. Thornton, this is Sheriff Cassandra Rosier from Summersville down in Nicholas County. I'm sorry to bother you so early, but I've got to ask you some questions about your son, Ricky."

"Oh lord, it's about Ricky," the man said to someone. Cass heard a female voice in the background ask, "What's he done now?"

"Mr. Thornton, I need you to talk to me. You can catch your wife up on the conversation after we hang up. I need to ask you where Ricky is. It's important."

"Far as we know, he's down at our cabin on Plum Blossom Lake in Fayette County. Why?"

"Has he ever said anything to you about doing harm to his ex-wife?"

"To Sam? He'd better not. She's the best thing that ever happened to him. Stupid kid!"

"Do you hear from him much?"

"Only when he needs money. And he's needed a lot lately. We had to cut him off. We've had all kinds of people calling us lately trying to collect on his debts, wanting to know where he is. At first we tried to protect him, but after a while we gave up and just gave everyone the address where he's living. We're law-abiding people, Sheriff. I'm happy to give you that address if that's what you want. It's 3988 Old Plum Orchard Road. It's one of only four cabins that are right on the beach—a nice little A-frame at the east end of the lake. He's probably trashed it by now. We're afraid to go down there and look. If you can do something to straighten him out, you'll have our full support."

"Thank you, Mr. Thornton. I hope it doesn't come to that. Just so you know, Sam's missing. We have reason to believe Ricky has her."

"She's with Ricky? Why would she...." The full import of Cass's revelation hit the man. "Oh. Oh, I see!" he said in a concerned, anguished voice. "Want us to go down there and check?"

"No, no. It would be better to let us take care of it. I need to ask you to please not call him or tell him about this conversation. If he calls you, please contact me immediately. If you were to warn him or reveal that we're looking for him, it could turn out very badly for Sam—and for you. You folks could be charged with aiding and abetting."

"Don't worry about us," Mr. Thornton said quietly, sounding as if he was about to cry. "You just find that Sammy girl. We love her to death. Ricky never deserved her in the first place. You have our 100% support."

"Thank you, sir." Cass's heart went out to Ricky's parents. "I promise I'll call if I have news one way or the other."

Chapter 65

The Previous Evening.

If Sam ever felt like cursing, it was now. Only steps away from being free and Ricky had thrown her and Charlene under the bus. Tony looked at Ricky and asked, "What cha mean, she's the one with the money?"

"Sam's rich! She's the one I was getting your money from. That's why I brought her here."

Tony looked at Sam. "That true, lady? You the one who was gonna help out Mr. Numbnuts here?

"Sam answered carefully. "I was considering loaning Ricky some money, but now that he's revealed himself to be such a sniveling coward, I'm not sure anymore."

"She's got millions," Ricky cried. "And it's sitting in the bank over in Summersville. You better watch out. She's has a black-belt in *Taekwondo* too. If I was you, I'd tie her up right now, just like I did."

"He tie you up?" Tony asked.

Sam nodded. "Yes, until just before you and your friends came."

"How come you was loose when we showed up?"

"Because I convinced him he was better off letting me go. He was trying to extort a million dollars from me."

Tony looked at Ricky in surprise. "A million bucks?"

"He told me he owed you over six-hundred-thousand and needed some money for himself. But the money he believes is in the bank at Summersville isn't there. It's already invested. I couldn't get my hands on a million dollars by Monday if I wanted to. He finally got the message and was letting me go. When you came in, I was on my way home and he and Charlene were on their way to Mexico."

"That's not true," Ricky wailed. "She said she'd get your money first thing Monday morning. Ain't that true, Charlene!"

Thrown under the same bus as Sam, Charlene wanted nothing to do with it. "No it ain't true, Ricky," she said. "What Sam said is the truth. And just so you know, we're done. We get out of this and you better pray you never see me again."

"Good luck with that," Sam mumbled to herself. "I'll prove it, she said. He told me he had over thirty-thousand dollars to go to Mexico with. I'm betting it's in his briefcase. Probably either in the bedroom or in the Escalade in the garage. If he wasn't headed to Mexico, why didn't he try to buy his finger with it?

"God damn you Sam," Ricky shouted.

Tony looked at the Professor. "Go check it out."

The Professor returned from the garage with Ricky's briefcase in hand. "It's locked," he said.

"What's the combination, Numbnuts?" Tony asked as he walked over, kneeled in front of Ricky and put the briefcase on the floor.

Ricky was defiant—not about to give up the last of his fortune without a fight. "I don't know," he said, "That's not my briefcase." Sam watched Tony pull his gun from its shoulder holster and place it against Ricky's kneecap. He said in a calm, level voice, "You get one chance at this, Ricky. You already lost a finger. How do you feel about never walking again? You got three seconds to start spittin' out numbers, and they better be the right ones. 3... 2...

"No! No! No!" Ricky screamed as he pushed himself hard against the back of the couch. "1-9-5-3 on the left, 4-0-5-5 on the right."

Tony lowered the gun, spun the dials, then opened the latches. He raised the lid to reveal stacks of $20's, $50's and $100's. "Ricky!" he said with mock surprise, "You been holdin' out on us. Your old-lady's right. You'd still have that finger if you'd a gave us this." He closed the briefcase and handed it to the Professor. "Count it," he commanded.

"God Damn you, Sam," Ricky said again.

Pauly, you and the Professor tie em up," Tony indicated Ricky and Charlene. "Put our little loving couple here on the couch and put Mrs. Money Bags in the chair. "I gotta make a phone call." Tony fumbled for his cell phone and strode toward the door.

*

Once the trio was tied, Pauly took advantage of Tony's absence. "Hey Ricky, you got any booze around here?" he asked. Ricky directed him to the tall antique wardrobe standing in the corner of the living room that served as Ricky's liquor cabinet. Pauly opened the ornate, Early American-style door and extracted a fifth of Jack Daniels that was three-quarters full. "Anybody else want a shot?" he asked, raising the bottle. The Professor shook his head and the captors remained silent. Even Ricky wasn't tempted. "How bout you, little dolly?" Pauly asked Charlene, "You wanna oil the old hinges a little?" Charlene fearfully shook her head no.

Within minutes Pauly became obnoxious and began tormenting the girls. He stood in front of Charlene and said, "Hey baby, you got a nice rack goin' on there." He wet his finger and ran it down her exposed cleavage as far as he could. "Them twins are peekin' outa that blouse real good. And them jeans, baby, you fill em out just right. Pauly took another pull straight from the bottle than said, "Stand up, baby, let's take a look at that ass. Oh, sorry, you can't stand up." He laughed and said, "Just gonna have to stick with your tits, I guess." He looked at the Professor. "She looks good, right?"

"She does indeed," the Professor confirmed quietly.

"I don't know about you, Prof, but I'd like to see a little more. Whadda ya say?" The Professor nodded and said. "I think a good non-clinical examination would be nice."

Pauly unbuttoned the top button of Charlene's blouse. She struggled against her restraints and whimpered, "Please don't, mister. Please don't."

"Hey, call me Pauly. We're all friends here, right?" He undid the second button then pulled her blouse away from her and looked down. With a cat-that-got-the-canary grin he said, "Well would you look at this, Prof, she ain't wearing no bra. Wanna see em?"

The Professor grinned back.

Pauly opened the third button, then the fourth and fifth. Then he jerked the shirttails out of her blue jeans and threw the blouse fully open. She sobbed as Pauly said, "Man-ohh-man would you look at these babies. He reached out and fondled her right breast and at the same time leaned in and mouthed the nipple of her left. "Look at that baby stand up," he said. "Hey Prof, I think she likes me."

"What about the other one?" the Professor asked, nodding toward Sam.

"Let's find out!" He turned to Sam. "How bout it little darling? You got a nice rack too?"

"My rack is none of your business," Sam spat venomously. She shriveled at the thought of the man touching her.

"It is if I say so. You're a little wildcat, ain't cha." Pauly was beginning to slur his words.

"Enough of a wildcat that if you touch me, when this is over I'll hunt you down and make you pay."

"WooHoo!" Pauly mocked Sam's bravado. "We got us a tough girl here. I like tough girls. Let's see what cha got, tough girl."

As Pauly fumbled with the top button of Sam's blouse, she tried to remain stoic, fighting off the impulse to cry. She didn't want to show any sign of weakness. But despite her best effort, a single tear spilled and traced a path down her cheek. She took some satisfaction from the fact that it was not from fear or embarrassment, but rather from anger born of her immense frustration at not being able to reach out and strangle this vile man.

Pauly wasted no time. He quickly unbuttoned the blouse buttons and roughly extracted the bottom of the blouse from Sam's slacks, just as he had done with Charlene. Then he threw the blouse back…only to expose a white, modest, completely opaque, lace-trimmed silk bra.

"One more layer to go," Pauly said as he fumbled in his pocket and pulled out a pocket knife. He ran the back of the blade down her cleavage and was about to cut the narrow piece of fabric that held the two sides of her bra together when Tony walked back in.

"What the hell are you doin'?" Tony thundered when he saw Sam's open blouse. He looked at Charlene, sitting fully exposed, and asked, "What you trying to pull, Pauly?"

Pauly, clearly fearful of Tony's wrath, said, "We're just takin' a little look-see, that's all. We ain't hurtin' nothin'."

"Cover them ladies back up," Tony said darkly, "and go get our bags from the car. We're gonna be here a while."

While Pauly went about his task, Tony called the professor into the kitchen. Sam could overhear what was said. "…So the boss says we get the money, put the fear of God into the women, and let em go. Then we beat feet back home. The boss wants to talk to Ricky personally. We're supposed to bring him back with us. It don't sound too good for Ricky."

"So what's the plan?" the professor asked.

"We stay here til Monday. If me and the rich bitch work somethin' out that gets us the money, we're on our way back to New York with Ricky. If it turns out she ain't got the money or can't get it, then we dump all three of them in the lake and get back to civilization."

*

After Pauly lugged the gangsters' bags in, Tony gave out the assignments. Pauly, you stay out here with Ricky and the Girlfriend. And I better not come in here and catch you messin' around again. Professor, you stay here and make sure Pauly minds his P's and Q's. And neither of you's better fall asleep."

What Tony did next surprised everyone. He went over to Sam, tore away the duct tape that held her captive in the chair, checked her wrist bindings to make sure they were secure, then put his huge arms under her and lifted her free from the chair as easily as if she were a little child.

"Where you goin'?" Pauly asked?

"There's a bedroom with a nice big bed back there and I'm gonna be in it. Any questions?"

There were none, except for the thousand or so that suddenly screamed in Sam's brain. As Tony carried her down the hall to the bedroom she thought, *Dear God, please help me. Cass, Cass, where are you? Hurry! Please, please hurry!*

Chapter 66

Still suffering some of the after effects of the concussion, Sam's mind slowly swam up through layers of consciousness. She remembered were she was and opened her eyes with a start, fearful of what her condition might be. To her immense relief, she found herself still bound, but more importantly, still fully clothed. Only her shoes were missing. The big gangster who had seemed so intimidating last night had thrown a warm comforter over her. As far as she could tell, he never laid a hand on her.

Tony was still asleep in an overstuffed chair across the room, his head thrown back at what looked like an uncomfortable angle, his mouth agape. Through the edges of the curtains, Sam could tell it was fully light outside. She looked at the alarm clock on the night stand. It read 8:46 a.m. She didn't want to wake him. The longer things went, the greater the chances that Cass would come to the rescue.

She thought about what had transpired last night after Tony picked her up and carried her to the bedroom. "What are you going to do?" she asked fearfully after the man dumped her unceremoniously in the middle of the bed. Bound or not, she was prepared to resist. Too her surprise he said, "I'm gonna talk to ya. I didn't want to leave you out there with that dumbass, Pauly.

"That's all?"

"Yeah, that's all. Look, you're a damn good lookin' piece of ass and I'd love to screw your brains out, but I don't want to give you no reason to not cooperate. If I hurt ya it ain't gonna help nobody. Besides, I don't force broads to do me. I like it when they like it, see. Ain't no fun otherwise."

The man seemed sincere. "So what do you want from me?" she asked.

"Money," Tony said. "You cover Ricky's debt and keep your mouth shut and all a you's is outa here—cept for Ricky that is. My boss wants a little talk with him."

"You going to kill him?"

"Not my call, lady. All I know is that he's goin' back to New York with us. You got enough dough to cover Ricky's debt?"

"How much does he really owe you?"

"Two hundred and eighty grand. That's includin' interest and everything. As far as we're concerned, you already paid us forty-eight-grand last night when you told us about Ricky's stash. So the rest would be two hundred and thirty-two grand."

Sam shook her head in disgust at Ricky's perfidy. "Yes, I can get that much," she said.

"Can you get your hands on it by Monday?"

"Not in cash, that would raise too many eyebrows. I'd suggest we do it by wire transfer. I can have the proceeds wired directly into any bank account you want anywhere in the world. It takes about an hour, but the minute it's transferred you can confirm it."

"Yeah, my boss does that kinda stuff all the time. So what we gotta do?"

"We have to go to the bank and arrange it through their wire transfer office. However, I have one condition."

Tony shook his head. "You ain't in no position to be makin' no conditions."

"Then we won't have a deal."

Tony stood and looked at Sam balefully. "Look, I'm tryin ta be nice here, lady. If I wasn't I coulda just left you in there with Pauly."

Sam nodded. "I appreciate what you've done. But you're a gangster and you're asking me to trust you. I'm sorry Tony, I can't do that. Would you? All that I'm asking is that I and Charlene's safety be guaranteed."

Tony looked skeptical. "So whatcha tryin' to say?"

"When I walk into that bank on Monday I want Charlene and only you or one your men with me. Once I make that transfer, that money's gone. I can't take it back. As soon as the transfer's confirmed, your man walks out of that bank and Charlene and I stay. We're not coming back here Tony. We're not putting ourselves in harm's way again."

Tony thought it over, then asked, "So what's to keep you's from calling the cops on us?"

"Two things. I'm a Christian. If I swear something before God I always keep my word, no matter who, no matter what. You can ask Ricky about that. The second is that I'm not stupid. I don't want to die and I don't want Charlene to die either. If I were to betray my oath to you, you or someone else like you would try to kill me, right?"

"You better believe it."

"I don't want to have to look over my shoulder in fear of the Mafia the rest of my life. If we do this, we both walk away and nobody has to be the wiser. I'm positive that Charlene will feel the same way. I'm an attorney. I make deals all the time. This is a take it or leave it deal. Either it happens that way or it doesn't happen at all.

Tony was right. It was a huge gambit. She was in no position to bargain. But she had to make him think she was. If it didn't work, all that was left was her faith in Cass to be able to attempt a rescue—one that none of them might survive.

Tony paced the room in thought. Finally, he looked at Sam and said, "I'll have to clear it with my boss, but as far as I'm concerned, you got a deal. But if you screw me on this, Mrs. Thornton, I'll be back. And you'll look back on this little experience as one of your fondest memories.

*

Tony emerged from the hallway, carrying Sam as he had the night before. Pauly was in the kitchen frying some eggs while the Professor occupied the chair, keeping an eye on Ricky and Charlene. "Move your meat, Professor," Tony said. Suddenly he stopped. "Who opened up them curtains?" he thundered, starring out the window at a gorgeous view of the lake.

"I must admit that I did," the Professor said. "There are some wonderful examples of Pin Oak and Mountain Magnolia out there, and I wanted to see just exactly where we were. I checked carefully to make sure no one was there."

Tony dropped Sam into the chair with a thump. "Get em closed" he growled at the Professor. "Somebody could come wandering into the yard or some fisherman could see in here from his boat. Pauly, you finish what you're cookin' then get your ass outside where you can keep an eye on this place. We don't want the cops sneaking up on us."

Chapter 67

Prior to arriving at Plum Blossom Lake, Agents Clinger and Holmes summoned a special FBI hostage rescue team. In preparation for their arrival, Cass, the agents, and Sheriff McMillan of Fayette County drove a half-mile up South Shore Road to the base of the small hill that separated the Thornton property from its nearest neighbor.

They walked to the crest of the hill and looked down. Indeed, the road ended in front of the cabin.

Ricky's Escalade wasn't in the driveway, but an older maroon Chevy Lumina and a dark-colored Lincoln Town Car were. Did Ricky have company? It looked like it, but without walking up there and knocking on the door, there was no sure way to tell. They needed to get a look at the back of the house, and the only way to do that was from the other side of the lake.

After a rough, bouncy ride up the little-traveled road on the north shore, Cass, agent Clinger, and Sheriff McMillan, all of them dressed in camo, now lay concealed in heavy brush just back from the edge of the lake directly across from the Thornton Cabin. In the unlikely event of traffic on the little-traveled road, they'd left

Holmes to keep an eye on the vehicles that were parked precariously on the side of the narrow track.

The steep-roofed 'A'-frame home had wings built on to the left and right. The right wing appeared to be where the bedrooms were. The left wing was a two-car garage. Floor to ceiling windows on the lake side formed the rear wall of the cabin, giving occupants a panoramic view of the lake and the wooded hills beyond. With their binoculars, they would have had a clear view into the house were the curtains not drawn.

After watching the back of the cabin for more than an hour, Cass was ready to give up the vigil and suggest they go back and just walk up and knock on the front door to see if Ricky was there.

Then suddenly the curtains opened and they had a full view inside. They were looking into a large living room/family room combination and a sizable open kitchen behind. The only thing that separated the kitchen from the other room was a wide counter. Bar stools were pushed up against it on the living room side. A wide entryway beside the kitchen led to the front door.

Cass saw a man, obviously the person who had just opened the curtains, walking away from the windows. To her surprise, it wasn't Ricky. She spotted another man in the kitchen area. He appeared to be short and muscular with wavy dark hair. He was dressed in dark clothing and wearing an apron. *Where the hell's Ricky?* she wondered.

"I've got movement on the couch," Clinger whispered. Cass swung her binoculars there. She spotted Ricky sitting beside a redheaded woman who appeared to be asleep. *Why are they sitting like that?* Both were at a strange angle, upright but leaning unnaturally into each other.

Clinger, whose binoculars were more powerful, must have been wondering the same. "I think they're tied up," he said softly. "See how their legs are close together and angled kind of funny? It looks like their arms are behind them.

Clinger was right. *What the hell? Ricky's supposed to be the kidnapper!* "I'm not getting this," Cass said. "Any of you see Sam?" No one responded.

Then Sheriff McMillan said, "I think I recognize the woman on the couch. Looks a lot like Charlene Nay. If that's who it is, my daughter went to school with her. She's a local barfly whose only run-in with the law was a DUI two or three years ago."

"Sounds like Ricky's type," Cass said derisively.

With no sign of Sam, Cass's anxiety rose. Where the hell was she? The trio watched for several more minutes. Cass was about to make the call that they get back to their vehicles to talk about what they'd seen when suddenly a third man dressed in a dark suit appeared from the bedroom side. He was huge. At least six-foot-eight and wide. He had a high forehead that gave way to dark, thinning hair. Most surprising, he was carrying Sam.

"That's her!" Cass hissed to her companions. "What the hell's he doing?" The big man stopped in the middle of the living room and turned directly toward them. Something in his demeanor suggested he was angry. He turned and deposited Sam in a chair on the other side of the room and gestured at the man who had opened the curtains. The man sprang to the side of the windows and rapidly drew the curtains closed again.

"Oh God," Cass whispered. "Why was he carrying her?" Anybody get a good look at her?

"I did," Clinger said quietly. "She was tied up too. But she was alive and that's the most important part. But we've got another problem."

"What?" Cass demanded.

"I recognized the big guy from when I worked organized crime out of Manhattan. It's Big Tony Lazaro. He's a capo for the Bustinari crime family. Drugs, loan sharking, gambling, girls... "

"This has to have something to do with Ricky," Cass said. Let's get out of here and figure out what to do."

Agent Holmes was waiting, anxious to hear their report. "At least we know your friend's alive," Clinger said as he brushed dirt and grass from his camo pants.

"Thank God," Cass said. "The question is, how are we going to get her out of there? Ricky Thornton is one thing, but a whole gang of professional bad guys is something else."

"It all works the same way," Clinger said. "You just have to move faster and be smarter.

"Either of you see any guns?" Sheriff McMillan asked.

"No," Clinger replied, "but with Big Tony there, I guarantee they'll have them. Sheriff McMillan, do you have a SWAT team?"

"I've got four deputies SWAT trained, but we've never put together a real SWAT team. My county could never afford it."

"Until my rescue team gets here, let's put your four men in the woods around the house. They can be our eyes and ears. Let me find out where my people are. Clinger punched a number out on his cell phone and wandered away from the group.

"How's Mary Ann," Agent Holmes asked.

"Last I heard, she's fine," Cass said. "We've got Barlow on a suicide watch until you feds can transfer him to your own lockup. They tell me he hasn't said a word."

"That was a nice, take-down, Sheriff," Holmes replied. Kinda like he walked into a right cross. You should be proud."

Cass smiled. "Just another day in Paradise. What's really important is getting my Sammy-girl out of that cabin alive."

Clinger strode back purposefully. "They'll be here within two hours—fourteen of the biggest, baddest federal agents you've ever met. In the meantime we've got to secure this place. Sheriff McMillan, you need to secure all roads coming in and out of here and evacuate the neighbors. We need to get all the boats off that lake. "Sheriff Rosier, I watched you work yesterday. You're welcome to join the team, albeit at the rear. You'll be helpful once we have the victim free."

Cass nodded.

Clinger looked at McMillan and asked, "Sheriff, do you have access to a good boat?"

"The department doesn't own one, but I know a couple of guys who do. Why?"

"Because we're going to need one."

Chapter 68

"What do you think?" Cass asked. She stood behind Agent Clinger, dressed in tactical clothing including a flak-jacket and helmet. The FBI SWAT team leader knelt low directly in front of Clinger.

They were concealed in the trees at the apex of the little hill they'd been at before. Klinger swept the property with his binoculars and said, "I can't see the guard. That worries me." McMillan's deputies posted in the trees around the cabin had reported that occasionally someone came out of the house and patrolled the grounds. It wasn't always the same man. The reports confirmed that at least one of the men was armed.

Clinger tapped the SWAT team leader on the shoulder. "Seen enough, Agent Parsons?"

"Yes," the agent replied. "Let's go back and set up the team. Thank goodness for these woods, we can get practically right up to the house without worrying about being seen. We'll just have to take our chances with the guard."

*

The deep throbbing roar of a powerful speed boat engine could be heard halfway down the lake. It was a foreign sound on Plum Blossom Lake, were boats were restricted to a sedate, wakeless speed.

A young couple dressed in practically nothing cavorted in the back of the boat as the driver swung the craft wildly from one side of the lake to the other. The boat sped past the Thornton property, made a wild turn at the end of the lake and returned. The noisy visitor was easily heard inside the cabin. The Professor pulled back the corner of the curtain and peered out. "Just a bunch of kids," he reported to Tony. That boat's creating an interesting Doppler effect. Notice the wavelength shift as the boat gets further away. Looks like they're headed back down the lake."

Tony shook his head. "You and your science talk, he said. How come you always have to show off with that brainy shit? Then they listened as the boat turned again. "More of your Doppler effect," Tony said as the noise increased. But this time it sounded kind of funny, like it was changing directions over and over. Tony strode to the window, pulled the curtain aside and watched for himself.

Sure enough, the crazy kids were zipping back and forth, creating huge wake waves that were sure to make shoreline property owners angry. When the boat reached the front of the Thornton property, the driver threw the helm hard-over and headed straight for shore. To Tony's horror, it made a beeline for the little dock in front of the cabin. The boat stopped and the guy in back jumped out and started to tie up.

"Get Ricky over here," Tony barked. Pauly and the Professor each grabbed one of Ricky's arms, hauled him to his feet and dragged him to where Tony was standing. By the time he got there, the chick in the barely-there bikini was out of the boat with a beer can in her hand and goosing around with the guy trying to tie the boat off. Tony held the curtain open a little wider so Ricky could see and asked, "You know who they are?"

"Never seen them before."

"What they doin' here?"

"Your guess is as good as mine. Nobody's supposed to use those docks except the property owners."

The mystery of their purpose was solved when the driver exited the boat carrying a large picnic cooler and a blanket.

"God damn' kids," Tony growled. "Pauly, go out there and run the little bastards off. Keep your heat hidden. Don't want them callin' the cops cause somebody pulled a gun."

Pauly holstered his pistol at the middle of his back and pulled his shirt over it. He parted the curtains, found the sliding glass door and stepped out on the low deck. He gestured to the boaters. "Hey you kids get out of here," he shouted. This here's private property."

The girl, practically falling out of her swimsuit, smiled broadly, raised her beer can to Pauly and shouted back in a slurred voice, "Hey, Mister. Howyadoin'? Come on out and join us. Wanna beer?" She stumbled a little but caught herself. She was clearly several sheets to the wind.

Pauly looked at where he knew Tony was watching. He grinned and nodded toward the revelers. Tony sternly shook his head no. Pauly's grin faded.

"Hey, look here," Pauly said as he stepped off the deck and began walking toward the boaters. The driver was opening the cooler while the girl started ditty-bopping to music playing over her iPod. God, she looked good. Maybe Tony would just have to keep himself company for a while.

*

"What's that crazy idiot up to now?" Tony asked the Professor. The Professor peered between the curtains on the other side of the room.

"I don't know," the Professor said, "but it doesn't look like he's in much of a hurry. I think he's going to try to fulfill his biological imperative. You want I should go out there and take care of it?"

"Not yet. No sense letting anybody know there's more of us in here. Just keep an eye on him and let him have his fun. I'll deal with him later."

*

Pauly grinned as he sauntered toward the boaters. The little broad was putting on quite a show. But the closer he got the more things looked a little strange. At twenty feet his eyes told him that this chick wasn't as young as he thought. Neither was the driver. These weren't exactly kids. But hey, she looked good, very fit. "Hey, you's guys," Pauly said with a grin, trying to get them to pay attention. About ten feet away from them, Pauly heard a noise from behind and to his left. He looked that way but saw nothing. *Probably a deer or somethin'*, he thought. When he looked back at the boaters he found himself looked straight into the barrel of an AR-15.

*

"GUN!" the Professor shouted.

"What?" Tony spun on his heel and leapt for the curtain, drawing his automatic as he did. Suddenly the front door of the cabin, the one he'd come through last night and nearly taken off its hinges, slammed open again. Tony turned and saw two dark, round objects come rolling across the floor of the entryway. Then more crashed through the kitchen window. In an instant the whole world seemed to erupt in a series of blinding flashes and deafening explosions. Tony staggered backward, completely disoriented. The confusing flashes and incredible noise nauseated him. He pointed his gun in the general direction of the entryway just as his heel caught in the carpet and he fell backward, spoiling his aim. The back of his head hit hard against the frame of one of the windows. Stars exploded in his head as his vision faded and all became quiet. Very, very quiet.

*

The Professor saw the flash/bangs rolling across the entryway and realized instantly what was happening. He had to get out through the sliding glass door. He threw his forearm up to shield his eyes from the flashes he knew were coming and leapt toward to where the sliding glass door was. He could do nothing to protect his ears. He was surprised to suddenly see the curtains billow out at the exact spot where the door was. The barrel of an AR-15 assault rifle poked through the curtains, then a helmeted, body-armor-clad body parted the curtains and stepped through. The professor saw the letters FBI on the front of the body armor. The helmeted head turned toward him as the rifle barrel swung his way. He raised his pistol and fired. The intruder went down. Then movement in his periphery drew his vision to the entryway. A number of the fearsome, black-clad, helmeted bodies were pouring in the front door. They pointed guns at him and appeared to be shouting but he couldn't hear what they said. He swung his pistol in that direction. Something smashed into his wrist, causing his hand to convulse on the trigger. He felt the recoil but in the same instant, the sensation was swallowed by excruciating pain. His weapon flew from his grasp as his horribly mutilated hand seemed to explode in a blossom of blood. Then something slammed hard into his chest followed in the next instant by another. His legs begin to crumple. His head turned toward the intruders and as he did, he caught the intense red beam of a laser sight squarely in his right eye—and in that moment, the .223 caliber AR-15 round obliterated its target and the Professor was no more.

*

"Hey?" Pauly shouted as he instinctively reached back to draw his gun. As he did he felt two sharp pains in his chest then his whole body contorted as an electrical shock robbed him of all control over his muscles. "Aruhhhhhhhhhh," he cried as his body stiffened and he pitched forward on his face. As the electric shock went away, he groaned and rolled to his back. He found himself looking up into the face of the woman in the bikini. Instead of a beer, she was holding the pistol-like control unit of a Taser.

"You done fighting? she asked. "If not, I can shock you again till you are."

Pauly shook his head fearfully. "I'm done," he said through gritted teeth.

"You got a weapon?"

"Behind me, in my belt. Who are you guys?"

"FBI," the woman said. "In case you haven't figured it out yet, you're under arrest.

"Damn," Pauly cursed. "Can I tell you that you still look smoking good in that bikini?"

"You're a real horn dog, aren't you." The agent gave him another jolt of the Taser just to let him know how much she appreciated the compliment.

*

The darkness lasted only a few seconds. Tony felt himself coming around. He could tell he was lying down, his head hurt like hell. His neck was bent at an awkward angle against the window frame. *What just happened?*

He opened his eyes. *What the...?* Several men dressed in helmets and body armor stood above him pointing guns. A half-dozen red laser dots danced crazily across his head and chest. The men were saying something but with the ringing in his ears, he couldn't understand. One turned to speak to someone else and Tony saw the letters on his back. 'FBI.'

Now it all made sense. He turned his head and spied the Professor sprawled awkwardly in front of the back door. His fixed eyes, a spreading pool of blood, and a small, dark, dot in the middle of his forehead told the tale. Tony realized he wouldn't be going home to New York after all. He sagged in resignation and said, "I give up."

*

It was over. Sam's hearing was beginning to come back. Within moments of the apocalyptic eruption of noise and fury, Cass was at her side, freeing her arms and legs and checking her to make sure she was okay. The room was a confusing mass of people, all dressed in helmets and flak-jackets and boots and gloves. Sam felt as if she were in the midst of a gun-filled video game scene.

Someone who appeared to be a medic or doctor hovered over her, trying to use a stethoscope while someone else tried to take her pulse. She waived them off and for the first time since being bashed over the head by Ricky, was able to push herself out of the chair and stand, scarcely believing how good it felt to be able to move her arms and legs freely.

Other medical personnel administered to the agent who'd been shot by the Professor. The .32 caliber bullet entered the side where the agent was not protected by body armor. But it failed to pierce his Kevlar undervest. Rather, it traced a path between it and the flak jacket, doing no serious damage.

The ringing in Sam's ears was nearly gone. She could hear conversations almost normally. She turned to Cass and said, "I look like crap. My hair's a bloody mess, my makeup is a fond memory, and I probably smell like last week's lasagna."

Cass laughed. "Sammy, my dear, you're the best-looking thing I've smelled in a long time." She threw her arms around her and gave her a prolonged hug.

Suddenly Sam heard Charlene scream, "Ricky!" Last Sam had seen him, Ricky was tied up on the couch next to Charlene. Sam's view was blocked by a forest of milling law enforcement officers. She stood and worked her way to where she could see what was going on.

Charlene was frantic. Tears streamed down her face as she held her hands to her mouth. Two paramedics had Ricky off the couch and on the floor. One administered mouth-to-mouth while the other performed CPR. Sam couldn't tell why. Then she noticed the wound. It was small, located high on the left side of his chest. Every time the paramedic giving the CPR pushed down, frothy blood bubbled up through the wound. Sam rushed to put an arm around Charlene. "What happened?" she asked.

"I don't know," Charlene wailed between sobs. "One minute he seemed fine, then he just slumped over. That's when I saw the blood on his shirt."

Clinger had the same question for Charlene: "What happened?" She gave him the same answer. He looked at the SWAT team leader.

"Wasn't us," he said, holding his hands up in denial. "The only one we took down was the guy in the glasses. And he gave us no choice."

A new paramedic came rushing in with a portable defibrillator. It was just like in the movies. Sam watched Ricky's body convulse as the shock was administered. "Got a rhythm," the paramedic who had been giving mouth to mouth said. He held a stethoscope to Ricky's chest. He's breathing but his right lung is filling. We've got to get a tube into him fast. Somebody call and confirm that the chopper's on its way."

Sam watched as the paramedics struggled valiantly to save Ricky's life. What a year ago would have been a frantic, catastrophic moment for her was now one of strange detachment due to the awful, stupid things Ricky had done. *So many bad choices*, Sam thought, shaking her head. An unbidden tear slipped down her cheek, not so much for Ricky's condition as for her sense of loss over what might have been.

Chapter 69

"So he just came wandering out of the woods?" Sam was thoroughly taken with Cass's recitation of Dr. Barlow's capture. They sat at Sam's kitchen table, sipping morning coffee and dunking donuts in the time-honored law enforcement fashion. Sam couldn't believe she'd taken up such a habit.

"That's exactly what happened," Cass said. I was behind him so I couldn't see it, but Eric said his jaw nearly dropped right off of his face—froze him as stiff as a board."

"How's Mary Ann doing?"

"As well as can be expected. Her brother's flying in tomorrow. Compared to our other victims, she got off easy. What's the latest word on Ricky?

Sam sighed. Even though she was detached, thinking about Ricky's awful situation still made her sad. "Looks like he's going to make it. But it will be out of a hospital bed and straight to prison for him. I talked to Clinger. They're going to offer Charlene a deal to testify against him. I hope so. In a lot of ways she was just as much a victim as I was. What's the latest on Barlow?"

"We've still got him on a suicide watch. We're waiting to hear what Stewart wants to do, whether he wants to take the case to a grand jury or go for a preliminary hearing. You're his special investigator, what do you think?"

"I'd vote for the grand jury. We have more than enough evidence to go straight to trial." Looks like we're going to prosecute him for murder first then the feds can try him for the kidnapping charges.

Cass hesitated, considering her next question. "I'm almost afraid to ask this, but do you know what your plans are? I hope this little serial killer adventure and Ricky's stupid kidnapping stunt aren't going to drive you out of Summersville and back to New York."

Sam sighed. "I've been thinking about that too. New York was a wonderful experience. I learned more there than I ever thought I would. Ricky made it a little bit of hell, but Harold and Nancy Howell are wonderful people and I wouldn't trade my experience at the law firm for anything.

"But to be honest with you, it's felt really good to be back home. I love being close to you and Katie. In New York I never had time for anything except my practice. There just wasn't time for a personal life. Looking back, that was a major part of what killed my marriage. Back there, all I did was help rich people who couldn't get along divide up more money than they ever needed. Here I've been helping real people with things they never would have been able to do for themselves. I've never felt the real purpose of the law more strongly than I've felt it right here working on the evening gown murders case."

Cass was encouraged. Maybe what she was going to ask wouldn't be as hard as she imagined. "I'm glad you feel that way because there's something I want you to think about. "Doyle Stewart's getting old. This trial is going to be pretty hard on him. He sure could use your help getting through it. But there's something else. He's been in the job for over thirty years and I have it on good authority that he wants to retire. Are you dead set on going back to New York or could I convince you to stay around here for a while, at least long enough to help Stewart get Barlow put behind bars for the rest of his life?"

Sam smiled. "Funny you should ask," she said. "I'm not going back to New York. I sent my resignation letter to the law firm yesterday. I think Katy needs her Aunty Sam to be here in Summersville, not sending her birthday cards from some big city hundreds of miles away. I'm now officially jobless. So what do you say—want to hire me as your babysitter?"

Cass flew out of her chair and gave her friend a huge hug. "Oh, Sammy, I'd love to!"

"So about this county prosecutor thing," Sam asked as Cass sat back down, "when did you say he's up for reelection?"

"You?" Cass asked with surprise as she pointed her finger at Sam.

"Like I said, as of yesterday I'm officially unemployed. If Doyle Stewart retires, why not?"

"Why not indeed." Cass grinned. "He's up next year. We'll start on your election campaign first thing tomorrow morning."

IF YOU LIKED THIS BOOK, COULD YOU DO ME A FAVOR?

One of the most valuable assets any author can have is fans who are willing to tell others about his writing. I encourage each of you to tell others about *All The Pretty Dresses* by submitting a review to Amazon, Goodreads, Smashwords and other sites that accept reader feedback. Thanks.

WANT TO BE FIRST ON THE LIST FOR THE NEXT CASS ROSIER/SAM MARTIN BOOK?

All you have to do is sign up for my free monthly e-newsletter. *You'll be given advance notice of the next book's releas*e. If you've bought this book AND you sign up for the newsletter, you'll receive a promo code that will make the next e-book in the Cass/Sam series available to you for HALF-PRICE. If you sign up for my monthly e-newsletter and have purchased both *All The Pretty Dresses* AND *Wage$ of Greed*, you'll receive a special promo code that will allow you to receive the next Cass & Sam book FREE during the first two weeks after publication!

To **read the first chapter** and sign up for the newsletter, Visit my website at www.stevenjclark.com.

These offers apply to e-book purchases only and only apply if the books subject to the special offer have not been purchased pursuant to a different discount price promotion. For information on special offers to purchasers of print versions, contact the author at sjc@cut.net.

(THE SECOND BOOK IN THE CASS ROSIER/SAM MARTIN SERIES IS CURRENTLY UNTITLED, GO TO THE WEBSITE AND READ THE FIRST CHAPTER THEN WATCH FOR A SUMMARY OF THE BOOK IN THE NEWSLETTER. SUBMIT YOUR TITLE SUGGESTION, AND IF I USE IT, YOU'LL RECEIVE A FREE AUTOGRAPHED PRINT EDITION COPY. PROJECTED PUBLICATION DATE, DEC. 2014)

WHAT'S NEXT FROM AUTHOR STEVEN J. CLARK?

Wage$ of Greed

(E-book release scheduled for Oct., 2014)

Brief Synopsis

It seemed like such a good plan in the beginning—make it appear that the gas wells out on the reservation had gone dry when they were actually still working. Red Gannon, owner of Gannon Oil, Inc, and Dave Blackthorn, Gannon's Chief of Security, would pocket millions in no time. And all that money would be *off the books*.

Suddenly two explosions shatter everything and send millions of dollars worth of gas up in smoke.

Unbeknownst to the conspirators, the misery their plan causes to residents of the Shiprock area, a Navajo community located just a few miles west of the bustling Four-Corners city of Farmington, NM, has spawned creation of a dangerous paramilitary group; the Native American Liberation Movement (NALM). The group's agenda; either get the wells running again or rid the reservation of them entirely.

Caught squarely in the middle is Navajo Attorney Danny Whitehorse who represents dozens of affected families. The well explosions force him to file suit against Gannon Oil long before he is ready—and opens the gates of hell. Danny is forced to run for his life while trying desperately to learn the truth about the dry wells—a truth that could put Gannon and his henchmen in prison for the rest of their lives.

Wage$ of Greed (WOG) is an edge of your seat, John Grisham meets Tony Hillerman thriller that weaves an intricate tale of murder, intrigue, avarice, and nail-biting suspense intertwined with fascinating bits of Navajo culture and religion. And, oh yes, there is a nice touch of romance thrown in for good measure.

WOG is the first installment in a series of mystery/thrillers set in and around the Navajo reservation. This book is a tribute to the late best-selling author, Mr. Tony Hillerman. Just prior to Mr. Hillerman's death, he paid me the ultimate compliment when he reviewed *Wage$ of Greed* and gave me written permission to invoke his name in the promotion of this work.

For your enjoyment, I have included the first chapter of *Wage$ of Greed* below. Want to see more? Read the first **three** chapters on my website at www.stevenjclark.com.

Wage$ of Greed

Chapter 1

"BOOM!" The explosion sent ear splitting sound waves reverberating off the vertical walls of the deep, isolated wash located fifteen miles southwest of Shiprock, New Mexico. Sheer thirty-foot tall dirt walls confined the sound to the immediate area, but there was no hiding the fire and smoke of the spreading mushroom cloud that curled hundreds of feet into the air.

"Perfect!" Eddie Sam exclaimed as he sprinted from behind the bend in the wash where he, Albert Horseman and David Nez had sought protection.

"Aieeeee. There's nothing left," Sam heard Horseman shout as the trio skidded to a halt at the edge of the ten-foot-wide crater.

"Where'd the pipe go?" David Nez asked. Two hours earlier, while Eddie attached the detonator to the three explosive-filled five-gallon fuel cans, he'd watched his friends cobble together a collection of rusty pipes into something that approximated a natural gas wellhead.

This was their first full-size test and it had come off perfectly. As he stood at the edge of the crater, Eddie thought of all it had taken to reach this day. A collection of discarded timers on his back porch testified to the difficulty of finding one he could modify into a safe and reliable detonator. In the end, it was the simplest and cheapest kitchen timer from Wal Mart that did the trick. The only metal parts were the timing spring, the bell and the clapper. With a wire soldered to the clapper and another to the bell, when the timer reached '0' the clapper struck and the electrical circuit was completed. But that had to happen only when they wanted it to. The slightest contact between the bell and the clapper at the wrong time and Eddy and everyone around him would be dead in an instant.

Getting the mix of fertilizer and diesel fuel just right was a challenge. He first tested a quarter cup of fertilizer and a quarter cup of diesel in a frying pan on his kitchen stove. He used the bare ends of an extension cord to ignite the concoction. The "Whoosh!" that resulted wasn't so much an explosion as a ball of fire that boiled up and rolled across the ceiling. With singed hair and eyebrows, Sam found himself beating out a half-dozen tiny fires that threatened to burn his trailer to the ground. It was the last experiment he conducted indoors.

"What a difference," Eddie said to his companions. Their largest previous test used three peanut butter jars to simulate the gas cans.

"It's like dynamite compared to a fire cracker," Horseman agreed.

"Where's the pipe?" Nez asked again.

"Let's go find it!" Eddie said. "Albert, you and I will head south, David, you go north.

The banks on both sides of the arroyo near the blast were cratered by the shrapnel from the explosion. They had to search for some distance to find anything recognizable.

"Found one," Horseman called. He pointed. A three-foot-long mangled piece of pipe was sticking out of the dirt wall more than ten feet up. They were ninety-feet from the crater.

"Right here," Eddie heard David shout from the other direction. He was nearly a hundred-yards the other side of the crater. He was pointing at a twisted length of pipe on the floor of the wash.

There should have been more. Apparently the main body of pipework had been blown over the sides of the wash and now lay scattered on the desert floor above.

"Man, that was huge," Nez exalted when they reassembled at the crater. "I say we do it now—tonight!

"No. " Sam replied. "We all agreed this would be only a last resort. We wait until after the next NALM (**N**ative **A**merican **L**iberation **F**ront) meeting. If we don't hear what needs to be said, then we go."

"I don't understand you," Horseman replied. "You just buried your grandfather and yet you want everybody to sit back and keep taking it?"

The comment brought an all too familiar stab of anger and pain. Five years ago, when Gannon Oil drilled the gas well on his grandfather's land allotment, the well money transformed his grandfather's life. He and Grandmother moved out of the old family *Hooghan*, into the new pre-fab government house. There was enough money for a pickup truck and for food bought from the store in Shiprock. Grandfather sold off his flock of sheep. They kept a few chickens around, but only because Grandfather liked chickens.

But then the oil company turned off the well and the flow of money ceased. His grandparents went from riches to rags in a matter of weeks. The pre-fab house was heated with propane and had no fire place. When the money ran out, so did the propane. There was no more money for store-bought food. Eddie didn't know it, but when the chickens ran out, grandfather was reduced to hunting Jackrabbits to feed himself and his grandmother. It was a wonder they hadn't come down with Tularemia. The truck had long-since run out of gas, so there was no way for them to ride to town to buy food, gas or anything else. But grandfather was silent about all this.

In January, the moon of Crusted Snow, Sam discovered the depths of his grandparents' misery. Visiting their place for the first time in more than a month, he was concerned when grandfather failed to answer the door. Breaking Navajo courtesy traditions that respected people's privacy in their own home, but knowing that grandfather was quite hard of hearing, Sam opened the door and called in, "Grandfather, it is your grandson, Eddie. Are you here?" He stepped in and closed the door against the bracing, cold wind. But closing the door did nothing to take away the chill.

"This house is too cold," he said to himself. Then he realized it was also dark. The sun had set more than a half hour before, but not a light burned anywhere inside. *What happened to the electricity? This is definitely not right.* He called out again, louder this time. "Grandfather, it's your grandson, Eddie. Are you home?"

Silence.

He turned to leave then thought he heard something. Was it his grandparents or had some evil spirit, of which the *Diné* believed in many, somehow gotten into the house. Hesitant and watchful he walked toward where he thought the sound had come from.

He found his grandparents covered in blankets in their bed. His grandfather's gaunt eyes recognized him but the man was so weak from hunger and cold he could barely raise his arm to gesture for Eddie to come in. Tears flowed from the old man's eyes. "Your Grandmother," he rasped out, "I think she is dead."

Grandmother had died the day before and the old man was too weak to raise himself off her deathbed to go for help.

Grandfather ended up in a nursing home in Shiprock but only for a few months. He never fully recovered. He missed his wife of more than 50 years terribly. On the last day of his life he told Eddie how he wished he had never allowed the *Bilagaana,* the Whiteman, to drill the gas well on his land. He grasped Eddie's hand and in a tortured whisper said, "The well is cursed with an evil spirit. Before you sing me onto the Shining Path, promise me that you will get rid of the *Bilagaana* well before anyone else comes to live on my land."

Eddie leaned over and whispered the great secret he carried, of his plan to get rid of the well if the oil company wouldn't turn it back on. The old man's grip on his arm tightened. His eyes lit up for the first time in months. Into the night, grandfather and grandson sang the warrior's battle song so loud and long that a nurse finally came and shushed them. The next morning grandfather was dead. As far as Eddie was concerned, Gannon Oil had killed both his grandparents as surely as if they had held a gun to their heads and pulled the trigger.

Standing on the floor of the arroyo, Eddie ached for revenge—ached for justice. But the warrior in him told him to act smart; to act like *Ma'ii,* the Coyote. "Don't worry, Albert," he said. We will listen carefully at the next NALM meeting. Then we will decide whether to use what we have learned to make the well on my grandfather's land disappear. We will burn this desert down around Gannon Oil's ears if we have to! But now we'd better get out of here. Who knows what kind of attention that explosion will draw?"

THANK YOU! LET ME AUTOGRAPH YOUR COPY

I want to personally thank you for your interest and your support. I will be happy to autograph print copies of this book so long as you send it to me with a self-addressed, fully pre-paid return shipping means. I will happily autograph books bought at or brought to any public book signing or other event such as conferences or conventions. The address books and all other mailed communications should be sent to is:

New Horizons Press/Publishers
HC13 Box 3071
Chester, UT 84623

FOLLOW THE AUTHOR ON FACEBOOK, TWITTER, LINKED-IN AND OTHER SOCIAL NETWORKS.

ABOUT THE AUTHOR

Steven Clark is the former Publisher and Editor-in-Chief of a national trade newspaper for the Manufactured Housing industry and has written extensively for local and regional newspapers. After being raised in Utah, he spent most of his adult life in California, Texas and Tennessee. Steve and his wife, Lauri, now reside in a tiny town in a high mountain valley in central Utah. *All The Pretty Dresses* is the first of three books planned to be released by Clark this year. Look for *Wages of Greed*, in early Fall and the next book in the Cass Rosier/Sam Martin series by the end of 2014. Mr. Clark reminds you to please leave your review on Amazon, Goodreads and other sites that accept your reviews. He welcomes your email contacts at sjc@cut.net and invites you to like/follow him on Facebook, Linked-In and Twitter

Made in the USA
San Bernardino, CA
02 August 2014